NOT QUITE A SCANDAL

The Audacious Ladies of Audley
Book 2

BLISS BENNET

Copyright © 2024 by Jackie C. Horne

All rights reserved. No part of this publication may be reproduced, distributed, or transmitted in any form or by any means, including photocopying, recording, or other electronic or mechanical methods, without the prior written permission of the publisher, except in the case of brief quotations embodied in critical reviews and certain other noncommercial uses permitted by law.

Cover design by L1graphics

Model cover photograph © 2024 by Jessica Boyatt
Quaker Meeting House:
Burford Quaker Meeting, Oxfordshire, England
Honeysuckle blossom photo: Scisetti Alfio/Shutterstock.com

This is a work of fiction. Names, characters, and incidents are the product of the author's imagination or are used fictitiously. Any resemblance to actual events, locales, or persons, living or dead, is purely coincidental.

ISBN ebook: 978-1-7378455-3-9
ISBN Paperback: 978-1-7378455-4-6

For permissions requests, please contact the author:
bliss@blissbennet.com

NOT QUITE A SCANDAL

The Audacious Ladies of Audley
Book 2

An inheritance lost. A betrothal threatened. A scandal brewing...

Outspoken Bathsheba Honeychurch knows how difficult it is for an unmarried woman, even a Quaker, to successfully champion political change. Her solution? Wed best friend Ash Griffin and begin remaking the world. But the arrival of Ash's worldly cousin with unthinkable news puts Sheba's dreams for the future suddenly at risk...

The death of Noel Griffin's grandfather exposes an appalling betrayal: Noel is *not* the heir to the Silliman earldom, despite what the late earl raised him to believe. Still, the only honorable course is to accept his widowed grandmother's bitter charge: find the true heir, disentangle him from his religious community, and tutor him in the responsibilities and privileges of a title Noel assumed would be his. He certainly won't allow a presumptuous, irritating Quakeress to keep him from his duty—no matter how fascinating he finds her...

When scandal threatens both their reputations, can Sheba and Noel look beyond past dreams and imagine a new world —together?

PRAISE FOR BLISS BENNET

"Good Lord, is this a fine romance…. romantic, funny, touching, and extremely well-researched…. perfect."—*All About Romance*, "Desert Island Keeper"

"savvy, sensual and engrossing"—*USA Today Happy Ever After*

"Bennet may be a fledgling author but her book stands stalwart with… *Devil in Spring* by Lisa Kleypas, *My American Duchess* by Eloisa James, and *A Lady's Code of Misconduct* by Meredith Duran…. I was very much taken with her assured writing, complex and unusual characterization, and verve for storytelling."—*Cogitations and Meditations*

"A refreshing change of pace from other historical romances." —*Romantically Inclined Reviews*

"This has been the year of finding incredible new voices in Historical Romance for me and I can now add Bliss Bennet to the list!"—*Passages to the Past*

"This pleasing romance… round[s] out its story with precise historical flair and genuine feelings."—*Publishers Weekly*

"Steamy historical romance with witty and memorable characters and an intriguing plot…. [W]ill keep readers turning pages from beginning to end."—*Night Owl Reviews*

"[Bennet's] finest achievement is the heroine who remains unconventional to the end even when she cooperates in the most conventional of romance fiction's elements: the HEA."—*Heroes and Heartbreakers*

"effervescent. . . . a series well worth following."—*Historical Novel Society Indie Reviews*

"[Bennet has] the rare, and becoming rarer, ability to create main characters who reflect their times and are in turn uniquely, likably themselves."—*Miss Bates Reads Romance*

"A beautifully written love story that has everything you want in a great historical romance: heart-wrenching emotion, heartbreak and a great HEA… Cannot wait for the next one in the series."—*The Reading Wench*

"Catnip for the historical romance reader."—*Bookworlder*

"The human nature of the characters was genuine, even a little understated…. I cried at the end, a sure sign of emotional investment."—*Novels Alive*

"A delightful read!"—*InD'Tale Magazine*, Crowned Heart of Excellence

"Bennet creates the most enticing, delightfully imperfect characters. Watching them finally achieve their happy ever after is bittersweet—you're happy they're happy, but… you weren't done with them yet…"—*USA Today Happy Ever After*

FOR MADDIE

Justice innovator to the world
My own sweet star

PROLOGUE

Leicestershire, England
August 1816

"Bathsheba? Bathsheba Audley Honeychurch! Come here this instant and explain why there's a bull in the midst of my ballroom!"

From the top of Audley Priory's grand staircase, fourteen-year-old Sheba Honeychurch suppressed a groan. Five pairs of adolescent eyes, some widening in amusement, others in dismay, flicked between her and their sharp-tongued grandmother, who stood, arms crossed, foot impatiently tapping, in the center of the grand hall below.

Of course, Lady Audley knew that none of her other granddaughters had had anything at all to do with the appearance of nearly two tons of hungry bovine inside—inside! How had the bull gotten inside?—Audley Priory. Only wild, rattle-brained Sheba—or so her cousins had begun to call her—would ever find her efforts to do a good deed metamorphose into such unmitigated disaster.

Why, she'd left that bull grazing contentedly in the back garden, nowhere near Grandmother Audley's ballroom! Why had the silly thing taken it into its head to wander inside the Priory? And just hours before the start of the annual summer ball, too, the ball that would cap the Audley cousins' two-week visit to the Priory. Perhaps Sheba shouldn't have allowed herself to become so distracted by Elizabeth Heyrick's pamphlet on the plight of Britain's factory workers. But, still, it was too bad of the creature to wander away from where she'd left it!

A low moaning moo, followed by a snuffling snort, resounded from the back of the house.

"Dilks, make sure that ballroom door is shut tight. We don't want the animal to have run of the entire house!" Grandmother Audley commanded the Priory's no-longer-quite-sprightly butler.

The sight of a sword in the trembling hand of said butler sent Sheba racing past her cousins down the steep flight of stairs. "Oh, grandmama, the poor thing! How frightened he must be! Don't allow Friend Dilks to hurt him!"

Grandmother grasped Sheba's arm before she could rush to the poor creature's defense. "The bull? How frightened *the bull* must be? What of Mr. Dilks? Or of Mr. Tillson, whom I sent to chalk the ballroom floor? And what of poor Jenny, who had that great snorting animal yank the flowers she was arranging right out of her very hands? What is the world coming to, when a gel cares more for the sensibilities of a beast of the field than for her own fellow men?"

"I am sorry, grandmama. But it was not well done of the servants to leave the doors to the terrace open. How else could Wellington have got in from the garden?"

A handful of sniggers sounded from the landing above.

"Wellington?" Grandmother Audley pinched the bridge of her nose. "Naturally, you've given the creature a name."

"Well, Friend Underwood called him Brownie," Sheba admitted. "But I thought the old fellow deserved a nobler name than *that!*"

Another moo, this one louder than the first, lowed. From the gallery above, one of her cousins—Polly? Connie?—giggled. Oh, how they all laughed at the scrapes misfit Sheba found herself in during this first summer visit to their Grandmama's! They'd all been coming to the Priory for years, but Sheba's mother had never allowed it. Jane Honeychurch had not wished her only child to be exposed to the vanity and emptiness of the transitory enjoyments of an aristocratic world she herself had left far behind when she'd joined the Society of Friends.

But Mother was gone now...

Sheba pressed her lips tight, fighting against tears. Young ladies of the *ton* did not sob, nor show any other strong emotion, grandmother insisted. And Sheba certainly didn't wish to give her cousins yet another cause to tease...

If only Father hadn't thought it so important for Sheba to develop closer ties to her mother's family! She'd never have been sent to Audley Priory for this strange summer visit otherwise. She felt such a square peg, completely unable to fit into the round holes girls like her cousins, brought up in the Church of England, inhabited with such ease.

Sheba scowled, her toe kicking against the lush carpeting. Why should she care what they thought? The principles her mother had instilled told her she'd done the right thing, no matter how her cousins might laugh and tease.

"Underwood?" Grandmother frowned. "Mr. Underwood, the tavern keeper in Uppingham? What was he doing with a bull?"

"He'd bought the poor emaciated creature to use in a bull-baiting!" Sheba's fists tightened. "Have you ever seen a bull-baiting, Grandmama?"

Lady Audley shuddered. "No, I have not. Nor, I dare say, have you."

"Certainly not! But my teacher, Friend Heyrick, wrote a pamphlet about the horrible practice, so I know all about them.

Do you know, they wrap a chain about the miserable creature, and tie it to a stake, and then set vicious dogs to worry and maul it? And to protect itself, the bull must worry and maul the dogs in its turn! Oh, how could I just stand by when I could stop such an atrocity?"

"How could you indeed?" Grandmother echoed, a hand rising to her temple.

"Then you understand why I had to free the poor creature," Sheba said, even though she didn't think Grandmama had meant *quite* the same thing.

"I understand why you *thought* you had to take it," Grandmama answered. "But what I don't understand is how the beast came to be in the *ballroom*?"

"Because I couldn't just leave him behind in Uppingham! What if some of the villagers who'd been looking forward to the disgusting spectacle found him and dragged him back to Friend Underwood? I could never allow any of God's creatures to be treated with such barbarous cruelty as that man intended."

"Oh, merciful heavens!" Grandmama Audley dropped into the footman's chair. "I thought we'd seen the last of crusading Audley women after we lost poor Jane."

Sheba frowned. No one in the Society of Friends back in Leicester would have spoken so slightingly of her mother. But Grandmother Audley, who had raised her daughters in the Church of England, had never been happy that her youngest had joined the Friends. Especially not after Jane Audley Honeychurch began preaching in public soon after her own daughter's birth.

If only Sheba could be half as persuasive a speaker as her mother had been! But unlike Jane Honeychurch, Sheba had not yet discovered a gift for the ministry.

Still, the poor bull deserved her best effort. Sheba raised a fist in the air. "God sent the animals for our use, but not for our abuse!" There, that sounded almost as ringing as her mother's finest sermon.

"Was he abusing the animal, then?" Anna, at seventeen the eldest of Sheba's Audley cousins, laid a hand on her shoulder. She must have followed Sheba downstairs.

By all rights, Anna should be angry with her. After all, the ballroom *was* being decorated for a dance being held in honor of Anna's just-announced betrothal. But her good-natured cousin just gave Sheba a sympathetic smile.

"What else would you call setting a pack of vicious dogs on an innocent animal?" Sheba declared. "If only there were laws to defend innocent beasts from the barbarous cruelties to which they are exposed, I might have summoned a magistrate, but—"

A pounding on a door at the back of the Priory was met with a mournful bellow from the ballroom.

"Dilks!" a rough voice cried. "The damned bullock's here someplace! You can hear its blethering all the way to Ayston!"

"Please tell me you did not just up and lead that bull away without due compensation to its owner." Grandmama pulled a handkerchief from her sleeve and waved it against the heat. "There may be no laws to protect an animal from its master, but there are certainly laws against stealing another man's property."

"What else was I to do?" Sheba flushed. "Remonstrance and appeals to his better feelings proved fruitless. And the cruel fellow only laughed when I offered him fifteen shillings, the entire sum my father gave me before I left Leicester, to purchase the beast. How was I to know a bull cost ten times as much?" Instead, she'd used those fifteen shillings to pay a farm boy to bring the bull to Audley Priory. The lad hadn't needed to know that the animal did not *precisely* belong to her...

The butler reappeared from the back of the house, an unhappily familiar figure in tow.

Grandmother sighed. "Mr. Underwood, I presume."

The publican took off his hat and nodded. "Aye, my lady."

"You've come in search of a certain animal, I take it?"

"It isn't yourn, my lady. Nor ern, neither." He waved his hat in Sheba's direction.

"No, I dare say it is not."

"Grandmama, you can't mean to give Wellington back to this, this... this barbarian!" Sheba set her body between the tavern keeper and the ballroom. She might only be fourteen, and a girl, but if he tried to push past her, she'd show him how an Audley lady could fight!

"Wellington?" Underwood's forehead wrinkled. "It's Brownie I'm after."

Another roll of sniggering floated down from the stairs. Sheba glared at her cousins and stamped her foot.

"Sheba, control your temper." Grandmother sighed again as she rose from her seat. "Mr. Underwood, does my granddaughter speak the truth? Are you planning to bait the creature currently making itself at home in my ballroom?"

The man's face split in a wide grin. "By'r Leddy! The ballroom? That's a sight they'd pay good money to see!"

"And I'll pay good money to have the creature removed," Grandmama Audley said. "Immediately."

"Grandmama, no!" Sheba exclaimed. "Not unless he promises he won't set the dogs on poor Wellington!"

Underwood snorted. "As I told the young miss here, the bull cares no more for a fight than a crow cares for Sunday."

"How can you say such a thing? It is true, he has no words to tell us how he suffers. But the voice of your conscience should be sufficient reproach!"

"What of the young miss's own conscience, eh?" Underwood stepped closer to Sheba. "Pomfering a beast what's none of her own? The magistrate'll have something to say about that!"

"How much did you pay for the bull, Mr. Underwood?" Cousin Anna asked before Sheba could tell the publican what she thought of such a mean, petty threat.

"Twenty two guineas." He patted his pocket. "I've the bill 'o sale right here."

"And if we reimburse you for Brownie's loss, will you agree not to bring the magistrate into it?" Grandmama asked, wiping her handkerchief against her furrowed brow.

How dare the man make Grandmama worry so! Still, Sheba couldn't help but demand, "And not use the proceeds to purchase another animal to take its place?"

"Lady Audley won't countenance bull-baiting, nor cock-fighting, nor any other such cruel spectacle, not on her lands, nor anywhere in the vicinity," Anna added.

Underwood gave them a considering look. "Happen I would, iffen you were to make it twenty-five. Set out a pretty penny for the advertisements in the *Chronicle* and the *Journal*, I did."

Sheba's face flamed with outrage. "What, are we to *pay* the fellow to do what's right? How can you—"

"Be quiet, gel. It is no longer your concern." Grandmama Audley shooed a hand at her cousins, who must have drifted down from the landing while Sheba had been engrossed in defending poor Wellington. "Back upstairs, the lot of you, or I won't allow you to stay up and look in on the dancing tonight."

Sheba frowned as several of the girls squealed and ran back toward the landing. That's all any of the silly gooses had talked about for nearly a fortnight, how much they longed to catch a glimpse of the elegant gowns and gloves, headdresses and jewels that would adorn the figures of the ladies attending tonight's ball.

Sheba had no use for such empty-headed, frivolous extravagance. Her mother had always counseled her to avoid pride and immodesty in apparel, and to shun the vain and superfluous fashions of the world. Decent plainness and simplicity in dress had been good enough for Jane Honeychurch, and it was good enough for Sheba, too.

Yes, it would take more than Underwood's empty threat to keep her from speaking her mind.

Sheba stepped closer to Lady Audley. "Grandmama, I don't think you've considered—"

"What I think is that I'll be sending you right back to your father in Leicester if you do not stop this endless arguing! Upstairs, immediately!"

"Aye, needs a good yambering, that one does," Underwood had the gall to opine.

Sheba ground her teeth, searching her mind for an appropriate set-down. But Delphie, the cousin closest to Sheba in age, as well as the most sympathetic, laid a restraining hand on her arm. "Come, Sheba dear. You'll only give Grandmother a megrim, arguing so. Once she's made a decision, she never changes her mind. Besides, Cook promised to send up some of the lemon biscuits and ginger cake she's made for the guests tonight for our tea. You don't want Connie and Lizzie to eat them all, do you?"

Sheba didn't care what Connie or Lizzie or Polly thought of her. But if she were to alienate Delphie, the only cousin besides Anna who did not openly mock her strange ways…

Delphie held out a hand.

Sheba took it, but not without first throwing one last look of disdain at the man who would treat a poor bull with such inhumane cruelty.

His smug, triumphant smile, the indifference of her chattering cousins, the dismissal of her grandmother, it all made her seethe. How utterly unfair! Why should anyone care more about the cut of a gown, or the flavor of a cake, than the fate of a fellow living creature? Why were there no laws preventing men like Underwood from perpetrating such disgraceful cruelties upon poor unoffending beasts? And why was nothing being done to find work for all the men who had served so nobly during the war? Or to provide for the widows and children of those who had died in it? Or to ensure the workers in mills like her father's were paid a fair wage? How could any man feed his family when the Corn Laws inflated the price of grain, and the Game Laws took away his right to hunt on what had once been common land? Why should laws supposed to help everyone lead to such suffering for so many?

If only other people knew what she knew, really knew and *felt* the many ills of the world as she did! Surely, then, they'd be as compelled as she was to fix them.

But somehow she could never seem to make anyone really *listen*. Not like her mother had…

Sheba was still seething with frustration and self-reproach late that evening when Anna stole away from the ball to entice her cousins up into Audley Priory's attics to play at some silly wishing game she'd invented out of whole cloth. Telling them a ridiculous story about how it was an old ancestral tradition of intrepid Audley ladies past. But Sheba wasn't fooled. Anna just wanted to escape the tedious inanities of the ball.

Still, when Anna instructed them all to confide to the scraps of paper she handed about the most secret desire of their audacious Audley hearts, Sheba did not hesitate.

Not a wish for a handsome husband, as all the other girls were likely scribbling. Nor anything as base as mere land, or jewels, or wealth beyond compare, either. No, not even for the spiritual guidance for which her mother had often enjoined her to pray.

No, what Sheba wrote in a bold hand that slashed over the paper was this:

To live up to my mother's example, and make people want to change the world.

CHAPTER 1

April 1824

Noel Griffin—plain *Mister* Noel Griffin now, not the fifth Earl Silliman, nor even Baron Ruxford, not anymore, thank you very much, Grandfather—was having a bad day. A deucedly bad day, preceded by a disagreeable fortnight, capping a damned difficult year. And spring had only just sprung...

Noel tapped his whip against his boot as he stared back at the small cottage, one of a group of newly constructed residences on the eastern side of the city of Leicester. Inside, he'd discovered his long-lost uncle's wife, fluttering and twittering as if he'd been a fox set on stealing every precious egg from her henhouse rather than the deliverer of bounties far beyond her imagining.

But of her son, the man whom he'd come to Leicester in search of, there'd not been the least sign. Damn the whelp's sorry hide.

"My lord, will you be staying the night?" his coachman asked. "Or heading back to London?"

Noel glared down at the tops of his boots, still gleaming despite the past day's travels. A small sop to his valet, the persistence of that gleam. Poor Nelmes had been severely downcast since the shocking news that his master had been demoted from heir apparent to heir presumptive had raced through Silliman House, faster than a flame through tinder. Noel had been trying ever since to show his appreciation that the poor fellow hadn't up and decamped at the first whisper by paying due attention to all the sartorial niceties, no matter how little he cared about fashion himself.

"My lord?" the coachman repeated.

His valet wasn't the only servant having difficulty adjusting to the change in his master's fortunes. Noel set a hand on his elderly coachman's sleeve. "I realize old habits are hard to break, Stinchcomb. But if you wish to remain in my employ, you must give over this 'my lord-ing' me. Now take the carriage back to the Blue Boar Inn and get the horses settled. I've one more stop to make before I retire there for the evening."

"Very good, my lo— Very good, sir."

The coachman creaked back up onto the driver's seat and clucked the team back down Leicester's high street, busy with afternoon traffic, on toward the inn they'd passed earlier in the day. Noel followed on foot, but instead of stopping at the hostelry, he swung north, toward the ancient church of St. Nicholas and the even older massive stone arched wall dating back to Roman times that ran behind it. His newly discovered aunt had invited him to wait in her parlor until her son returned from attending a meeting of a newly founded anti-slavery society, but she'd been so obviously discomposed by Noel's presence, he'd chosen to set off in pursuit of young Manasseh Griffin—good lord, what an embarrassingly Biblical name!—himself.

Noel might have been interested in attending the anti-slavery meeting himself, especially given the appalling discoveries he'd made about the Silliman estate holdings during his grandfather's long illness. But family matters must take precedence over personal preference, at least for the nonce. Once he returned to town, though, he'd ask his secretary to find out if a similar society existed in London, and when it next met...

Noel passed the church, then by a field his nervously chattering aunt had informed him was known as Holy Bones, locals believing the place must have once been a site of ancient pagan sacrifice due to the plethora of oxen skeletons that had been excavated in its environs. The street that lay beyond had once been called St. Clement's, from its leading to that church, Mrs. Griffin had added, but had since degraded into the charmingly named Dead Man's Lane.

Hardly a propitious location for the site of a house of worship. But perhaps the members of the Society of Friends didn't have the luxury of being overly fastidious.

Noel made his way down the narrow lane, then through an even narrower passageway to a tall gabled structure built of coursed stone rubble. Its oversized sash windows, twelve panes over twelve, loomed twice the height of the nail-studded timber double doors they flanked. So high they almost reached to its half-hipped stone roof, giving the building a wide-eyed, comical appearance. If its doors had been open, it would have looked decidedly surprised. Just like himself, no doubt, after the Silliman solicitors' shocking announcement that Noel, despite his grandfather's years of assurances to the contrary, was *not* the rightful heir to the Silliman earldom.

Noel gave a self-deprecating snort. It wasn't like him to indulge in such nonsensical flights of fancy. But recent events had put him in a decidedly strange humor.

He stepped up onto the rough timbered porch, then paused. Was this the correct place? Did one knock at the door of a Quaker house of worship? Or just step right in? The sect *was* known for not standing on ceremony...

Before he could decide which course would be the more proper, the door flew open and a thin, cloaked figure ploughed right into him.

"Umph!"

"Oh!"

His arms grasped at the figure—a slim, lithe, but decidedly feminine one—before the force of her movement could send them both tumbling from the porch. The brim of a silk bonnet brushed against his cheek and the scent of soap tickled against his nose as her arms windmilled and flailed, sending printed pamphlets tumbling to the porch. A sudden gust of wind sent several skittering across the timbers.

"Oh, catch them, do!" the young woman cried.

Noel knelt and scrambled to stop the papers closest to him, stifling the unexpected flutter her surprisingly throaty voice raised in his chest. *Immediate, Not Gradual Abolition*, he read as he smoothed a gloved hand over a crumpled page. *An Inquiry into the Shortest, Safest, and Most Effectual Means of Getting Rid of West Indian Slavery.*

Ah. The right place, then.

Together they managed to retrieve the bulk of the pamphlets before they flew away on the April breeze. Shoving the ones he had collected under one arm, he rose, then held out his opposite hand to help her to her feet.

Where was that scent of honeysuckle coming from? The vines twisting over the nearby fence were barely in bloom.

As her long-lashed eyes met his, Noel felt the breath catch in his throat.

His own eyes roved her face, her figure, trying to understand what about such a plainly dressed woman had provoked such a response. Surely not the long, oval face, with its high cheekbones flushed with embarrassment. Nor the slim, swanlike neck, no matter how elegant. The pouting promise of those lips, pink as a summer sunset? The blue of those eyes, dark and deep as the open sea?

The way she stared as brazenly at him as he stared at her?

In his suddenly tight chest, his heart gave a mad, almost sideways leap.

What in the hell?

Noel Griffin, reputedly the most civil, and above all, impassive of London's gentleman, was staring, gasping like a hooked fish, like a damned besotted schoolboy, at a lady whom his rational mind told him did not come even close to numbering among the most handsome women of his acquaintance.

He blinked, then shook his head, trying to rid himself of the ridiculous, embarrassing fascination. But still the feeling, a great gaping *yearning*, held him tight in its grasp.

"Can you tell me, ma'am, if the meeting of the Leicester Anti-Slavery Auxiliary has concluded?" he asked, struggling not to trip over his own words. "I'm looking for a Mr. Manasseh Griffin, whom I understand is in attendance."

"Ash?" A sudden jerk of the lady's head brought her eyes to his. "How do you know Ash Griffin?"

He didn't even notice it, the door of the chapel creaking open again behind her, so caught up in staring at her he was. But the gloved hand that came to rest atop the lady's shoulder could only have been attached to someone who had come from inside.

He forced his eyes away from the deep blue ones pinned just as fixedly on his own, only to be hit with yet another blow. A gentleman with the same hazel eyes, narrow blade of a nose, and slight cleft of the chin Noel saw each time he looked in the mirror. A few years younger than himself, no doubt, and with a far more affable expression on his somewhat rounded countenance. But a Griffin all the same.

"Is this fellow troubling you, Sheba?" the young man asked.

He hadn't believed it, that this deucedly bad day, nay, this entire damned difficult year, could grow even worse.

But it could, and had.

For here he was, smitten by the very lady he'd been warned would prove the greatest stumbling-block to all his carefully laid plans.

The lady—the entirely unsuitable lady—whom his aunt had

informed him was almost engaged to his cousin.

How in the hell was he to disentangle Manasseh Griffin not only from his mistaken religious beliefs, but also from the influence of this bewitching Quakeress?

If only Jane Audley Honeychurch, a preacher and dream prophesier of no little renown in the Religious Society of Friends, had still been alive, her daughter might have had some warning that all her life's plans were about to be tossed to the winds this fine spring day in the fourth month of the year of our Lord 1824.

Oh, sixth day had begun uneventfully enough. In the morning, Sheba had written her daily letter to one of her many Audley cousins—this one to Philadelphia, offering her condolences at the death of Delphie's grandmother-in-law—then taught reading and simple sums at the school she'd established for the children of the workers at her father's hosiery mill, her favorite part of the day. In the afternoon, she'd spoken at the Leicester Friends' Women's Meeting for Discipline on behalf of a deeply repentant Mary Wheeler, who had been in danger of being disowned for marrying without permission, then attended a gathering of the Leicester Ladies' Committee, where women of various religious persuasions discussed how best to raise funds for the indigent Irish. Just before dinner, she'd visited both Naomi Mayfield and Jane Landry, reading aloud to each infirm woman from the Bible and listening to their cares and concerns.

After dinner, though... Yes, after dinner was when it all began to go wrong. Instead of the reward she'd promised herself for a full day's work—rereading William Garnon's memoir of his time serving as the first government chaplain in the African colony of Sierra Leone—she'd squabbled yet again with Ash.

Not, as they had so often during the past year, over how—or

even whether—to try and convince the elders of Leicester Meeting that she and he were well-suited to wed. Nor even about Sheba's growing sense that she was being called to widen the scope of her teaching, perhaps traveling as far as the East, or even to Africa. No, this argument had been about the antislavery pamphlets her friend and former teacher, Elizabeth Heyrick, had just published. The Leicester Anti-Slavery Society, an auxiliary of the national Anti-Slavery Society established just the previous year, was to meet later that evening, and Sheba had assumed Ash would be happy to distribute copies of the pamphlet to his fellow Auxiliary members. But Ash, no doubt wary of what he deemed the radicalness of the publication's arguments, had proven difficult to pin down.

Sheba would have been happy to distribute the pamphlets, but the national Anti-Slavery Society didn't allow women to join, and the men of the Leicester Auxiliary had followed their example. Foolish, the lot of them! Not only mistaken about abolishing the cruel institution gradually, rather than immediately, as Friend Heyrick's pamphlet urged, but also blind to the myriad contributions that women could make to the cause. If her mother had still been alive, *she* would have shown them the error of their ways. Why could not Sheba?

She'd helped Ash to see the rightness of sharing Friend Heyrick's pamphlets, after Papa had excused himself to his library and his beloved books and Ash could no longer dodge the fervency of her importuning. At least, she'd *thought* he'd come to agree with her. But Ash was always so determined to avoid an argument, Sheba sometimes mistook his appeasement for actual assent. As she must have done this evening. Why else would the pile of pamphlets still be lying on the table in the front hall nearly an hour after Ash had left?

In her irritation, Sheba had snatched them up and marched through the cool fourth month air to Soar Lane without even stopping to put on a shawl. Perhaps that's why she found herself shivering now as she gazed up at the brown-haired man standing across from her on the Meeting House porch, clutching the pamphlets she'd dropped when she'd crashed into him in her rush to leave the Meeting House without being noticed.

Had she met him before? He wasn't a member of Leicester Meeting—Sheba knew every one of them by name—nor of any other Meeting in the Midlands, either, she'd guess. No Friend would be dressed in such fashionably elegant attire. Even without a hat—oh, had she knocked it clear off his head when she'd bumped so unceremoniously into him?—the man cut an exceedingly fine figure, with his shiny polished top boots and fine woolen coat, his silver-topped walking stick and silky cravat tied in an intricate, showy knot.

No, he must be stranger. Why, then, had his hand in hers as he pulled her to her feet felt so familiar?

And why was he staring at her now as if she'd done him some grievous harm?

"Is this gentleman troubling you, Sheba?"

Sheba started. She hadn't heard the door to the Meeting House open behind her, hadn't even heard Ash stepping onto the porch.

"No, Ash. As usual, I'm the cause of the *contretemps*." She scooped up the high-crowned beaver hat that had fallen to the porch, then brushed a spot of dirt—oh, she'd left her gloves at home, too!—from its brim. "There! As good as new."

"Think nothing of it, ma'am," the stranger said as he took the hat from her. Certainly not a member of their Society, then, using that honorific rather than simply naming her "Friend."

His hands, naturally, were encased in gloves, gloves of the finest kid.

Ash grabbed her hand and pulled it to his side. To hide her poor breeding in going out without gloves of her own? Ash disliked it so when she forgot propriety in her rush to accomplish some suddenly remembered task.

"Have you lost your way, Friend?" Ash asked the stranger with a little less of welcome in his tone than Sheba was used to hearing. "Or are you in search of a member of the Meeting?"

"The latter. Although I believe I have found him. You are Manasseh Griffin, are you not?"

"Indeed, I am. And your name, Friend?"

The stranger bowed. "I am Noel Griffin, sir. Is there somewhere we might speak in private?"

"Griffin?" Sheba exclaimed. "Are you some relation of Ash's?"

"A cousin, in fact."

"Cousins!" Her gaze bounced back and forth between the stranger and Ash. Yes, even in the waning light, she could trace a resemblance. That light brown hair as sleek as an otter's. Those eyes flickering between green, gold, and amber, depending on how they caught the light. Ears a bit smaller, hands a bit larger than one expected to find on a gentleman. Closer to thirty than to Ash's nineteen, she'd guess, with the look of a mature man rather than one who had just shed the awkwardness of adolescence.

But the stiffness of his bearing, the sternness of his expression —nothing about *those* would ever put one in mind of Ash's father, pious William Griffin, much less Ash, the familiar, friendly boy who had been Sheba's playmate and companion since childhood.

Sheba blinked, then turned back to Ash. "You never told me you had any relations on your father's side."

Ash frowned. "I didn't know I had."

"So I understood from your mother, when I called at your home earlier this evening."

Noel Griffin's voice sounded nothing like Ash's, either. All short, sharp, precise syllables, as if each word had been honed on the edge of a knife. Just like Grandmother Audley's. No wonder the sound raised all Sheba's hackles.

"Shall we return there, or shall we adjourn to the Blue Boar, where I've taken rooms?" he continued. "I've a private parlor where we may speak undisturbed."

Ash, uncharacteristically, said nothing in response to his newfound cousin's question. He need not be intimidated by the older man's polished manners and elegant dress. Sheba gave his hand an encouraging squeeze.

Why, after all this time, had this cousin chosen to seek Ash out? He must have some news about their family to impart. For good, though, or for ill?

Behind them, the door to the Meeting House opened again. Ash's fellow members of the Anti-Slavery Auxiliary milled out onto the porch, several holding copies of the pamphlet she'd left in a pile on the table just inside the door. Good. At least something worthwhile had been accomplished this evening.

"All to rights, Friend Griffin?" Isaac Farrand, one of the Meeting's elders, asked.

But Ash and the stranger both remained silent—each waiting for the other to speak?

"This man has come in search of Friend Griffin, on family business," Sheba jumped in to cover the awkward pause. "Might they speak in the Meeting House, if your gathering has concluded?"

"Family of the late William Griffin?" Friend Farrand asked.

The stranger nodded.

"Indeed, then, Friend Griffin." The elder handed Ash a large key. "Thou wilt return it before Meeting for Worship?"

Sheba might find the plain speech still practiced by Isaac Farrand and many other Leicester Friends antiquated, even occasionally silly. But the haughty look of disdain that crossed Noel Griffin's face at the sound of Friend Farrand's "thou wilt" made her temper flare. As if the older man's words had been intended as a personal affront, rather than a reflection of the Friends' belief in the spiritual equality of all people. What right did he have to look on his elders with such obvious contempt?

Ash only gave a jerky nod. "Yes, Friend Farrand. Thank you."

Sheba stepped inside the Meeting House before Noel Griffin could think to send her away. The Meeting might not yet have granted Sheba and Ash approval to marry, but she could still stand as Ash's friend in the face of whatever news his cousin had to impart. Orderly Ash hated any kind of change, and Sheba couldn't help but feel that the presence of this arrogant stranger boded upheaval of the most disruptive sort.

Noel Griffin took off his hat and examined the interior of the Meeting House with a critical eye. "I've never been inside a Quaker church. How plain it all is! And how odd, to sit on benches instead of pews…"

Sheba bristled. "It is not a church, it is a Meeting House. We do not force the poor to sit in the back, nor line our coffers by making the rich pay for the privilege of a padded pew. For are we not all children of the same great parent, and stand equally in need of His assistance?"

Ash threw Sheba a pleading glance—yes, it made him uncomfortable when she championed their faith to the worldly, but she would not let that keep her silent—before turning back to his cousin. "I take it, Friend Griffin, you are not a member of our religious society?"

The gentleman snorted. "Hardly. Your father may not have told you, but he, like all his Griffin ancestors before him, was raised in the Church of England."

"*All* his ancestors?" Sheba asked. "Even those born before the sixteenth century, when most English were of the Catholic persuasion?"

"Sheba, please, such quibbling is hardly helpful." Ash pressed her down onto a bench, then gestured his cousin to take a seat on the other side of the aisle. "You were speaking of my father, friend?"

"Yes. William Griffin's decision to abandon his family and take up with a dissenting sect was the cause of the estrangement between himself and our grandfather."

"Grandfather? I have a grandfather, as well as a cousin?" Ash leaned forward, all eagerness and curiosity. How Sheba's heart ached for him, knowing how dearly he still mourned his father, whom they'd lost to influenza nearly six years ago. What a gift it would be to discover a previously unknown grandfather, even one who did not share their own religious beliefs.

But Ash's cousin shook his head. "I have been sent to inform you of our grandfather's passing. He died three months ago, on his estate in Devonshire."

"His estate? Then your grandfather was a man of property?" Sheba's mind worked furiously. "Is that why you've come? Did he make some bequest to Ash, in spite of the family estrangement? Ash cares little for riches for his own sake, but he does have three younger sisters to keep clothed and fed. His own father is gone, too, you know, and he helps his mother support them."

"Sheba," Ash protested, humility and hurt lacing his tone. Unkind, to remind him of William Griffin's death.

"Ash had to begin working at a far younger age than either he or his mother wished because of it," Sheba could not help but add. This stranger should know how good a man, how deserving a man, his cousin was. "He serves as a clerk in my father's hosiery factory. But his true talents do not lie in totting up sums. Even a small bequest would allow him to give over such ill-fitting work and spend his time instead ministering to our fellow Friends, as the Lord intended."

"Sheba, please." Ash pressed a hand to her shoulder, a reminder not to embarrass him by prattling on as she was too often wont to do.

But his cousin's raised eyebrow told her it was too late. "A *small* bequest? I suppose a Quaker might regard it so."

Sheba frowned. Did he mean to insult them?

But the strange expression on his face—not so much disdainful as simply lost—stopped her quick rebuke before it could spill over her lips

Sheba's hands grew cold. Something here was wrong. Deeply wrong.

She reached out to Ash, but he had already risen from the bench. As had his cousin.

"Quakers may have no regard for rank, but I have been taught to honor my superiors," Noel Griffin said through lips pulled painfully tight. "Especially the head of my house."

With a flourish of his hat, Ash's cousin bent into a deep bow. "Welcome to the Griffin family, my lord. Manasseh Griffin, fifth Earl Silliman."

CHAPTER 2

"Ash, an earl? Impossible!"

Noel's hat beat an impatient tap-too against his thigh. Who did this Bathsheba Honeychurch think she was, butting into his cousin's affairs, chivvying them both into this strange church when they had far better have spoken in private? She should have left them alone to discuss family business that was certainly no concern of hers.

A pushing, presumptuous chit, precisely the type of woman he least admired.

Why, then, did his eyes keep flicking in her direction?

"My father never mentioned having any connection to the aristocracy," Manasseh Griffin said, the frown lines about his eyes not detracting at all from the easy geniality of his expression.

Noel would have been far more comfortable speaking about such difficult family matters without an audience. But his cousin seemed to be in no hurry to send Miss Honeychurch away, damn the boy. As thick as thieves, they were, his aunt had told him, and had been ever since childhood, even though she was three years his cousin's senior, twenty-two to Manasseh's nineteen.

Everyone expected they would soon marry, her aunt had strongly implied.

Noel humphed under his breath. Not if he had anything to say about it. The sooner he could disentangle his cousin from a match so unsuited to his true rank, the better.

"Surely, Friend Griffin, you must be mistaken," his cousin added when Noel failed to counter his assertion.

"Yes, of course! This gentleman has simply set upon the wrong Griffin." Miss Honeychurch's ungloved hands flew through the air like a flock of starlings startled into sudden flight. Could the young woman not sit decorously still? "Here in Leicester, there are at least three other men with the same surname. And there must be a hundred, if not more, throughout the whole of England."

"There are certainly many Englishmen who share the name Griffin," Noel acknowledged. "But I doubt Manasseh is as equally a common sight in the parish records."

Miss Honeychurch stepped between Noel and his cousin. "How do you know that Manasseh is the Christian name of the man for whom you search? If, as you say, the families have been estranged, how would yours even know it? Surely you must be mistaken."

"I assure you, ma'am, I am not mistaken." How strange. The lady was acting more like a protective elder sister than a supportive helpmeet. Or like a hen clucking and fluffing her wings to warn off predators from a defenseless chick. And his cousin was allowing her to do so, too, and without the least objection. Did the fellow always defer to the girl?

Noel disliked being uncivil, but perhaps incivility was the only language such a pushing woman would understand.

He turned his back on her and addressed his cousin. "Charles Reginald Griffin, fourth Earl Silliman, had three sons, the second of whom was named William Henry. As was your father, was he not?"

Manasseh Griffin nodded.

"William Henry Griffin, the earl's second son, was born on

November 23, 1764. Again, as was your father?"

Another nod.

"And your father sired one son and three daughters before his passing in 1818? Or so he dutifully informed his mother by letter after the birth of each."

For the first time, his cousin's face lit with interest. "His mother? Is his mother still living, then?"

"Yes. And quite eager to make your acquaintance. It was she who sent me in search of you." By all rights, a chore the Silliman solicitors should have undertaken, not Noel. But his grandmother thought having a family member, rather than a complete stranger, convey the news would be kinder to Manasseh Griffin. If her request demonstrated that Lady Silliman cared more for the feelings of a grandson she'd never met than the one with whom she'd lived for more than a decade—well, he'd do better not to dwell on such an uncomfortable insight.

"Why, though, did this grandmother make no effort to acquaint herself with Ash sooner?" Miss Honeychurch demanded. "If, as you claim, she's known of his existence all these years?"

Noel grimaced. The baggage *would* pick up on the part of the story that did his family the least credit.

But his cousin deserved to know the truth. Or at least that part of the truth which related to himself.

Noel set his hat carefully down on the bench. "It was always understood amongst us that Uncle William had died as a young man at sea, and died without issue. But apparently that was only a fiction put about by the earl when your father left the Church of England. After their estrangement, Lord Silliman would not allow anyone to even speak the name of his son in his hearing, never mind acknowledge the fact of his continued existence."

"Only a fiction? How polite you are, dressing up a wolf in sheep's clothing." Miss Honeychuch's eyes flashed. "The man lied about his own son!"

"Does not my cousin's ignorance of his ancestry suggest that *his* son did the same?" Noel countered. "And lied not just to his child, but to his wife, too, if my aunt's surprise when I informed her of his aristocratic connections is to be believed?"

"I'd advise you to keep a more temperate tongue," his cousin said, his tone mild but unwavering. "My mother, like all faithful Friends, places integrity at the center of her life."

Thank goodness the fellow had at least *some* backbone. "My apologies, cousin. I spoke out of turn."

"And I am far too prone to provoking people, as Ash is often kind enough to remind me now that my mother is no longer here to do so," Miss Honeychurch said with a surprisingly self-deprecating smile. The unexpected dimpling of her cheek made Noel blink.

Miss Honeychurch had lost her mother, too?

Manasseh Griffin cleared his throat. "We would all do better to think before we speak, I believe. Friend Griffin, I wonder—"

"Please, enough of this 'Friend' business." Noel summoned the semblance of a smile. "You may call me Noel. Or Griff, if that would not be too awkward, given our shared surname. We are cousins, after all."

"Distant cousins? Or close?"

"Ash and I are second cousins," Miss Honeychurch interposed. "Before she married, Ash's mother was a Honeychurch."

His newly discovered aunt had failed to mention that detail. But still, he could best Miss Honeychurch there. "Manasseh and I are even more closely related. My father and his were brothers."

A wistful smile flit across his cousin's face. "I've been blessed with an abundance of sisters, but no brothers. What of you?"

His sister's tiny face, those baby fists furled against fever and pain...

Noel shook his head. "No. I have none of either."

"But cousins can sometimes grow as close as brothers, can they not?"

Ah, the boy was looking for connection, perhaps even for a model of adult masculine conduct he might emulate. Noel would happily take on such a role, especially if it detached his cousin from undue female influence. Especially the influence of a certain impertinent, interfering young Quaker.

Careful to keep his eyes from flicking again in Bathsheba Honeychurch's direction, he set his hand to his cousin's shoulder and gave it a light squeeze. "I would like nothing better."

"But I still do not understand why I should have anything to do with our grandfather's title," his cousin said. "Since my father was not, as you've explained, the eldest son."

"Our Uncle Charles, who was the eldest, died before his thirtieth birthday, and left no legitimate issue. As the only son of Grandfather's second son, you fall next in line to inherit."

"But Ash can refuse the title, can he not?" Miss Honeychurch interrupted. "Or bestow it upon some other member of your family? You, perhaps?"

Noel would not allow himself to flinch, no matter how sharply her words bit. She could hardly know how he'd urged the family's solicitor to rake through peerage law for a way to make his grandfather's promise that Noel would be the one to inherit the earldom a reality. How, after the lawyers had only shaken their heads, he'd pored over dusty legal tomes for hours himself, searching for some loophole that could make truth of the earl's self-deceiving lie. How the words "no person that hath any Honor of him and a Peer of this Realm, may alien or transfer the Honor to any other person" echoed in his brain every night when his head met his pillow, every morning when he first opened his eyes.

No. He was not the Earl Silliman, nor would he ever be, not unless Manasseh Griffin predeceased him without male issue. And Noel would give no man any reason to accuse him of wishing for such an outcome, let alone doing anything in his power to hasten it. Noel knew his duty. He would see this raw young cousin trained up properly, to do his own duty to their family, to the title, and to all who depended upon both. To act otherwise would be to forfeit not only the respect of his peers, but even worse, his own.

"Impossible, ma'am," he finally mustered the calm to assert. "Surely Quakers are not so isolated from the rest of the world as to be ignorant of the laws of primogeniture?"

"We are not ignorant of worldly ways," his cousin said, laying a hand on Miss Honeychurch's arm before she could give free rein to the temper he'd intended to provoke by his less than civil question. "It is only that they are so distant from our own beliefs and experiences, they can be difficult to fathom."

"I understand, cousin. But you will soon become accustomed to them once you remove to London."

"London?" Miss Honeychurch exclaimed, her blue eyes widening. "You wish Ash to go to London?"

His cousin clutched at a bench, his face growing suddenly pale. Ah, yes. The true import of Noel's news was finally starting to sink in.

"But what of our plans to marry, Ash?" Miss Honeychurch whispered. "And my calling to teach the children of the oppressed? You know the Church Missionary Society will never allow an unwed woman to travel to the East, or to Africa..."

Noel felt his own face blanch. Miss Honeychurch wished his cousin to go a-proselytizing in foreign climes? It seemed he'd arrived just in time to save Manasseh Griffin from the most rash, impracticable scheme he'd ever had the displeasure of encountering.

"Our grandmother awaits us in London, Manasseh. You must come and take up your rightful place in society."

Miss Honeychurch set a hand on his cousin's back, her face grim. "Ash *has* a place in society. In the Society of Friends. There is no need for him to travel to London."

"I'm afraid I must disagree with you, ma'am. The Earl Silliman must take his seat in the House of Lords when Parliament is in session. And he must administer his estates, none of which lie in Africa, or even here in Leicestershire. Hundreds of people depend upon his so doing."

Once again, he turned his back on the forward, managing chit, speaking directly to his cousin. "The countess, our grandmother, instructed me to bring you to London immediately, so we may begin to familiarize you with your new responsibilities. I've already asked your mother to pack you a bag. Although you needn't bring much; heaven knows you can't appear in such plain garb when we introduce you to the *ton*."

"The *ton*? Ash, surely you won't—surely you can't—" Miss Honeychurch took a step back, then another, her easy self-assurance slipping away like shadows into shade.

Ah, yes. She, too, was finally beginning to understand what this change in her childhood friend's fortunes truly meant. Not just for Manasseh Griffin, but for herself.

Noel would not allow himself to wonder why the satisfaction he'd anticipated at hearing the dismay in her voice failed to materialize.

"I don't know, Sheba," his cousin finally answered with a slow shake of his head. "I must speak with the Elders, and with my mother, and seek their advice. And then pray on what is best to be done."

"What's best to be done? Surely there can be no question of your going to London!"

"Miss Honeychurch. You must see that a man, an honorable man, cannot simply turn his back on his family, nor on his responsibilities."

He had deliberately softened his tone, but his words did not seem to reassure her. Nay, instead they seemed to recall her to her more belligerent self. "His family? What of Ash's responsibilities to his mother and his sisters?"

"His new position will allow him to better fulfill those

responsibilities," Noel answered, schooling himself to patience. "His income as Earl Silliman will allow him to support any number of female dependents."

"Mere money," she scoffed. "As if filthy lucre has anything to do with fulfilling one's familial responsibilities."

"Sheba," his cousin cautioned.

"Money may not be of the greatest import, ma'am but I challenge you to show me a man who can support his dependents without any income at all," Noel challenged.

"Now, Friend Griffin," his cousin said, his tone placating.

"Ash has an income," Miss Honeychurch said, paying not the least heed to his cousin's attempts to calm the waters.

"A clerk's pittance?" Noel scoffed. "Hardly enough, I'll warrant, to keep a household of women fed, clothed, and sheltered in any degree of comfort."

"Perhaps not up to your lofty standards. But I assure you, neither Ash's mother nor his sisters find their way of life lacking. Friends eschew the luxuries and excesses of the worldly."

"Sheba, cousin, such squabbling is unseemly, and hardly necessary…"

Noel barely heard Manasseh Griffin's mild admonishment, caught by the storming scorn in Miss Honeychurch's eyes. Eyes that flashed as blue and hot as a strike of summer lightning. He stepped closer, heedless of the scorch.

"My cousin may eschew any personal or private luxury he wishes, for himself or on behalf of his sisters or mother. But he cannot ignore his responsibilities to the earldom. He has a duty to his dependents, and to his country. He is a nobleman now."

Miss Honeychurch gave a distinctly unladylike huff. "As if a nobleman is any different from any other man with dependents or responsibilities."

Perhaps he should have expected it, that mix of incredulity and disdain in Miss Honeychurch's voice. She was, after all, a Quaker. Even Noel, who knew little of the sect, understood its members scorned traditional social hierarchies, purporting to believe in the equality of all men before God. Still, the few Quakers with whom he'd come into contact had all been businessmen, attuned to the practical benefits of cultivating aristocratic connections. Though he'd never seen one doff a hat nor bow to a gentleman whom most of English society would deem his social superior, neither had he ever witnessed one so openly scorn the distinctions of rank.

"The duties of a nobleman far exceed those of any ordinary working fellow," he bit out. "My cousin is a peer of the realm now, like it or not. There is nothing he, nor I, nor even you, Miss Honeychurch, can do to change that."

"A peer of the realm?" Was it temper that made the color rise in Miss Honeychurch's face? Or fear? "Do not all peers have to swear fealty to the Church of England?"

"If they are to take their seats in Parliament, yes."

So violently she shook her head, Noel was astonished every pin in her hair did not fly to the corners of the church. "Impossible! No Friend will ever swear an oath."

"A ridiculous prohibition," Noel countered. "Surely no intelligent man would allow such a minor inconvenience as swearing to tell the truth to stand in the way of doing his duty to his king."

"Minor inconvenience? When the Bible admonishes us to 'Swear not, neither by heaven, neither by the earth, neither by any other oath: but let your yea be yea; and your nay, nay; lest ye fall into condemnation'?"

"You display your ignorance by interpreting that verse so literally, Miss Honeychurch. For did not God himself show the unchangeable character of his purpose by guaranteeing it in his own oath to Abraham?"

Miss Honeychurch's eyes narrowed. "My mother would say you're splitting Biblical hairs. A Friend speaks the truth to all, including men in positions of power. To swear an oath would be to suggest that there is one standard of truth for daily living, and another for the court. Ash cannot swear an oath, and so he cannot be named a peer. You will never change Ash's mind on this matter, I assure you."

"And I assure you that I will."

Lord! Every nerve in his body hummed, as if the lightning in her eyes had been more than metaphorical, as if it had struck him right between his own. If he didn't stop this, stop right this instant, he just might shake right out of his own skin.

Or grab Miss Honeychurch and shake her free of her own...

A loud crash jerked him free of her spell.

He turned to find an overturned bench, the hat which he had set atop it now slowly rolling across the floor.

"Cousin Manasseh, surely you must see—"

"Ash, surely you will not—"

But the only sign of the man they importuned was the door to the Meeting House, slamming shut in his wake.

What bliss, to hear the clock in Soar Lane's Meeting House finally strike twelve! All around Sheba, her fellow members of the Leicester Society of Friends were shaking hands with their neighbors, signaling that Meeting for Worship had finally come to an end. She offered a repentant hand of her own to old Hannah Darby, who sat on the bench to her left. The elder had spent the better part of First-day worship casting disappointed glances at Sheba, who had been fidgeting impatiently beside her during the entire morning.

Why was it so exceedingly difficult, if not impossible, to settle her mind to silently wait upon God? Sadly volatile, this temperament of hers, even on the best of days, as her mother had been wont to remind her. And completely ungovernable for the past two, her thoughts and feelings roiling as if she were a pot of water set over a briskly burning fire. Because for two whole days, Ash had assiduously avoided her. Or what was more likely, his haughty cousin had deliberately kept him from her company. Worried, no doubt, that she'd offer opinions far different than his own about what Ash should do about his unexpected, and most unwelcome, inheritance.

She craned her neck, searching for him amongst the clusters of Friends exchanging greetings and farewells in the wake of the Meeting. He shouldn't have rushed off like that on sixth-day evening, leaving her alone with his disconcertingly cold cousin. Noel Griffin, caught up in his ridiculous London propriety, had insisted on accompanying her all the way home, as if she had been a child unable to find her way through a city teeming with ruffians rather than a grown woman navigating streets she had traversed without incident for more than a decade. But forcing Ash, who so hated change, and who hated arguing even more, to listen to her and his cousin brangling so, well, it had not been her best moment.

She'd felt guilty afterwards, even though it had been Ash who had abandoned her. If she'd read the presumptuous determination in his cousin's cold hazel eyes correctly, Noel Griffin would think nothing of bending friendly, obliging Ash to his own will. She could only hope that Ash—or, at least, one of the Meeting's less compliant elders—had sent the disdainful lordling packing.

"Friend Honeychurch." Hannah Darby's voice creaked almost as loudly as the bench from which she rose. "Approaching public worship with a mind crowded with thoughts of outward things, and resuming such thoughts with avidity upon First-day Meeting's conclusion, is not likely to fill up the interval to profit. Little wonder thou wast never called to the ministry as thy good mother was."

Sheba stared at her hands, clenched tightly in her lap. Why should she resent members of the Leicester Meeting who felt called to remind her how short she fell of her mother's godly example? Did she not remind herself of the same nearly every single day?

As a child, she'd taken it for granted that she, like her mother before her, would be called to the ministry, would spend her young adulthood ministering to her fellow Friends rather than settling into an early marriage. Friends believed that exercising such an invaluable gift should be the central purpose of life, whether the person called was a man or a woman. Emotional entanglements, especially romantic love, would only prove a distraction from such vital service. Her own mother, called to lay down her life for His sake, had spent her early adult years traveling and preaching, not marrying until she was nearly five-and-thirty.

But unlike Jane Honeychurch, her daughter had never received the least sign of a religious calling.

During adolescence, Sheba had often felt as useless as an ox ploughing lines in the sand. Until the day she was called to understand that her dearest friend Ash would make a fine minister, especially if he had Sheba as his helpmeet. His friendly, open manners led young and old not only to confide in him, but also to listen to, and act on, his counsel. Even if Sheba were never called to the ministry herself, once she married Ash she could carry on her mother's work within the Society of Friends by supporting his.

And as a married woman, she would gain more respect and authority in the many charitable organizations outside the Society, too. Including the Church Missionary Society, the organization that had sent several men, and a handful of married women, to Africa and the East to teach and to spread the Gospel.

Her mother had traveled to preach, had she not? If she and Ash were to journey overseas, perhaps she could finally begin to live up to Jane Honeychurch's example.

But was such a desire a true leading from God? Or only the

selfish desire of a guilty heart?

A squeeze of bony fingers against her hand jerked Sheba's attention back to the Meeting House.

"Be certain thy actions are guided by love, not ambition or prideful righteousness." Hannah Darby laid a wrinkled hand atop hers. "Those who are willing to be led by the only true guide, Bathsheba, are seldom kept without a knowledge of the way,"

A painful flush rose over Sheba's cheeks. How could the elder see so easily into the most shameful parts of Sheba's mind?

"I thank you for your wisdom, Friend," Sheba answered, even as her eyes wandered the congregation. In search of Ash, she hoped, rather than from a wish to avoid Hannah Darby's too-knowing eyes. "But I must find Friend Griffin—"

There, just rising from the bench at the back of the room, stood Ash's mother, retying her youngest daughter's bonnet as Patience mustered her other sister toward the Meeting House porch.

Sheba glanced to the benches on the opposite side of the aisle, where the men sat. But of the sole Griffin brother there was not the least sign.

"Bathsheba? Bathsheba Honeychurch? Art thou listening, child?" Hannah Darby exclaimed as Sheba jumped up from the bench.

"Will you excuse me, Friend? I must speak with my Aunt Abiah without delay."

"Oh, what an impatient disposition is thine!" Hannah Darby exclaimed. "Have a care, lest the violence of thy impulses lead thee astray."

"I will, Friend Darby, truly I will." Sheba gave the woman's hand a quick squeeze before rushing down the aisle.

But by the time Sheba had caught up with Abiah Griffin on the Meeting House porch, she was already deep in conversation with Friend Satterthwaite and Friend Tanner, both members of the Leicester Women's Meeting for Discipline.

"Bathsheba, how do you do?" Elizabeth Heyrick, Sheba's former teacher and current mentor, stayed her just before she reached Aunt Abiah and the others. "Was Manasseh able to share copies of my pamphlet with Friend Farrand, or any of the other members of the Leicester Anti-Slavery Auxiliary?"

"Oh!" Sheba slapped a hand to her mouth. "The pamphlets! I nearly forgot them amidst all the tumult of the past few days."

"Just as well, Bathsheba," Rebecca Sattherthwaite interrupted, cutting a disapproving glance at Elizabeth. "Far too worldly behavior for a Friend, to be printing up tracts about matters of so little concern to the Society."

"The perpetuation of slavery in our colonies is the concern of every moral creature," Elizabeth said, the mildness of her tone at odds with the certainty of her words.

"We already forbid the practice amongst our members," Rebecca Satterthwaite said. "Let those of other religions look to their own principles."

"But we are all implicated in the vile practice, whenever we purchase sugar made from the forced labor of the enslaved," Sheba argued.

"Come, come," Mary Tanner held up a quavering hand against the long-standing argument. "It little becomes us to argue, especially with dear Abiah in such need of our support."

"Ah, yes. Poor Abiah!" Rebecca Satterthwaite turned her pitying gaze on Ash's mother. "To discover thine own husband had kept such secrets! If William Griffin were still alive, we would surely have called him to task for withholding the truth from thee."

Sheba pressed closer to her aunt and laid a comforting hand on her sleeve. Friends valued truthfulness, but Rebecca Satterthwaite's candor could sometimes be altogether too cruel.

"For all that Abiah's husband and Bathsheba's mother so fervently believed their children would one day be called to wed,

I believe we were wise to counsel them to wait before marrying."

Sheba fought back a huff of frustration. Neither Rebecca Satterthwaite nor Mary Tanner had been at all encouraging two months ago when Sheba had formally requested approval from the Women's Meeting to marry Ash, after he'd finally turned nineteen. Why should it matter that no deep inward promptings of the Holy Spirit had led her to choose him? Had they not been the best of friends since childhood? And had they not always been taught it was far better for a marriage to be based on friendship rather than on silly romantic ideals?

But the consensus of the elders of the Women's Meeting had been that Sheba and Ash should wait. They must be patient, and listen for a divine leading first, to ensure that such a marriage would be in accordance with the will of God, without whose blessing there could be no true happiness.

The elders' lack of encouragement about her proposed marriage made Sheba reluctant to confide in them her wish to teach in foreign lands, for they would insist she wait for a divine leading here, too. A leading they, just like her mother, assured her she would hear if she would cultivate the habit of frequent retirement and contemplation rather than rushing about like a whirlwind, busying herself with worldly concerns. Only when she could quiet her mind would the still small voice of the Lord be inwardly revealed.

Why should it be so easy to know what other people should do, how they should act, but so difficult to quiet the rill of her wayward thoughts and listen patiently for that still small voice of the Lord? A voice that always seemed just out of her reach…

"Friend Honeychurch, how fares your father?" Rebecca Satterthwaite asked, intruding on Sheba's worries. "Did he not accompany you to Meeting this morning?"

Blood rushed again to Sheba's cheeks. Of course Friend Sattherthwaite noticed Joseph Honeychurch's absence from First Day Meeting for Worship.

"Father had his nose buried in a report from the Gas Company when it was time to leave, and I could not convince him to set it aside. Aunt Abiah, where might I find Ash?"

Instead of answering Sheba, Abiah Griffin cast Rebecca Satthertwaite a worried glance. Sheba's father might not care overmuch at being chastised by the Committee for Discipline for allowing temporal concerns to keep him from First Day Meeting, but Ash's mother, just like Ash, disliked being the target of the elders' disapproval.

"If only Joseph Honeychurch would follow Manasseh Griffin's example," Mary Tanner said, blinking rheumy eyes. "Abiah's son never shirks First Day Meeting."

"How can you say so, Mary, when he is not here this morning?" Rebecca Satterthwaite protested.

"I hope the news from London you received has not made him ill?" Elizabeth ventured.

Ash, ill? Surely not. But still upset with Sheba? Only too likely...

With a disposition far easier than hers, Ash usually forgave her frequent outbursts of temper quite quickly. But Sheba's determination to take up his cause with his cousin, and without allowing him a moment to speak for himself, must have made him unhappy. Was he still avoiding her?

She'd called at the Griffin house Seventh Day morning, and again the same afternoon, hoping not only to apologize but also to offer Ash the wealth of ideas she'd devised for how best to explain to his cousin why he could not leave Leicester. But both times, Patience had told her he was too busy consulting with his mother, and with the Meeting's elders, to have any time for her. And Patience herself was far too busy watching over her younger sisters to spend time in idle gossip, either. Sheba would just have to wait until the morrow, Patience insisted, after First Day Meeting for Worship, if she wished to speak with her brother.

Had his sister not told Ash of her visits? Or had his far-too-worldly cousin kept him from attending Meeting?

No, she couldn't believe it. The Griffin family had always been diligent in First-day worship. And after receiving such unsettling news as his cousin had brought, they would certainly need all the support and advice their friends could give.

"No, Ash is not ill," Abiah finally answered, her eyes shying away from Sheba's. "My son is not in town at present."

Sheba stepped back, her palm reaching for the cool stone of the Meeting House wall. Ash had left Leicester? Without even a word to her?

"Do not say he is traveling on First Day, Abiah?" Disapproval laced Rebecca Sattherthwaite's voice. "I never would have thought it of him."

The look in Abiah Griffin's eyes was not one of worry, now, but of guilt. "No, not on First Day. Ash and his cousin left last night, on urgent family business. For London."

CHAPTER 3

Noel's grandmother, Frances Griffin, Lady Silliman, still sprightly at the age of seventy two, tripped down Silliman House's grand staircase, delight limning her lined face. "Ah, my dear, you've returned at last. And you need not tell me who you've brought with you, for your cousin is the very picture of his dear, dear father. Oh how I have longed for the day when I would finally get to meet my poor William's only son. Here, sweet boy, bend that handsome head of yours and let me give you a kiss."

Lady Silliman laid a passing hand on Noel's sleeve, but all her attention was fixed on the man she'd sent Noel to find: Manasseh Griffin, the true heir to the earl of Silliman. Before their grandmother's appearance, his cousin had been gazing about the grandeur of Silliman House's entrance hall, eyes wide with awe. But at the dowager's welcoming words he gathered himself and offered their grandmother a shy smile. Brushing past Noel, Lady Silliman curled a hand about her newly discovered grandson's neck, pressing her lips to his ruddy cheek.

Noel shoved his hands into the pockets of his coat. So similar, this scene, and yet so different, from when he'd first been brought to Silliman House nearly twelve years ago. His grandmother had been just as welcoming to him, but Noel, unlike Ash, had been all stiff wariness, still reeling from the loss of his father only a few months earlier, his mother and sister the year before. The news that his Uncle Charles, his father's elder brother, had died unexpectedly, too, leaving Noel next in line to inherit his grandfather's earldom and estates, had only convinced his fifteen-year-old brain that accepting affection from anyone, especially a family member, would be the course of a fool.

No, Noel had been far more at ease with his stern, dispassionate grandfather, a man who had not had more than a word for him when he'd been merely the son of his own youngest son, than with a kindly grandmother who fussed and fretted about his tender feelings, feelings he'd far prefer to ignore. Noel had lapped up the earl's disdain for strong feelings —Frenchified, effeminate, the mark of the undereducated and ill-bred, he often scoffed. His grandfather had taught Noel instead to value intellect, rationality, strategy and planning. A true gentleman would always shun dangerous and self-indulgent emotional display.

All lessons that Manasseh Griffin seemed never to have encountered. For if his cousin felt the least bit of discomfort in the face of Lady Silliman's effusive welcome, Noel could not detect it.

"Grandmama." Ash accepted the countess's kiss, then took the tiny woman's hands in his own, the corners of his eyes crinkling. "You cannot know how very happy I am to make your acquaintance."

"And I yours, my dear boy."

"May I call you Grandmama? Or would you prefer Beldam? Good-dame? Eldmother?" Ash smiled as he offered his handkerchief to Lady Silliman, whose eyes had begun to tear.

Noel supposed he shouldn't be so surprised by his cousin's easy manner. After spending the last few days traveling with Manasseh Griffin—a journey made far longer because of his cousin's refusal to travel on Sundays—watching him smile and chat and charm every single person they encountered, he'd realized that his cousin's disposition was markedly different from his own. Far more similar to their grandmother's, in fact, than Noel's had ever been.

Noel shook his head at the unworthy flicker of resentment that observation engendered. If his grandmother could gain influence over his cousin, make him wish to please her, it was only to the good. Someone more personable than Noel could better persuade him to give over his Quaker ways and adopt manners and beliefs more fitting to an earl.

Lady Silliman dimpled even as she dabbed away her tears. "Grand*mother* will suffice, at least for when we are *en famille*, Manasseh."

"Ash, if you please, not Manasseh. It is what my family calls me."

"Ash? But that is nothing like Manasseh."

"For that you must fault Bathsheba—my mother's cousin, whom I've known since we were both in leading strings. When she was a child, Sheba couldn't pronounce my Christian name, and called me Ash instead. And such was, and is, the force of her personality that my family could not but follow her lead."

"Ash it will be, then. But you will, of course, be Silliman to me when we are in company," Grandmother declared, patting at his cousin's waistcoat as if she could not keep herself from checking that her long-lost grandson truly stood before her in the flesh, and was not simply a flight of her wishful fancy. "It will take us both a while to accustom ourselves to it, but it is best to begin as we mean to go on. You are the earl now, and calling you by your proper name in public will be the first step in bringing society to recognize you as such."

You are not *the earl now...*

It is your duty, sir, your duty to your family, to find the rightful heir and bring him to London...

You must call him Silliman...

Your grandmother wishes it...

Months later, those words, and the apologetic expressions on the faces of the Silliman family solicitors as they offered them, still shot arrow-sharp shafts of shame. Even worse, the memories engendered a nearly uncontrollable need to rant and rage at his poor, conflict-averse grandmother. How could she have left it to Mr. Rackham the elder and his son to inform Noel of his grandfather's lie?

Noel pressed his hand around a spiral in the wrought iron of the grand staircase until its curves bit against his palm.

Though she might avoid conflict, Lady Silliman always knew how to navigate social conventions to her own, as well as her family's, advantage. And so Noel had swallowed his unbecoming anger and followed her advice, passed on to him by Mr. Rackham the elder, to call his newly found cousin by the title that had once belonged to their grandfather.

Ash, though, had not welcomed Noel's deference. It was not the way of Friends, his cousin had explained, to use titles or honorifics of any kind. No *Lord* this, not even any *Mister* that. Given name only, or given and surname together, or Friend and surname at the most, he'd insisted whenever Noel had tried to address him with the least formality.

Noel could only hope that Lady Silliman could persuade his cousin of the impracticality of trying to steer such a course through the tumultuous waters of the *ton*.

"Grandmother in public, then, and Granny in private," Ash declared with a wide grin. "Yes, it will be just as you wish."

Lady Silliman gave his cousin's arm a playful swat. "Granny? Oh, go on with you, you silly boy!"

Noel blinked. Had his oh-so-proper grandmother just *giggled*?

"Now do come into the drawing room, so we may discuss how to best begin to introduce you to society. There will be some awkwardness, at first, as everyone expected—" Lady Silliman glanced quickly away from Noel, then gave a slight wave of her hand. "But we will paper it over easily enough."

Noel and his cousin shrugged off their greatcoats and handed them to the footman.

"Oh, what is this you're wearing?" Grandmother declared, hands flying to her cheeks as she caught sight of Ash Griffin's Quaker garb. "Heavens, your grandfather would turn over in his grave to see a descendant of his sporting about London in such a poorly-cut coat. Noel, you must take your cousin to Schweitzer and Davidson before we begin to introduce him about town. Oh, how handsome you will look in a figured silk waistcoat—hunter green, do you think? Or perhaps a dark blue?"

"Grandmother," Noel cautioned. It had been difficult enough convincing his provincial Quaker cousin to come to London. Appeals to wealth, appeals to power and self-interest, none had moved his cousin in the least. Appeals to family duty and sentiment had worked a bit better. But only after explaining how many people depended on the earldom, and emphasizing how much broader scope a peer had to do good in the world than did a lowly factory clerk, had he been able to persuade his cousin to leave Leicester.

Ash had been stubbornly resistant, though, to changing his plain garb for something more suited to his new rank. Noel had chosen not to push, at least for the time being.

"What, you think me unhandsome?" Ash asked, striking a hand to his chest in mock-hurt. No, his personable cousin did not need Noel to manage their grandmother.

"Unhandsome?" Grandmother chuckled again. "You silly boy. One look in your mirror will tell you the ridiculousness of any such fear."

"But I suppose I shouldn't care," Ash added with a winsome grin. "Sheba is always warning me that charm is deceitful, and beauty vain."

Noel frowned at Ash bringing up yet again one Miss Bathsheba Honeychurch. During their time on the road, he'd had to suffer a veritable litany of "Sheba says," and "Sheba believes," and "I wonder what Sheba would think of that?" at the hands—or rather, from the lips—of his cousin. The novelties of the road should have distracted his cousin from all he'd left behind, especially the irritating Miss Honeychurch. But the further they traveled from Leicester, the more frequently he uttered her name, as if it were some sort of verbal talisman, a reminder of an identity to which he must know he could no longer cling.

And at each utterance of "Sheba," an image of the annoying Miss Honeychurch would rekindle in Noel's own brain, forcing him to blink away surprisingly vivid memories of flyaway flaxen hair, animated hands tracing through the air, blue eyes snapping with intelligence and intransigence in equal measure.

At least Ash had called her *cousin*, not *betrothed*. Thank heavens for small favors.

"Unhandsome? With those bright hazel eyes and that enchanting blade of a nose?" Lady Silliman smiled. "Both just like your father's, and *he* was once known as one of the fairest men in all the *ton*. I declare, if you had put me in a room full of strangers, I would have known you for my grandson in a trice."

His cousin laughed and shook his head.

"Oh, you do not believe me? Come and see for yourself, then."

Lady Silliman slipped her hand in the crook of Ash's arm and drew him into the library. Over the mantel, a family portrait held pride of place. His grandparents and their six children, three sons and three daughters, the boys remarkably similar in coloring and expression, all blond and ruddy with aristocratic confidence and good humor.

"Do you see how much you favor them? Your father, as well as your uncles?" she asked.

Ash stepped closer, studying the portrait intently. "Indeed, I do. And perhaps one day I may look as distinguished as does this grand personage presiding over the whole—my grandfather,

I presume? I regret that the estrangement between him and my father prevented me from ever knowing him. You must miss him dreadfully, ma'am."

Did she? The late earl had been a proud, unyielding man. And he'd made his wife live a lie each time he presented Noel as his rightful heir. Even worse, he'd forced her to deny her own flesh and blood, prevented her from knowing Ash and his sisters, her own grandchildren.

Noel had never once heard her upbraid the man, never even openly disagree with him. But surely she must have resented him, resented the lies he'd made her live, the self-denial he'd made her daily bread.

Just as Noel resented her for rejecting those lies, laying waste to everything he'd assumed about himself, everything he was, everything his grandfather had promised he would be…

Noel's jaw clenched. Enough. Feeling bitter, aggrieved—it accomplished nothing, changed nothing. He had a duty to fulfill, a duty to his family, to his grandmother and to his cousin. For the next two years, until his cousin gained his majority, he would teach Ash—teach *Silliman*—everything their grandfather had once taught him about the responsibilities and privileges of being a peer of the English realm.

And when Silliman turned twenty-one? What in hell was he going to do with himself then?

Noel pulled at his cravat, as if it, rather than the question, were causing the sudden tightness binding his throat.

"Yes, it is difficult to reorient one's life after such a forceful presence is taken from it," Lady Silliman said, admirably diplomatic to the end. "Still, it is a comfort to have the Zoffany painting of him as a young man hanging in the gallery at Ruxford Hall, as well as this family portrait here in town."

"I am glad, Granny." His cousin turned back with eager interest to stare up at the painting. "I cannot wait to show it to my mother and my sisters. And especially to Sheba. She always thought it a pity my father never had his likeness drawn. She offered to take one, many times. But Father always thought it too frivolous to sit for her."

His grandmother shot Noel a concerned glance. He was not the only one, it seemed, noticing how often her grandson uttered that unwelcome name.

"Your mother—she did not wish to accompany you to town?" Lady Silliman asked instead.

"No, Mother and the elders all thought it better that she and my sisters remain in Leicester, at least for now. No need for all of us to be exposed to the worldly ways of London society…" His cousin trailed off, looking a bit lost as he gazed about at his unfamiliar surroundings, so much more sophisticated and elegant than the plain rooms in which he'd lived with his family.

"Worldly ways?" Lady Silliman frowned. As the daughter of a duke, she'd been raised in even loftier surroundings than were to be found in Silliman House. She likely knew less about Quaker customs and manners than Noel did.

But his cousin did not seem to notice their grandmother's confusion. "I wonder if I might trouble you for ink and some paper. I'd like to write to my mother, to inform her of my safe arrival. And to Sheba, too—"

"Certainly you must write to your mother. But not to your cousin. It is improper for any young man to correspond with an unmarried girl."

His cousin's smile was puzzled. "Improper?"

"Yes, improper. You would not want to raise unwarranted expectations, would you? Oh, how I long to introduce you to my friends, and to their sons and grandsons, the young men who will soon become yours. But it seems we have some work to do first, to teach you how to go on. Write to an unmarried girl indeed…"

"But Noel kept me so busy I had no chance to speak with Sheba before we left for town," Ash protested.

Yes, his cousin was right. Noel had done all in his power to keep his cousin away from the girl after that initial meeting. He'd suspected Sheba Honeychurch would do all in her power to persuade her almost-betrothed to remain in Leicester.

Not because he didn't trust himself in her company.

"Sheba's never visited London before. But she's always wanted to judge for herself whether the concerns members of the Society of Friends express about the evils of public places of amusement commonly enjoyed in town are truly warranted."

Noel's stomach swooped. Bathsheba Honeychurch, here in London? No. Impossible. Her father, the Quaker elders—surely they would never allow a young, unmarried girl to rush off in wanton pursuit of a not-quite suitor. A veritable scandal it would be, and not just among the *ton*.

Although why his first instinct should be to worry about whether Miss Honeychurch might earn the disapprobation of her fellow Quakers, rather than about what malevolent influence she might exert over his cousin, he could not begin to fathom.

"I hope you will allow me to receive her letters, Grandmother," Ash continued. "She is my oldest friend, you know, as well as my cousin, and I love her dearly."

Noel's jaw clenched. *I love her dearly?* As a friend, and a relation, yes. But as something more?

"Come, my dear, you must be fatigued from your long day's journey. Let me show you to your bedchamber so you may rest and refresh yourself before dinner," his grandmother said, no doubt changing the topic to avoid answering Ash's question. "I have begged off all social engagements for the coming fortnight so we might all become better acquainted, and discover what gaps in your education and training we will need to address before we introduce you to society. I do not know what hours you kept in Leicester, but here we dine at seven o'clock. Oh, as a Quaker, were you allowed to keep a timepiece? If not, there is a mantel clock in your bedchamber which you may consult. Or shall I have a footman summon you when the time is nigh?"

Ash grinned. "Timepieces are certainly allowed, Granny, even pocket watches. Although we Friends tend to frown upon the fancy chains and fobs which fine gentleman are all too apt to sport."

"Ah, more's the pity. Still, as long as you agree to wear the Silliman signet and carry your grandfather's timepiece, I suppose we may allow it. Surely, though, you might consider…"

Lady Silliman glanced back towards Noel before ushering his cousin from the room, a glance replete with questions. Was affability and charm the true heart of the new earl? Or did a core of Griffin stubbornness—a stubbornness that would lead Ash Griffin to cling to unfashionable, inconvenient Quaker beliefs—lie beneath? And who, precisely, was this Miss Bathsheba Honeychurch whom her grandson kept mentioning?

Noel didn't have any answers. At least, not yet.

But he would make it his business—his duty—to find them.

"And what is your impression of the young man? Is he likely to stand with us, or against?"

Noel, bleary-eyed from trying to make heads or tails of Grandmother's less than meticulous household account books, blinked at the welcome sight of his personal secretary. Michael Pinney stood in the doorway of Silliman House's library, shaking the rain from his beaver hat and fastidiously wiping a few stray drops from his pristine kid gloves.

"At last! What kept you so long?" Noel had summoned his secretary from Ruxford Hall, the Silliman family seat in Devonshire, more than a week ago, the very day after he and Ash had arrived in London. "A well-sprung coach should have had you here in three days."

Pinney grimaced. "A disagreement with Ruxford Hall's steward over the best means of mitigating the spring flooding. And then not one, but two bridges between Plymouth and London washed out by these pestilential rains, sending me miles and miles out of my way. Almost enough to make me wish myself back in the Caribbean, such a dreary deluge without cease. No one told me it rains in England almost as much as it does in Nevis. At least tropical downpours and thunderstorms there pass in an instant, leaving sunshine in their wake. Unlike *here*, where one can never shake oneself free of the damned damp chill. But enough about the tiresome weather. Tell me everything about the new earl."

Noel smiled as Pinney threw himself into a chair opposite the desk, taken as always by the engaging manners of his lively young secretary. He'd hired Pinney more than a year earlier, shortly after his grandfather's second stroke. Grandfather, of course, had his own banker, two secretaries, multiple land stewards, and an entire firm of solicitors to advise him on matters relative to the estate. But not one of them would make any decision, nor take any action, without first receiving a direct order from the earl.

Orders that the poor man, bedridden and mute in the wake of his apoplexy, had for months been completely unable to give. Polite, but evasive, they'd been, Grandfather's myriad advisors, whenever Noel had tried to reason them into acting.

At the time, Noel had believed them too set in their ways, and too afraid of his irascible grandfather, to take direction from anyone besides the earl. Later, he'd wondered if their reluctance had stemmed from their knowledge, or suspicion, of the falseness of Grandfather's claims about the identity of his true heir. Friends and acquaintances—even his own purported heir—had been fooled by the earl's lies, but a nobleman's solicitors could have known the truth. Such men might be willing to hold their tongues to appease an employer, but few would act in a way contrary to the law.

As the months passed and his grandfather's physicians grew less and less sanguine about the earl's chances of recovery, Noel realized he needed an advisor completely loyal to him, not one beholden to his grandfather, to help him navigate the Silliman estate advisors' continual naysaying and delays. To his great satisfaction, he'd found that man in Michael Pinney. At their first meeting, Noel had been taken both with Pinney's quick mind and engaging manners; in the year since, he'd been continually impressed by the depths of his knowledge of the law, as well as his continual good spirits in the face of Noel's increasing frustration with the intransigence of his grandfather's advisors.

"A cheerful, accommodating sort of fellow, my young cousin. I believe you will like him. He and Lady Silliman are already fast friends."

Loyal to a fault, Pinney would likely ask to continue in Noel's employ. But his skills were far too valuable to be wasted on a mere Mr. Griffin. He'd be a calm, steadying influence on the wide-eyed new earl.

"But is he likely to go along with our unorthodox scheme? Will he accept the substantial financial loss to the estate that emancipating the men and women on those damned plantations will inflict? You know I won't work with any man who isn't appalled by the prospect of slaveholding." Pinney, the son of an English planter and his enslaved mulatto mistress, had witnessed the horrors of the vile institution first-hand.

"The fact that my cousin was raised Quaker, and that he belongs to Leicester's anti-slavery Committee, bodes well, I believe," Noel answered. "He'll not wish to be known to his co-religionists as a slaveowner."

"Quaker?" Pinney gave a bark of laughter. "Is that why your grandfather pretended his middle son never existed? Because he turned Quaker?"

Noel nodded. "Grandfather never spoke of him, or to him, after. Nor his son to him. Or so my grandmother told me."

Noel had had a similar urge after discovering, quite by accident soon after his grandfather fell ill, that two West Indian sugar plantations, worked by more than fifty enslaved women, men, and children, numbered among the Silliman estate's holdings. What an insult to his father's memory! Late in his naval career, James Griffin captained one of the first ships committed to suppressing the recently-outlawed slave trade, and had given his life fighting to capture a Portuguese slaver and free its human cargo.

Noel had rushed to upbraid his grandfather over the revolting discovery, determined not to speak to the earl ever again if the man refused to rid the estate of such a foul inheritance. But by that time, Lord Silliman was too far gone to care whether his grandson shunned him.

"Blast your Uncle William for not staying decently drowned at sea! Or for siring a son instead of only daughters. Your plans to gradually free the men and women on those plantations would be close to becoming a reality if not for that one very inconvenient fact."

"*Our* plans," Noel reminded his secretary. Pinney knew far more about the legalities of emancipating the enslaved in the far-flung British colonies than Noel, or any of Grandfather's many advisors, ever would.

"Your plans, my plans, it little matters. Not now that…" Pinney trailed off.

"Not now that all decisions related to the estate, including whether to maintain its slaveholdings or no, have been taken out of my hands," Noel finished. *Damn it to hell and back.*

Pinney sat back in his chair and offered a wry smile. "And now Uncle William's Quaker son is the rightful owner of those benighted plantations. How my father would be swearing down the house at such an ironical turn! Did I ever tell you of the time two Quaker ladies who had come to Nevis to preach harangued him and the other slaveowners on the island for perpetuating the evil practice? Right after Sunday services it was, outside the church in Saint John Figtree. I must have been all of five or six, and Father, pugnacious soul that he was, attempted to debate the matter, arguing that allowing me, his quadroon son, to attend services alongside him, as well as planning to send me to England to be properly educated, should be evidence enough of the beneficent, civilizing influence of a pious Christian master. Alas, the Quaker ladies were not at all convinced."

Noel snorted. Hardly a surprise, that. Not if the ladies had been anything as fierce as the righteously indignant Bathsheba Honeychurch...

"If he was raised Quaker, then I'm guessing your cousin will be just as eager to dispose of those two plantations as you are," Pinney added. "Do not Quakers disown any member involved in the evil institution?"

"Yes, another point in our favor. But a more significant point against—my cousin is only nineteen."

Pinney frowned. "If he's not yet of age, then the trustees will not allow him to dispose of any assets, not if they believe it against the estate's interests."

"And he won't be of age, not for twenty-one long months."

Pinney frowned. "Yet another reason, I suppose, for you to put off looking to your own finances?"

Pinney had been urging Noel for months to move some of the naval prize money his father had bequeathed him from government bonds to riskier, yet more lucrative, investments. Because in the wake of his disinheritance, Noel had no lands, no estates to provide for his financial future.

But Noel kept putting Pinney off. Because the late earl had scoffed at money earned from manufacturing as ungenteel? Because Noel's plan had been to keep the monies his father left him safe in the four percents, ready to finance the careers of any younger sons he might father? Or because some soft, hurt part of him still could not believe his grandfather could betray him so?

Even the challenge of Pinney's raised eyebrows could not shake Noel free of this strange disinclination to take charge of his father's money. Why would his secretary not let him ignore his own interests if he wished?

Noel offered Pinney a dismissive shrug.

"No?" Pinney challenged. "Then I've several new prospectuses for you to consider—two mining concerns in South America, a gas company proposing to light cities on the Continent, and a new insurance group backed by Rothschild and Gurney."

One by one, Pinney slapped the prospectuses on the desk in front of him. But Noel only gave each a cursory glance.

"I even came across several men interested in developing faster steamships, and others proposing to use such ships to encourage leisure travel. Since boats are a particular interest of yours, you really should consider—"

A knock at the library door interrupted Pinney's recital, saving Noel the trouble of explaining—or avoiding explaining—his strange reluctance to look to his own finances.

"Excuse me, sir. Is the new earl at home to callers? There is a woman downstairs wishing to speak with him."

Noel frowned. "A woman? Or a lady?"

The butler hesitated for a moment. "A gentlewoman, I believe, sir."

"A *young* gentlewoman, is it, Thomas?" Pinney raised an amused eyebrow. "Accompanied by her marriage-minded mama and all her female relations, no doubt. And here I was, thinking you'd make sure to keep your cousin's presence in town a secret, at least until your grandmother deemed his manners suitable for polite society."

"The gentlewoman is unaccompanied, Mr. Pinney." The stiffness of the butler's posture indicated even more clearly than words his disapproval of such immodest behavior.

The skin at Noel's nape began to prickle. "A young woman,

you say? Blonde hair, about so high? Quite plainly garbed?"

The footman blinked. "Yes, sir. Lady Silliman instructed she is not at home to callers, but as we've had no such direction from the earl, or from yourself, I did not wish—"

Noel jerked from his seat. "Thank you, Thomas. I will see to the matter myself."

"Plainly garbed? A lady from your cousin's past, then, rather than from his future," Pinney offered as he followed Noel to the staircase. "When you informed me the young lordling had been raised Quaker, I confess I pictured a sober, sanctimonious sort, not someone trailing abandoned lovers in his wake. Or is she perhaps his wife? Must I begin researching the finer details of annulment law?"

Noel scowled. "Not a lover, nor a wife, although she once entertained pretensions of becoming the latter. Just an interfering baggage of a cousin who needs to be sent on her way with a flea in her ear."

"Ah, even more intriguing," Pinney drawled. "A lady who can discompose Noel Griffin, the most self-contained gentleman of the *ton*. An attractive baggage, as well as an interfering one, is she?"

Noel paused on the stairs and turned back to Pinney with a scowl. "You had far better spend your time wheedling the settlement documents from Grandfather's solicitors than sharpening your wits on me. If the West India properties were never entailed, there's still a chance that my cousin can convince the trustees to sell them now, rather than waiting until he's old enough to make the decision himself."

Pinney sobered. "Indeed. The solicitors will likely be more forthcoming, though, if they believe I am acting on his behalf rather than yours."

"Then tell them you are. My cousin has proven more than happy to follow my recommendations so far, and I'm certain the two of you will suit. Come back this evening, after dinner, and

I'll introduce you."

Pinney nodded. "Thank you, sir. You know if the situation were different, I'd be eager to continue in your employ."

"I know, Pinney. But a gentleman without land or title has little need of a personal secretary. Now, off with you, before I put a flea in your ear, too."

"I'm going, I'm going. But do not be too hard on the young lady. You can hardly blame her for not wishing to give over her sweetheart, especially now that he's inherited a title and properties worth thousands of pounds." Pinney's brows waggled.

Noel had not taken Miss Honeychurch for the greedy, grasping sort. Could his own ridiculous attraction to the chit have addled his judgment? The prospect of an earl's fortune could turn the head of any young lady, even a Quaker one.

Or perhaps it was simply the political power of an aristocratic title the girl coveted.

No matter. Whether in pursuit of affluence or influence, Miss Honeychurch would just have to covet the Silliman heir from afar. It was Noel's duty to do everything in his power to keep her away from his cousin.

CHAPTER 4

"Miss? Miss? 'Twas Number nineteen you wanted, weren't it, now?"

The doubt in the voice of her cousin Constance's coachman made Sheba frown. She'd been staring up at Silliman House through the carriage window, trying without success to imagine poor Ash at ease in such an ostentatious place. Made of brown brick, the terraced London town house stood four stories high and four windows wide, each sash window set under a flat gauged arch. Curved iron balconies wrought in fancifully elaborate scrolls and flowers framed the first-floor windows—how ridiculously tiny, those balconies, whatever use could they be?—while a columned porch with an open pediment painted stark white set off a pair of double doors stained a dark, austere brown.

The sight only convinced her all the more of the rightness of her decision to follow Ash to town, even if she'd had to foist her company on her reluctant cousin Connie to do so. If this were the type of place his newly discovered family expected Ash to live, what other evils of their worldly society would they demand he embrace? And would he have the strength of character to deny them?

The footman Connie insisted must accompany her on the

short ride from Clapham to Mayfair jumped down from his perch next to the driver and gestured towards the door of the town house. "Shall I see if the family is receiving, Miss?"

Sheba opened the carriage door, let down the steps herself, and jumped down to the pavement before the surprised footman could offer a hand. "No need, Friend. I'm certainly able to knock on a door myself."

The footman frowned, as if inclined to argue. Connie—or her overbearing, querulous husband, more like—must have instructed him not to leave her side.

She patted the man's arm. "Truly, Friend, I'm perfectly capable of conducting a social call on my own. You needn't worry that I'll complain to Colonel Wingfield that you failed to do your duty. Not an easy man to work for, my cousin's husband, I dare say?"

The footman snorted. "Seen that already, 'ave you, miss?"

"Hard not to, I think. But he'll have no call to upbraid you on my account. Now please tell the coachman to walk the horses and call back for me in a hand-while."

"A hand-while?"

"A few minutes, Friend."

"Very good, miss," he said with a chuckle before rejoining the coachman atop the carriage.

Grasping the ring of the ridiculous door knocker at number nineteen—some sort of pagan god, was it meant to be, with a rapper coming out of its ears?—Sheba banged it against the brass plate.

A stately footman, all braid and frogs and patronizing condescension, gazed at Sheba, then looked past her, as if wondering where the rest of her party might be. Connie had urged her to wait until she was free to accompany her. But after watching how Connie's bed-bound husband constantly demanded her attention, Sheba knew it would be fruitless to delay.

Sheba also knew, from her yearly visits to her Grandmother Audley's, that unmarried young ladies of quality should not bustle about London without proper chaperonage. But her worries for Ash wouldn't allow her to wait even a day longer. She didn't need Connie's approval, or Connie's husband's, or anyone else's, not when she knew what was right. Besides, she had a promise to keep...

"I am here to see Manasseh Griffin, Friend. Is he at home?"

The footman cleared his throat. "Lord Silliman? The new earl?"

Sheba frowned at the unfamiliar, and unwelcome, honorific. The servants in an aristocratic household would never risk calling their master by his given name. But she need have no such scruples.

"Manasseh Griffin, yes. Would you please inform him that Bathsheba Honeychurch from Leicester has come to call?"

The footman cleared his throat again, then pulled the door wide. "Won't you step in? I will see if he is at home."

"Thank you, Friend."

The footman, his posture perfect, ascended a curved stone staircase without once laying a gloved hand on its elegant wrought iron balustrade.

Sheba paced the marble floors of Silliman House's grand entrance hall, a room clearly designed to impress upon all visitors the rank and wealth of its owners. On its paneled walls, gilt-framed mirrors and grand portraits depicted austere Griffin ancestors in garments long out of fashion. Framing the front door, two oversized urns decorated with figures from what she assumed must be classical myth, all wreathed heads and scandalously flowing tunics. And above it all, a chandelier of bronze and gold, ornamented with a crown of stars, each of its candleholders held aloft by fierce winged griffins.

Sheba could not but shake her head. Such love of vain decoration! How Ash must cringe every time he passed through.

And what was that sitting on a console table under the staircase, inside that glass case? A miniature ship? Made not out of wood, as a proper ship would have been, but of some white material she couldn't quite place. How very odd, to find such a prosaic thing set amongst the grander ornamentation of the rest of the hall…

But when she stepped closer and crouched down to bring her gaze to eye-level, to better examine the unusual object, her breath caught at the artistry and skill of its creator. Three masts rose from the ship's planked deck, each equipped with elaborate rigging she could imagine would be ready to raise sail at a moment's notice. An intricately carved figurehead of a lion, mouth wide with a roar, gave fair warning to oncoming vessels from its perch on the ship's prow. A raised anchor, a row of longboats hung above the deck, ropes coiled at bow and stern, even a row of minute buckets, each with handles made from the merest slips of thread—all details which attested to the fact that the model's creator had known what it was to live upon the sea.

Sheba had never been aboard a ship of any kind herself, but she could almost imagine what it must be like, just by looking at the lovingly created reproduction.

"A replica of His Majesty's Ship *Swiftfire*. A beauty, is she not?"

Sheba, startled by the low voice behind her, jerked and spun. Her shoulder knocked against the console table, which might have sent the small model toppling if Noel Griffin had not reached out a long arm to steady it.

His eyes fixed, though, not on the ship, but on Sheba.

He stood far too close to her person. Yet the wall behind her gave her no room to step away.

For a long, silent moment, he stared down at her, his narrow, patrician face impassive, his hazel eyes unblinking. Only a little taller than herself, with a build slightly leaner than Ash's, yet quite imposing all the same. What could it mean, that odd look in his eyes?

She stared back, the strangest prickling raising the tiny hairs on the back of her neck.

Did he think to intimidate her, staring at her so? Well, her mother had taught her through example not to allow any man to cow her. Especially not one as top-lofty as Noel Griffin. With a scowl, she pulled her shoulders back and raised her chin, stretching to her full height.

He took a quick step away, as if only now realizing how inappropriately close to her he had stood. The warmth in his gaze disappeared, replaced by an air of aloof detachment.

Sheba looked away, turning her attention back to the small ship she had nearly overset. She'd not noticed before the row of canons peeking out from behind the tiny windows on the ship's side. Not a vessel designed for peaceful commerce, as she'd initially assumed, but for military combat.

"A beauty? Not a word I would use to describe a vessel designed to wage war," she said, breaking the uncomfortably tense silence hanging between them.

"Ah, but the original was not always engaged in battle, Miss Honeychurch." He raised a finger, as if he wished to run it down —down her cheek? No, of course not. Down the ship's tiny rail, most like. But the glass case would not allow it.

"If you could but ride her decks on a clear, sunny day," he said, tapping that finger against that case, "light clouds scudding over your head, sails billowing in a steady wind, I dare say you'd recognize the beauty in her."

"As have you? Are you a man of the navy, then, Noel Griffin?" She could not keep her voice entirely free of scorn, raised, as were all Friends, to believe that war and the guidance of the Holy Spirit were utterly incompatible.

"No," he said, his eyes narrowing. "But my father was. The *Swiftfire* was the last ship he captained."

She almost missed the pained expression that flickered across Noel Griffin's face, so quickly did he hide it behind a mask of impassivity.

"May I say I am glad you chose not to follow in your father's footsteps?" she blurted, trying to banish the unwelcome burst of sympathy the sight of that expression raised. Noel Griffin was her adversary, not her friend. "If more men would cease to learn war, the world might come closer to achieving the universal establishment of peace."

"It was not my choice. My grandfather would not allow it."

"A wise man, your grandfather, to guard against placing his dependence upon fleets and armies."

Noel Griffin's lip curled. "Ah, I had forgotten. You Quakers are a pacifistic lot."

The sarcasm in his tone raised Sheba's hackles. "'All bloody principles and practices do we utterly deny, with all outward wars, and strife, and fightings with outward weapons, for any end, or under any pretense whatsoever, and this is our testimony to the whole world,'" she recited the lines her mother had taught her, her chin held high.

"An easy stance to take now that Napoleon is no longer alive to spread the desolation of war among the civilized nations." A swift wave of his hand cut off the rebuttal rising to her lips. "But I doubt you came to London simply to debate the merits of Quaker pacifism with me, Miss Honeychurch."

"No. Indeed not."

"May I inquire, then, what has brought you to town?"

"I have come to attend the Friends London Yearly Meeting, which is to be held later this month."

"Not, though, at Silliman House. To what do we owe the pleasure of your presence here?"

Sheba squeezed her reticule between her gloved fingers. What an annoying, officious man!

"Knowing I would be in London, Ash's mother and sisters asked me to pass along their letters to him, and to write back and inform them how he is getting on. He left Leicester so abruptly, we could not all help but worry about him. Myself especially. As he must have told you, he has long been my dearest friend."

"Indeed," Noel Griffin said with the slightest of nods. "In London, however, it is not considered at all the thing for a young lady to come calling upon an unwed man. But perhaps manners are less refined in Leicester."

"If Ash had taken up his own lodgings, perhaps such a petty restriction would be merited," Sheba answered. "But he is living here, at Silliman House, where his grandmother also resides. Surely it is not improper to call upon a man in the bosom of his own family?"

"And did you bring your family with you? I confess I am curious to meet the lady and gentleman who had the rearing of my lady crusader."

Sheba bristled, not at the epithet—had she not always longed to be branded a crusader, just as her mother had so often been?—but at the mocking tone in which he'd uttered it. "My father remains in Leicester. But I can assure you I have his leave to be here."

A fool's errand, her disapproving father had termed it, to remind Ash that his elevation to the peerage need not interfere with their plans to marry and travel abroad. Yet Joseph Honeychurch would not forbid her from going. Just as he had once respected his wife's calling to travel and preach to her fellow Friends, so too, did he respect his daughter's need to act as she felt called to. Sheba could not bring herself to tell him—how could she, when she could barely even admit it to herself—that no still small voice of truth inside her had insisted she follow Ash to London. No, only the promise she had made to Ash's father to look after his only son after he died....

Father had supported her, even in the face of all the Leicester Meeting elders who cautioned her against succumbing to the temptation of mistaking her own will for that of the Creator's.

While Father would not agree to accompany her himself—far too busy with the work of his mill in Leicester, especially now that he was short one clerk—he did make all the arrangements for her travel to Connie's home in Clapham, and provided her with the funds necessary for her upkeep in town for a good part of the spring.

Noel Griffin raised what was obviously meant to be a sardonic eyebrow. "You seem to have misplaced whatever companion your father must have sent with you in his place."

"My father's coachman has returned to Leicester."

"You are in London entirely without chaperone, then?"

Sheba toed the carpet under her skirt. "I am staying with my cousin, Constance, the wife of Colonel Wingfield."

"And this Mrs. Wingfield, she did not accompany you today?"

How the man did pry! "A simple social call hardly required her presence."

"And so you came by yourself, hoping the news would spread." His now cold hazel eyes narrowed. "Do you deliberately court scandal, in the false hope that it will force my cousin's hand?"

Sheba frowned. "Force Ash's hand? To do what?"

"To marry you."

Sheba sputtered. Did he truly think that she, that any Friend, would *force* another to do something against his will?

"Come, Miss Honeychurch. Such a pretense of outrage little becomes you. My aunt informed me that you have long expected to become my cousin's wife."

"Yes, both my mother and his father believed Ash and I would be called by the Holy Spirit to marry, and impart our religious beliefs to the next generation of Friends."

"Yet Abiah Griffin assured me her son has yet to make you a formal offer. Might he have failed to receive such a calling?"

Sheba's fingers, suddenly hot and damp, flexed inside her cotton gloves. Ash was not the only one who had not received the prophesied calling...

"You believe you know Ash better than I?" she challenged, raising her chin to stare straight into his mockingly narrowed eyes. "After only a few days' acquaintance?"

"Perhaps not," he acquiesced, even as his ungloved hands fisted defiance against his hips. She was reckoned tall for a woman, and she'd not taken him for an imposing man. But when he stepped closer, the tips of his boots almost touching the hem of her skirts, his lean, acetic face looming above hers, she shivered.

"Even so, I would caution you against bruiting it about town that the two of you are engaged, or that your calling on him unchaperoned is a sign of some understanding between you. You will likely find *your* reputation, rather than Silliman's, tarnished by such scurrilous gossip."

What an overbearing, interfering beast! To imply that she would stoop to gossip, to fomenting *scandal*, to achieve her ends!

Sheba's hands fisted on her own hips as she stepped closer, willing him to move back. Her mind raced, searching for the most stinging set-down her principles would allow her to utter.

But he did not give even an inch of ground.

Neither would she.

She cataloged his narrow face, the barest hint of a cleft in his clean-shaven chin, the puff of his lips, turned down in slight, but unmistakably supercilious, disapproval.

But behind that superciliousness she glimpsed something vastly different. Melancholy? Grief?

And even beyond that, beyond what looked remarkably like sorrow, hid something yet deeper, something she could not quite puzzle out, or even come close to naming.

A bustle at the door jerked them free from their mutual staring. Several footmen, arms overflowing with boxes and bags, gave way to a laughing Ash.

Sheba's tight shoulders, her fisted hands, relaxed for the first time since she'd stepped into Silliman House. How familiar her friend looked, and how dear!

An older woman who shared his warm hazel eyes and ruddy apple cheeks hung on his arm. His grandmother, no doubt. Thick as thieves, they looked, chuckling and smiling as yet another footman helped them off with their hats and coats.

Ash had never appeared so at ease clerking at her father's factory.

Some inadvertent sound of dismay must have escaped her mouth. Ash looked up from the lady beside him, his eyes growing wide as he caught sight of her.

"Sheba? Whatever are you doing in London?"

"Leicester Meeting has sent Miss Honeychurch as their representative to the Yearly Quaker Meeting," Noel Griffin answered on her behalf.

Sheba brushed past the annoying man, hands held out to Ash. "When they heard I would be traveling to town, your mother and sisters asked if I would carry letters to you. Oh, how good it is to see you, my friend!"

Ash took her hands in his and gave them a warm squeeze. "And you as well, Sheba."

Nine days, nine long days without even a glimpse of her best friend. They had never, not in their entire lives, spent so much time apart. Ash rarely left Leicester, and even Sheba's yearly summer visits to Audley Priory, which had begun after her mother's death, only lasted a week.

Oh, how she had missed him!

She scrutinized him from head to boot, looking for any sign of anxiety or disquiet. But he wasn't rubbing one hand roughly over the other, or pulling at the bottom of his waistcoat as if it didn't quite fit, as he was wont to do whenever he felt discomfited. And whatever was he wearing? A ruffled shirt, a bright red waistcoat, an obviously newly-purchased black frock coat?

Help my poor son resist the allurements of this mundane world, Bathsheba Honeychurch. And the weaknesses of his too-obliging nature. When I am no longer here to guide him, let him draw on your strength, help him to walk in the truth and the light. Swear it, Sheba!

Six years ago, she had made Ash's father a solemn promise—not an oath, he must have been half out of his mind with pain to ask a Friend to swear an oath—a promise which she had striven each day of her life thereafter to fulfill. Keeping that promise had often been a struggle, given Ash's overly complaisant nature. Even when amongst their friends and family, she'd often had to remind him not to succumb to his regrettable tendency to give in to the demands of others to avoid wrangling and squabbles.

Had William Griffin extracted that deathbed promise from Sheba because he'd feared his Silliman relatives would invite his son back into the fold? Had he suspected Ash might one day even be proclaimed the Silliman heir?

Her eyes fixed again on Ash's peacockish attire. Had she failed his excellent father already?

She pulled her hand free of Ash's and brushed a tentative finger against the silk, not linen, of his foppishly-knotted cravat. "Whatever would your father say, to see you like this?" she whispered.

A slight blush rose on Ash's cheeks. But a gentle clearing of the throat behind him prevented him from answering.

"Grandmother, may I introduce my cousin and friend, Miss Bathsheba Honeychurch? Sheba, my grandmother, Frances Griffin."

Noel Griffin raised that supercilious eyebrow again, not this time at Sheba, but at Ash.

"Ah, Lady Silliman," Ash added, with an anxious look at his grandmother.

But the older lady did not raise any objection to what appeared to be a social faux pas. "How kind of you to call, my dear. Silliman has often mentioned your name, as has Noel."

"Have they?" She glanced back over her shoulder at Noel Griffin. Unlikely that he'd shared anything with his grandmother that would redound to her credit.

"Indeed they have. But we did not expect to see you in town. Silliman told us you had never once traveled beyond the Midlands."

"I hadn't. But the privilege of participating in the annual London Meeting is not something I could refuse." Sheba smiled. "But enough of me. How happy you must be to acquaint yourself at long last with your grandson! You must have quickly discovered what I have long known; he is the kindest and most conscientious of men."

Ash's grandmother looked taken aback—by Sheba's direct manner? Or by her refusal to grant her a deferential curtsy?

"I am quite taken with how much you resemble Ash's sisters," Sheba rushed on, "especially Patience, the eldest. You both have such kind eyes. Patience offered to take up my teaching duties at the school for the children of the laborers at my father's factory whilst I am in London, if her sister Abigail would join her. Even dear Phoebe, who is but eleven, pledged to visit Friend Mayfield and Friend Landry and read to them from the Bible in my absence. Oh, how you must be longing to meet them, Friend Griffin, after all these years!"

"Yes, certainly." Frances Griffin looked a bit startled, as so many did when Sheba rattled on in that heedless way. But the older woman recovered quickly. "I do hope your journey from Leicester was a pleasant one?"

"Yes, I thank you, it was."

"And your maid—did you send her to the kitchens for refreshment? Noel, will you have her fetched? How unfortunate that we had no word of your impending visit! Silliman and I are quite taken up with engagements at the present. If you were to leave us your direction, we might send a card informing you when we are next receiving."

Ash's grandmother slipped her hand around his elbow. "May I borrow your arm, Silliman? I confess our morning's outings have quite fatigued me. Good day to you, Miss Honeychurch."

Sheba must look as ridiculous as a fish tossed up on the bank, her mouth gaped so. She rushed over to the ornate balustrade of the grand staircase and stared up at her rapidly disappearing friend. "But Ash, I came all this way—"

"Leave your direction with the footman, Miss Honeychurch. My grandson will return your visit in due course."

Ash gave her the most fleeting of apologetic glances. "*Soon, I promise*," he silently mouthed.

Sheba watched with a shrinking heart as Ash and his grandmother turned the corner of the staircase landing, the elderly woman leaning heavily on his arm.

"Your carriage, I believe, Miss Honeychurch?" Noel Griffin waved an arm toward the still-open front door, where Connie's footman now stood, hat in hand.

Sheba paused, then pulled the letters from Ash's family from her reticule and set them alongside the model of the *Swiftfire*. She groped inside it again, this time pulling out a pencil, and then a bit of pasteboard Connie had insisted she take with her. Her hand shaking, she scribbled hastily on its back.

She could feel Noel Griffin's eyes on her the whole time.

"My cousin's card, with her direction. You will give it to Ash, if you please, and tell him I will be expecting his call."

Her fingers prickled as his ungloved hand drew the card from hers.

She glanced back at the now-empty staircase before returning to meet his cool hazel gaze.

Who would prove the more formidable opponent in this quest for Ash's soul? His grandmother? Or his cousin?

Five days. Five whole days since brazen Bathsheba Honeychurch had elbowed her way into Silliman House, fairly bursting with sanctimonious self-righteousness, determined to distract his cousin from his new position as head of the Silliman family.

And somehow Noel still could not get the blasted creature out of his head...

Noel had been hard-pressed to put Ash off from returning the interfering baggage's visit. But he'd done it, making up engagement after excuse, all to keep his cousin from racing off like a lapdog panting in pursuit of its mistress. Did the boy have no spine at all?

And Miss Honeychurch—she treated his cousin less like a lover than as a child in need of her moral guidance, just as she had when he'd first met her in Leicester. Chiding Ash for his choice of dress, invoking the memory of his father to shame him. Might she be one of those women who would take pleasure in a husband whom she could treat as one more item to add to an ever-growing list of projects requiring her attention and oversight?

Noel repressed a shudder. He'd not wish such an overbearing wife on even his worst enemy.

Foolish, it would be, to allow his easily-swayed cousin to visit the girl without him. But he found himself strangely reluctant to encounter her again. Something about Miss Bathsheba Honeychurch discomfited him in a way he could not quite understand. Even now, his fingers tingled with the memory of how he'd almost reached out to trace the line of her narrow brow, the curve of those wide, chiding lips as she stood gazing down at the replica of his father's ship, wonder and admiration in her eye. Thank heaven his grandfather had instilled in him the necessity of physical as well as emotional self-control. Embarrassing beyond measure if he'd actually *acted* on such a ridiculously unruly impulse.

But instead, he'd spoken to her with harshness, even cruelty.

Accusing her of wishing to entrap his cousin into marriage, of intending to spread scandal in order to do so. As if Ash, who could not go an hour without singing the girl's praises, were completely misguided in his opinion of her.

Directing his anger at her for his own unwelcome attraction, evidently, instead of at himself, where it rightly belonged.

Not well done. Not well done at all.

But disconcertingly necessary for his own peace of mind...

"Is there anything more you would like to know about your English estates, my lord, before we turn to the earldom's holdings abroad?"

Noel pulled his attention back to Mr. Rackham the elder, one of the gentlemen appointed trustee to Lord Silliman until he reached his majority. He sat across from Noel, Ash, and Michael Pinney at a long table in the Silliman House library, with Mr. Rackham the younger and Mr. Rackham the eldest, Ash's two other trustees, to each side.

Noel's cousin, who had been diligently taking notes during each morning's meeting, set down his pencil with a smile. "Holdings abroad? Do not tell me we've invested in some French lace manufactory! Or are speculating in Dutch tulip farms? How unpatriotic! Should you not dispose of such holdings immediately, and reinvest the profits in some good English land?"

Like each one of Ash's earlier attempts to instill some degree of levity into the week's dry proceedings, his cousin's latest joke fell on unreceptive ears. All three Rackhams simply blinked, cleared their throats, then paged anxiously through the papers on the table in front of them, as if some key to understanding this lighthearted new earl might lie within.

Noel supposed he might have warned the trio that in his cousin they would find a character far different from that of their dour grandfather. But he doubted they would have listened. Ever since Grandmother had informed them that Ash, not Noel, was the true Silliman heir, none of the Rackhams had paid Noel the least mind. They'd even looked askance at his attending these meetings—he, after all, was decidedly *not* the Silliman heir, and even worse, would be the first to benefit if the current heir were to die without issue. But not even Rackham the eldest had been brazen enough to insist that he leave outright, not when his cousin insisted he attend.

Noel fought back a petty smile. Thank heavens they were none of them related to bold Bathsheba Honeychurch.

"The late Lord Silliman did not hold with *foreign* investments, my lord," Mr. Rackham the elder finally answered. "Your holdings abroad are of a colonial nature. East India Company shares, a small estate in Ireland for the breeding of horses, and a thriving shipyard in Quebec. All quite profitable, as you will see from this summary of the past decade's income from each."

"Do not forget the two plantations in Nevis," Noel added as Rackham handed yet another sheet of figures over to his cousin.

Pinney raised an eyebrow. Michael had urged him to tell his cousin of the estate's involvement in slavery, but Noel had held off, not wishing to be accused by the Rackhams of improperly influencing the new earl. But if his cousin had paid the least attention to the perorations on the evils of the institution he claimed Bathsheba Honeychurch was especially adept at giving, it would not take him long to ask…

"Nevis? Is that in America?" Ash inquired.

Rackham the youngest rattled his sheaf of papers. "No, my lord. In the Indies."

"The West Indies," Pinney could not resist adding.

His cousin paled. "The estate owns sugar plantations?"

"Yes, my lord. Your grandfather sent his son to the Indies to explore possible investment, then purchased the plantations from a West Indian gentleman shortly after his return," Rackham the eldest said.

A deep coldness invaded Noel's chest. He'd always assumed

those plantations had been in the family for several generations. His *grandfather* had bought them? And Noel's own father had been involved in their purchase?

Impossible! Shortly after the abolition of the trade in slavery in 1805, James Griffin had requested to be stationed off the coast of Africa, so he might participate in the capture of slave ships the new law authorized. He would never have recommended his own father purchase slave plantations.

"Which son was sent to the Indies?" Noel bit out. "My father?"

"No, the new Lord Silliman's." Rackham nodded to Ash. "It was shortly after Mr. William returned from Nevis, I believe, that the unfortunate break with his family occurred."

Noel and Pinney exchanged a loaded glance. He could not imagine a man who had turned Quaker recommending any such purchase. Had his father's decision to buy them in spite of his son's advice proven the straw that broke William Griffin's back?

Ash frowned, a finger tracing down the columns of figures. "This income, it comes from the sale of sugar?"

Yes, Ash, make the connection, see the patterns...

"Yes, my lord."

"But sugar plantations are worked by enslaved Africans, are they not?"

All three Rackhams nodded.

"Do you mean to tell me that my grandfather's wealth was built on the backs of enslaved people? The estate, to which I am heir, *owns* human beings?" The dismay in Ash's voice rose with each appalled sentence.

"Indeed, my lord," said Rackham the younger, as imperturbable as his father and grandfather. "Your holdings in Nevis have turned a pretty profit for the estate over the years, even if the price of sugar has gone down somewhat since the end of the war."

"Merciful heaven! If my mother were to hear of this—The elders—If Sheba!—" His cousin paled. "Can they be freed?"

That was an unexpected turn! Although perhaps Noel should have anticipated it, given those pamphlets that Bathsheba Honeychurch had been waving about when he'd encountered her on the Leicester Meeting House porch. *Immediate, Not Gradual, Abolition* was it not?

Now it was Rackham the younger's turn to turn peaky. "Such an ill-advised action would hardly be in the fiduciary interests of the estate, my lord."

"Then can they be sold? The plantations, I mean, not the slaves. Sold to a reputable planter, one we can be sure will not ill-treat them?"

"They can, if the properties were never added by your grandfather and his eldest son to the entail," Pinney said. "I have asked the Rackhams to look into the matter for you, but as yet they have given no definitive answer."

Rackham the elder frowned at Pinney's presumption before turning back to Ash. "The plantations were not added to any existing entail. But with newly-purchased properties, it is far more common for a separate entail to be created than an existing one be amended. We are consulting with the late earl's solicitors to see if any such document exists."

"Even if it does not," Mr. Rackham the younger added, "we would be remiss in our duties as trustees to allow any such sale. The properties have contributed significant income to the Silliman estate since their purchase."

"But I'll be cast out of the Meeting!" Ash's voice shook. "Friends are forbidden from owning slaves."

Mr. Rackham the eldest pulled down his glasses and glared over their rims. "Quakers might be so forbidden. But surely, my lord, you are aware that a peer must accept the sacrament as a member of the Church of England."

Ash gripped the table, his knuckles turning white.

Damn it all to hell. He'd specifically asked the trustees not to remind his cousin about the necessity of giving up his religious beliefs.

"Are there not some peers of other religions?" Ash asked.

"Yes, the Duke of Norfolk is a Catholic. But he cannot take a seat in Parliament," Mr. Rackham the eldest replied. "Only peers who have subscribed to the Thirty-Nine Articles of Religion are given a voice in the government."

"I can't vote in Parliament? But voting, and having access to the king to advise him on matters of state, are the only privileges of a peer Sheba will think at all worthwhile."

"Access to the sovereign is a privilege rarely exercised, my lord," Mr. Rackham the eldest could not seem to help but quibble. "Especially by one who does not share our King's religion."

Noel flicked his eyes at Mr. Rackham the younger and gave a minute shake of his head.

"Grandfather, Lord Silliman, let us set aside this matter for the nonce," Rackham the younger counseled. "We have far more important—"

A footman knocking at the library door interrupted Rackham's attempt to calm the waters. "Mr. Griffin, a Lord Stiles has come to call. I informed him you were otherwise occupied, but he insists it is a matter of some urgency."

Stiles! Noel had not seen his old schoolfellow in more than five years. His friend's diplomatic posting must have finally ended. How propitious that personable Spencer Burnett, Viscount Stiles should return to London just now. He'd be the perfect man to help introduce Ash into aristocratic society.

"Send him up directly." Noel waved a hand at the footman, then turned back to the Rackhams. "Sirs, might we continue this discussion tomorrow? Lord Stiles is an old friend, one I particularly wish my cousin to meet."

Rackham the eldest turned to Ash. "Is that your desire as well, my lord?"

Noel gritted his teeth against the obvious snub.

"What?" Ash, clearly caught up in his own thoughts, struggled to pull his attention back to the room. "Yes, tomorrow, I thank you."

By the time the Rackhams had finished collecting their papers, Stiles had already reached the landing outside the library. "Griff!" He held out a hand, then pulled Noel into an embrace. "Thank Christ you're in London. I've need of you, friend."

"Stiles." Noel slapped his friend on the shoulder, then pulled back to examine him more closely. Five years ago, Noel had warned Spencer Burnett against accepting a position in Sierra Leone, knowing painfully well from his own father's time in the West African Naval Squadron how deadly such an office could prove. One of the worst postings in the Navy, every sailor said, given the prevalence of deadly tropical disease. But Stiles, stubborn man, had ignored Noel's every warning.

His friend stood before him now, hale and hearty, with the deep tan far more characteristic of the sailor than the diplomat. But deep lines furrowed his forehead, and his bracketed lips pressed in a tight line.

"Damn, but it's good to see you again. Tell me what I can do to help."

Stiles paused, his lips twisting grimly. "I'm sorry to cause you pain, Noel. But is it true that you've been displaced in the line of the Silliman inheritance?"

Noel gave a sharp nod.

"And your cousin, one Manasseh Griffin—do you know where I might find him?"

Ash stepped into the passageway. "I am Manasseh Griffin."

"You know my cousin?" Noel asked.

"Only by name. My wife's cousin, Bathsheba Honeychurch, mentioned him in her last letter."

"You are the Lord Stiles who married Philadelphia Fry?" Ash held out a welcoming hand.

Spencer Burnett had first been betrothed to charming Anna Fry, Philadelphia's older sister. But Anna had died of a fever only a few weeks before the ceremony was to be held. The two fathers, eager for an alliance between their families, had substituted one sister for the other, regardless of her wishes, or of Stiles'.

Unsurprisingly, the match had not prospered. At least if Stiles' continual rushing off to London, and then his mad dash to Africa, all without his wife, were any indication.

"Yes, I am." Stiles gave his cousin an assessing glance. "Last week, Miss Honeychurch wrote asking Delphie to serve as her chaperone while she visited London. Delphie apparently agreed, and left our estate in Surrey yesterday. But she—" Stiles paused, pulling fitfully at the thumb of his glove—"she failed to leave her direction. I wonder if you might know where Miss Honeychurch is currently lodging?"

Noel gave a silent snort. His friend, who five years ago had left his wife without as much as a backwards glance, had now raced up to town in pursuit of her, without even an inkling of where she might be? And looked as anxious about that lack of knowledge as a sailor's wife during a storm?

Noel patted his waistcoat pocket, the pocket in which he'd slipped the card Bathsheba Honeychurch had asked him to give to Ash. The card he'd kept for himself, even after sharing its information with his cousin. "I just may be able to help you, my friend."

CHAPTER 5

Five days. Five interminable days spent in the company of cousin Connie and her irascible invalid of a husband in their tiny cottage in Clapham. Every moment in expectation of Ash returning her call.

But he had not come.

And she missed him, her oldest friend. Missed his good cheer, the easy way he had of making everyone around him comfortable and content. And most of all, his down-to-earth common sense, which often kept Sheba grounded when higher flights of fancy tempted.

Did he miss her?

Sheba would have suspected Noel Griffin had kept her direction from him if she'd not received one brief note, meticulously penned in Ash's copperplate hand, asking for her forbearance whilst he attempted to learn about his new duties and responsibilities as an earl.

The note did not mention whether those duties and responsibilities were at all in conflict with his duties and responsibilities as a member of the Society of Friends.

Or the promises he had made to Sheba.

Help my poor son resist the allurements of this mundane world, and the weaknesses of his too-obliging nature…

A knock on the cottage door sent Sheba rushing to the drawing room window. But the angle was wrong; whoever was calling stood inside the alcove in front of the door, hidden from Sheba's sight.

Unable to wait for Connie's single manservant to respond to the summons, Sheba rushed into the passageway and yanked open the door.

Her shoulders fell. Not Ash.

But when she realized just who was standing on the step before her, she broke out into a smile.

"Philadelphia? Thank heavens you've come! I believe I'll run mad if I have to spend another night under the same roof as Saint Connie and her tediously melancholic colonel."

Sheba grasped Philadelphia Burnett's arm and pulled her into Connie's cottage. Sheba had written to Delphie before Connie, asking Delphie to serve as her London chaperone. As the wife of the son of an earl, Delphie would be more likely to move in the same social circles as Ash's newly discovered family than a mere Constance Wingfield could. But Delphie had put her off, urging her to ask one of their other Audley cousins instead. And since time was of the essence, Sheba had had to settle for a grudgingly acquiescent Connie.

Had Delphie come to serve as her chaperone in London after all? What had changed her mind?

"Unkind to speak so of our cousin, or her husband," Delphie chided, then set a kiss on Sheba's cheek.

"I know. Poor Connie! I do so wish she'd listened to us and waited until a more suitable gentleman offered. The Colonel is not at all a pleasant man, I fear."

"And what are you about, answering the door of a house not even your own?" Delphie asked as she set down a valise in the passageway.

"Because if I waited for a servant to do it, you'd have been standing on the step for the rest of the afternoon." Sheba pulled the door shut behind them. "The colonel keeps all his dependents occupied every minute of the day catering to his every whim. And then, if someone knocks more than once at the door, he complains of the noise. Come in, come in!"

Amongst their many Audley cousins, Delphie had always been Sheba's favorite. Quiet and kindly, she'd never laughed at the many scrapes in which Sheba's inflexible principles and impetuous temper often landed her during their annual visits to Audley Priory every summer. But after Delphie had been unceremoniously married off to Spencer Burnett, Delphie and Sheba had rarely been in company together. Delphie had been sickly during the early years of her marriage—and no wonder, married to a man who, if Sheba had correctly read between the lines of her cousin's letters, cared far less for her than she did for him—and then had lived in seclusion with her husband's grandmother after Spencer Burnett left the country to take up some foreign diplomatic post.

Today, though, Delphie looked as healthy and blooming as she had before her marriage. Sheba smiled and gave her cousin a hug.

"I'm surprised that Constance agreed to host you even for a few days if that is the case," Delphie said as she shrugged out of Sheba's embrace, and then out of her pelisse. "Does Colonel Wingfield not keep a manservant?"

"Oh, yes, but Dobbs is always being sent off on one sleeveless errand or another," Sheba answered as she pulled on the ribbons of Delphie's bonnet, then tossed both bonnet and coat on an empty chair. "And the colonel makes Connie dance attendance on him every moment of the day. Do you believe he's not allowed her to leave the house, not once in the five days I've been here? Well, we did warn her what a mistake it would be, marrying such a decrepit specimen of a man, war hero or not. Poor dear Connie!"

Sheba moved to shut the front door but then paused on the

threshold. "But where is your carriage? Surely you don't intend us to walk all the way to Mayfair. Oh, of course, you've sent your coachman to the Plough Inn, as the colonel keeps no stable. How long will the horses need to rest before we can set off again?"

She'd be so much closer to Ash in Mayfair. He could hardly put off calling on her then.

"Will we be staying at Morse House with your father-in-law? Or have you rented a townhouse of your own? How droll it will be if Henry Burnett expects me to 'my lord' him every time we meet. Do you remember how shocked he was when I called him by his name rather than his title at your wedding?"

A low groan from Colonel Wingfield interrupted before Delphie could answer. "Oh, the noise, the noise! You have no compassion for my poor nerves..."

Connie's quiet murmurs attempted to soothe her fretful husband. With some success, for a change, for Connie soon appeared in the passage and waved them into the front parlor. "Philadelphia! What a pleasure to see you, and looking in such good health, too. Are you unaccompanied? If only you had sent word—"

"Ha! You see, Con, even Delphie can act precipitously when the occasion warrants," Sheba proclaimed.

Connie frowned, then glanced back towards the passageway. "*Must* you speak with such vigor, Sheba? It is not at all becoming, especially in a lady."

Despite being younger than all the Audley cousins, Connie had always felt it her duty to upbraid Sheba for her unladylike ways. No one had ever made Con promise to help her cousins resist the allurements of the mundane world. Still, she hoped Ash did not feel as put upon by Sheba's guidance as Sheba did by Connie's...

"Calm yourself, my dear," Delphie, ever the peacemaker, said. "I've come to deliver you from our termagant of a cousin."

"Oh! We are to stay at your father-in-law's townhouse! On Hanover Square, is it not? Only a brief step from Silliman House, where they've taken Ash."

"Ash? Who is Ash?"

"Manasseh Griffin," Connie said with a sigh as she sank into a chair. "The young man whom Sheba so rashly came to town to pursue."

"Not to pursue, Con. To rescue!"

"And from whom does Mr. Griffin need rescuing?" Delphie asked.

"From his newly-discovered relatives, of course. Especially his top-lofty sobersides of a cousin. They all think to make him as unfeeling as themselves, only concerned with rank and wealth and their precious family name."

"To have a concern for one's family and its standing in the world hardly seems unfeeling," Connie reproved. "And the gentleman is a peer now. His responsibilities must be enormous."

"His responsibilities should be what they always have been: to the truth, and the light. To making the world more just." Sheba's fists clenched on the arms of her chair. "Someone must remind him of what truly matters."

"Perhaps what truly matters to him is not the same as what truly matters to you," Connie answered. "Not everyone shares your lofty ideals, nor your rash, impractical means of achieving them."

"Rash! Impractical! Why—"

"Mrs. Wingfield? Mrs. Wingfield!" the Colonel called. "Is it not time for my afternoon tisane?"

"Please excuse me for a moment, Philadelphia. I just need to see to the colonel—"

"Mrs. Wingfield!"

"Yes, my dear. Cook will have it ready in an instant," Connie called, then bent to Delphie's ear. "Thank heavens you've come,

Philadelphia. Our cousin's intemperate manners are cutting up the poor colonel's peace most dreadfully. When I return, we can discuss what's best to be done with her."

"What's best to be done with me?" Sheba threw up her hands in disgust. "As if I am not even in the room!"

Delphie smiled in sympathy. But in sympathy with Sheba, or with Connie?

Once Connie was out of earshot, Sheba knelt beside her other cousin's chair. "Please, Delphie, can we not remove to Mayfair immediately? Ash's cousin insists they cannot spare the time to pay social calls, but I know that's not the true reason he hasn't come. Noel Griffin just doesn't want him to see me."

"Sheba, I know you're intent on marrying this young man, but I don't understand why? When you speak of him, it's almost as if you regard him as a child in need of your guidance, rather than an adult who will help you navigate the difficulties of married life. Why does Ash Griffin matter so much to you?"

Sheba's hands fisted in her lap. Why must everyone question her so?

But if she wished Delphie to uproot her life in the country and serve as her chaperone in town, did she not owe her cousin some explanation?

She stared at hands, unfurled her fists, as she gathered herself, searching for the words to show her cousin the truth of her need.

"No one has ever been as kind, or as patient, with me as Ash has," she said after long, quiet moments of contemplation. "He's always been my pillar, counseling me to slow down and think before I act. And I help him, too. Help him to stand up for his principles when his too obliging nature would lead him astray. Even if I hadn't promised his father I would, I'd give Ash anything he needed. Happily. Freely. For he is the kindest person I know."

"You care deeply for him, this Ash."

Sheba bent her head. "I cannot imagine a future without him."

"Oh, my dear." Delphie laid a palm atop Sheba's head, stroked a soothing hand over the spill of her hair. "If only we all had the power to turn the futures we imagine into reality..."

"But I could, Delphie," Sheba said, taking her cousin's hand in hers and squeezing tight. "I know I could. Know I can, if you will but agree to help."

"Are you so very certain, then, you're not following in Connie's footsteps, and mine? Choosing a husband for all the wrong reasons?"

Sheba took a deep breath. "I don't wish to wed Ash because I need to feel needed, like Con did. And Ash cares for me, just as much as I care for him."

The unspoken words—*unlike your husband*—hung heavy in the air between them.

Until Delphie at long last gave a sigh, a smile—melancholy, but a smile nonetheless—playing over her lips. "Then let us discuss how best to bring you and your young man back together."

Sheba spent the rest of the afternoon trying to convince Delphie of the necessity of decamping for Mayfair without delay. But her cousin seemed strangely reluctant to leave Clapham. They argued back and forth, Sheba explaining over and over the importance of staying in town, Delphie putting her off with excuse after excuse, Connie interjecting her own quelling admonishments about the impropriety of Sheba's pursuing Ash to London, round and round in circles until Sheba thought she would go mad.

An inadvertent word of Delphie's finally revealed that her cousin had left Surrey without making any arrangements at all for where she—where *they*—would stay. Her husband, unsurprisingly, kept no lodgings in London, and though her father-in-law did, Delphie refused to ask if they might share them. Sheba knew that Henry Burnett was not the most pleasant of men, but still, could Delphie not tolerate a bit of unpleasantness for Sheba's sake?

The sun was beginning to set when a knock sounded from the front of the house.

"Oh, this time it surely must be Ash!" Sheba rushed to the passageway and pulled open the door.

And at long last, Ash it finally was. Oh, the familiarity of that smile—how it warmed her after all these days in far less than congenial company.

She felt an answering smile break across her own face. But before she could throw her arms about him in welcome, he cleared of his throat and nodded over his shoulder.

He had not come alone.

No, he was accompanied—ugh!—by his stiff stick of a cousin. As elegantly turned-out as he had been in Leicester, the bottle green of his coat drawing attention to the highlights in his hazel eyes, his light brown hair glinting in the afternoon rays of the spring sunshine. Those green-gold-amber eyes glared at her with barely-concealed disdain. Much as Malachi must have stared at the priests of Israel who dared to set polluted bread upon the Lord's altar.

How could such an expression, one so different from that on the face of his far more affable cousin, be the least bit becoming?

She blinked away the disturbing thought. No. Noel Griffin was *not* more attractive than his cousin. Certainly not.

But who was this third gentleman? She did not recognize him at first. Not until he rose from his bow and she caught sight of his deep brown eyes, eyes she was far more used to seeing crinkled in laughter than creased with care. The last time she'd seen him, he'd been far more pale, and far more elegantly dressed, but surely she was not mistaken…

"Miss Honeychurch. You will remember Viscount Stiles?" Noel Griffin nodded in the not-quite-stranger's direction.

"Spencer Burnett?" The man who had abandoned England, and Delphie, after the death of their only child.

Delphie's husband gave her a stiff nod. "Bathsheba Honeychurch. I am come in search of my wife. Might you know where she is to be found?"

Sheba glanced over her shoulder, back toward the parlor. Did Delphie know her husband had returned to England? And how did he know Ash and his cousin?

"Sheba, Viscount Stiles and my cousin Noel are old schoolfellows," Ash said, anticipating her question as he so often did. "From your letter to his wife, Stiles heard of my good fortune, and, knowing of our friendship, came to Silliman House in hopes that I might know where to find you. And with you, we hope, Lady Stiles. Is she within?"

So Delphie *did* know her husband had come home. And had shared *Sheba's* secrets with him, a man she wasn't at all certain her cousin should trust...

"Why did Philadelphia come to town without informing you?" Sheba could not help but ask.

Despite sporting a tan more likely to be found on a laborer than on the face of a man of rank, Spencer Burnett's cheeks colored at her question.

"If you would invite us in, Miss Honeychurch, we might avoid conducting our personal business where all on Clapham Common can hear," said Noel Griffin, all sarcasm and superiority and implied but never overtly-stated insult. At least, not in front of his cousin or his friend.

Still, she could not deny the validity of his point. More than one person walking Battersea Rise had stopped to stare in their direction.

Intelligent, and strategic, too, this cousin of Ash's. She might even admire him—his mind, that is, not his person—if he weren't so intent on thwarting her plans...

Since Connie's manservant had still not made an appearance, Sheba collected the visitors' hats and gloves, setting them on the console table in the passageway before leading the three men to the drawing room. Would her cousin be pleased, rather than appalled, by her husband's unexpected appearance?

"Delphie, we have visitors. May I introduce my particular friend, Manasseh Griffin? And his cous—"

"I am sorry to have to contradict a lady," Noel Griffin interrupted, regret not at all evident in his tone. "But my cousin's proper title is Earl Silliman."

Sheba bristled. "As I have told you, Noel Griffin, the use of such titles is not the Friends' way."

"It may not be *your* way, Miss Honeychurch, but I do not believe your cousin shares your religious persuasion. What if she were in company with others who expect a well-bred lady to know and use proper honorifics? Do you wish her to embarrass herself?"

Sheba could not quite contain her derisive snort. What a mindless rule-follower he was!

"Come, we are all family here." Ash moved between Sheba and his odious cousin. How he hated for people to argue! "Or perhaps will be, one day."

Sheba struggled to contain her grin. Ash had not given over the idea of their marrying, then, despite the arguments his cousin must have surely made against it. But what did his new position mean for their plans to minister and teach in foreign parts? If she could only speak to him in private!

"No one will take it amiss if Lady Stiles simply calls me Ash, as Sheba has done this many a year," her friend added. "Manasseh is a bit of a mouthful, is it not?"

Yes, keep reminding your cousin that a relationship of years will not be toppled in a mere fortnight, no matter how much he meddles.

"It seems our parents share a proclivity for foisting unusual, and unwieldy, names upon their children, my lord," Delphie said with a smile. "My given name is Philadelphia."

"A beautiful name for a beautiful lady. I am pleased to make your acquaintance, and look forward to furthering it during your time in town."

Sheba's stomach sank as she watched Ash take her cousin's hand in his and kiss it. "What, are you already embracing town manners, Ash? What would Friend Aldham, or Friend Howgill, or any of the other elders of the Meeting think to see you now?"

How tightly Noel Griffin's lips pursed! Because she had rebuked his cousin in company? Or because the rebuke came from a mere woman?

No matter. No Friend should shy from pointing out the errors of their ways to a straying member of the flock. And truly, what was Ash about, acting the gallant so? As if he were a royal courtier rather than a sober gentleman! She stepped between Ash and Delphie, not wishing to give him any further opportunity to exercise these worldly new manners on her cousin.

"Miss Honeychurch, I understand you are in need of a chaperone, as well as a place to lay your head during your stay in London," Spencer Burnett redirected the conversation. "Now that I've found her again, I'm certain Lady Stiles will join me in inviting you to accept our hospitality. At this late point in the season, lodgings can be difficult to come by, but Noel's—ah, Lord Silliman's secretary is working to find several from which we may choose."

Lodgings in London! Sheba nearly quivered in excitement. "How good of you, Spencer Burnett. I thought we were to stay at Morse House, but rooms of our own—oh, that will be even better."

She clutched Ash's arm and gave it a squeeze. "We'll be able to see each other every day, Ash!"

Ash's arm stiffened under her hand. Instead of echoing her

excitement, Ash only nodded to Spencer, and then to Delphie. "We are both in your debt, my lord, my lady. Cousin." How stilted his voice was!

Sheba frowned as a strange, unspoken tension filled the room. Ash would not meet her eyes. Delphie, seemingly just as uncomfortable as Ash, would not meet her husband's. And Noel Griffin—well, he could not seem to stop staring at Sheba, disapproval written all over his pale, proud face. Disapproval, and something else, too, something Sheba could not quite make out...

What secrets were they all keeping?

"Griff will make arrangements for us to view the different houses tomorrow afternoon," Spencer Burnett said. "I've taken rooms for the night at the Plough here in Clapham, and will bring a carriage round early in the morning. Make certain you are packed and ready to depart, Miss Honeychurch. Delphie, you will accompany me back to the inn."

Delphie started at her husband's high-handed command. Not quite fearful, no, but clearly not comfortable with her newly returned husband, either. Sheba tried to catch her eye, silently asking for her approval of her husband's plan. But Delphie kept her eyes firmly fixed on her lap.

"Philadelphia, my dear, why do you not stay with us here for the night?" Sheba had been so caught up in the swirling tensions between the room's occupants, she had not even noticed Connie's return. "If you don't mind sharing a bed with Sheba, that is."

"I don't wish to be an imposition on you, Connie, nor on the colonel." Delphie's tone was almost as stilted as Ash's had been. Oh, why could not anyone simply tell the truth about their feelings?

"No imposition at all. The colonel has decided to dine in his room and retire early this evening, so I am entirely at your disposal. And we do have a lot of catching up to do, don't we, cousin?" Connie's eyes, gleaming with speculation, rested not on Delphie but on her long-absent husband.

Yes, between them she and Connie would dig out the truth of Delphie's feelings for Spencer Burnett. And then Sheba would know whether to accept or decline the man's generous offer.

But first, she had to find a way to speak with Ash without his officious cousin intruding. How else could she discover his intentions about their marriage, and about Sheba's plans to travel overseas to teach?

"Will you not stay to dine with us, Ash?" Sheba asked. "As skilled a housewife as Connie is, surely she'll be able to stretch a meal to feed us all."

"Thank you, Sheba, but I don't—"

"You are too kind, Miss Honeychurch," Noel Griffin interrupted. "But my grandmother expects us to dine with her tonight. We'd best be off before it grows too dark to ride."

And before Sheba had a chance to offer the least persuasion, Noel Griffin had chivvied Ash into making his bows, collected their hats and gloves, and herded him into the passageway.

"I will see them out," Connie said, leaving her two cousins alone in the drawing room.

Of course, Noel Griffin would not allow her a moment alone with Ash. Pushing, managing man!

Sheba closed her eyes and took a deep, calming breath. Difficult, but necessary, to wait in stillness on the Lord for the renewal of patience and strength. For the light that arises out of the darkness. For guidance on how best to help Ash.

And to help Delphie, too, if, as Sheba was beginning to suspect, her cousin had come to London not just, or even primarily, to help Sheba, but to escape her newly-returned husband.

Noel Griffin should—would—have no place in her concerns.

No matter how she curious she was about that sad, vulnerable look in his eye…

CHAPTER 6

"A letter for you, Miss Honeychurch."

The morning light glanced through the tall windows in the Conduit Street lodgings Noel Griffin's secretary had found for them, winking off the polished silver of the salver held out by the footman, and off the shiny buttons of his coat. Yet more examples of the worldly vanities which the *ton* regarded as necessary, that tray, those buttons. How much time the members of fashionable society spent on their furniture, their apparel, even the apparel of their servants!

"Thank you, Joshua," Sheba said as she took the note from the footman. "But it is Friend, not Miss, Honeychurch, if you would."

How uncomfortable her request made the poor fellow. But Sheba had no time to reassure him, far too eager to discover the identity of the writer of the note.

Eagerness quickly gave way to disappointment. It was not from Ash.

Sheba sighed. She'd assumed that once they all removed to town, she'd spend most of the daylight hours with her oldest friend. But she'd not seen him, not once these past four days.

No. She'd been left, instead, to play awkward chaperone to Delphie and her estranged husband.

And for four days, Delphie kept herself aloof, taking almost comical pains to ensure she was never alone with that husband. Sheba's cousin never said a word about what she felt at Spencer Burnett's unexpected return, just as she'd never confided her feelings about his earlier abandonment, or about the child they had lost. Still, Delphie's detached, brittle presence told Sheba enough. Her throat ached to see her cousin still in such pain.

"From Connie?" Delphie asked with a nod toward the note Sheba had allowed to fall into her lap.

"No, from my old teacher back in Leicester. Con was kind enough to forward it." Sheba took up the letter again and read the few lines which Elizabeth Heyrick had penned. "She wishes me to bring a copy of her pamphlet to her London publisher, and to inquire whether they might be interested in printing an edition. Do you know in what part of town I would find Gracechurch St—

Joshua, the footman, cleared his throat. Another note to deliver, not to her, but to Spencer Burnett.

Sheba tapped her fingers against her half empty teacup, waiting for Spencer to finish reading. "From Ash?" she couldn't keep herself from asking when he set it down without speaking.

"No. From an acquaintance just returned from Sierra Leone. Sharing a rumor that Sir Charles MacCarthy's forces have been routed by the Ashantee."

Sheba had little interest in battles or war. But the word Ashantee caught her ear. Weren't the Ashantee an African people?

"Charles MacCarthy? Who is he?" she asked.

"The Governor of our British colonies in Africa. So many of us tried to warn him how foolish it would be to start a needless conflict with the major power in the region. But it seems he did not listen."

"You, warn him? Were you posted to Africa, Spencer Burnett?"

"Yes. Did Delphie not mention my work in Sierra Leone?"

Spencer's eyes flicked to his wife.

But Delphie didn't look up, far too occupied with crumbling a bit of toast between her fingers. "As I did not know myself where you'd been until you returned to England, I could hardly share such information with my cousin."

Sheba flinched at the coldness of her cousin's words. How could Delphie not admire her husband for undertaking such difficult work?

From her reading about the missionaries in Sierra Leone, Sheba knew such a posting must have been challenging in the extreme. Surely such work, such a commitment to helping the Black settlers from Britain and America, as well as those set free there from slavers' ships the navy had captured, suggested that the Spencer Burnett who sat before them now was a far different man than the frivolous, trifling fellow Sheba remembered from her cousin's wedding.

Did Delphie not think so?

"How successful, do you think, is the British Navy's African Squadron in suppressing the slave trade?" she heard herself ask, curiosity overtaking worry that Delphie might find her interest in Spencer's work a betrayal. "And what sort of aid does the British government offer the people they've rescued from the inhumane captivity of slavers' ships? Oh, did you ever meet William Garnon, or any of the men and women sent to the colony by the Church Missionary Society?"

"Yes, I met several of the missionaries during my time there." Spencer grimaced. "I'm afraid many of them found the life overly taxing, and looked for solace in the bottle far more often than was good for them."

"The bottle? Do you mean alcoholic spirits? Surely not William Garnon!"

"No, Garnon had more self-possession than many of the others. A real loss when he succumbed to fever. And his wife! Poor lady, first to lose her husband, and then her first child to stillbirth only one day after. A boy, it was, just like—"

He bit off the sentence, his lips pinching tight.

Beside Sheba, Delphie stiffened.

Sheba glanced between the two, neither willing—or able?—to meet the other's eyes. She'd known without Delphie having to saying a word how much the death of their child had pained her, still pained her. But she'd never suspected Spencer might harbor an equally deep hurt…

"Philadelphia." Spencer rubbed a restless hand over his chest. "I'm so very sorry. I didn't mean to remind you—"

Before Spencer could offer the remainder of his apology, a footman knocked on the dining room door. "My lord, Lord Silliman awaits you in the drawing room."

"Ash? At last!" Sheba jumped from her seat and dashed past the footman, grateful to have an excuse to escape their unspoken pain, pain she seemed unable to fix.

Maybe now that she'd left them alone, they'd finally talk. Finally share the grief that still troubled them both, instead of holding onto it in silence…

She opened the drawing room door to the sight of Ash, shuffling from boot to boot by the drawing room fireplace. With a sigh, she allowed her worries about Delphie and Spencer to momentarily ebb.

She watched, unobserved, as Ash fidgeted and shrugged, as if his coat fit uncomfortably across his shoulders. No wonder! Instead of the unstructured flannel jacket and plain waistcoat in gray or black he usually wore, today he sported a tightly-fitted wool tailcoat of deep blue, a silk striped waistcoat, and shiny top-boots adorned with ridiculously useless tassels. And was that a jewel of some sort on his fancifully-tied cravat?

"Ash." Sheba held out both hands, struggling to keep her dismay from her voice. "I began to fear we would never see you again."

Her friend gave her fingers a light squeeze. "My apologies,

Sheba. Despite the aristocracy's reputation for dissipation and indolence, it turns out that a great deal of work is required to oversee an earldom. My cousin and I have been cooped up with my men of business every morning since we last met."

He cast an apologetic glance not at Sheba, but over her shoulder.

Someone else was in the room. Someone whose eyes must be staring right at her, if the shiver of unwelcome awareness skittering down her spine was any indication.

With feigned unconcern, she cast a glance over her shoulder. And yes, there stood Noel Griffin, staring not at her but out the drawing room window. But the swing of the tails of his coat belied the pretense he'd been gazing at the street all the while.

Why should the thought of those green-brown eyes fixed on her person discompose her so? She need not care what Noel Griffin thought of her.

And nor should Ash, either. Especially not when it came to the religious principles they'd both long embraced.

"Working every morning and visiting a tailor every afternoon?" she chided, putting her back to Noel Griffin to brush her palms against the lapels of Ash's excessively showy waistcoat. "Do you intend to turn peacock, allowing them to dress you in such clothes?"

"Miss Honeychurch." Noel Griffin had turned from the window to offer her a short, stiff bow. "As outspoken as ever, I see."

"Friend Griffin." Her throat clenched at his less than courteous greeting. But she fought the urge to stifle her own words, tipping up a defiant chin instead. "As supercilious and high-handed as ever, I see. Could you not trust your cousin to call on an old friend without your supervision?"

"We have not come to call upon you, ma'am, but upon your chaperon. Ah, Stiles, there you are. Ten o'clock, just as promised."

"Griff. Silliman." Spencer offered the two men a bow. "Just let me send the footman for my hat and gloves, and we'll be off in a trice."

Sheba's shoulders fell. Ash had come to see Spencer? Not her?

"Where are you off to?" she asked, trying to keep any hint of desperation from her voice.

"Tattersall's Repository." Ash's eyes shone with excitement. "I want to get there early, to make sure the horses we inspected yesterday won't be auctioned off before I've a chance to bid on them."

"Yesterday? On First day? Did you not attend Meeting?" Sheba could not quite keep the shock from her voice, even knowing how much Ash hated to be criticized, especially in front of others. Oh, how she hated to embarrass him! And she was no weighty Friend, to be admonishing another, especially when her own behavior was so often lacking.

But if you do not, who will? her mother's voice whispered silently in her ear.

He'd been away from Leicester for less than a fortnight, and already he had fallen so far into worldly ways. How much longer before he soared so far out of her reach, she'd not be able to keep her promise to his father?

From behind Spencer, Delphie cast her a sympathetic glance. "It's a fine morning for a walk, Sheba. Tattersall's is no place for a lady, but perhaps we could set the gentleman as far as Hyde Park?"

"Oh, yes!" Sheba reached out to squeeze Delphie's hand in appreciation. She knew what it must have cost her cousin to voluntarily agree to spend time in her husband's company. "I'd like that above all things."

Noel Griffin did not look at all pleased by this proposed addition to their party. But Sheba dashed from the drawing room to collect her hat and gloves before he could raise any objection.

As they stepped onto the Conduit Street pavement, Delphie

slipped her hand inside Noel Griffin's elbow. "Do you typically spend the spring months in town, Mr. Griffin?"

Sheba smiled her thanks to her cousin. Even if she'd wished to avoid walking with her husband, Delphie could have engaged Ash in conversation, rather than Noel Griffin. But she'd chosen Ash's cousin, leaving Sheba free to claim her old friend.

Sheba laced her gloved hand through Ash's elbow and pulled him ahead of the rest of the group. Away from the disquieting weight of Noel Griffin's gaze...

"Tell me everything! Now, quickly, before the others have a chance to catch us up. What are they like, your Silliman relations? What do they expect of you? Are you able to keep to your principles, at least in ways other than in dress? Or do they insist you put your religious beliefs aside in favor of their own? How long do they wish you to remain in London? And how do you manage to live in such a needlessly ornate place as Silliman House without being put to the blush?"

Beside her, Ash chuckled. "A walk of less than a mile hardly gives me time enough to answer even half your questions, Sheba."

"Well, if you had deigned to call on me before now, I could have asked you some of them already."

Ash stared down at his boots. "I'm sorry, Sheba. But I've hardly had a moment to draw breath, never mind time to make a social call, what with my grandmother trying to school me in how to go on in society, and Noel and the family solicitors teaching me about the duties of the earldom, the people who depend on our estates, the properties that we, that I—"

Why had he stopped speaking so abruptly? Because he, like her, did not know which way to turn now that they'd reached the end of Bond Street?

"Down Piccadilly, then through Green Park," he said, gesturing with his free hand.

Sheba frowned. When had he a chance to become so familiar

with the streets of London?

"But visiting your oldest friend is not the same as making a social call, is it?" she said, her tone far sharper than perhaps was wise. "And I could have helped you; after all, I do spend a week every summer with my mother's mother. She is a countess, too, you know."

"But expectations about behavior when one is amongst family must be different from those in aristocratic society, do you not think? And even if you'd ever moved much in such grand society yourself, I doubt you would have made much of an effort to conform to its rules, especially if those rules contradicted your own principles."

His smile, easy with affection, usually soothed her. But today, it only annoyed. "And you will? Conform to such rules, even when they go against your own principles?"

Ash shifted uneasily under her hand. "It's not as cut and dried as you make it out to be, Sheba. It's important to make my grandmother and my cousin happy, too, not only myself."

"And will they only be happy if you completely abandon your beliefs?"

"No, of course not. We just need time, time to understand one another. Lady Silliman is such a lovely person, kind and affectionate, and so eager to welcome me into the family. And to introduce me to her friends and acquaintances, and to their sons and daughters, just as soon as I've learned enough to not embarrass myself with my provincial manners. I don't wish to disappoint her."

Their sons and *daughters*? Was Ash's grandmother already matchmaking on his behalf?

Ash waited for a break in the rush of carriages and drays before drawing her across Piccadilly to the entrance of Green Park. "I know you'll love her as much as I do, Sheba, once you have a chance to become acquainted."

"*Will* we have a chance to become acquainted? Or has your

cousin already warned her against me?"

Ash glanced back over his shoulder, as if worried his cousin might overhear him. But Spencer, Delphie, and Noel Griffin had still not crossed Piccadilly. "Noel never mentions your name, at least not in my presence. I cannot say what he has told my grandmother out of my hearing, though."

Do you deliberately court scandal, in the false hope that it will force my cousin's hand?

If Noel Griffin had the effrontery to abuse her so abominably to her face, she doubted he would have the least scruple in abusing her to all his relations.

"Have you told her of our plans? That we hope to be married once we can gain the approval of the Meeting? And that we hope to travel abroad?"

Ash dropped her arm and turned away, his gaze fixed on the fountain burbling in Green Park's shallow reservoir. Deliberately refusing to meet her eyes.

Beneath her breastbone, her lungs constricted, making it impossible to catch her breath.

"Ash?" she finally managed to whisper. She set a hand on his sleeve, searching for reassurance. But he shrugged it away with an impatient huff and stomped up a rise leading to the park's lodge. Sheba chased after him until he stopped beside two large stags cast in bronze which framed the lodge's entrance.

"Why did you follow me to London, Sheba?" he asked, his forehead wrinkling. "When I expressly asked you to give me time, time to figure out how to best reconcile what I've been with what I must become?"

"Asked me to give you time? When? You never even deigned to call to say good-bye, so eager were you to rush away to town."

"In the note I sent you! Did I not ask you to be patient, to give me a chance to meet my new relations, and to learn what is expected of an earl? But no, you couldn't trust me to find my own way, not without you to tell me what to do and how to be."

The uncharacteristic harshness of his tone made Sheba's own frustration rise. "A note? I never received any note. Did you leave it with my father, or one of the housemaids? Or ask your mother to give it to me?"

"No. But I was assured it would be delivered." He looked over Sheba's shoulder, his expression troubled.

She followed the direction of his gaze and caught Noel Griffin staring at her. But as soon as she caught his eye, he immediately jerked his attention back to Delphie.

"I suppose in all the chaos of our hurried departure, it was simply overlooked," Ash said.

Sheba's jaw clenched. Overlooked? Or deliberately held back by his cousin?

If the latter, Ash must not have shared what he had written to her with Noel Griffin. For his cousin, even more than Ash, would have wished for Sheba to remain in Leicester.

Served him right to have his sly machinations backfire in such a spectacular manner. Did he not know that lying lips are abomination to the Lord, but they that deal truly are his delight?

Sheba frowned. What Noel Griffin did or didn't know about God's word simply did not matter. What was important was to make things right with Ash.

"I'm sorry I didn't receive your letter, Ash. But even if I had, I still would have come."

"I was right, then. You don't trust me to find my own way."

"Certainly I trust you. But I promised your father I would help you keep to the path of truth and light. Your circumstances may have changed, but your commitment to that path cannot. Should not."

The stubborn set of Ash's lips told her he was not at all happy to be reminded of the task his father had set her. But he offered no further protest.

Thankful for once for his too-obliging nature, Sheba gentled her voice. "Will you try, then, now that I am here, to make time for me? So that I may help you to, as you say, reconcile what you've been with what you must become?"

He crossed his arms over his chest. "Only if you promise to treat me as a peer, and not as a troublesome younger brother in need of constant guidance and correction."

Sheba frowned. *Did* she treat him as a younger brother?

Hardly the behavior of a Friend, who should regard her future spouse as an equal...

This evening, when she could sit alone in her bedchamber, she would try to open herself to the Divine Spirit, to listen expectantly and patiently for guidance on how to treat Ash with respect even while keeping her word to his father.

"Sheba? I need your promise," Ash repeated. "As well as your promise to respect my decisions, and not try to persuade me to act against my sense of what is right."

Sheba crossed her arms, hugging herself tight against the bite of his words. Did he truly think she had so little respect for him?

"A true Friend would never try to persuade another to do what he does not feel called from within to do," she said, trying to keep the hurt from her voice. "I only wish to help you to listen to the light within, rather than allow yourself to be constantly swayed by the need to please others. As I promised your father I would."

"Miss Honeychurch."

She'd been so focused on her conversation with Ash, she'd not realized his cousin had caught them up.

She shivered—in surprise, of course, not because the sound of Noel Griffin's voice sent a rill of awareness trickling down her spine.

"Lord Stiles has taken his lady to find a hackney coach, as she is feeling fatigued after walking up the hill. Please, allow me to bring you to them."

He extended a gloved hand.

Sheba paused, strangely unwilling to offer her own.

She gave herself a quick shake. Noel Griffin might be a crafty, even manipulative man, but there was no need to fear setting her hand in his.

"Will you be at home tomorrow, Ash?" she asked as Noel Griffin's fingers curled about hers. "Delphie and I would be pleased to return your call and be introduced to your grandmother."

"Our grandmother is not yet receiving," Noel Griffin said. "Not until she's certain Silliman has all the rules of acceptable ton behavior etched into his memory."

"Which will be before the week is out, if the rout party she's planning for this coming Friday is any indication," Ash said.

"A rout party?" The surprise in Noel Griffin's voice suggested he'd had as little knowledge of the event as Sheba. "Already?"

"Yes. Only a small gathering, so I might practice my new manners before the far larger ball when I'll be officially introduced to society." Ash gave Sheba a wry grimace. "Wish me luck?"

"You don't need luck, Ash," she said, reaching out with her free hand to give his shoulder a reassuring squeeze. "No one who knows you could ever find you a disappointment."

His bent head and shy smile—what welcome reassurance that treating him like a child, rather than an equal, had not scuttled their friendship entirely.

"Come, ma'am." Ash's cousin tucked her hand inside his elbow. "You would not wish to leave your cousin waiting. Silliman, we'll meet you at Hyde Park Turnpike."

In silence, Noel Griffin led her back through Green Park towards Piccadilly. What was that scent tickling at her nose? Something sharp and spicy, yet with an undercurrent of citrusy sweetness—oranges, perhaps?

Did he wear eau de cologne? What a worldly indulgence, to sprinkle oneself in scent.

Yet somehow, shockingly appealing. Sheba allowed herself the momentary indulgence of a short, surreptitious sniff.

He looked down at her, the merest hint of a question in his melancholy eyes. A question she could not begin to answer.

She tipped her head to gaze instead at the clouds drifting lazily across the clear summer sky. She and Noel Griffin might spar and spat, but she'd never once thought of him as a troublesome child, had she?

"How well you look this evening, my dear." Grandmother patted a gloved hand against the lapel of Noel's tailcoat, then linked her arm through his, drawing him down Silliman House's grand staircase. "A new waistcoat? Ah, I see how it is. You wished to make Ash more at ease, having to order so many new garments, and so made a few purchases of your own. How kind you are to show such care for the feelings of your cousin."

A wry smile tugged at the corners of Noel's lips. Grandmother always would cast the actions of others in the most sympathetic light. But his purchase of the embroidered silk-satin waistcoat had little to do with any kindness to his cousin. Grandmother might not remember, but Noel certainly knew that Ash's first introduction to society was also the first time Noel himself had appeared amongst his peers since word of his being supplanted in the Silliman line of succession had spread beyond their family. No need to confide that he'd donned the showy garment in the vain hope it might serve as a kind of armor against—or at the very least, a bit of distraction from—the prurient gossip of the *ton*.

Or even worse, as a way of provoking a certain outspoken, sanctimonious young lady of his acquaintance. One whom he'd managed for the better part of a week to allow his cousin to see only in the company of others, and for as brief a time as politeness demanded.

A task far easier than he'd anticipated, as Ash seemed almost as reluctant to spend time with Miss Honeychurch as Noel was willing to grant it. But the managing chit had finally outmaneuvered them both, arranging for her cousin Lady Stiles to call on his grandmother during her first at-home since she'd returned to town. Noel had only discovered after the fact that Grandmother had invited Lord and Lady Stiles, as well as their guest, to tonight's party, without knowing just who that guest might be.

It would be Noel's duty to keep said guest from entangling Ash in any private conversation, as well as to put a period to any rumors she might be spreading of a tentative betrothal between them.

Noel brushed his fingers against his uncharacteristically gaudy new waistcoat. While he'd dragged Ash from bootmaker to tailor to hatter over the past week, assembling a wardrobe far more appropriate to his cousin's new station than his usual sober Quaker garments, Ash had tried to explain why his co-religionists, including Miss Honeychurch, frowned upon ornamentation of every kind, especially ornamentation of dress. Something about it manifesting a worldly spirit contrary to the letter and spirit of Scripture, a spirit productive only of vanity and pride. In proportion to the attention men paid to outward decoration and the vagaries of fashion, so did they suffer loss in the value and dignity of their minds—or so his cousin opined.

The sober dictates sounded odd ringing forth from such a cheerful, laughing boy. Noel could imagine them easily enough, though, uttered in the pontificating voice of one Miss Bathsheba Honeychurch.

When his cousin had laughed at the shawl-collared waistcoat the tailor at Schweitzer and Davidson had urged upon him, a garment tastefully embroidered with silk flowers in a cream just a shade darker than that of the fabric but embellished with sparkling silver spangles more appropriate to a lady's gown than a gentleman's vest, some devilish impulse had Noel instructing the tailor to add the gaudy item not to his cousin's account, but to his own.

He'd certainly not purchased the damned thing in the hopes of impressing Bathsheba Honeychurch. Why, then, should the prospect of her haranguing him for his questionable sartorial choices set a spark of anticipation flaring in his chest?

"Noel, dear," his grandmother said as they reached the bottom of the staircase. "I have something I would ask of you."

At the unfamiliar sound of his Christian name on his grandmother's lips, disquiet doused that anticipatory spark. The late Lord Silliman had always demanded his wife call Noel "Ruxford," the courtesy title used by the Silliman heir, rather than by his more informal font-name.

Yet another falsehood his grandfather had foisted on them all.

"What is it, Grandmother?" he asked.

Lady Silliman plucked a few drooping petals from a floral arrangement decorating the entryway table, her eyes carefully avoiding Noel's. "During the late Lord Silliman's time, you always stood beside us when we greeted our guests. But I wonder if it would be better, perhaps, to allow the titled members of the family to perform that function by ourselves tonight."

The titled members of the family...

Noel swallowed, then forced himself to answer with as much equanimity as he could muster. "Will not my absence suggest to our guests that I harbor ill-feelings towards my cousin?"

"Perhaps." Lady Silliman pulled several roses from the footed vase and laid them decoratively on the table beside it. "Better that, though, than to give them any reason to persist in the mistaken notion that it is you, and not your cousin, who has inherited the title."

The mistaken notion that it is you...

Why? Why had she never told him? Why, even after her husband's death, had she left it to the family solicitors to inform him that all he had ever worked for had turned, like the apples of Sodom, to ash in his mouth?

Noel's jaw clenched so tightly, he feared his teeth might crack.

"Noel. My dear." His grandmother laid what he supposed was meant to be a comforting hand on his lapel. "You are a valued member of this family, and always will be. And you are still the heir to the earldom. *Ash's* heir."

As if either were any consolation.

"Heir presumptive, not heir apparent," he added with a grim smile. "And as soon as Ash marries and begins to fill his nursery, not even that. I was never the true heir, no matter how often, or how long, Grandfather put forth such a falsehood."

No matter how often you pretended it was true, too...

Lady Silliman's hand fell to her side. She, unlike her husband, had never uttered the lie herself, at least not that Noel could recall. But she'd never openly challenged the earl, either. Never once publicly repudiated his false claims, or made more truthful declarations herself. No, she'd only watched and waited, waited until her husband's death to undercut everything Noel had been taught to believe about himself. About who he was, and who he would someday be.

Could she not understand how galling it was even to attend this damned rout? To have to bow and chatter as he watched the malicious enjoyment of his own misfortune flicker in the eyes of the gossip-mad guests? Or worse still, the pity in those of the more kind-hearted?

Yes. The tight expression on her usually smiling face, the way her tiny body seemed to shrink even further into itself—yes, she understood. Yet she offered no words of apology, only pulled her shoulders back, her stance firm.

She, just like his grandfather before her, expected him to do his duty, to his family, to his cousin. Do what she knew was right.

What Noel, even in spite of his frustration and anger, felt was right, as well.

He set his jaw. Enough. The heart should keep its own bitterness to itself, not rain it down like acid upon the innocent heads of others. Especially not upon those it loved.

He cast about the entrance hall, looking for some suitable distraction.

"You will be glad to hear I was able to convince my cousin to give over his dull Quaker headgear for a more suitable beaver," he said, reaching for a shiny top hat sitting on the console table by the front door. "Mr. Lock was accommodating enough to send over a good supply."

Grandmother gave him a long, considering look before at last taking up his lead. "Do not Quakers insist on wearing their hats inside? Please tell me you reminded your cousin how improper it would be to don such a thing at an evening party."

Ash, who must have come down before them, popped out of the drawing room and snatched up the hat in question. "What, after being goaded into purchasing this fashionable fribble, I'm not even allowed to parade about with it on my head? But perhaps it would look better on your lovely curls."

With a flourish, he set the hat in question not atop his own head, but on Lady Silliman's.

"Oh, do take it away, you silly boy! How Draper will scold if the feathers she arranged so becomingly are set awry." Grandmother's gloved hands fluttered about the intruding headgear, but the affection in her smile could not be mistaken. How easily his cousin could make her laugh. "Set it down this instant and give me your hand. Our guests will be arriving any moment."

Noel took the curly-brimmed beaver from Ash and gave his cousin their grandmother's arm in return. For a man raised amongst the sober Quakers, Ash Griffin certainly did like to tease.

He could hardly imagine pious Miss Honeychurch enjoying

Ash's verbal mischief as Grandmother did. Surely a quieter, more sober sort of gentleman would be more to such a woman's taste.

Noel shook his head. The preferences of Ash's childhood friend were little to the point. All Noel need concern himself with this evening was how best to keep Bathsheba Honeychurch from monopolizing the attention of his cousin.

And perhaps devising a plan for turning that attention to something—or someone—else?

CHAPTER 7

From the opposite side of the drawing room, Noel kept a wary eye on his cousin as Ash and Grandmother offered the hospitality of Silliman House to each new arrival. Despite his grandmother's reluctance to have him greet the guests, too, he'd been poised to step in if the new earl made the least social stumble. But his cousin conducted himself with admirable aplomb, not once falling back into his eccentric Quaker habits. He called each nobleman by his proper title, rather than awkwardly naming each "Friend"; bowed in proper deference, but only when such deference was called for; and, most importantly, refrained from blurting out any stingingly blunt truths as Bathsheba Honeychurch was all too wont to do, at least if the complaisant countenances of their guests as Ash welcomed them were to be believed. Thank heavens the chit's influence over his cousin had not extended *that* far.

Even the Earl of Morse, one of the *ton*'s highest sticklers, did not come away from his introduction to Ash with a frown. That gentleman was not likely to remain sanguine for long, though, not once Miss Honeychurch and her chaperones arrived. Viscount Stiles, the earl's only son, was as different from him as chalk was from cheese. Yet another reason for Noel to keep his eyes peeled for the arrival of Miss Honeychurch's party—he had forgotten to warn Stiles his father would also be in attendance this evening.

But after a clumsy footman knocked over two bottles intended for the guests, Noel had to go in search of the key to the wine cellar which had somehow gone astray. And then had to divert a dowager who was about to mistake a departing Michael Pinney for a footman, assuming that anyone with skin darker than her own must of course be at her beck and call. And then lend a sympathetic ear to several of his grandmother's cronies, who button-holed him to natter endlessly on about their bevy of unmarried granddaughters and grandnieces who had all recently made their social debuts, and whom he must be certain to introduce to his most charming young cousin at the earliest opportunity.

Given all the distractions, it would hardly have been surprising if he'd missed Stiles' party. But even with his back to the door, he could not mistake the unsettling, yet enticing, prickling that hit his nape about an hour into the party. Because of course all of Noel's senses continued to heighten into taut, anticipatory awareness the instant Miss Bathsheba Honeychurch entered a room. Damn him for the veriest of fools.

He watched over Lady Chaveley's shoulder as Grandmother graciously welcomed the new arrivals, then quickly and deftly drew Ash's attention away to another set of guests. Miss Honeychurch did not seem at all satisfied with that. Far too used to having Ash dance attendance on her, no doubt. But could she truly expect to hold any young man's attention, especially one as unused to the glittering splendors of the ladies of the ton as was his cousin, when dressed in such a plain manner?

Unlike the elegantly-attired Miss Debenham, with whom his cousin was currently conversing, nay, unlike every other lady in the room, whose gowns all featured fashionably large puffed sleeves and wide, gored skirts, hems one and all elaborately trimmed with lace, flounces, or rouleux, Miss Honeychurch wore a dress almost austere in its simplicity. A simple brown silk with plain capped sleeves, a demure, untrimmed neckline, and a skirt shockingly bare of embellishment of any kind. No jewels hung from her ears or neck; no flowers or feathers or ribbons adorned her severely-dressed light blonde hair. Completely unadorned, was Miss Bathsheba Honeychurch, dressed without the least intention of calling attention to her person.

And yet the animation of her expression—why, even from clear across the room, she glowed, incandescent as the heart of a bonfire.

A bonfire by which every fiber in his being longed to be warmed…

"Mr. Griffin, good evening. Fine night for a party, fine night indeed."

Noel started as this genial greeting from one of his grandfather's old cronies. Happily, the man only spared him a quick nod before turning toward the more enticing refreshment table.

How long had he been staring at her? Noel clenched his teeth. Damn his brain for fluttering off into such ridiculous flights of fancy when it should instead be planning how to mitigate the damage an outspoken Miss Bathsheba Honeychurch, let loose amongst the genteel guests at his Grandmother's party, was all too likely to cause.

Noel made his excuses to Lady Chaveley and moved to intercept his old friend and his troublesome house guest.

"Neither Miss Honeychurch nor I wants for conversation," he heard Stiles say as he drew closer to the viscount and his ladies. "If we strike up a lively debate, we'll be certain to draw the attention of someone of interest."

"Lively debate is always welcome, but please, no arguments in the midst of my grandmother's drawing room, Stiles." Noel set a welcoming hand on his friend's shoulder, then offered his wife and Miss Honeychurch a perfectly correct bow. He would not allow his gaze to linger on the latter, no matter how his wayward senses urged him to drink his fill. "Ladies. Welcome. May I introduce you to some of my grandmother's acquaintances? Lady Butterbank has just arrived, and you see Mrs. Staunton and Mrs. Chaveley there, by the window. I believe you will find them—"

"Stiles. How surprising to find you in town."

Beside him, both Stiles and his lady stiffened. Damn. Morse had not waited long to force his presence upon them.

"Father." Stiles offered his father a perfunctory bow. "I did not know you would be in attendance this evening."

The earl offered an even more perfunctory nod of his own in return. "Lady Silliman knows what is due to rank and family. Lady Stiles, good evening."

Stiles' wife bent into a gentle curtsy. But Miss Honeychurch, unsurprisingly, did not. Stubborn, stubborn lady.

"And this woman, I suppose, who refuses to offer proper deference to her superiors, must be your cousin, Miss Honeychurch."

Noel fought against an inexplicable urge to set his body between Bathsheba Honeychurch and the scornful gentleman looking down his aristocratic nose at her with such clear contempt.

"And you are Henry Burnett," the lady answered, not needing Noel's championing in the least. "Well do I remember you from my cousin's wedding. How pleased you must be to have your son safe back in England."

"Must I? One would suppose so, wouldn't one?" Morse glanced between his son and Miss Honeychurch, as if he couldn't decide which of the two was less worthy of his regard.

"Lord Morse," Noel said, hoping to diffuse what was looking to become a most uncomfortable exchange. "My grandmother was not sure you would be able to join us so early in the evening. Parliament has adjourned for the day?"

"Lords has, although the Commons continues to blather on.

How some men do enjoy listening to themselves pontificate! And what is this that I hear of you staying at a hotel, Stiles? The furnishings at Morse House may not be in the first state of fashion, but they should be good enough for a man who has spent the past few years living in an uncivilized hovel."

"Thank you, sir, but we do not wish to impose," Stiles answered. "We have taken lodgings in Conduit Street."

"Ah, I was not aware. As you did not deign to wait upon me when you first arrived in town to inform me of your plans. How many days have you been in residence? Four? Five?"

"My apologies, sir," his wife interposed before Miss Honeychurch could utter whatever rebuke was clearly hovering on her lips. "We have been much occupied with readying our lodgings."

"Indeed. I must admit, I cannot quite understand how a visit to the billiards' rooms at Charing Cross, nor the cudgel-playing at Spa Fields, nor the animal-baiting at Westminster Pit, might contribute to one's domestic arrangements. By wagering on the outcomes, perhaps?"

Beside him, Stiles gave a barely audible growl. His friend had often hinted at how overbearing his father could be, but Noel had rarely had the chance to witness the earl's behavior himself. The late Lord Silliman might have insisted on having his own way, too, but at least he'd never insulted Noel in public.

"Lord Stiles has been kind enough to offer us his company as I introduce my cousin about town," Noel explained. And in return, Noel had offered his friend a sympathetic ear, listening to Stiles' worries over how best to win back the regard of his long-estranged wife. Not that Noel had much advice to offer there; the amount of time and effort people devoted to affairs of the heart had always struck him as pointless, if not outright silly. But Stiles seemed sincere in his desire not just to reconcile with, but to gain his wife's affections. She, however, did not seem to have thawed much to him in the days since they'd discovered her in

Clapham.

Perhaps he could distract Miss Honeychurch from his cousin by suggesting she play matchmaker for hers?

"Noel Griffin has been encouraging Ash to wager?" Miss Honeychurch whispered to her cousin, even as her indignant eyes fixed on Noel. "How could he?"

Noel repressed a flinch. Perhaps not, if the suggestion came from him…

"I also heard tell of a visit of a far different sort, though," the earl continued. "To the Colonial Office?"

Given Miss Honeychurch's interest in anti-slavery work, the knowledge that Noel had facilitated a meeting between his friend and those responsible for setting policy for the African colony of Sierra Leone could not but redound to his benefit. But just as Stiles had not informed his wife—or his wife's cousin—of his recreational pursuits, neither, it seemed, had he told them of his political ones.

Noel gave himself an invisible shake. There was absolutely no reason why he should care a tuppence what Miss Honeychurch thought of him.

"Mr. Griffin, I have heard that Silliman House boasts a particularly fine pianoforte," Stiles' wife said, once again trying to diffuse the tense conversation between father and son. "Are we to have music this evening, do you know?

An unpleasant smile crossed the elder Burnett's face as he turned his attention to Noel. "Mr. Griffin? Ah, you refer to Lord Ruxford here."

Noel pressed his lips tight, the honorific sounding both comfortingly familiar and painfully grating in his ear. One could not expect the *ton* to refrain from gossiping over something as tantalizing as a falsely-bestowed courtesy title. But he'd not imagined anyone would be so gauche as to bring the subject up to his face.

"Although you are Ruxford no longer, I understand," Morse

continued. "A sad business, this, being displaced by an upstart claiming to be a long-lost cousin."

"Displaced?" Miss Honeychurch had spoken so softly, he doubted anyone besides himself had heard.

His brow furrowed. How had she not realized that Ash's elevation had been at Noel's expense?

Stiles and his lady must have refrained from discussing his past with her. And he supposed a Quaker would hardly indulge in the *ton*'s gossip mill, the only other likely source of the painful information.

Her gaze lit on Noel, speculation animating her features.

"I suppose you have thoroughly investigated his antecedents?" Lord Morse asked, the polite enquiry in his tone gratingly at odds with the insult of his words. "It will not do to allow some imposter to claim the title so ably held by your esteemed grandfather, sir."

"Ash would never push himself forward!" Miss Honeychurch exclaimed. "He doesn't even want the title! Noel Griffin was the one who came in search of him."

"Indeed, my lord, it was I who informed my cousin of his patrimony," Noel confirmed. "There is no doubt that Manasseh Griffin is the son of my father's elder brother, and thus the rightful heir to the Silliman title."

"And here we all were, assuming the man dead all these years. Your grandfather played a dangerous game, keeping such a secret. And for what? In the end, it has all come to naught."

"Naught? A family has been reunited after years of estrangement," Stiles' wife protested.

Morse shook his head. "Better a family remain estranged than to have a weak heir set at its head. Ruxford—no, I suppose we must call you plain Mr. Griffin now, as you are no longer entitled to the courtesy title your grandfather was brazen enough to bestow on you—has been displaced by a barely educated pup! I cannot understand what the late Lord Silliman was thinking. A nobleman should keep his heir close, train him up properly to his duties and responsibilities, not ignore him and set another in his place. And said heir should be grateful for the attention he bestows."

"Might I trouble you to fetch me a glass of wine, my lord?" Lady Stiles asked, as clearly aware as Noel that Lord Morse's final barb had been directed at someone besides the now non-existent Lord Ruxford. "The room grows close."

Lord Morse frowned, then gave a perfunctory bow. "I will have a footman sent over directly, ma'am."

"My apologies, Griff," his friend offered after Lord Morse moved out of earshot. "My father can be remarkably blunt."

"It is I who should apologize to you. I meant to warn you that grandmother had sent him a card, but I fear I was distracted by the loveliness of your companions this evening."

Noel's clumsy attempt at gallantry clearly did not impress Bathsheba Honeychurch. But his next attempt to turn the conversation away from the awkwardness of his lost courtesy title—an offer to introduce Stiles to an undersecretary at the Colonial Office, so that Stiles might speak to him of his concerns about Sierra Leone—certainly did. Ridiculous, to be so warmed by the unfamiliar look of curiosity, rather than the usual scorn, lighting those blue eyes.

"Come, shall we have some music?" Lady Silliman bustled through the drawing room, urging her guests toward the passageway. "If you will all step into the music room..."

"Sheba?" Stiles offered his arm to Miss Honeychurch.

She hesitated, her eyes fixing with curiosity on Noel's, as if wishing to ask him more about what she'd just learned. But then she caught sight of Ash escorting one of the young ladies to whom his grandmother had introduced him earlier in the evening. Quickly threading her arm through Stiles', she pulled him in Ash's wake.

If only they had thought to invite a member or two of the

Anti-Slavery Society tonight. A conversation with Wilberforce, or even Buxton or Stephen, would have been even more compelling a distraction than the gossip about his lost inheritance.

Alas, Grandmother disliked guests with manners so uncouth as to regularly introduce controversial topics into polite conversation. So for now, he'd have to fall back on his first plan —pointing out how desperately Stiles needed help in winning back the regard of his wife, while subtly suggesting Bathsheba Honeychurch was the only one who could assist him. Stiles had cast him in a better light than she was wont to regard him; perhaps she wouldn't be able to resist such a call, even if it came from him.

He winged an arm to Lady Stiles. "May I direct you to the music room? Your husband tells me you are quite the proficient. I confess I am eager to hear you play."

And not at all eager to confess his keenness to avoid yet another dull and frivolous evening party by matching his wits against her young cousin.

Much to Sheba's dismay, the Silliman rout party had taken a musical turn, one which Ash had somehow contrived to escape. Her gloved fingers tapped against the seat of the chair upon which Delphie insisted she perch, waiting for the latest in a long line of young ladies to finish performing upon Silliman House's polished pianoforte so she might go in search of him.

Unlike Sheba, Noel Griffin seemed to have little difficulty keeping his attention on the music. She glanced at him from the corner of her eye, poised on the chair to Delphie's left, as elegant and immobile as the statues of the bronze stags by which they'd conversed in Green Park on Monday. How could Ash never have mentioned, not even once, that his cousin had been brought up to believe himself the rightful Silliman heir?

Was that why he donned such a stiff facade? To protect himself from the pain of his family's cruel betrayal?

She jerked her eyes back at to the pianoforte, fighting the unwelcome ache in her throat. No, anyone who would lie and manipulate to get his own way, as Noel Griffin's withholding of his cousin's letter demonstrated, could be naught but cold, proud, unfeeling.

Still, the memory of how he sometimes stared, unseeing, down at his hands, the hint of melancholy she caught, glinting through a quickly concealed chink in that impassivity…

No. A man who would hide behind such a carefully crafted reserve could never appeal to a Friend, one raised to value the truth above all.

Such a person should—would—far prefer a man like Ash, a man with an easy, open temper.

But still, Ash's easy temper could be a problem, too. For despite his promise to make time for her, she'd not seen him even once since their walk on Monday.

Sheba clapped politely as the latest young lady finally finished her turn. How many more songs must she sit through before she could escape Delphie's supervision and go in search of Ash?

"Miss Honeychurch?" Ash's grandmother stood beside the pianoforte's thankfully-empty bench. "Might you give the company an air?"

Sheba blinked. "It is not the Friends' way, Frances Griffin, to —"

"Perform in company," Spencer Burnett interrupted before Sheba could explain that music did not tend to promote the most important object of education: the improvement of the mind. "But my wife is well able to serve as substitute. Philadelphia? Might we tempt you to the instrument? I would be more than happy to turn the pages for you."

A slight flush washed over her cousin's cheeks.

"Thank you, Lady Stiles," Ash's grandmother replied. "You are too kind."

Spencer Burnett offered his wife his arm and led her to the pianoforte. Among the Audley cousins, shy Delphie was the one least likely to put herself forward. But her husband seemed determined to pull his quiet wife out of her self-effacing shell.

Yet another point in the man's favor.

Yes, Sheba's initial wariness of Delphie's husband had entirely given way over these past few days as she'd witnessed him try, time and time again, to gain back her cousin's wary trust. Unlike Sheba, whose mother had declared music but a sensual gratification, and worse, its study a distraction from the religious duties and retirement she wished her daughter to cultivate, Delphie's family had always encouraged her to pursue her musical interests. Obviously aware of how much Delphie loved music, Spencer had taken her to the opera at Covent Garden, to Flight and Robson's to hear the new Apollonicon organ, and to concerts not only at Hanover Square, but also at the Argyll Rooms. He asked Delphie about her favorite composers, then gifted her sheet music of their latest works, or procured copies from the wives of his many friends that she might transcribe. He'd even brought them to John Broadwood & Sons, encouraging Delphie to choose a pianoforte to rent during their time in town, since their lodgings had no instrument.

And he complimented her, too, not with false flattery but with a sincere appreciation for Delphie's true gifts—her insightful yet practical solutions to each problem they encountered while setting up their lodgings; the kindness she showed each potential servant they interviewed, even if she did not intend to hire them; even the way she would occasionally drift off into her own dreamy imagination in the midst of a conversation, a habit many others found annoying.

No, the Spencer Burnett of eighteen hundred and twenty-four was a far different man than the one she'd met at Delphie's wedding. Indeed, how could a man who had spent years working in Sierra Leone not but be changed by such an experience?

Delphie seated herself in front of the instrument, taking noticeable pains to avoid coming into physical contact with her husband. How sad to see her cousin so isolated, so stiff with resentment and hurt...

Noel Griffin shifted to Delphie's empty seat, his eyes fixed on the couple by the pianoforte. "My friend makes little progress there, I think," he whispered.

"Spencer told you he wishes to reconcile with my cousin?" Even though she whispered, the pitch of her voice clearly rose.

He shot her a sidelong glance. "Shocked, are you, that Stiles would share such intimate concerns with the likes of me?"

"Not that Spencer would confide in a friend, no. Only that you would care enough for another's feelings to welcome the confidence—"

Her gloved hand shot to her lips, pressing in vain to contain the unkind words.

"I may not spout my feelings about with the abandon of a whale spouting air, Miss Honeychurch. But I assure you, I care. I care deeply about the happiness of my oldest friend."

She blinked up at him, trying to hide her shock. "As do I."

He tilted his head so that his lips were beside her ear. "Then perhaps we might offer them both a helping hand?"

The start of the music kept her from asking him what he had in mind.

Thank heavens, Noel Griffin withdrew to a decorous distance. She took one deep breath, then another, willing her uncomfortably pounding heart to still.

Delphie played and played, with far more proficiency than most of the evening's other performers. Even Sheba found herself lost for long moments in the beauty of the music.

Someone, though, was not as enraptured by Delphie's playing as was the rest of the room. Why was Ash walking alone past the doorway of the music room?

Playing in company meant Delphie would be far too self-conscious to keep a wary eye on Sheba. Rude, perhaps, to leave in the middle of her cousin's performance. But she couldn't let the opportunity to slip away to speak to Ash—nor to escape Noel Griffin's uncomfortable presence—pass her by.

"If you will excuse me for a moment?" she whispered before carefully edging out of her seat and slipping towards the door.

But by the time she reached the passageway, Ash was no longer in sight. She searched for him in the library, in the dining parlor, and the drawing room, all to no avail. She finally found him downstairs in the entrance hall, engaged in conversation with two gentlemen to whom she had not yet been introduced.

She made her way down the grand staircase, waiting for a chance to draw him aside.

"In the great question of emancipation, the interests of *two* parties are involved: the interest of the slave and that of the planter," a portly gentleman opined. "You cannot expect to foment change unless you take both into consideration."

"But it cannot for a moment be imagined that these two interests have an equal right to be consulted," a younger gentleman answered.

Indeed. As if the slaveowners had any moral rights at all comparable to the enslaved themselves!

"Not an equal right, perhaps, but certainly an equal influence," the first gentleman replied. "Nay, a far more powerful influence, that of the planter."

"But if we defer emancipation until the planter is sufficiently alive to his own interest to cooperate in the measure, we will forever despair of its accomplishment," the second protested.

Why did Ash not add his own arguments to such a vitally important discussion? Sheba cast him an admonishing glance. Did he not see her? Or was he simply choosing to ignore her?

"Yes, the cause of emancipation calls for something more

decisive, more efficient than mere words," she heard herself say as she stepped closer to the group. "We must end the hypocrisy of pretending to commiserate with the enslaved, whilst bribing the slaveowner to keep them in slavery by purchasing the products of their labour."

The portly gentleman's eyes widened. But then, as if choosing to be amused rather than offended by her interruption, he lifted a single eyebrow. "Perhaps, if *all* would unite in such a resolution, ma'am. But what can the abstinence of a few individuals, or a few families, do towards the accomplishment of so vast an object?"

"It can do wonders," Sheba declared. "Great effects often result from small beginnings. Your resolution will influence your friends and neighbors; each of them will, in like manner, influence their friends and neighbors; the example will spread from house to house, from city to city, until among those who have any claim to humanity there will be but one heart and one mind, one resolution. Is it not so, Ash?"

"Silliman?" The other gentleman turned to Ash, clearly interested in hearing the opinions of this newcomer to society. "Do you share this lady's opinion of the matter? Or do you agree with your late grandfather's stance?"

His late grandfather's stance? Did Charles Griffin take the same view as the portly gentleman, that slavery should be abolished only gradually?

And why should such a question make Ash glance at her with such a wary look in his eyes?

"We all wish for the end of the institution, without doubt," he finally offered. "But even the most well-intentioned men differ about how best to achieve that goal."

What a mealy-mouthed, appeasing thing to say! Especially as she knew his actual view of the matter was far different.

"There is but one course of action that will achieve the goal of immediate emancipation: refusing to purchase slave-produced goods," she insisted, her voice far too loud, even to her own ears. But she could not seem to stop the haranguing torrent of words, even as they drew the attention of the other gentlemen in the room.

"My friend Elizabeth Heyrick has written all about it in her latest pamphlet. I've been to call on her London publisher, to gauge their interest in publishing a new edition," Sheba added.

"Called on a bookseller? A woman of business are you, ma'am?" asked the portly gentleman with a chuckle.

"In the City?" Ash whispered, casting an anxious glance toward the other two gentlemen. "By yourself?"

"Should I have waited for you to call?" she whispered back. "You know I can never just sit about twirling my thumbs when there is work to be done."

"If you will give me your direction," she said in a louder voice, turning back to the portly gentleman, "I would be happy to send you a copy of the new print—"

"Silliman." The crowd of gentlemen moved aside to make way for Ash's grandmother, the exaggerated tranquility of her expression a silent but clear rebuke of Sheba's forward, unladylike behavior. "Miss Debenham is quite taken with the portrait of the first earl. She'd be so pleased to hear the story of its painting from you; you tell it so much better than I. Come, she's waiting in the gallery."

"Certainly, Grandmother. If you will excuse us, gentlemen? Miss Honeychurch?" Ash bowed, then took his grandmother's arm and walked down the passageway.

She felt a hot flush crimson over her face. How easily he left her behind...

The rest of the company cast Sheba a few looks—some curious, some contemptuous, some utterly outraged—before trailing after their hosts.

Why could not one single thing seem to go her way?

She scowled up at the portraits of other past Silliman

ancestors hanging from the entrance hall walls. Redolent with disapproval, they seemed, as they sneered down at her, those heavily bewigged and bejeweled ancestors of Ash's. *How dare a woman of such plain dress and outspoken disposition despoil our ancestral home?*

Sheba scrunched her face tight for a few long moments, then slowly released it, struggling to regain her calm. Despite promising to spend more time with her, Ash continued to choose avoidance rather than confrontation. She was beginning to feel as ridiculous as a dog trying to catch its own tail, chasing after him to so little effect.

Perhaps it was time to start exploring whether it would be possible to teach in foreign lands even without a husband.

A whisper of movement behind her made her start. She wasn't alone?

She spun and—of course—discovered Noel Griffin leaning against the newel post of the grand staircase. His arms across his chest, a glint of something in his hazel eyes she might have almost thought amusement, or even warmth, if she didn't know him better.

When they'd first met, she'd thought Ash and his cousin shared *all* the same features. But now that she looked a little closer, Noel Griffin's lips, not pulled into a narrow line for once but quirking at the corners with what she could almost imagine might be *affection*—those lips were far different from Ash's, weren't they?

She crossed her own arms over her chest, embarrassment making her temper flare. "Are you here to lecture me again? Tell me how ill-bred it is to argue over contentious topics?"

"No."

His one-word reply brought her up short. "No?"

"No." Noel Griffin pushed himself away from the staircase and strode towards her. "I honor anyone who calls for decisive action to bring an end to slavery, and who challenges others to move beyond complaisance and to do their part."

A soft "oh" escaped her lips. Noel Griffin embraced the anti-slavery cause?

He was so close, she could see the intricate embroidery on his waistcoat. And were those *spangles* amongst the stitchery?

"Such a gaudy garment doesn't suit you in the least," she heard herself say. "Why ever did you choose it?"

Did he actually *chuckle*?

"Would you believe me if I said it was because I knew it would provoke your sharp tongue?" he said, his eyes alight with far-from-holy amusement.

Her "oh," this time, was silent. But the pounding of her heart was so loud, she wouldn't have been surprised if they heard it all the way back in Leicester.

He stared at her then, the strangest expression blooming over his narrow, sharp-edged face. All confusion and puzzlement and —

And *longing*?

The hairs all along her bare arms began to tingle.

"Would you—"

"Do you—"

They stumbled and tripped over each other's words, clumsy with unfamiliar awareness.

Noel Griffin waved a hand. "My apologies, Miss Honeychurch. What did you wish to say?"

What *did* she wish to say? She searched the shadowed planes of his cheeks, the roil of color in those strange, changeable eyes, as if she might find the answer in a face that no longer looked quite as distant as she'd once believed it to be.

"Does it pain you, no longer being known as Lord Ruxford?" she finally heard herself ask.

His eyes widened at the shockingly blunt question. But he gave her no answer.

Had that been her intention, to offend him? So that she could push him—and these disturbing feelings he seemed to engender—away?

Or had she hoped he *would* answer? Hoped he would share something meaningful of his true self, something he kept protected, hidden, even, perhaps, from himself?

"It is only, if someone told *me* I wasn't to be called Bathsheba any more, I would have felt quite upset," she continued, somehow unable to keep the words from tumbling from her mouth. "So I wondered if you might feel the same..."

Could that be a smile threatening to challenge the austereness of his expression? "An unusual name, Bathsheba. 'And it came to pass in an eveningtide, that David arose from off his bed, and walked upon the roof of the king's house. And from the roof he saw a woman washing herself; and the woman was very beautiful to look upon.'"

Very beautiful to look upon... Why should a Bible verse sound so strikingly different when spoken by Noel Griffin than by one of the elders at Meeting?

"It's not that I'm overly fond of the name—who would wish to be called after a woman known for being taken in adultery, whatever could my mother have been thinking?" she said, the words spilling out of her mouth faster than a stream after spring snowmelt. She brushed aside the momentary sense of guilt at speaking ill of her exemplary mother. "I might have preferred to be called Esther, or Ruth, or even Jehosheba. *She* at least saved her nephew from execution..."

How surprising, to see the corner of his lip turn up in amusement.

"I'll admit, I have been wondering about the origins of your name. Your mother must have been thinking about Bathsheba as mother of Solomon, rather than as temptress of David."

"Temptress? You think Bathsheba deliberately tempted the king?" Sheba declared, annoyance flaring. Yes, far more welcome, annoyance, than this discomfiting tingling *awareness...*

"All the paintings I've seen depict it so. Although one does wonder why so many artists seem compelled to paint that particular scene, rather than other moments in the biblical Bathsheba's life. Is it because they can still claim to be pious, even when depicting a female nude?"

Nude? Painters depicted the biblical Bathsheba without clothing?

Sheba flushed, her eyes fixed on his. Not because his were immodestly straying down her person. But because she seemed quite unable to stop imagining those eyes studying the unclothed bodies of her painted namesakes.

And, much to her own bewilderment, picturing herself in their place—

"Ah, Sheba, there you are."

The sound of Spencer Burnett's voice sent her spinning away from Noel Griffin, a marble struck by a welcome taw.

She sputtered as air refilled her lungs. Had she truly been holding her breath?

"Thank you, Griff, for tracking her down." Spencer clapped a hand to his friend's arm before turning back to Sheba. "We're ready to bid the company goodnight if you're amenable. I've asked a footman to gather our coats and summon a hack."

"A hackney? For such a short distance?" She'd have far preferred a nighttime walk, which would have given her the chance to gather her scattered senses unobserved.

"Yes, Delphie's been rather done-in by the day's exertions." Spencer tilted his head, his eyes shifting between her and Noel Griffin. "Let me just go and collect her from the music room. I'll be back in a trice."

Without even waiting for her reply, he left her alone again with Noel Griffin.

"Poor Philadelphia," Sheba said, quick steps taking her to the model of his father's ship and putting some much-needed distance between them. "It must be exhausting, always hiding one's true self away from others. Not just from strangers, but from one's own family, too. No wonder she is so tired."

"A circumspect young woman, your cousin. Particularly so in regards to her husband?"

"Yes," she said, giving a silent thanks that he'd followed her lead, shifting the conversation away from more confusing ground. "She must see that Spencer Burnett is no longer the callow man she married. But she's wary of placing her trust in him again."

"And you think him deserving of that trust?"

She frowned. "Do you not?"

"Yes, but he is *my* oldest friend, not yours. I may be biased in favor of his happiness, rather than the well-being of your cousin."

Sheba crossed her arms. "I believe this may be the one time when you and I agree, Noel Griffin."

He gave a huff redolent with amusement. "The one and only, no doubt."

"Oh, assuredly."

"Beyond all question."

Sheba fought back the smile teasing at the corners of her mouth.

"During this past week, my cousin's husband has done nothing that should cause her to mistrust him. His every action seems designed to ensure her comfort and well-being. And she is sympathetic to him, of that I have no doubt."

"But she is wary of his intentions? And perhaps, too, of her own feelings?"

"Yes," Sheba said, blinking in surprise. She'd not imagined Noel Griffin could be so insightful, especially about the feelings of a woman.

Could he see as easily into hers?

"I have tried to convince her it is her duty to reconcile with him, as I know my mother would," she said, stepping away from the model ship to stare up the staircase, as if she might summon Spencer and Delphie simply by willing it. "But my cousin refuses to listen."

Sheba chose to ignore his half derisive, half amused chuckle.

"And whenever he's about, she insists she cannot do without my company," she said, more to the newel post than to him. "She'll say almost anything to ensure that the two of them are never alone. She doesn't seem to see that her avoidance is hurting herself, perhaps even more than it's hurting him."

"Your cousin is lucky to have someone like you, who loves her so much."

Sheba rubbed a finger over the wrought-iron balustrade, trying not to frown. She was far more used to being criticized by the members of the Meeting for the strength of her feelings than being praised for it.

"Delphie deserves some happiness, after all she's suffered. And she could be happy, if she would just set aside her anger and try to forgive."

"But Spencer will never be able to win her over if she refuses to spend time with him."

"No."

"Then perhaps you and I should work together to ensure they do."

Sheba whirled, prepared to upbraid him for teasing so. But his expression held none of its earlier amusement. Could he be in earnest?

"Work together? When you despise me so?"

"I may think you a poor match for my cousin, ma'am, but I would not go so far as to say I despise you," he said, his dry tone at odds with the gleam in his eye. "Besides, our being at odds over your relationship with Ash will only work to our advantage. Your cousin will never suspect us of colluding against her."

"Colluding! But I would never play my cousin false!"

"Say plan, then, rather than collude. Between the two of us, surely we can devise some pleasant outings and gatherings during which we can contrive to give them time alone."

Sheba's brow furrowed. "Contrive? That sounds almost as bad as collude! Has not Ash explained the importance to Friends of always telling the truth? My mother taught me that integrity demands avoiding even that which is misleading, even if technically true."

Noel Griffin crossed his arms. "To have a strategy one does not share with others is not the same as lying or misleading."

She gave a reluctant nod. He was right, no matter how loathe she might be to concede the point.

"What, then, should our first outing be?" he asked.

Oh, how much of London she wished to see! "A visit to Smithfield Market, to see if the conditions of the animals there are as terrible as Elizabeth Heyrick asserts? Or perhaps the Foundling Hospital? No, I know! The Newgate Prison, where Friend Elizabeth Fry is doing so much good for the incarcerated women!"

Noel Griffin laughed. "All ideal sites for the promotion of romantic feelings, to be sure. Although if your cousin shares your philanthropic interests—"

A throat cleared behind them. "Sheba. We are ready, if you are?"

Delphie took the coat held out by the footman and shrugged into it herself before her husband could offer to help.

"Certainly, cousin," Sheba said, exchanging a significant glance with Noel Griffin. Yes, he had noticed her cousin's standoffishness, too.

But he'd also somehow managed to scoop up her cloak from the footman, too, unlike his slowtop of a friend.

"You will send Philadelphia an invitation, then?" she asked in as even a tone as she could muster as he set the silk about her shoulders and pulled the hood with unexpected gentleness over her hair.

He nodded.

"My cousin is far more eager to promote my interests than her own pleasure, I fear. She'll be less likely to refuse an outing if Ash is also of the party," she hinted. There. She could be both strategic *and* tell the truth.

"Yes, Griff, do invite your cousin to whatever it is you have afoot," Spencer interrupted, handing Sheba a glove she must have dropped. "My wife is eager to further her acquaintance with him."

"Anything to please you, Stiles." A wry expression played across his face as he offered them a parting bow. "Miss Honeychurch. Until we meet again."

Sheba nodded, then swept past the footman toward the hackney waiting by the door, fighting the urge to look over her shoulder to see if those green-gold-amber eyes were still fixed on her.

She'd never thought she and Noel Griffin would share the same opinion about anything. And yet here they'd were, agreeing over the need to help Spencer win back the trust of his wife.

And to work together to reconcile the two.

Not quite the arrogant tyrant she'd originally thought, then, this Noel Griffin.

But just because a man wasn't as evil as one had originally thought, that didn't make him a *good* man, she reminded herself as Spencer handed her up into the carriage. He'd still withheld Ash's letter from her, had he not?

Not an evil man, no. But surely a dangerous one, if he could make her forget to ask about something as important as that...

CHAPTER 8

"How very unexpected." Delphie frowned at the note a footman from Silliman House had just delivered to the Conduit Street drawing room, then glanced up at Sheba.

"What is it? My father? Ash?" Sheba asked, tossing down the missionary papers she had been reading and rushing to Delphie's side.

"No, dear, no. Just an invitation from Mr. Noel Griffin, asking if we would accompany him and his cousin to the theatre this evening. But does not the new earl share your religious objections to dramatic performances?"

"An invitation to see a play?" Sheba set an arm about Delphie's shoulder and skimmed the note she held. Written in a neat, decisive hand, the hand of a man not prone to trifling hesitancy or delay. He'd certainly not waited to implement their plan to bring Delphie and Spencer back together, even though they'd only first discussed the idea last night.

If only he had thought to consult with her first! Plain Friends refused to attend the theatre. Because they did not wish to encourage men to assume false characters as all actors were required to do. And because playgoing accustomed its patrons to light thoughts and injured their moral feelings, by exciting a craving for stimulants and external objects of amusement unbecoming of a true Friend. Neither her family nor Ash's had ever frequented Leicester's sole theatre. Surely Ash must have explained as much to his cousin?

"Do you think it might be a ploy?" Sheba asked, her eyes narrowing. "A way to appear open to my spending time with Ash?"

"I'm not sure I understand your meaning, Sheba. Does not your young man also object to the theatre?"

"Yes, but Noel Griffin must have realized by now how accommodating Ash is, how he'd hate to refuse to attend a pleasure outing his cousin had taken pains to arrange. He must know me well enough by now, though, to suspect that unlike Ash, I won't give over my principles simply to mollify others, and thus would likely refuse the invitation. Oh, I can picture him even now, gloating over his own cleverness at sticking to the letter of our agreement while simultaneously thwarting my desire to spend time with Ash."

"Agreement? You have an agreement with Mr. Griffin, do you?"

Sheba bit her lip. She didn't wish to lie, but as Noel had said, not revealing all of one's plans was not the same as telling an untruth…

"We have agreed to stop acting as if we are enemies. For Ash's sake."

"An encouraging development." Delphie must have seen something odd on Sheba's face, for she quickly added, "I mean, that Mr. Griffin should care for the feelings of his cousin. Perhaps some day he'll even come to love him as dearly as do you."

Sheba did love Ash. Of course she did.

"Although Mr. Griffin's love for his cousin will be of an entirely different nature than your own," Delphie added as she sat down on the settee, examining once again the note in her hand.

"How should it differ, the love of one's fellow man from the love of one's spouse?" Sheba asked, kneeling to sit by Delphie's feet. She'd often puzzled over this vexing question, longed for a mother whom she could ask. For she never felt entirely quite satisfied by the answers the elders gave.

But perhaps Delphie could help where the elders had not?

Because unlike her other Audley cousins, Delphie never laughed at her questions, or shrugged them off as unimportant. Delphie listened, then took time to consider, to weigh Sheba's concerns against her own feelings and experiences. And then she'd share what she'd discovered, even if they were words she knew Sheba would not wish to hear.

If only all of their Audley cousins could be as committed to the truth...

Sheba rested her forehead against her cousin's knee, waiting for Delphie's mind to settle.

"I wonder," Delphie finally said, her voice filled with diffidence, "if one should feel something more for the person one marries than the love of one's fellow man. Not just the affection one feels toward a friend, but a passionate affection, as one sex to the other?"

Sheba frowned. "But is it not wrong to make the beauty or comeliness one's object in considering a life partner? Whoever thinks to build a marriage on such shaky ground, the Lord will surely blast it."

"Something your elders counsel?" Delphie asked.

Sheba nodded.

"One certainly should not make beauty or comeliness one's *only* object, I think," Delphie said after another long, considering pause. "But I don't think it wrong for attraction to play *some* part. How else are you meant to choose one particular person from the vast multitudes of one's fellow men to wed if you don't feel a particular attraction to one over the others?"

"You felt such an attraction to Spencer? Even though you married him out of duty, when Anna could not?"

The apples of Delphie's cheeks pinked. Had Sheba hurt her, mentioning the sister she had lost? She reached out and squeezed her cousin's hand.

Delphie stared out the window through unseeing eyes. Lost in her own world, again, as she was all too wont to do.

It was no use trying to yank Delphie back by force. So Sheba waited for her cousin to return.

As the clock struck the hour, Delphie blinked, as if she had just woken from sleep. "Yes, I felt an attraction to Spencer. I would never have consented to marry him if I had not."

Sheba frowned. Had shame, rather than hurt, made Delphie's cheeks fire? Shame that she'd coveted her sister's betrothed? Why, then, did she sound almost pleased by the fact?

"My father and his may have chosen for me, but in the end, I chose him, too," Delphie added.

"But one isn't meant to choose one's husband," Sheba said, fixing on the one word in her cousin's declarations that she could understand. "One should wait for the counsel of the Lord, wait for the inner Light to move one towards another."

"But does the Lord never choose to move one towards a person for whom one has an attraction?" Delphie asked with a gentle smile. "Do you, for example, have no liking for the person of Lord Silliman?"

Sheba sat back on her knees and frowned. Liking for Ash's person? Why should the question make her stomach quiver, as if she had just swallowed a slightly fusty bite of bread?

Delphie's palm smoothed over Sheba's brow. "It will be difficult, I think, to enjoy the marriage bed if you do not."

Sheba jerked free of Delphie's hand.

"Enjoy the marriage bed? You enjoy the marriage bed, Delphie?"

This time, Delphie's cheeks flushed nearly scarlet.

"Someone recently reminded me of the words of St. Paul," she finally said after a long embarrassed pause. "'Let the husband render unto the wife due benevolence: and likewise also the wife unto the husband,' for 'the wife hath no power of her own body but the husband: and likewise also the husband hath no power of his own body, but the wife.' To render one's spouse due benevolence means more than just submitting to duty, I think. Benevolence suggests a true disposition to promote the happiness of the other. Yes, I think a wife can, and should, find pleasure in the marriage bed."

Sheba stared up at her cousin, her mind awhirl. How intimate, how vulnerable, it all sounded! And yet the yearning in Delphie's voice suggested it was something she *wanted*. Something she had once had, and liked, and yearned for still.

Had Spencer refused to offer her that due benevolence? Was that why she insisted on keeping him at arm's length?

Or had he given her such pleasure, and the vulnerability of it, of entrusting her person to a man who had abandoned her, frightened her far too much to welcome it?

Sheba pushed a wisp of hair that had pulled free of her chignon back behind her ear. Even if either were the case, what advice could she, unmarried, untutored in the ways of conjugal love, offer either of them?

Could one find pleasure in the marriage bed if one had felt no real moving in the truth toward another? If she had no attraction to Ash's physical person?

And did it matter if she didn't? A union of minds and spirits, that was the most important thing in a marriage, surely...

Delphie sighed. "We've come a long way from the original question. So tell me, should I send Mr. Griffin our regrets?"

Sheba rose and strode to the window, watching the mid-day rush of pedestrians and horses and carriages. "The elders always encourage us not just to blindly follow their teachings, but to test them out against our own experience. Noel Griffin's invitation will allow me to judge for myself whether playgoing has as pernicious an effect as I've been taught to believe."

"Are you quite sure, my dear?" Delphie asked.

The challenging light in Noel Griffin's eyes as he proposed that she and he join forces to help Spencer win back his wife flashed across her mind. She kissed her cousin's cheek. "Thank you for considering my feelings, Delphie. But I am quite sure."

Delphie set her own lips against Sheba's temple before pulling free of the embrace. "Then would you fetch my writing desk, so I may answer Mr. Griffin's note forthwith?"

"Yes, and what's more, I'll run it down to the footman to deliver as soon as you've finished, too."

Not before, though, she added a postscript with a plan of her own...

"Whitechapel? But are we not to attend the theatre?"

After a drive far longer, and far more tedious, than she had expected, Sheba could not escape the stuffy Silliman carriage soon enough. But Delphie hesitated on its top step, blocking Sheba's way.

In spite of her wariness of attending a play, Sheba had looked forward to tonight's outing, especially the carriage ride. She'd planned to sit next to Ash and apologize for her behavior at last night's rout. And after he forgave her, as she was sure he would, she'd whisper to him her plan—her and his cousin's plan—to allow Spencer and Delphie time alone this evening. And, of course, remind him to guard against the dangers of attending a stage-play, and ask him to help her resist the temptations that they had been warned theatre-attendance fostered: an unhealthy excitement of mind, and an unwitting embrace of false morals.

But Delphie invited—no, insisted—Sheba take the seat between herself and Spencer rather than sitting beside Ash, giving Sheba no chance to share any sort of confidences with him. And, much to Sheba's surprise, Delphie monopolized the subsequent conversation, too, chatting with Ash and Noel Griffin about the weather, the difficulties of travel, the health of their grandmother, and that of Ash's mother and sisters back in Leicester. Sheba tried to turn the conversation several times away from such idle small talk, but all to no avail. Both Ash and his cousin deflected her every attempt, each offering little but polite platitudes in return. Noel Griffin would not even inform her of what play they were to see, insisting it remain a surprise.

And then Sheba's foot, tapping against the carriage floorboards in frustration at the inanity of their inconsequential talk, had accidentally brushed against Noel Griffin's. His eyes flicked to hers, a heat far greater than such an innocent mistake warranted simmering in their depths before it disappeared behind his typical guarded reserve.

She'd jerked her slipper back beneath her skirts, her pulse pounding in her ears. Why did she allow him to discompose her so?

"Delphie, please, would you step down?" Sheba resisted the urge to give her dithering cousin a push. "My first visit to a theatre will end before it's begun if you don't move out of the way."

"Whitechapel, though?" Delphie asked again, her eyes flickering warily up and down the busy street filled with bill-men, orange-sellers, and theatre-goers of all ranks and stations.

From the pavement below, Noel Griffin offered her cousin a gloved hand. "Not all of London's playhouses are to be found in the west end, Lady Stiles. I assure you, you'll be perfectly safe here."

Finally, her cautious cousin set her hand in his. Spencer quickly moved to her side, setting himself between her and the push of the crowd.

"Miss Honeychurch?" Noel Griffin extended his hand a second time.

Sheba would have far preferred to have Ash's help. But he had

Not Quite a Scandal

jumped down from the carriage the moment it had stopped and rushed over to read the playbill posted by the theatre's door.

Admonishments against the lusts of the flesh had never made much sense to Sheba. Why should anyone find it difficult to resist such a weak urge as a carnal appetite? But as she stared down at Noel Griffin's hand, slim, elegant in its neat kidskin glove, the very tips of her fingers began to tingle. Was this what the elders had been warning of, this strange, breathless awareness, this eager anticipation of another person's touch?

She forced herself not to allow her hand to linger in his.

"I think you will find tonight's performance of particular interest," Ash's cousin said as they walked toward the door of the theatre.

Sheba's gaze jerked to his face. Yet another spark of challenge lit his hazel eyes.

"Will I?" Had Noel Griffin selected a play particularly designed to offend? Surely not, not when he had invited his old schoolmate, and that schoolmate's wife, to the performance.

But perhaps the offense would only be to a Friend?

Sheba glanced suspiciously over Ash's shoulder at the playbill posted by the theatre door.

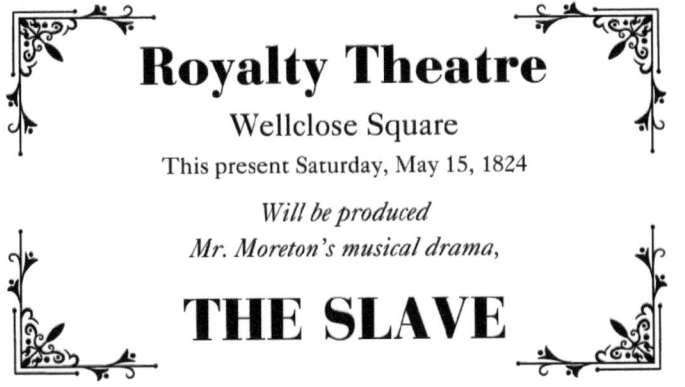

Royalty Theatre

Wellclose Square

This present Saturday, May 15, 1824

Will be produced
Mr. Moreton's musical drama,

THE SLAVE

Sheba's hands fisted in her skirts. Who could think to find pleasure in watching the sufferings of one unjustly deprived of his freedom?

"It won't just be you experiencing something for the first time, you see," Noel Griffin's finger tapped against the names of the actors listed on the playbill. *Gambia (the Slave), Mr. Keene, a Gentleman of Colour*, she read.

"No Black man has ever before appeared on the London stage, or so my secretary informs me," he continued. "And this Mr. Keene does quite a creditable job, if the reviews are to be believed. Although I understand he is an American, so England cannot take all the credit."

Sheba balked. "Is the man *owned* by an American? Is he being forced to act?"

"No, of course not. The English, unlike the Americans, do not condone slavery here."

"Although we condone it in our colonies."

Beside her, she felt Ash start. Was he as wary of this play as she?

Noel Griffin's brow furrowed. "I thought my choice would please you. The play is all the rage among the anti-slavery set."

"Excuse me," Ash interrupted. "I must go and pay for the seats my cousin has reserved for us."

He bowed and dashed through the crowd milling about the entrance to the theatre.

Not so wary, then. What had upset him, then?

"Delphie, stop dilly dallying and come see!" Spencer waved from the vestibule. "Glass chandeliers over the boxes, gas lights on the stage, and a ceiling painted like the summer sky! I doubt you've ever seen the like."

Sheba glanced over her shoulder as Delphie urged her towards the theatre door. Noel Griffin had chosen the play deliberately with her in mind? And not with the intent to antagonize, but the wish to please?

The clapping from the boxes and the pit of the Royalty Theatre had barely begun to subside when his cousin rose from his seat beside Noel. "Lady Stiles, your glass is empty. Allow me to fetch you another from the refreshment room before the next play begins."

"Silliman, send the footman," Noel said with a frown. His cousin kept forgetting a man of his position had others to take care of such mundane tasks.

"Yes, but then I'd miss the chance to speak to Mr. Davenport-Devenport, and to Lord Pierson, both of whom have been waving from their boxes," his cousin replied with an easy smile for Lady Stiles and a raised eyebrow for Noel.

Oh. Yes. It was time to set their plan—well, actually, Miss Honeychurch's plan—into action.

Spencer's wife offered a gracious smile of her own. "Thank you, then, my lord. More lemonade would be most welcome."

Miss Honeychurch jumped up from her own seat. "I'll come, too. I'd welcome a chance to move about after sitting still so long."

"A turn about the lobby would be most refreshing," Noel agreed, offering her his own arm before she could reach for his cousin's. The fewer chances Bathsheba Honeychurch had to exert her influence over Silliman, the better.

If only she were attempting to exert her influence over Noel. He could have dismissed her far more easily, then, regarding with contempt any overt attempt to win him to her side. But Bathsheba Honeychurch, honest to a fault, would never deign to charm or flatter the likes of him, even if doing so might ease her own path. No, she treated Noel with equal parts candor and contempt, clearly as indifferent to him as he wished she were to Ash.

If only he could feel just as indifferent towards her! But even the touch of her small, gloved hand against his sleeve made the hairs on his arm tingle with sudden animal awareness. And when a careless gentleman jostled against her, he immediately pulled her close to his side, not for an instant caring how it might look to Ash, who trailed behind them, or to any gossiping member of the *ton* attending tonight's performance.

A waft of honeysuckle hit his senses, made him draw in a deeper breath. He wouldn't have thought a Quaker would use perfume or fragrant soap, but the scent was definitely coming from her. He had to summon all his self-restraint to keep himself from burying his nose in her severe chignon, the curve of her elegant neck, searching out the source of the elusive aura.

He gave himself a mental shake. Enough. A grown man did not allow his animal urges to dominate his rational brain. Especially not in public.

He should consider instead what she might have thought of the play. He'd found it fairly ridiculous—what enslaved man, once emancipated, would go and sell himself again to free his former master from debtor's prison?—but pictured himself playing devils' advocate if she'd found it just as lacking, lauding it to the skies just to annoy her. Because arguing with Bathsheba Honeychurch filled him with a vigor he'd not felt for months. He might not be able to indulge his physical desires, but he could surely allow his intellectual ones free reign without anyone being the wiser.

Instead of making their way to the refreshment room, Noel guided Miss Honeychurch through the throng of late-arriving playgoers to the theatre's front door. Outside, the Silliman carriage awaited, just as they'd planned.

"Shall I send the footman to inform Lady Stiles you've taken ill?" Noel asked as the fellow jumped down from beside the driver to open the carriage door.

"As I've told you several times already, Noel Griffin, I do not lie." What a pugnacious tilt of the head Miss Honeychurch had! "Robert, you may inform my cousin, whom you will find in the second box on the left side of the theatre, that once I learned that the next play was to be a burletta, I could not countenance remaining. And Ash Griffin and his cousin kindly offered to see me home. Please tell them we'll send the carriage back for them in due course."

"Very good, ma'am," the footman said as he lowered the carriage steps. Of course, she would call the footman by his given name, rather than the more general, and convenient, "John footman."

"A bawdy farce?" Miss Honeychurch gave a shudder of distaste. "Whatever were you thinking?"

Behind him, Ash chuckled. "Yes, I didn't think *Cherry Bounce* would be quite to your taste."

"Although it would have been amusing to see your reaction to Mr. Holland's performance," Noel said. "His new song, charmingly entitled 'Clump's Farm,' reportedly features the most amazingly life-like imitations of a variety of barnyard animals."

She shuddered again, her frown deepening.

What might she look like if he could ever bring her to laugh?

He shook off the thought and held out his hand. Ignoring his polite offer, she scrambled up the steps all on her own.

She could hardly ignore the surprise he'd arranged to have waiting in the carriage, though.

"Connie?" Miss Honeychurch laughed and threw herself into her cousin's arms. "But what are you doing here?"

Mrs. Wingfield, whom he'd had his coachman retrieve from Clapham after he'd delivered them to the theatre, carefully extricated herself from her cousin's enthusiastic embrace. "Mr. Griffin wrote to me of your scheme to help Delphie and Spencer, and the need for a proper chaperone for you in Delphie's absence. Happily, Colonel Wingfield retired early this evening, which left me free to offer my help."

"But why? What need have I for a chaperone when Ash is here?"

Mrs. Wingfield sniffed. "Did your father teach you nothing of proper behavior? As if it would be at all the thing for an unmarried lady to ride in a carriage at night with two unmarried men! Thank heavens Mr. Griffin has more of a concern for your reputation than you."

Taking advantage of the two cousins' bickering, Noel pulled Silliman away from the carriage. "I noticed that you changed the subject when Miss Honeychurch began to preach about the evils of colonial slavery during the first intermission. You haven't told her about the estate's slaveholdings yet, have you?"

His cousin frowned, pulling the brim of his hat down over his brow.

"Well then. If you're set on avoiding the conversation, you needn't accompany us if you don't wish. I'll be happy to make your excuses."

Ash cut a glance toward the carriage, then back to the door of the theatre. "Lord Pierson *has* been eager to introduce me to White's, which grandmama says is the club our grandfather frequented. Perhaps some of his old friends will share their memories of him with me."

Since you have hardly spoken of the man, Noel heard, though the words never passed Silliman's lips.

"Then go and seek him out," Noel replied, ignoring his cousin's unspoken question. "I am happy to see the ladies home."

And even happier to keep his cousin from spending additional time in Miss Honeychurch's company.

Noel climbed into the carriage and took his seat opposite the ladies. "Enjoy the rest of your evening, Silliman," he called out the window, then gave the coachman the signal to drive on.

"What, is Ash not coming with us?" Miss Honeychurch turned to gaze out the window at the rapidly retreating theatre.

"No. He has other commitments tonight."

He should have been pleased by the confusion and frustration playing across her face. But somehow, he was not.

"Tell me, ma'am, how did you enjoy the play?"

She threw herself back against the squabs with a huff. "I must own I was extremely disappointed. The theatre was needlessly grand and dazzling, and I had no other feeling during the performance besides wishing it were over."

"Sheba! How ungrateful you are. You should be thanking Mr. Griffin, not just for the invitation, but for selecting a play particularly intended to appeal to you."

"Why should you think a play about a man unfairly enslaved should appeal to me? Or to anyone?"

"Because that unfairly enslaved man is the play's hero?" Noel offered.

"But a gentleman of colour, a free man, enacting the part of a slave? How that must pain him!"

"As you are unfamiliar with the theatre, you may not understand that actors do not take on the feelings of the characters they depict," Noel explained. "They know they are just performing a part."

"I disagree." Miss Honeychurch's hands whipped about the carriage, like a ship's sails on a windy day. "The trick and trade of representing what he does not feel must make him at all times an actor, and his looks, and words, and actions, will be all sophistication, not honesty. Such evil will be likely to continue with him throughout his entire life!"

"Several of my acquaintances in Clapham who are involved in the new Anti-Slavery Society have praised Mr. Moreton's play," Mrs. Wingfield offered, setting a settling hand over Miss Honeychurch's. "They say it impresses upon the world that noble sentiments may take root even in the bosom of a slave."

"Noble sentiments? You mean sentiments that continually affirm how very acquiescent to his enslaved state Gambia is?"

Miss Honeychurch exclaimed.

"Acquiescent? When he declares 'I am a slave:—in that all human wretchedness is comprehended?' " Noel asked.

"Yes, but does he not also say 'there is a state worse than slavery—liberty engendered by cruelty'? Yes, indeed, Gambia is the very model of an acquiescent slave. He's loyal not to his own people, but to his owner, and gives up his interest in the woman he loves simply because that owner loves her, too. Why, he even exchanges his own freedom to free his rival from prison! No wonder English audiences appreciate him so."

Even in the dim light of the carriage, Noel could see the blush overtaking Miss Honeychurch's narrow face. He'd never seen a woman whom indignation became more. Nor argued with one who sent such a rush of awareness racing down his spine.

"Gambia's character may be more designed to flatter English audiences than reflect the true feelings of any actual enslaved man, I'll grant you that," Noel conceded. "But is it still not a challenge to those among our countrymen who are all too ready to believe the claims of West Indian plantation owners that Africans are by nature inferior to Europeans? And that it is too dangerous to free them from the planters' purportedly benevolent care? Does not such a noble depiction of a man of color help to begin to change their minds?"

"Intelligent men should be moved by rational arguments, not false sentiment."

"Yet every day we witness our fellow men being swayed more by their hearts than by their minds."

"How foolish!"

Just as foolish as Noel finding the disdain in the curl of those surprisingly lush lips the least bit compelling.

"Foolish, yes, I agree. Yet true nonetheless. Anyone who wishes to persuade another to his cause needs to use all methods at his disposal. Including appealing to his emotions. I would think someone truly committed to the cause of abolition would welcome any tool available to persuade others to his side."

Instead of immediately taking issue with his argument, she paused, as if searching for the answer to a challenge he'd not even realized he'd made.

"Are you implying that my commitment to abolition is lacking?" she finally whispered.

A veritable villain, he felt, as he watched a lost look of dismay pall those lovely, lively features. He'd intended his words to provoke, not to diminish. Not to hurt…

"My goodness, Delphie and Spencer must know by now that you've abandoned them," Mrs. Wingfield interjected before he could figure out how best to apologize for his offense. "Do you think he'll be able to convince her to remain and watch the afterpieces with him? Or will she insist they leave at once?"

Noel gave a silent thank-you to Mrs. Wingfield for the welcome change in topic, and kept his peace for the remainder of the carriage ride back to Mayfair. He might share Miss Honeychurch's anti-slavery sentiment, but his goal was to detach the argumentative Quakeress from his cousin, not to find himself tangled up in feelings for her himself.

"Noel Griffin, will you please remind Ash that London Yearly Meeting begins next week? On Fourth-day at ten." Bathsheba Honeychurch set her gloved hand in his for just the merest moment as she stepped lightly down from the carriage onto the Conduit Street pavement. It took a surprising degree of restraint to keep himself from reaching out and curling his fingers around it, from pulling her lithe figure closer to his.

"Yearly Meeting?" he asked.

"Yes, of the Society of Friends. Representatives are appointed from Meetings all over Britain to travel to London once a year to meet and discuss how best to promote and maintain our society and religion in life and practice."

Of course, she had said she'd come to town for that Yearly Meeting, hadn't she, when she'd first visited Silliman House. "My cousin has not mentioned being appointed by your Meeting."

"No, he wasn't. But any Friend who is a member of a Monthly Meeting may attend. Since we've never traveled to London before, we've neither of us had the opportunity to attend. Ash must looking forward to it almost as much as I am."

She paused on the front step to give him a considering look. "On second thought, please don't bother to remind Ash. Tiresome, is it not, being asked to play intermediary? Messages and missives so easily go astray..."

Her dismissive expression, as if he were not worth the attention she'd pay a creeping worm—damn it. Ash must have mentioned the note he'd written her before leaving Leicester. The note he'd entrusted Noel to deliver.

The note which Noel, without a second thought, had tossed onto the fire burning on his aunt's drawing room grate.

He swallowed against a sudden heaviness in his chest. Why should it matter what she thought of him? He'd always cared far less about others' opinions than whether he lived up to his own morals and values.

Yet somehow he could not stop himself from craving the good opinion of plain-spoken, honest-to-a-fault Bathsheba Honeychurch.

It had been unworthy of him, failing to deliver that letter. Unworthy of him, and of her.

He reached over her shoulder, his pulse flaring at her sudden proximity, and tapped the knocker against the front door.

"I will remind him, Miss Honeychurch," he said, taking a deliberate step back. "And will ensure that any message you send him will reach his hands. You may depend upon it."

CHAPTER 9

"Miss Honeychurch? The earl will be down in a moment. He asks that you make yourself comfortable in the library until he is ready to join you."

Sheba stepped into Silliman House's front hall, trying hard not to stare at the unfamiliar man who had opened the door. He was clearly not a footman, for he wore no livery. In fact, he was dressed in the clothes of a gentleman. Yet with those liquid brown eyes, close-cropped black curls, and skin several shades darker than the fawn-colored waistcoat he wore, what else could he be but a servant?

"Michael Pinney, at your service, ma'am. Once secretary to Baron Ruxford—Mr. Noel Griffin, I mean—and now the same to the new Earl Silliman."

"Secretary?" The incredulity in her tone—where had it come from?

She might have missed the grimace that crossed his face, so quickly did he repress it in favor of an impassive politesse.

What a slight to Michael Pinney, the all-too-obvious doubt in her voice. She, who had not only been raised to believe in the equality of all people, but who also claimed to be committed to the anti-slavery cause, had been shocked to discover a Black man had been entrusted with the role of secretary to a nobleman? Her cheeks burned with shame.

"I'm sorry, Friend Pinney, for the disbelief in my tone. It was poorly done of me to cast doubt on your abilities in such a manner."

Michael Pinney blinked for a moment without speaking. "Unusual, Miss Honeychurch, for an Englishwoman to even recognize such a slight, never mind apologize for it. But then again, Mr. Griffin did mention you were the most—ah, shall we say, *unconventional?*—lady of his acquaintance. I'm pleased to finally have the opportunity to confirm the fact for myself. May I take your coat?"

Sheba blinked, too. Noel Griffin had spoken of her to his secretary?

"No thank you, Friend," she answered. "Ash and I are to take the Griffin carriage to London Yearly Meeting. We must leave soon if we are not to be late. I'm sure he won't be much longer."

At least she hoped he wouldn't be. She'd not seen hide nor hair of Ash, not since their night at the theatre four days ago.

She'd sent him several notes since then—one offering an apology for her behavior at his grandmother's party, another reminding him when Yearly Meeting was to be held, a third to ask if they might share his carriage to Devonshire House in Bishopsgate today, as Delphie had other plans for theirs (plans that did not include Spencer, alas). But despite Noel Griffin's assurance that he'd not interfere with their communications, Ash had not responded to a single one.

She pressed a fist under her ribs, trying with little success to stay the maelstrom of frustration, impatience, and hurt whirling away in her gut.

Ash could not be in London and yet refuse to attend Yearly Meeting, could he?

"How long, Friend Pinney, have you been in Noel Griffin's employ?" she asked, turning back to the secretary. "Do you enjoy working for him? Do you reside here at Silliman House? Or do you have a family with whom you live? Oh, are you involved in the anti-slavery cause?"

Michael Pinney laughed. "Not just unconventional, but inquisitive, too, I see. Where to begin? Lord Ruxford hired me a little over a year ago, soon after the late earl's first stroke. As I'm sure you know, he assumed he would succeed his grandfather to the title, and wanted a secretary not already beholden to that grandfather to see to his affairs."

Pinney opened a door at the left-hand side of the entrance hall and ushered her inside.

"But why are you to work for Ash, and not for his cousin?"

The room into which he ushered her contained far fewer books than any chamber named "library" should hold. Instead of bookcases, its walls were lined with paintings. No, portraits, the features of their sitters so similar to Ash's and his cousin's, they surely must be Griffin ancestors.

"Because it would be too difficult for a secretary unfamiliar with the family's holdings to guide the new earl, especially as he has so little knowledge of the proper running of an estate. And because Mr. Griffin has no need of the services of a secretary, no longer being a man of property himself."

Sheba frowned. "Ash's inheritance has left his cousin destitute?"

"No, he has a small inheritance from his father, one that will support him well if he'd only take the trouble to invest it wisely. But come, you shouldn't tempt a mere secretary to tell tales on his employers. Why do you not say something of yourself? Lord Silliman's told me you are much involved in charitable works in your community."

"No more than Ash and his sisters. In my absence, Patience and Abigail have been kind enough to oversee the school we opened for the sons and daughters of the people who work in my father's factory."

"You do not share the fear that seems common among

Evangelicals that such education will lead to revolutionary tendencies among the laboring classes?"

"A member of the Society of Friends is not the same as an Evangelical, sir. In fact, I believe so strongly in the need for an educated populace that I've long considered traveling overseas, to teach the basics of writing and reading, and the principles of Christianity, to those far less fortunate than even our own English poor. Perhaps to the Indies, or even to Sierra Leone."

Friend Pinney's easy expression hardened. "I assure you, Miss Honeychurch, no West Indian planter would allow you anywhere near those they've enslaved. And as for the children freed from slaver ships and resettled in our African colony, what makes you think they would welcome being taught by a European, one with the same color of skin as those who stole them away from their homes and families? Would not an intelligent child be quick to wonder if such a wicked people serve a wicked god?"

Sheba started at Michael Pinney, wondering how to answer such shocking questions. She'd been worried about whether teaching overseas might be a selfish indulgence of vanity rather than a true calling of the spirit, worried, too, that Ash's new social position might prevent her from going. But she'd never even considered that those she thought to help might not welcome, might not even be in need of, what she hoped to teach…

"But Friend Pinney," she finally managed to say, "do you not think—"

"That will be all, Pinney," a voice from behind them ordered. "You may return to your duties."

The tone of those words, though both quiet but firm, left no doubt of the speaker's expectation of being immediately heeded.

Ash's grandmother, a polished cane in hand, slowly crossed the room towards them.

"Very good, my lady." Michael Pinney gave a respectful bow,

then shot Sheba a commiserating glance before leaving her to contend with Frances Griffin. The secretary, no doubt, had heard rumors of the lady's antipathy to Ash and Sheba's not-quite-engagement.

Even despite the embarrassing start of, and end to, their conversation, Sheba would have far preferred to remain with Friend Pinney than struggle through a private meeting with Ash's grandmother. The older woman's disapproval was almost palpable.

But Frances Griffin did not chide her. "My husband, myself, and our six children," she said gazing up at a portrait hanging over the fireplace, affection and sorrow playing in turn over her features. "The girls are all married and tending to their own families now. But my poor boys are all dead and gone, along with their father."

Sheba's hands clenched the silk of her best gray gown. "'And this is the comfort of the good, that the grave cannot hold them, and that they live as soon as they die. For death is no more than a turning of us over from time to eternity.' Or so writes William Penn. When I lost my mother, his words gave me no little consolation."

"A wise man, my dear. And yet, as a creature still caught in time, I feel the loss of them every single day."

Sheba kept quiet, allowing the woman the grace of silence to gather her composure.

"You'll be most interested in the middle boy, the one holding the cricket bat," the older woman finally said, pointing to the center of the painting. "The current Lord Silliman's father. An active, cheerful child, my Will, far more concerned with proving himself on the pitch than worrying over the state of his soul, as you and yours are wont to do."

"Ash's father was a good man. In whatever he did, his guiding principle was to make it redound to the glory of God, and to hasten the coming of the Redeemer's kingdom on earth."

"A paragon of virtue, you make him sound. Quite unlike the rowdy boy I knew so well. Please, tell me, what was he like as a man? Not just as a member of your religious community, but as a husband, and a father?"

Sheba thought for moment before speaking, weighing the older woman's need for comfort against the necessity of truth. "Stern. Quick to call his children, as well as his wife, to fault. But quicker by far to upbraid himself for his own failings. He cultivated a habitual quietude of mind that encouraged Ash and his sisters—nay, encouraged us all—to listen carefully for the promptings of the divine within."

A look of disappointment flitted over the older woman's face. Had Sheba misspoken? What would a woman who was not a Friend value most in a son?

"He was also a dutiful man," she added. "He served on many of the committees tasked with the running of our Society, and attended to his responsibilities with thoughtfulness and care."

Ash's grandmother laid a hand on Sheba's arm. "But was he kind? Did he love his children? His wife? Did they love him?"

Sheba glanced at the older woman, then back up at the painting. It was difficult to recognize the sober, dutiful man she had always known in the face of the smiling boy he had once been. "Ash could tell you better than I," she finally said.

"Ah, but Silliman would not wish to hurt my feelings. I fear he'd only prevaricate or temporize rather than cast his father in a less than flattering light."

"I see you are coming to know your grandson quite well, ma'am." Although if she knew him as well as Sheba did, she'd give over calling him Silliman. How galling Ash must find it, to have a name specifically designed to call attention to the false belief that he was somehow superior to the rest of mankind, just by the mere accident of his birth, continually foisted upon him. And by one who was supposed to care for him, too.

But Ash's grandmother had clearly not bothered to ask Ash his opinion on the matter. "An affectionate, kindly boy, so eager to please everyone around him. Especially a newly-found grandmama. But you, Miss Honeychurch, have no such scruples. A plain speaker, or so both of my grandsons tell me. So I put greater credence in your words than in Silliman's. Please, tell me the truth of the matter."

Sheba smiled. The lady had likely not meant her description to be a compliment, but Sheba could not take her words as anything but. "Did your son ever tell you that his name was once drawn for the militia? Just before the end of the war with Napoleon, it was. The Lord Lieutenant of Leicestershire resolved to revive the county troop, and William Griffin was among those chosen by lottery to serve. Being a Friend, and faithful in his testimony against bearing arms, he of course refused. And as he had not enough money to pay the fine, nor goods that might be taken in recompense, he was sentenced to a month in gaol for that refusal."

"Gaol? My dear Will?" Ash's grandmother pressed the tips of her fingers against her mouth.

"Yes. And every day, do you know who visited him there?"

"His wife? The minister of your church?"

"Ash," Sheba said. "After he finished his schoolwork and his chores, Ash went and sat in that dim, dingy gaol and read to his father from the Bible, all of his own accord. Not out of a sense of duty, or because his mother or any of the elders asked it of him, but because he loved his father. And his father loved him in his turn. He was all of nine years old at the time."

"Then that is all that I could want for Silliman. Or for any of my grandchildren. To love and be loved by their parents." The older woman's eyes turned to Sheba. "That, and to find a suitable partner with whom to share his adult life."

Ah. Ash's grandmother was finally coming to the point.

"Suitable, yes," Sheba agreed. "Young people should be joined in marriage with persons of similar religious inclinations, suitable dispositions, temper, sobriety of manners, and diligence in business."

Ash's grandmother blinked. "Is that what your religious society tells you? What of similarity of rank and birth? What of fortune?"

"Fortune should not matter. Friends advise parents not to make it their first, nor their chief care to obtain large portions or settlements when seeking marriage partners for their children. And as to rank, why, Friends believe that all people are equal in the eyes of the Lord."

"In the eyes of the Lord, perhaps. But in the eyes of society? A footman is hardly the equal of an earl."

"The daughter of a mill owner should be a suitable wife for either a footman or an earl."

Ash's grandmother blinked. "Should she? What a very singular opinion."

"An opinion that I'm sure you'll find Ash shares."

Did he, still, though? Or had the influence of his grandmother, the influence of this worldly society in which he now moved, brought him to question the values on which he'd been raised?

She tapped a suddenly anxious foot. What could be taking Ash so long?

"Do they look like their father?" his grandmother asked, redirecting the conversation rather than openly rejecting Sheba's confident assertion. Not as willing as to accuse Sheba of having scandalous designs against her grandson as Noel Griffin was, it would seem. "Silliman's sisters, I mean. Do they have the Griffin countenance? Here, you can see it more clearly in this portrait of my husband's own father, which was painted when he was not yet twenty."

Ash's grandmother gestured to the other side of the library, where a smaller painting hung on the wall between the room's only two bookcases.

Sheba crossed the room to examine the picture more closely. She'd expected to see a single man, but the artist had chosen—or been instructed to?—paint two figures. The older, although clearly still a very young man, was obviously the Silliman ancestor to whom Ash's grandmother had referred. Dressed in finery far too splendid to actually be engaged in practicing archery, as the painter had depicted him. In his left hand he held a bow, while his right reached for an arrow from a stack held by a small boy who stood at the very edge of the painting.

A small *Black* boy, whom the artist had painted staring up at Ash's ancestor with an expression part fawning admiration, part submissive deference.

Would not an intelligent child be quick to wonder if such a wicked people serve a wicked god?

Gambia's character may be more designed to flatter English audiences than reflect the true feelings of any actual enslaved man.

Pinney and Noel's words raced through Sheba's head. The admiration and deference of the boy in that painting—surely the young boy must have been far from feeling anything like...

Sheba's stomach roiled. What was such a painting doing here, hanging in the Silliman family townhouse?

"The third earl? And who is the child beside him?" she choked out.

"The boy? Oh, some servant or other, I suppose."

"A servant? Or a slave?"

Ash's grandmother frowned. "I suppose it could be either. The estate did own several plantations in the West Indies at one time, I believe."

Sheba could barely get the words past the choking sensation in her throat. "*Did* own? Or *still* owns?"

The obvious disgust in her tone must have startled the older woman, for she took a step back, her face creasing with alarm.

But the answer to Sheba's question came not from Ash's grandmother, but from a voice behind them.

"Still owns."

She whirled. Ash stood by the door, dressed in garments far less splendid than those in which his ancestor had been depicted. But still far too fine for a man who was supposed to follow the Friends' commitment to forbear pride and immodesty in apparel.

Her eyes flicked to Noel Griffin, who stood behind his cousin in clothes almost as fashionable as Ash's. Sheba frowned. Why was Ash's cousin squeezing his shoulder?

And why were Ash's fingers gripping the frame of the door so tightly they were turning white with the strain?

"Now do you understand why I can't attend Yearly Meeting?" he bit out, his tone harsh and clipped. "I've inherited not only a title and estates here in England, but two sugar plantations on the island of Nevis. I'm a slaveowner, Sheba. And until I reach my majority, my trustees will not allow me to emancipate them, or sell them, or to do anything to the people they insist I *own*."

And with that ugly revelation, Ash turned and fled the room.

The expressions flashing across Bathsheba Honeychurch's face—shock, dismay, disbelief, anger—should have given him fair warning. Grandmother was certainly keeping her distance from the younger woman, as if well-aware of the shell on the verge of detonation they had in their midst. Yet Noel found himself stepping past Lady Silliman, further into the library, as if his mere presence beside Miss Honeychurch could somehow mitigate the calamity of his cousin's dreadful revelation.

But the self-righteous young woman needed no such comfort from anyone. Especially not from Noel.

"How long has he known? How long?" she demanded, her eyes afire with indignation.

"A fortnight."

"And he's kept it from me, all this time?"

"I fail to see what concern the Silliman estate's holdings should be to you," Frances Griffin said, her tone stiff with offense.

"Besides, there is nothing to be done about it," Noel said with a weary shake of his head.

Sheba Honeychurch's eyes narrowed. "You may think there is nothing to be done, but I'm certain Ash will find a way."

So certain, those words. But the crack in her voice—was she beginning to doubt his cousin?

"I assure you, there is nothing to be done. At least not until Ash—Silliman," he amended after his grandmother cleared her throat "—comes of age."

"Nothing to be done? The grand and mighty Lord Silliman, a peer of the realm, a belted earl, can do nothing? What use is such a title if he cannot even free the people your ancestors enslaved?"

"Miss Honeychurch." Grandmother took a cautious step towards the agitated young woman. "I hardly think such a topic of conversation appropriate—"

"No, you wouldn't, would you? Not when you can walk by this painting every day and not recognize the abomination it attempts to hide!"

"Abomination? My father-in-law, an abomination?" Grandmother's voice wavered between confusion and outrage. "You go too far, miss."

Miss Honeychurch shrugged. "I must speak as I find."

Family duty would have him side with his grandmother. But in his heart Noel could not help but take Miss Honeychurch's part. He hated catching sight of that picture every time he looked up from his estate work, an ugly reminder of the Silliman family's connection to the slave trade.

If Noel had been the new Lord Silliman, he'd have made the change, even at the cost of upsetting his grandmother.

But he wasn't Lord Silliman, was he? Nor ever likely to be.

He swallowed back his frustration. Whether he held the title or no, he had a responsibility to protect his family.

"Miss Honeychurch. Please have a care when speaking to my grandmother."

But his request only seemed to inflame the woman. "What, so you can both continue to ignore what is right in front of your eyes? Can you not see the grandiosity of the garments in which your ancestor was painted? So clearly meant to show the supposed superiority of the man who wears them! And the falsely fawning expression of the poor boy, as if he is so very happy to serve his white master? How can you look at this painting and forget the truth it tries so hard to hide?"

Foolish, to respond to such an excessive, immoderate diatribe. And yet the question still came tumbling from his mouth. "What truth?"

"The truth of the cruelty of slavery. That painting would have us believe it natural, inevitable, that purportedly superior Europeans should rule over Africans. And even worse, that Africans should be grateful for that mastery. But people like your great-grandfather enslaved Africans not out of benevolence, but for their own benefit, and through violence and rapine. This painting is a fraud, a vile falsehood, one that you perpetuate by giving it a place of honor in your home."

How she blazed, with the beauty of an avenging angel, all just and stern. Noel had to look away before her righteousness incinerated him.

Instead, he stared at the painting, disgusted anew at the obsequiousness of the boy's smile, the deference of his posture, his position at the very edge of the canvas, as if he barely deserved the small space the artist had granted him. Just as Sheba Honeychurch said, the entire design of the painting encouraged its viewers to forget to ask where the boy had come from, and why he was smiling so fawningly at his purportedly benevolent master.

Yet another lie his family conspired to persuade him to embrace…

"Miss Honeychurch, have a care. You would not wish those in the *ton* to label you a fanatic," his grandmother cautioned—or warned? Would Grandmother deliberately spread scandal about Ash's outspoken friend?

"I understand, now, why God chose Ash to inherit this title rather than you, Noel Griffin," she said, thrusting an accusing finger at Noel's chest. "You would have done nothing to mitigate the sufferings of the people you dare claim to own. But Ash will not long allow such an injustice to stand. He knows his duty."

How utterly galling, that even in the face of the utter unfairness of her accusation—hadn't he been working for months on plans to gradually emancipate the people on those damnable plantations?—he should still find himself so painfully attracted to her.

"Sheba—"

His grandmother's timely interruption saved him from betraying his ridiculous infatuation. "Duty? What do you know of duty, Miss Honeychurch?" she said, her voice ringing with unfamiliar heat. "An earl has a duty to his name, to his family and his dependents. Noel has been taught to understand this, and will teach Silliman in his turn."

"How can a man ever teach another about truth and duty when he has been brought up under false pretenses?" Bathsheba Honeychurch protested. "His own family lied to him. Lied to him for years, telling him he would inherit his grandfather's title. And now you expect him to pretend again, pretend that duty to family is the highest good, and teach that so-called truth to his cousin? How can he, when his own family was the one who betrayed him so?"

Noel's chest tightened. How could she have known? How could she see so clearly what he'd rarely even allowed himself to acknowledge?

And how dare she say out loud what he had been struggling so hard all these months to repress? He pressed his lips tight and clenched his hands, though whether to keep himself from shaking her until her teeth rattled, or jerking her against him and pressing his mouth to hers to stop the flow of those wrenchingly honest words, he could hardly tell.

"Enough!" Yes, far better to be angry than to reveal how deeply her words bit. "You know nothing of what I would have done or not done if I had been the one to inherit."

"Oh? You would have immediately freed the slaves your grandfather and great grandfather and who knows how many ancestors before you dared claim to own, would you?"

"Michael Pinney and I were exploring ways to begin to free the men and women forced to work those plantations, the moment the title was mine."

Behind him, he heard his grandmother gasp. But the time for keeping secrets from his family was over.

"But, as you so kindly point out, Miss Honeychurch, the title never belonged to me. Alas, the rightful Lord Silliman, unlike myself, is not yet of age." Noel's words hissed against his teeth. "You might be able to persuade him of the righteousness of your cause, but his trustees will never allow him to take any action they consider to be against the financial interests of the estate. They won't even consider selling the plantations, never mind incurring the loss of the thousands of pounds freeing those who work them would incur. No matter the shame such ownership brings to the Silliman name. No matter the insult to the memory of my father, who lost his life captaining a ship charged with interdicting illegal slavers off the African coast."

"Noel," his grandmother whispered. "Do not speak of it. You must not speak of it."

How odd to feel so lightheaded, so unmoored. As if finally giving vent to his resentment and anger had sent him dangerously adrift. If he no longer had family honor to cling to, who was he? Who could he ever hope to be?

He clutched at the back rail of a chair, trying, trying without success to keep the appalling giddy dizziness at bay…

Until he heard her simple declaration.

"I honor you, Noel, as would my mother. Honor you for speaking the truth. No matter how difficult, or how painful."

He stared, ensorcelled by the expression on Bathsheba Honeychurch's face. Oh, he'd seen its like before, directed at his cousin, all kindness and compassion and sympathy. But to be the object of it himself, why, that was an entirely different experience. She looked at him as if there were nothing the least disgraceful, only honor in revealing such family secrets. Nothing to be ashamed of in finally giving the bitterness of his loss free reign.

She looked as if for the first time she saw him as a person in his own right, rather than only as the villain who had foisted the unwanted burden of a title and estate upon Ash and herself.

That look filled a space inside him he'd never known had been empty. Empty for years…

He started as she laid a gentle hand on his sleeve. She stared up at him, making sure she had his full attention before she spoke. "And ye shall know the truth, and the truth shall set you free."

The softness of her tone, the admiration in those blue eyes, the warmth of the small hand—how he wanted it, wanted *her*, all for himself.

"Miss Honeychurch? Do you not have a meeting to attend this morning?"

The clipped tone of Lady Silliman's words only gradually broke through the haze of that surprising, shocking longing.

Sheba blinked, then shook her head, gathering her scattered faculties far more quickly than Noel did. "Indeed. I thank you for the reminder, Frances Griffin. Would you please tell Ash that

I think he would be welcome at Meeting, despite the evil this inheritance has forced upon him? I bid you good-day."

His eyes followed her as she left the room, his ears straining for the sound of the front door closing behind her.

Why did the tension in his shoulders, in his back, his fists not ease when the door's shush finally reached his ears?

"Well. A painful episode, that," Lady Silliman declared, her eyes carefully fixed on the family portrait above the mantel. "But at least now the girl must realize how impossible any match between herself and Silliman would be."

How neatly his grandmother closed the door on an action—a person—not to her liking. A person who did not fit comfortably into the conventional, rule-bound world of the *ton*.

A world he wasn't sure he wished to belong to any longer, either.

Noel swallowed. "Indeed, ma'am. Impossible."

No, he could never allow Bathsheba Honeychurch to marry his cousin. But not for the reason his grandmother assumed. Not because he cared a wit for the shame and scandal marrying a lowly Quaker would cast on the Silliman title.

But because the only man he could suddenly stand to imagine marrying her—horrible, tantalizing, tormenting realization!—was himself.

CHAPTER 10

"Meetings for Worship and Discipline are duly attended by most of our Members, and though deficiencies are still remarked in the attendance..."

A shaft of late afternoon sunlight glancing through the high window of the Women's Meeting House in Bishopsgate caught Sheba's wandering eye, a far-too-tempting distraction from the droning voice of the Clerk of the London Yearly Meeting of Women Friends. When the list of nearly one hundred female representatives from every Quarterly Meeting in Britain, and from the National Meeting in Ireland, too, had been read aloud and recorded at the start of the first Sitting earlier in the day, Sheba had thrilled with pride to be gathering with so many fellow female Friends, all gathered to manage, order, and regulate the public affairs of their Society. Even sitting at the very back of the room—because she'd been late, having to walk rather than drive, with no Ash accompanying her—had not dampened her enthusiasm.

Paying attention this afternoon, though, as the Clerk read aloud from yet another Quarterly Meeting's responses to the nine Queries each was annually asked to answer, recounting whether members of their communities were acting in a manner consistent with the Society's religious professions, was proving more of a struggle.

The sun, hidden behind black clouds of rain for most of the day, almost seemed to halo the heads of all the women beside her. If only it had broken through earlier, rather than hiding behind the mizzling rain during her three miles walk from Mayfair to Bishopsgate this morning, perhaps she might not be so distracted by it now.

"An appearance of drowsiness in some Friends prevents a clear answer being given respecting becoming behavior during Meeting for Worship," the Clerk continued. "The remiss are reported to be under care…"

Under her breath, Sheba gave a wry huff. Drowsiness had never been her besetting sin. No, Leicester's elders were far more likely to chastise her for not sitting still than for nodding off during Meeting for Worship.

"Nothing appears but that Friends are preserved in love towards each other, and many are careful to avoid and discourage talebearing and detraction…"

Sheba stared at her lap, folding and unfolding her gloves between restless fingers. She could have made more of an effort to be preserved in love towards Ash's grandmother this morning. The grief carving such deep lines about Frances Griffin's mouth when she had stared up at the portrait of her family, so many of its members dead and gone, had moved Sheba, moved her deeply. Yet the woman's bewilderment at Sheba's dismay over that dreadful painting had infuriated her even more. Such self-willed ignorance was unconscionable, was it not? And most deserving of the admonishment Sheba had felt called to give?

And all such as behold their brother or sister in a transgression, go not in rough, light, or upbraiding spirit to reprove or admonish him or her, but in the power of the Lord, and the spirit of the Lamb, and in the wisdom and love of the Truth, which suffers thereby, to admonish such an offender.

The memory of her mother's words made Sheba hang her

head. Her words to Frances Griffin this morning had been driven far more by anger, and by shame, than by love. As if by berating the older woman for her prejudice, Sheba could paper over her own unfairly biased response to her first sight of Michael Pinney. She'd apologized to him, but truly, she owed the older woman an apology as well. Not for the words themselves, but for the rough, upbraiding spirit in which she'd uttered them.

And an apology to both of her grandsons. How often had frustration, rather than a true spirit of tenderness, led her to admonish Ash? And why had she allowed such partiality and false judgment to keep her from seeing the truth depths of his cousin's spirit?

"When any case of that nature comes to the knowledge of Friends, early care is taken to admonish such as appear inclinable to marry in a manner contrary to the rules of our Society..."

Ash would hate being admonished by the Elders. She could not forget his poor face, so tight with disgust and dismay as he told her of that wicked, wicked inheritance. Nor the indignant cast of Noel's, when she'd accused him—oh, how unfairly!—of not caring about the injustice of enslaving other human beings.

She would have reassured Ash that she'd not break off their agreement to marry if he'd not rushed off so. But would the Meeting refuse to allow them to wed? No, the elders could never be so cruel, not if Ash explained it was none of his doing, and that he'd emancipate every man, woman, and child so falsely claimed as property by his trustees as soon as he gained full control over his estate.

The Meeting might counsel them to wait to marry until he came of age and could do so, though.

Two more years was not such a very long time...

Why had Noel Griffin never married?

Sheba shifted carefully from side to side. There was no reason, none at all, to wonder about a matter that should be of no concern to her.

And yet his hazel eyes, so like, and yet so different from, Ash's—somehow, her mind kept flitting back to them, so pained, so very, very weary. How fixedly they'd stared at her after she'd upbraided his grandmother for lying to him all those years! As if he'd never expected anyone to consider how hurtful it would be, having been taught to expect one life, then to have that life pulled so unceremoniously from beneath him, as if he were no better than outdated carpet, set aside after the purchase of a more fashionable replacement.

As if no one had ever seen beyond the dutiful front he presented to the world, seen beyond to the lonely, grieving man behind it.

Before he'd donned that familiar cloak of protective anger and flung out his own stinging admonishments, she'd almost thought—what a ridiculous notion—he might embrace her.

Oh, why was this bench so hard? And the room so stuffy? She shifted yet again, trying without much success to avoid jostling the women packed in tight beside her.

Her impatient wiggle earned her not a rebuke, but a glance of sympathy from the woman on her left. "I think this is a young Friend at her first Yearly Meeting," the older woman said after the Clerk called for a brief pause.

Sheba gave a rueful nod. "My apologies for distracting you with my restlessness, Friend. I sometimes struggle to endure with composure what is necessary to bear. Sometimes, I fear, I feel so extremely impatient I cannot sit still, even if you were to promise me the world."

The older woman patted Sheba's hand. "Difficult for a young person to sit quietly and attentively for the whole of such a long day, is it not? Yet if thou takest care to prepare thy heart before attending tomorrow, and allow all immoderate passions to subside, patience will follow, and truth will be revealed."

"Thank you, Friend," Sheba said. "None of the elders from my own Meeting are here today, so your advice is very welcome. I am Bathsheba Honeychurch, from Leicester."

"Thou art very welcome, my dear." The older woman took both of Sheba's hands in hers. "And I am Mary Harlow, come to London from the city of Sheffield."

"Do you know, Friend Harlow, if any booksellers are in attendance today?" Sheba asked, forcing thoughts of the Griffin cousins from her mind. London Yearly Meeting was the perfect opportunity to make inquiries on behalf of Elizabeth Heyrick and her anti-slavery pamphlet.

"Ah, art thou in search of instructive reading?" Friend Harlow asked. "Hast thou met Friend Harriet Fry? She and several other Friends think to form a library association, to collect and lend instructive and improving tracts."

"I don't wish to purchase books, but to find a bookseller who also prints them."

The older women blinked, her brows drawing closer. In confusion? Or doubt?

"On behalf of a Friend in Leicester," Sheba hurriedly reassured.

"Oh. To be sure. Harriet Fry's husband, Edmund, perhaps?" Friend Harlow mused. "Or Friend Darton or his son? Though thou wilt find none of them here today, I fear. Far too engaged in the pursuits of business to attend Yearly Meeting, alas."

Sheba had already met with a William Darton, who had published several of her teacher's earlier works. He'd expressed interest, but had told her he must consult with his partner before making a decision. Nearly a week had already passed, though, without any word. Surely it would do no harm to talk with other London printers…

"Is thy Friend in Leicester a teacher?" Friend Harlow asked.

"Mine, yes, at one time." Sheba gave a wry smile. "I hope I am able to exercise the duties of my calling as well as she."

"Ah, if thou hast a concern regarding education, thou must

speak with William Allen, who plans to open a school for girls of the Society in Stoke Newington later this year."

"What of teaching beyond our borders?" Sheba asked, shifting from Elizabeth Heyrick's interests to her own. "In America, or the Canadian colonies? Or in the Indies?"

Friend Harlow's head tipped. "Hast thou read the report of the committee on promoting African instruction?"

"African instruction?" Sheba grasped Friend Harlow's arm. "In the colony of Sierra Leone?"

"Yes, my dear." Friend Harlow patted her hand. "Friend Hannah Kilham is there as we speak, teaching the children liberated from slave ships, and cultivating a grammar of some of the unwritten languages of Africa."

"Did Friend Kilham travel with her husband?"

"No, my dear. With the Thompson siblings, and Friend Richard Smith. Oh, they are beginning again—"

With a friendly smile, Friend Harlow turned her attention once again to the front benches.

Sheba sat down, clutching the seat of the bench to force herself still. An *unwed* female Friend was even now teaching in Africa? Did that mean *Sheba* need not marry if she wished to take on such work?

Sheba blinked when the Clerk finally finished reading the Lincolnshire Quarterly Meeting's responses to the Queries and adjourned the Meeting until tomorrow morning. Her mind had been racing so, considering an option she'd never thought possible, she'd not been paying the least attention to the concerns of the Meeting.

The silence of the assembled crowd broke, friend greeting friend amidst a veritable confusion of furled umbrellas and wet cloaks, damp clogs and soggy bonnets. Now that the business of the day had concluded, the social whirl could begin. For representatives came to London each May, not only to conduct business, but to meet and mix with Friends they only saw once a year. A continuous round of tea and dinner parties and after-dinner sermons from the most respected ministers in the Society—and a rare opportunity for the younger attendees to meet potential marriage partners—or so others from Leicester who had attended in the past had described it.

No one from Leicester had been selected as representative this year, though. And Sheba was the only one who had come from Leicester Meeting on her own behalf.

She followed Friend Harlow into the flow of the crowd out into the courtyard. The men, who had spent the day in their own Meeting House just across the yard, searched out for the girls and women to whom they belonged—or whom they hoped one day to belong.

Friends collected in twos and threes and groups even larger, preparing to make their way to their various lodgings and ready themselves for the evening's gatherings. Sheba spied more than one courting couple among the throng.

Why should she be noticing such a thing now? At the very moment when teaching abroad without marrying shifted from obvious cannot to tantalizing possibility...

Oh, why had Ash refused to come?

As they reached the front of the Old Meeting House, a bustling group of young people who shared Mary Harlow's apple cheeks and air of sensible good humor gathered about the older woman, all jostling for her attention.

"Didst thou meet Elizabeth Walker, Grandmother, who hast come all the way from New York? They say she will speak with all the younger members of the Society tonight after we dine."

"How very many certificates were granted for religious service abroad this year! Dost thou think the Divine Master will ever direct *thy* feet beyond the borders of our isle, grandmama?"

Friend Harlow laughed. "And who would train thee up in simplicity, and in plainness of speech, habit, and manners, should I receive just a leading and go traipsing about in foreign lands?"

"But thou would come back, Grandmama, just like Susannah's mother after she was called to the ministry," one of the younger boys asserted.

"Perhaps. But I would be gone for many, many years were I called to minister in other countries. Why, thou wouldst be grown and wed with babes of thy own by then!"

The children all clamored in protest at such an obviously distressing thought.

And it was distressing, was it not? Not just for the ones left behind, but for the one called to leave, too. To be parted for years from Elizabeth Heyrick and Friend Farrand, and Hannah Darby, and all the other Friends at Leicester Meeting. From Aunt Abiah and the girls. Even from her father, no matter how little a role he played in her daily life since her mother's passing.

Why had the pain of such partings never occurred to her? And not just partings from those in Leicester, but from her other relations, too. From Spencer, and Delphie, and Connie and all her other Audley cousins.

From Ash, if they were not to be married.

From Noel...

Do not give way to apprehension of your own creating, Bathsheba. Try to be still, and hope clearly to know what is best.

Sheba's jaw set. If her duty appeared plain, why should she draw back?

"Enough, children, enough! You will frighten away my new acquaintance with all thy bustling."

It felt wrong, to find the sound of Friend Harlow's voice so much warmer, so much more inviting, than the memory of her own mother's.

"Didst thou come today by thyself, Bathsheba Honeychurch?" the older woman asked as she placed an arm about the youngest child of the group.

"Manasseh Griffin, a fellow member of the Leicester Meeting, was to have accompanied me, but was unexpectedly detained." She raised her chin, which had unaccountably dipped. "I hope to see him here tomorrow."

"Well, thou art most welcome to come and dine with us at the Coventry's this evening. I dare say dinner will be served in relays, so great will be our numbers. One addition to the party will be of little concern."

"You are very kind, ma'am. But Miss Honeychurch's cousin, with whom she is staying while in London, will worry if she does not return."

Every nerve in Sheba's body pricked at the sound of that deep voice, the touch of the gloved hand confidently tucking her own into the crook of his elbow.

Even though neither hand nor voice belonged to Ash.

She met Noel Griffin's eyes, confused by the strange, disconcerting ache flooding her chest. A wistful lonely longing for something, something to which she could not even put a name.

"Ah, thy friend has come to collect thee," Mary Harlow said with a slightly puzzled smile. The fashionably dressed man beside her was obviously no member of the Society. "Well, we will see thee tomorrow, then, my dear. Remind me to introduce thee to Samuel Darton on Sixth-day, when we will all gather for Meeting for Business. Thee might procure a copy of the report I mentioned from him. And remember to prepare thy heart before thou comest! The benches will not seem so hard if thou but take thy seat with a willing spirit."

Sheba watched in silence as Friend Harlow and her party bustle from the Meeting House yard to Bishopsgate Street, their chatter and laughter echoing down the narrow passageway. They watched a final few stragglers collect their belongings and their friends, their steps echoing against the paving stones. Beside her, Noel stood silent, too, making no effort to hurry her along.

The sky darkened as they waited—for what, Sheba was not

quite sure—drizzle shifting once again into a light rain. Noel released her arm to shake open an umbrella she had not realized he'd been carrying, then lifted it high above her head. Raindrops pattered against the oilskin, and, more softly, against the back of his coat.

"Michael Pinney told me of your meeting," Noel said, tipping the umbrella so that it better shielded her from the increasingly heavy showers. "And that you had expected to take our carriage to this one. I did not wish to leave you without conveyance a second time."

When had Noel Griffin become kind?

She grimaced. Perhaps he had always been so. Which she might have seen if she'd only looked beyond her immediate, biased, dislike…

She shook herself. Time, then, for her to be kind in turn.

She moved closer, until the umbrella covered them both. "I'm so very sorry—"

"Please, accept my apology—"

Sheba grasped the hand holding the umbrella, a silent request that he allow her to speak first.

He nodded.

"What have you to be sorry for, Noel? I am the one whose good manners were so wanting this morning. Who am I to admonish your grandmother? It was badly done of me, badly done."

Noel's jaw clenched. "Perhaps. But your outrage was warranted. I should have insisted that the portrait be removed long before now. I rarely allow a bit of unpleasantness to interfere with doing what I know is right."

"Hurting someone you love is more than a bit of unpleasantness."

"Perhaps. But adhering to one's values and morals should be more important than the feelings of others."

"Your grandmother certainly thinks so."

He frowned. "My grandmother? But she is the kindest, most feeling lady I know."

"Kind?" Sheba fisted the silk of her damp skirts. "Was it kind of her to allow you to believe yourself the rightful heir to your grandfather's title? Kind to never tell you of the existence of Ash and his sisters? Kind to send you off to find him, the man who displaced you as heir, when the pain of discovering your family's deception must have still been as raw as a fresh wound? Did she think you had no feelings, just because you do not share them as easily with others as she does?"

Noel stilled, his eyes wide and unblinking. As if having another person recognize and acknowledge his emotions, his loss, brought relief, yes, but also a defenselessness he both welcomed and feared.

A defenselessness she recognized, because she felt it, too, staring up at him so.

Sheba shrugged free of his hand. "But there I go again, berating the poor woman when she is not even here to defend herself."

As she began walking towards Bishopsgate Street, she called over her shoulder, "If I promise to send her a written apology, do you think she will ever forgive me?"

"I believe so," he said, catching her up and tucking her under the cover of the umbrella again. Happy, it appeared, to follow her lead in lightening the mood. "Grandmother is not one to hold a grudge. Although you may wish to wait a day or so, to give her time for her feelings to settle. Especially now that my great grandfather's painting has been removed from the library."

Sheba came to a sudden halt. "At your direction?"

"No." He grimaced. "At my cousin's. Ash asked that it be hung in his bedchamber. How pleased Grandmother was, assuming the new earl's request stemmed from eagerness to pay homage to his Griffin heritage. Ash never denied it, though I suspect he had other reasons for making the change."

"Ash has a particular gift for smoothing everyone's ruffled feathers, even while doing what he knows is right."

"A happy gift. I envy him for it."

"It does win him many friends. But then, when I see how often such peacemaking comes at his own expense, I'm glad not to care what other people think of me as much as he does."

"His own expense?"

"Surely you must know how it will pain him, a daily reminder that his own forebears engaged in a trade that is anathema to him."

Yes. Ash would want it there, in his own chamber, a daily reminder of the hard choices he must make between duty to family and duty to what was right. A reminder that he could never erase the stain of enslaving others from his family's history. A reminder that he must, the moment he came of age, act to disabuse everyone in this creaturely world, a world into which he'd been thrust without asking, of the false notion that the people on those plantations were nothing but chattel.

The weight of his responsibilities—why had she not recognized them, appreciated them, before? Or given him the least credit for understanding the difficult path the Holy Spirit had called him to walk?

"He'll think it worth the while, though," she said. "Not just because he's pleased your grandmother, but because he's saved Michael Pinney from having to look at it as well."

The umbrella jerked in Noel's hand, sending a shower of raindrops coursing down to the pavement. Even in the dim evening light, she could see the color rising in his cheeks.

Sheba pressed her lips tight. She'd not intended to admonish him yet again. Why did she never consider her words before she spoke?

"Michael never took issue with the painting as you did," he finally said. "Never even mentioned it, not once in all the months we worked together in that library."

Noel kicked at a puddle, sending a spray of water flying into the street. "Stupid of me to think that placing his chair where he wouldn't have to look at it would somehow make it not matter."

Traffic on the main thoroughfare of Bishopsgate Street was still brisk, even in the early evening rain. He pulled her to his side as a crowd of boisterous young men—on their way to the theatre, or a music hall?—bustled by them towards Shoreditch.

The self-reproach drawing his lips so tight made something strange, unfamiliar, twist tight in her own chest.

"It is difficult, is it not, to enter into another person's concerns?" she finally offered.

He frowned. "Enter into another person's concerns?"

"Yes. To truly understand another person, his feelings and experiences, rather than looking half-blind through the scrim of one's own concerns. I've not been very good at considering our situation from Ash's point of view since you arrived in Leicester, Noel Griffin." She offered him a wry grimace. "I chafe at the way Connie always feels called to scold me and all our other Audley cousins, but I fear I've behaved much the same towards Ash. As his friend, I should try to understand his problems, rather than chafe at the restrictions they place on me."

"As his friend? Is that all you are to my cousin? His friend?"

She shivered at the sudden flare of heat in his eyes, even as she felt the blood warming her cheeks.

She pulled the umbrella away and dashed towards the shops below the Devonshire House Hotel. Surely that was the Silliman carriage waiting by the curb?

"A far more considerate man than I, my young cousin," Noel huffed—in apology?—as he caught up to her and opened the carriage door. "He'll make a better earl than I ever would."

By all rights, it should be Ash, that far more considerate man, here holding the umbrella above their heads, offering up his pains and fears for her safekeeping. Not his confident, argumentative, infuriating—vulnerable?—cousin.

How could Noel Griffin keep surprising her so?

"The meeting of your Society—it continues for a week entire, I understand?" Noel lowered the umbrella and gave it to a waiting footman, then held out a hand to help her into the carriage.

"A week and two days. The Meetings will conclude next Thursday."

"And has Spencer made a carriage available for your use for the duration?"

"I didn't think to ask. I can walk—"

Noel gave her a long look. "Four miles each way, every day for more than a week? A Silliman carriage will be at your disposal until then." He followed her into the vehicle and took the seat opposite. "As will I, on days when neither your cousin nor mine is available to accompany you from Mayfair to Bishopsgate and back again. What time tomorrow does the meeting begin?"

"At ten o'clock."

"Then I will call for you shortly after nine, unless you send word that you've made other arrangements. Perhaps I may even stay to observe for a while, if people who do not share your religion are allowed to attend."

"Yes, I believe they are. But why would you wish to?"

The corners of his lips tilted upward, slowly, so very slowly, until at last they revealed a broad, curiously inviting smile. A smile that made his typically stern countenance spark with life.

A smile directed solely at her.

"Because I can't help but wish to know what it is about the Society of Friends that could produce a woman as honest and outspoken as you, Bathsheba Honeychurch."

From the balcony in the Men's Meeting House, Noel could almost imagine he heard a collective sigh from the other attendees of this fourth sitting of the Friends London Yearly Meeting. A middle-aged Quaker—one Isaac Crewdson, as Sheba had whispered to him—had risen yet again from the row of elders facing the group to address the room. The fellow had already spoken several times during the afternoon, something Noel had not seen any other of the Quakers—neither the men nor the women, who had been invited into the Men's Meeting House for the Business Meeting—do. Still, none among the hundreds of Friends gathered below berated the man, or told him to stop opining.

If Grandfather had been in charge, he'd have shut the man down immediately. But these Quakers seemed to believe that decisions were best made when everyone shared their experiences and knowledge, and listened with respect to the experiences and knowledge of each, rather than just deferred to the highest authority in the room.

How much patience such a practice demanded!

Beside him, Sheba sighed, her hands playing restlessly over the balcony rail. No, patience was not one of Bathsheba Honeychurch's leading virtues.

"Would Friends again consider the subject of giving Friends with whom we had not had much opportunity of being acquainted certificates to travel upon the continent?" Crewdson said, in the nasal tones and over-enunciated vowels of a Mancunian. "The subject presses very closely upon my mind."

"Thank you, Friend, for sharing your concern," another man, acting in the position of Clerk, answered. "But we appear to have reached a sense of the Meeting on this matter. Would thou be willing to stand aside, Isaac Crewdson?"

Crewdson considered for a long moment, then shook his head. "I am led to stand in the way."

"May I visit with thee, Friend Crewdson, outside of the Meeting, and sit with thy concern?" a woman sitting amongst the other elders asked. "Another way might open to us if we pray and consider the matter further."

Noel quirked an eyebrow. Before offering to accompany Sheba to London Yearly Meeting, he'd pictured her hat-wearing brethren lined up in their pews—no, benches—much like the weightiest tomes on a shelf, all bent heads and solemn contemplation, moral pronouncements made manifest without a word uttered aloud. But each of the Meetings he'd attended had been filled with discussion and debate—lively, occasionally even heated, debate, challenging each listener to engage with ideas he may have never before even contemplated. Oh, there had been one or two occasions in which so many different views were expressed that no agreement could be reached, and the issue at hand had to be put by until a later Meeting. Or, like now, moments when one contrarian would not stop contesting an issue that the rest of the group considered decided. But far more often than he'd expected, the assembled Friends came to consensus on what action, if any, should be taken by the group.

It certainly took a lot of time to achieve that "sense of the Meeting," as Sheba called it, a decision about whether, and how, to act. Far longer than any nobleman who could just command his dependents, or a rector or curate to direct his flock. Yet Noel could only admire the respect these Friends showed one another, the care they took to consider opinions and ideas not their own, how ready they were to question their own assumptions rather than stand stubborn in the face of a rational challenge to a commonly accepted idea. And the honesty with which they spoke, an honesty and openness so different from what he was accustomed to finding among the society of the *ton*.

What might it have been like, to be raised among such people? If he'd not had it drilled into him to defer without question to the head of his family? If he'd not had to keep his ideas and beliefs to himself, but had been listened to with patience and respect? No, with a willingness to consider his ideas, even when they conflicted with those of his grandfather?

He glanced at Sheba from the corner of his eye. No wonder she expected—nay, demanded—her words be treated with deference. No, not deference, not like a nobleman would. But surely with a consideration few gentlemen of his acquaintance believed the opinions of a mere female deserved.

"We shall lay the matter over for now, Friend Crewdson," the Clerk said after consulting with his two advisors.

Isaac Crewdson nodded, then took his seat.

"Are there other Friends who wish to speak on the state of our Society?" the Clerk asked.

A man sitting in the center of the congregation rose. "I wish to call the Meeting's attention to the continuing evil of the Slave-trade. Friends have individually affirmed their abhorrence of the institution by the signing of myriad petitions. But I am moved to ask whether it is not our duty as a religious body, as advocates of humanity and justice, to make some public pronouncement against the continuance of so vile a practice."

Beside him, Sheba stilled. And remained still for the hour that followed, as various members of the Meeting rose to offer their thoughts on the issue. Some agreed with the first speaker; others counseling against breaking from Friends' traditional Quietist habits of disengagement from earthly affairs. Even those in favor of the Society taking a more public stance, though, did not all agree on what, precisely, that stance should be. A handful urged advocating an immediate end to the practice; more shared the gradualist approach favored by Mr. Wilberforce and his allies; still others counseled urging better treatment of the enslaved, rather than calling for their emancipation altogether, as a better first step into the public political debate.

"Friend Phillips publishes the Society's Epistles and tracts," an elderly woman said. "If we are to make a public statement on this matter, it should be through his press."

"But what of the Dartons? Or the Arch brothers?"

"Oh! Friend Harlow told me they rarely attend Yearly

Meeting," Sheba whispered, leaning forward to scan the crowed below. "But might they be here today?"

Noel frowned. Why should Sheba care about a pack of printers?

The sun on her hair, pamphlets raining about their feet...

Sheba's voice, confident, eager—My friend Elizabeth Heyrick has written all about it in her latest pamphlet. I've been to call on her London publisher, to gauge their interest in publishing a new edition...

She'd not yet found a willing printer, then. Not surprising, perhaps, given the radical nature of its argument. And her eager, yet distractible nature.

Might he earn her gratitude by offering to help?

"As the discussion today demonstrates, the Slave-trade, with its inseparable horrors, and the gradual but total abolition of Slavery, continue to be an object of deep interest to our Society," the clerk below declared. "But as there is no sense of the Meeting that the Divine Spirit is guiding us to make a public declaration, we will content ourselves with again commending in our Epistle the injuries of Africa and her offspring to the commiseration of every one amongst us. This Meeting adjoins to eleven o'clock tomorrow morning."

Before he could take up his hat and cane, Sheba had jumped up and raced for the stairs. He chuckled, then retrieved the reticule she had left behind in her hurry. By the time he'd caught up with her, she'd already reached the Meeting house door. So engaged was she in eager conversation with a thin man of a sober but kindly mien there, she seemed entirely unaware of how she was blocking the flow of her fellow Meeting members, eager to make their way to their evening engagements.

"But your firm has published essays on the evils of the slave trade in the past," she said to the man, hardly noticing as Noel took her arm and guided her out of the way of the throng. Her interlocutor, clearly more aware of the inconvenience they had been causing than Sheba, followed them through the door and out into the cobbled courtyard.

"My father did, Friend Honeychurch," the man said as he followed them into the paved courtyard. "But our firm has just agreed to distribute a pamphlet by a West India planter who argues for a gradualist approach to emancipation. From what you say about your friend's work, her argument is of a far more radical nature. I fear that it would not be profitable to commit our firm to such a risky venture."

"But did not we just hear Friend Allen warn against allowing efforts to gain a livelihood to endanger our own peace of mind, and what we know is right?" Sheba urged.

A troubled frown crossed Phillips' face. "Yes, indeed, Friend Honeychurch. And yet business failures reflect poorly on other Friends, and on the Society as a whole."

"But why should such a pamphlet endanger your firm's financial standing? Many Friends must share Friend Heyrick's conviction that immediate, rather than gradual, emancipation, is a just cause. Surely you have not been imposed upon by the wily artifice of the slaveholders to believe otherwise?"

"Sheba," Noel cautioned, his hand tightening about her elbow. Insulting a man whose mind you were trying to change would only make him cling all the more tightly to his own view.

"Gradual emancipation will only beget gradual indifference to emancipation altogether," she declared, proving that none of her elders had ever taught her the finer points of rhetoric.

He'd not thought he could feel anything but bitterness towards his grandfather, not after all the lies he'd told. How surprising, to discover a tiny tender shoot of gratitude poking its head through the acrid earth of grievance...

"I wonder if it might be possible to mitigate the risk?" Noel ventured. "Perhaps by sharing the cost of production with other printers and booksellers?"

Would she take exception to his interference?

"Oh, what a marvelous thought!" she exclaimed, surprising

him yet again. "I've already spoken to the younger William Darton about the project, although not yet to his father. And I've not met either of the Arch brothers, either. Are they here today? If not, could you tell me where I might find them? And share with me the names of any other friends involved in the printing trades?"

"Might some of the Evangelical publishers take an interest, too," Noel wondered. "Mr. Hatchard? Or Mr. Seeley?"

"Oh! Seeley and Son publishes tracts for the Church Missionary Society," Sheba exclaimed. "Surely they would find such a work worth publishing."

"And what of the Unitarians?"

"Are there any Unitarian presses in London?"

"I don't know, but I'm certain we can find out."

"If dissenting printers as well as Evangelical ones all joined together in such a project—why, Elizabeth's ideas would reach a far larger audience, then, would they not?"

The flush of pleasure on those high cheekbones, the spark of gratitude, even admiration, in those flashing blue eyes—Noel had to fight, hard, to free the breath caught tight in his chest.

"A conger, is it?" Mr. Phillips asked. "We all buy shares in the pamphlet, and share the risk of publishing it equally?"

Phillips' words sent Noel's eyes jerking free of Sheba's. How long had he—had they—been lost in each other's regard?

Sheba blinked, then took a reluctant step away from Noel.

Or was that reluctance only a figment of his ill-advised longing?

"Would you be more likely to join, Friend Phillips, if we were to make such an arrangement?" Sheba asked, turning her back on Noel to speak once again to the printer.

A hint of amusement played about the solemn Quaker's mouth as his eyes moved from Sheba to Noel and back again. "Aye, Friend Honeychurch. That I would."

CHAPTER 11

"No, no, my lord, not a hop, a *jeté*. We do not use only the one foot, like a child playing *marelle ronde*—or, as you English call it, the hopscotch. No, we leap from one foot to the other, like so. You see how it is done?"

Noel's lips quirked. Not at M. de Brunhoff, the amusingly exacting dancing master his grandmother had hired to teach Ash how to comport himself creditably in a ballroom. Nor at Delphie Burnett, with whom he had been partnered to provide an example of an accomplished couple to his inexperienced young cousin. But at Sheba, who was grimacing and pulling her hands away from Silliman's, her slipper safely back underneath her skirts. Ash, the clumsy oaf, had stepped on her yet *again*.

The plain brown silk of her dress rustled and shivered about her ankles. Was she rubbing her poor injured toes against the back of her calf?

The image of his own hand doing the same sent the incipient smile fleeing from his lips. He jerked his eyes away from her skirts and toyed with his sleeve-buttons, trying to keep the strength of his longing for Bathsheba Honeychurch safely hidden. Because despite spending the greater part of the last three weeks largely in her company, he seemed no closer to detaching her affections from his cousin and directing them to himself than he had been when she'd first come to town.

He'd thought—hoped? feared?—she'd return to Leicester once the Yearly gathering of Quakers in London concluded. But she'd been determined to attend the first public meeting of the Anti-Slavery Society, too, even after it was put off from May until June. He wondered at her father, granting his permission for her to remain in town for another month entire. Did not the man miss his only child?

Noel was grateful for Mr. Honeychurch's inattentive parenting, though, truth be told. For it had given him the chance to forge a truce of sorts with the man's daughter. If he'd asked Sheba, she'd likely even say they were friends, now, brought together not only by their efforts to find potential printers for her teacher Mrs. Heyrick's anti-slavery essay, but also by their redoubled efforts to reunite Spencer and Delphie. The four of them, accompanied occasionally by Ash, had spent hours and hours together exploring London these past three weeks. And on the handful of occasions they managed to entrap Delphie into spending time alone with Spencer, he and Sheba had visited London printers and booksellers, attempting to persuade them to join the publishing conger for Mrs. Heyrick's pamphlet.

Not the familiar London of the *ton*, perhaps, but the London that would most fascinate a Quaker: its philanthropic institutions, its scholarly lectures, and its dizzying array of prison houses, mental asylums, and convict ships. Once, Sheba had even dragged them to Smithfield Market, to witness for herself whether the animals there were treated with cruelty or no. After each outing, she'd scribble down a plethora of notes about what she'd learned, the outrages she'd witnessed, and how she thought each situation might be improved, notes she intended to share with her confidante and teacher back in Leicester.

Noel had argued in vain that such venues would not conduce

to romantic feelings. But Sheba refused to compromise her religious principles by attending what she deemed unduly trifling events. If she had been anyone else, he would have deemed such scruples punctilious, even ridiculous. Yet in her, the passion for philanthropy inspired a heady admiration he could hardly contain.

Nor could he help dreaming each night of what it would be like if even a sliver of that passion were ever directed toward him.

The few times he'd inadvertently revealed even a hint of his own longing, though, Sheba had shied away, skittish as a newborn colt. Had his slowtop of a cousin never even kissed her?

Each time, he'd hid his own feelings and retreated, too. Far better to continue to allow her to regard him as a friend than to send her fleeing his company altogether.

He caught her eye and raised an ironic brow, a silent reminder that she'd not have had to protect her toes if she'd only agreed to partner with *him* rather than Ash.

Her eyes narrowed, yet her cheeks bloomed with color.

He fought back a satisfied smile. Not entirely unaware of him as a man, that tantalizing blush hinted...

"Now, *mesdames et messieurs*, shall we try again? The *chasse* and *pas jeté assemblé*, *s'ils vous plaît*." The elegant Frenchman pulled his *pochette* from a long pocket in his coat then stroked his bow against its tiny strings.

Noel's fingers twitched as Sheba reached for Ash's gloved hand and gave it a squeeze. But she quickly released it and placed her fingers in Ash's palm at the level of their waists, as M. de Brunhoff had instructed. Unlike his cousin, Sheba seemed to have little trouble following the basic steps the dancing master modeled.

Noel took Delphie's hand, moving with her to model the correct steps for Ash and Sheba.

"Right-close-right, right-close-right, left-close-left, left-close-left, and again, right-close-right, right-close-right, and leap close —" Sheba skipped away with a squeak, just managing to avoid Ash's errant kick.

"Oh, my lord, no, no, no, we *jeté* to the *side*, not *towards* our partner…"

Noel aimed an amused glance at Delphie, but Spencer's wife seemed decidedly out of spirits today. Might she be missing her husband? She'd made a rather vague excuse for his absence this afternoon.

"Ash, do try a bit harder," Sheba scolded. "If you would only just *listen* to M. de Brunhoff—"

"I am listening." Ash groaned and tugged at his waistcoat. "But all I can seem to hear is Friends Farrand and Howgill warning us all against dancing's tendency to give birth to vanity and pride, and a thoughtless disregard for the important duties of life. And then I cannot seem to make my feet go where they should."

"You needn't make them go at all if you would just tell Frances Griffin you don't care to dance," Sheba said. "That your religion does not allow it."

Ash threw up his hands. "But how am I to gain anyone's respect if I can't do what they all do with such ease? If I refuse to partake of their pleasures, refuse to enjoy what others enjoy, I'll never gain a footing in this new society into which I've been thrust."

Sheba set a palm against his cousin's cheek. "Oh, Ash."

Noel had often wondered at everyone's claiming Ash and Sheba were the best of friends. From all he'd seen, she seemed to treat him more like a child than a mate of the soul. But those two short syllables, suffused with such affection, such tenderness, such sympathy for his pain and guilt and frustration —

If only she'd speak to Noel with such feeling in her voice…

"Besides, I can't disappoint my grandmother," Ash added. "She's taken such pains to make the ball a memorable one."

Sheba's face softened. "Then we must simply try again. Here, give me your hand."

She tried to pull him back into position, but his cousin stumbled, tripping over his own feet. Ash had never comported himself with the grace of a gentleman born and bred, but Noel had never seen him move with such awkwardness. All of the poor boy's usual ease seemed to have abandoned him in the face of participating in an amusement which he'd been brought up to believe excited only the most malevolent of passions.

Ash gave a plaintive sigh. "How is it that you are so much better at this than I am, Sheba?"

"Because I at least have seen ladies and gentlemen dancing before."

Noel blinked. "You have? Where?"

"At Audley Priory. My mother's family gathers there every summer, and my grandmother holds a grand ball to celebrate."

"The Countess of Audley is your grandmother?" Noel asked. How had no one ever thought to mention such a thing?

Sheba shrugged, as if being related to an aristocrat was of little moment. "One need only master a small number of basic steps to make a presentable showing at any dance, is that not right, *monsieur*?"

"Indeed, *mademoiselle*." M. de Brunhoff offered a tight smile. "Shall we try again?"

"Must we?" Ash nearly moaned.

Sheba's slipper tapped against the ballroom floor. "I'm more than ready to give this over whenever you are."

"But my grandmother—"

"Then stop dithering and give me your hand," Sheba said with a growl of frustration, a growl Noel found unexpectedly enticing.

But Ash certainly didn't. He jerked away before she could

catch him up again. "It is the gentleman who takes the lady's hand, not the lady who paws at the gentleman. How will I ever learn if you keep trying to lead?"

Noel felt the muscles in his jaw clench. Enough of this petty squabbling. One could never learn to dance with a partner no better than a misbehaving schoolboy.

Placing a hand on the small of Delphie's back, Noel steered her to stand opposite Ash. "I believe it would be easier, cousin, if you practiced with a more experienced partner."

Before Sheba could offer an objection, Noel set himself in front of her. "And if we tried a simpler dance. A waltz, perhaps, M. de Brunhoff?"

A look of relief passed over the poor dancing master's face. "As you wish, *monsieur*."

The restlessness Noel had felt all afternoon, being in Sheba's company but not the focus of her attention, settled as soon as he guided her hands up to rest against his shoulders. Unlike the more demure society misses with whom he typically danced, she kept her head held high, eyes not shying away from his. But the pink tint of her cheeks blazed nearly scarlet when he set his hands not on her elbows, as she was obviously expecting, but more daringly against her waist. That elusive scent of honeysuckle enticed his nose, and he could almost swear he felt the pulse of her blood coursing beneath his fingers, even with the weight of her silk gown and stays and his gloves between them.

"March, march, march, march, then *messieurs*, pirouette, *mesdames, pas de bourée, pas de bourée, pas de bourée*. Up, up, up on the toes, *oui, oui*…"

A satisfaction bone-deep settled over him at finally having Bathsheba Honeychurch in his arms. At being able to allow his eyes to roam without embarrassment or restraint over the sweep of her pert brows, the stretch of her lush mouth, the expanse of her graceful neck below that tip-tilted chin, confident and defiant in turn. He'd never had much sympathy for Goethe's self-indulgent Werther, but the romantic hero's assertion that "a maiden whom I loved, or for whom I felt the slightest attachment, never, never, never should waltz with any one else but with me" struck him as painfully apt.

He twirled her carefully, silently, unwilling to allow meaningless small-talk to distract him from a pleasure he feared he'd never stop craving.

She, too, remained quiet as the slow notes of the waltz enveloped them in a bubble of awareness, her blue eyes roving his face as his roved hers. She blinked, and blinked again, as if she could not quite understand what she was seeing.

"Ah, yes, my lady, with what elegance you dance!" M de Brunhoff cried as Ash and Delphie twirled past him. "Now, let us vary the posture, eh? *Messieurs*, place your right arm fully about your partner's waist, *et mesdames*, rest your hand and arm on your partner's shoulder."

Noel swallowed, then laced his arm behind Sheba's waist. Although he kept her at a decorous distance, the heat of her warmed his entire side. And when her hand crept up his shoulder, her corseted breast mere inches from his chest, that warmth turned molten.

He felt, as well as heard, Sheba's breath catch in her throat as his fingers tightened against her side.

The beat of the music, the tap of their slippers against the polished floor, the hum of pleasure he could not quite keep contained—Noel spun, and spun, dizzy with the turning, near giddy with longing.

"Pirouette, yes, pirouette. But *gently, seigneur*," M. de Brunhoff called out to Ash. "Your partner is not an ox under the plough, but a delicate flower, as precious as a *bébé* in your arms."

Noel did not realize the other couple had come to a halt until he nearly twirled Sheba into her cousin. That lady bit her lip, as if holding back a cry of pain. Had Ash abused her poor toes, as well as Sheba's?

"I beg your pardon, Lord Silliman." Delphie set a hand to her throat. "I fear all this twirling has made me quite lightheaded."

"Then let us stop for today," Ash said. "Come again tomorrow, will you, M. de Brunhoff, at the same hour? With only four more days before the ball, I'll need every moment of instruction you can spare."

"Very good, *seigneur*."

"Well, I'm fair parched after all that whirling about," Ash declared after the dancing master packed up his *pochette* and bid them good day. "Shall we adjourn to the back garden and call for some lemonade?"

"Thank you, but I am rather fatigued," Delphie demurred. "Perhaps if I may rest a bit before we dine?"

"Certainly, ma'am. Let us find a footman who can show you to a chamber."

Sheba shrugged free of Noel's shoulder, as if only now just realizing they were still entwined. He nearly growled at the sharp bite of abandonment, and had to force himself not to reach out and pull her back to his side.

Sheba moved to the doorsill, concern etching wrinkles between her brows as she watched her cousin ascend the stairs. "Do you know where Spencer Burnett has gone?"

"Did not your cousin say he had a business appointment of some sort?" he asked as he joined her by the door.

"I hardly think a simple business appointment would require him to take a valise. Or order all his belongings packed."

"Spencer's left town? Now? But I thought our efforts to bring him and your cousin back together were finally beginning to bear fruit."

She gazed at her hands, plucking at the fingers of her gloves. "As did I. Last week, after they returned from Greenwich Fair, they seemed as lovestruck as Rachel and Jacob."

Noel frowned.

"The story in the Bible? The Book of Genesis?" she clarified. "It took Spencer far less than the seven years of effort poor Jacob had to endure to win his love. Or so I thought. This past week, they spent so much time in each other's pockets, I was certain he'd convinced her to reconcile."

"But he hadn't?"

She yanked off her gloves and threw them on a chair. "They argued this morning. I couldn't catch the words, but even just the tone of their voices made me cringe. Angry, bitter, and then finally, painfully, silent. Not the silence of peace, but the silence that comes when hope has fled entirely."

"And then he left?"

"Without so much as a backward glance." Sheba stared after her cousin, long after she disappeared up the stairs. "And no matter how many times I ask, Delphie refuses to tell me anything. I *know* she loves him, and that he loves her, too. If only my mother were still alive! She would have brought them to see sense. But I don't even have any idea where he's gone…"

Noel paced to the ballroom window and stared at the sun gilding the low box hedges of his grandmother's garden. The first sunny day they'd enjoyed in nearly a week, but the warmth of that light could not touch him. To see Sheba Honeychurch, usually so filled with plans and possibilities, at such a loss—

"I'll find him for you."

Sheba yawned and stretched, blinking the sleep from her eyes. Why did her neck ache so? The mattress beneath her must be the most uncomfortable on which she had ever slept. She rolled her shoulders against what was decidedly not a featherbed. Not her bed in Leicester, then. Nor the one in Delphie's London rooms, either. In fact, not a bed at all, but the leather seat of a carriage.

A carriage? The last thing she could remember was driving away from Silliman House, weary unto death with trying to cajole Ash, appease his grandmother, and repress her disappointment at Delphie's dismissal of Spencer. And most difficult of all, ignore the strange new awareness of Noel Griffin that haunted her all evening, after only a single dance with the man.

She blinked again. Had she fallen asleep during the short ride from Ash's house to their Conduit Street lodgings? But the misty light of impending dawn suggested a far longer drive. Why were they still in the carriage?

She jerked upright, rubbing a hand against her cheek. Delphie sat across from her on the forward-facing seat, but her cousin wasn't looking at her. No, Delphie's eyes were fixed on the view beyond the lowered window, every line of her body tense.

Sheba shivered in the damp, chill air. The scent of newly-dug earth and fragrant summer flowers told her they were decidedly not in London.

Where had her cousin taken her?

"What time is it?" she asked as the carriage rolled to a stop. "Where are we?"

But Delphie made no answer. Opening the carriage door without even waiting for the coachman to lower the step, she jumped out into the chill of the early morning air.

Sheba shook her head at the strangeness of her cousin's behavior, then allowed the coachman to hand her down from the carriage. She winced as a sharp stone bit against the sole of her shoe. Evening slippers were not made for walking across the hard gravel of a country drive.

"Delphie? Philadelphia?" Sheba laid a tentative hand on her cousin's arm, but Delphie shrugged it off, walking over to lay her own gloved hand against one of the four stone columns that flanked the front door of an unfamiliar three-story manor. Staring up at its red brick walls as if mesmerized. As if within those walls lay all she might need to heal every pain, a balm more powerful than any to be found in Gilead.

"Philadelphia, you're frightening me. Tell me this instant, where have you taken me?"

Delphie pulled her shawl close about her and gazed up at the hipped roof, the white wooden cornice. "Home, Sheba. I've brought us home."

Sheba grabbed Delphie's arm again, this time yanking her right around so that she looked not at the house but at Sheba. "Home? Do you mean Beechcombe Park? You've taken us all the way to Surrey? Whatever for?"

She'd dragged Sheba off to the countryside when the all-important ball introducing Ash to aristocratic society was only four days away? What had Delphie been thinking?

A sudden hope caught the breath in her throat. Might Spencer be inside these brick walls?

But her cousin's answer quickly quashed that wishful thought. "Because it was a mistake for us, for you, to go to London. I should never have allowed it. Never have agreed to serve as your chaperone. I should have insisted you come to me here instead."

"Philadelphia! You're not making the least bit of sense. Why would I come to Surrey when Ash is in London?"

"Because your young man is no longer just Ash Griffin, a boy eager to follow your example and do your bidding! He's the new Earl Silliman. An aristocrat, a man with power, and privileges, and duties. And he'll hurt you when he leaves you behind."

Follow her example? Do her bidding? Sheba's cheeks burned at the implied insult. "Leave me behind? Ash would never leave me!"

"Sheba, stop being a fool. He must! How can someone be both an aristocrat and a Quaker? Is not the very heart of your religion a belief in the equality of all people? While the heart of aristocracy is the belief in the political supremacy of only those distinguished by birth. Can you not see? The two are entirely incompatible."

The unexpected harshness of Delphie's voice unnerved her. She stepped back and grabbed at the handle of the carriage door.

"Sheba. You must know that he'll have to give over his beliefs if he is to take his position in society."

"No!" Sheba's nails dug into her palms. "It would kill Ash to leave the Meeting."

Or if the Meeting disowned him for the West Indian plantations he'd inherited. She'd urged him to return to Leicester and explain the matter to the Meeting's elders, but each time she brought up the matter, he'd equivocate and evade. And pull further away from her...

"Would it? Or would it kill you? Will you give over your principles, your faith, for the sake of his title? Not just give them over, but take on their very opposite?"

Sheba felt her lips grow taut. "Ash would never ask such a thing of me."

"Perhaps not in so many words. He strikes me as a young man who does not enjoy brangling with others. But I can tell he's hoping you'll see the problem yourself and break off whatever informal engagement is between you of your own accord. Far less painful than having him spell out his change of feeling directly."

"Change of feeling? Ash? Who has been spilling such lies into your ears? Lady Silliman? No, she is too much the gentlewoman to ever be so unkind. I know—it's Noel Griffin who's been feeding you such poison! He hates me, Delphie, hates me with a passion!"

Oh, how petulant, how excessive, how utterly *false* those words sounded, even to her own ears. The memory of Noel Griffin's gloved hands in hers as they turned about the Silliman House ballroom, his expression stern, his eyes fixed on hers as if he couldn't bring himself to look away... It hadn't all been a lie, their rapprochement. He'd never speak behind her back, or try to persuade others that Ash did not care for her.

Noel Griffin didn't hate her.

She was beginning to fear his feelings might be quite the opposite.

Fear? Or wish?

Sheba clasped her elbows, pressing her arms tight against her belly. Were those her mother's gentle words echoing inside her head? Or her own?

No. It didn't matter. She would not allow herself to consider such a dangerous, selfish want. She belonged with Ash, was meant to marry *Ash*. Just as her mother and his father had always prophesied. She couldn't allow Noel Griffin or his inconvenient *passion* to make a hash of all their plans.

"He's lying if he says Ash's feelings for me have changed," she declared.

"Oh, Sheba, love. I don't need Lady Silliman, nor Mr. Griffin, to tell me what I can see with my own eyes. What anyone who has spent any time in company with the two of you together can see—Ash Griffin is not at all eager to pursue a connection between you. I cannot help but worry that he never really wanted to marry you at all."

The pity—no, the honesty—in her cousin's eyes infuriated her. "How could you say such a thing, Delphie? Why are you being so cruel?"

"All your energy and enthusiasm and idealism might be appealing to a man as conventional as Ash Griffin. But he'll tire of them, sooner rather than later. And I don't want you to tie yourself to the wrong man! Just as Connie has." Delphie hung her head. "Just as I did."

"Ash is not the wrong man! He loves me!" Sheba clapped a hand over her mouth. The strained insistence of those words—oh, how much doubt they revealed!

Delphie placed a hand on Sheba's arm. "If he truly cares for you, why has he still not come to the point of asking formally for your hand?"

Because he was ashamed of those slave plantations he had inherited. But she could not reveal that shame to Delphie. She shook her head.

"Why did he avoid doing so even before he inherited a title?" Delphie pressed.

Sheba flinched at the very question she'd been so assiduously avoiding. "Because he—Because I—Because his mother said—"

"Because, because, because!" Delphie's hands swept the air in exasperation. "Always another because, another excuse. Sheba, cannot you see how you're allowing your desire for what you want to blind you to the impossibility of having it? Hanging out after the earl will only cause you pain. Break it off now, before he is forced to openly break with you. Otherwise, I fear you'll embroil the poor man in a terrible scandal."

Scandal! Just as Noel Griffin had predicted, the first time they'd met in London.

"No, Delphie." Sheba shook her head, as if she could physically shake herself free of the painful truths spilling from her cousin's mouth. "Ash and I will find a way."

"Oh, my poor dear girl! As though society's rules don't apply to you, or him."

The rue in Delphie's eyes nearly eviscerated her.

"You're wrong, Philadelphia." Sheba's hands fisted by her sides. "You just want me to be as unhappy as you are."

"Unhappy? I'm not unhappy." But her cousin's refusal to meet her eyes belied the claim.

"Yes, you are!" Sheba lashed out. "You're unhappy and bitter and *alone*. A fool who sent away a husband who loves her! Don't think I didn't overhear your argument with Spencer Burnett yesterday morning. And now you want everyone else to be as lonely as you! You didn't leave London for me; you're just running away yourself!"

Her cousin drew in a deep breath, as if it took the greatest of efforts to gather her patience to deal with such a misguided girl. "We won't be lonely, Sheba. Not if we're here together. Cannot you see that leaving London is for the best? For both of us?"

How dare she! Sheba stamped her foot. "Philadelphia Audley Fry! Who are you to make such a decision on my behalf?"

"Because you'll be safe here, Sheba! It's what Anna would have wanted."

Anna? Delphie's long-dead sister? The eldest Audley cousin, who had looked out for all the younger girls when they'd gathered each summer at their grandmother's home? The sociable, vivacious young woman whose mere presence always seemed to set her introspective younger sister in the shade?

The sister who was meant to marry Spencer?

Sheba's eyes narrowed. "Anna? What has your sister to do with it?"

"I promised her. I promised Anna that I'd keep watch over you. Over you, and over all our Audley cousins."

No. Delphie should not allow a deathbed promise to lead her so astray...

Sheba shivered. She'd made such a deathbed promise, too, hadn't she?

But it was different. Her promise had been made to a wise and trusted elder, not to a sister only a few years older than herself.

And Delphie never said Anna had *asked* her to make such a promise—

"Why are you always trying to take Anna's place?" Sheba demanded, the words tumbling from her mouth before she even realized the truth of them.

"Because she cared for us!" Delphie's lowered her head for an instant, but then drew it back up. "And I promised her I'd keep you safe after she was gone."

"Safe?" Sheba scoffed. "Why would Anna ever ask you to keep us *safe*? If you made any such ridiculous promise, it's not because she asked you to."

"She did, Sheba! Just before she died, she asked me to help you, to protect you. She loved you, loved you all."

But Sheba just shook her head. "Surely you misunderstood what she was asking. Anna knew that loving someone isn't the same as wishing them safe. Safe? Anna was never safe! She was wild, and alive, and as far from safe as any person could be!"

"Yes, and what good did it do her? She's dead, Sheba. Dead, and gone. She left me, just like everyone else I love."

Delphie clapped her hand to her mouth, as if she could snatch back the terrible pain her words had revealed. Shove it back inside, deep inside, where no one, even herself, could see.

But Delphie was wrong. Sheba hadn't left her. Nor had Connie, or any of their other Audley cousins.

Her husband had left her before, that was true. But this time, Sheba was suddenly certain, it had been Delphie who had abandoned him.

After a long, tense, silence, Sheba finally spoke. "Anna had no choice in the matter. But you do. You didn't have to send Spencer away."

Delphie closed her eyes, then covered her ears, refusing to acknowledge Sheba's words. But Sheba jerked her around, yanked her arms down, forced her to look, to *listen*.

"Anna loved you, Delphie. Loved you, and loved us, too. But she wanted more for us, more for you, than just safety. Don't you remember, that night at Audley Priory, when she made us search our hearts for what we truly wanted, what truly mattered? She wanted us to *want*, Delphie. Not to hide away in the country, being *safe*."

"But all I wanted then was Spencer."

Delphie's eyes widened, as if she couldn't quite believe she'd allowed such an admission to escape her lips.

Oh, how the pain in her cousin's voice made Sheba's heart ache.

"I know," she said. "I could see it, even then."

Delphie turned away from Sheba, from the footman and driver turning the carriage toward the stables. She pulled her shawl close, as if her too-transparent feelings might be safely tucked behind it, too.

But Sheba would not let her cousin hide. Not any longer.

"And I still see it now," she said, her voice softening. "Have you never told him? Have you ever told him how much you love him?"

Delphie hung her head. "How could I? Spencer was meant to be hers. And he never wanted to be mine."

"So you've been hiding your feelings, hiding behind silence, all this time?" No wonder she and Noel had failed in their schemes to reconcile her cousin and his friend. How could they, when Delphie would not admit the truth of her feelings to Spencer, or even to herself?

"I had to! It was wrong for me to want what Anna had. To want him."

"Silence isn't meant for hiding, or protection," Sheba said, echoing the words she had often heard her own mother counsel. "We're meant to use it to seek clarity and truth. Isn't it time for you to find your own truth, Philadelphia?"

Delphie hung her head. "The only truth I know is that I can never be Anna," she whispered.

How could someone so kind, so caring of the feelings of others, be burdened with such a false sense of her own inadequacy?

Sheba brushed the backs of her fingers against her cousin's pale cheek. "No, Delphie. You can never be Anna. But what you can't seem to understand is that none of us even wants you to be. Not even Spencer."

Sheba moved toward Beechcombe's front door, then paused and turned at the top of the steps to stare back at her poor, misguided cousin. "How disappointed Anna would be," she said before brushing past a yawning footman who had come to open the door.

She was finished trying to make Delphie see what was in her own best interest. She needed to focus on her own self, her own future.

For Delphie was not the only one entwined in mistaken assumptions, was she?

Sheba needed to find a place to be alone, a place where she could quiet her heart and the hurry of her mind and listen for the still small voice of the spirit. The voice that says *this is the way, walk in it*.

Only then she would know what to do, about Delphie, about Ash.

About Noel Griffin.

CHAPTER 12

"Damned interfering jolterhead!" Noel crumpled the note he'd just received from Rackham the elder in one tight fist. For one of the few mornings during this rainy summer, the sun had broken through the clouds to warm the streets and rooftops of London. Yet Noel could take no joy in the change in the weather. With a snort of frustration, he tossed the crumpled note across the library.

It bounced off the carpet, nearly hitting Michael Pinney as he entered the room. Noel's—no, Ash's—secretary scooped up the errant missive and laid it back down on the desk. "Bad news, I take it?"

Noel growled. "After being asked nearly a month ago to consult with the late Lord Silliman's solicitors about whether an entail had ever been created for the plantations in Nevis, Mr. Rackham has finally done so."

"And?"

"It's just as we feared. Rackham is pleased to inform us that a new entail *was* specifically created for the plantations the late earl had purchased in Nevis. An entail by which the new earl is most decidedly bound. My cousin, though, is the last man so-constrained, and may break the entail if he wishes—only, of course, once he is of age."

"This is only a guess," Pinney said with a wry smile, "but does Rackham also advise that the new Lord Silliman instruct his solicitor to renew all the estate's entails immediately, including the one on the plantations? To ensure the family's holdings remain intact for future Silliman heirs?"

"Naturally. And though he usually refrains from troubling the ladies of a family with matters of business, he feels it incumbent upon himself to inform Lady Silliman of his recommendation. Surely the late earl's widow will see the wisdom of encouraging her grandson to do his duty to his family. The implication being that I will not."

Noel grabbed the cursed note from the desk and this time tossed it into the hearth. "As if there is no harm to the family's reputation in enslaving other human beings."

"Well, slave owning hardly disqualifies one from polite society, or a position of power. I've never stopped to count, but I'd wager a good percentage of the members of the House of Commons own property in the West Indies, or have relations who do."

"At least one in ten, if the membership in London's West India Association is any indication." Noel stared sourly at the balled-up note sitting smugly in the empty grate. Too warm for a fire today, damn it.

"Time to implement our secondary plan, then? Mitigation, since full emancipation is not an option? I've already written out the instructions to be sent to the overseers of both plantations."

"*Our* plan? Pinney, you seem to forget I am not the earl. Speak to Ash about your recommendations, not me. Or to Miss Honeychurch. She and he are the best of friends, and he is certain to listen to her advice, if not to mine or yours."

"Very good, sir," Pinney said with a knowing smile.

Noel huffed, then began to flip through the investment prospectuses Pinney had thrust at him back in May, when he'd first returned from Leicester. He hadn't given them more than a cursory examination since, too busy guiding Ash—and attempting to guide him away from Bathsheba Honeychurch—to spend any time considering his own financial future.

Banks. Mines. Insurance schemes. Bonds issues by the governments of Mexico, Guatemala, Peru...

Noel threw the bunch back on his desk, disgusted by his own lack of interest. Until one pamphlet that had been caught between two others slid free, and he caught sight of word *steamship*...

"Oh, you've finally deigned to look to your own financial concerns, have you?"

Noel's head jerked up. Pinney leaned against the mantel, amusement and exasperation playing in equal measure over his expressive face.

"I hope you don't make as free with my cousin as you do with me, Michael. The poor fellow is far too likely to take such sarcasm as true criticism than as a sign of affection or admiration."

"Don't you worry, sir. I'm teaching him not to allow others to impose on him, even myself. But the lesson has not yet quite sunk in, which is why I wished to consult you about this note."

"Note?"

"A letter, rather, addressed to the earl. I'm tempted to toss it on the grate, too, along with all the others you receive from perfect strangers importuning the estate for charity or patronage. But its writer claims an acquaintance with your friend, Lord Stiles."

Stiles. Damn it all to hell. He'd promised Sheba he'd find Spencer for her, but none of the inquiries he'd made in London over the past three days had born any fruit. And he'd not yet had any replies to any of the letters he'd sent to all Spencer's old cronies not currently in town, either. If Spencer didn't return to town before his grandmother's ball, Noel feared he'd have to set off himself in search of him.

"A friend of Stiles'?" he asked. "Who?"

"A woman named Sarah Gabbidon. She claims to hail from

Sierra Leone."

"Gabbidon? That's the name of the man with whom Stiles traveled from Freetown back to England. He's gone back to Sierra Leone, but he left a daughter behind, at a school in Clapham. He asked us if she might call on our assistance if she ever found herself in distress. And Stiles, damn him, seems to have left town. Are you certain the letter was meant for Ash, and not for me?"

"It is addressed to Earl Silliman. But I suppose she might share the general misunderstanding about just which Griffin has inherited the title."

Noel stilled. But the roiling rush of resentment and shame that had once accompanied any reminder of all he had lost failed to rise. "What kind of difficulties is she in?"

"None, as far as I can tell. She simply requests the privilege of an audience with the earl."

"To what purpose?"

"Her note does not specify, beyond saying it is a matter of interest to them—or you?—both."

Pinney handed him the letter. It had been written in a strong, confident hand, not the tentative loops one would expect of a schoolgirl. And its words contained none of the diffidence one would expect of a girl, either. Pinney was right: Miss Sarah Gabbidon's request contained no hint of the purpose behind it.

"Has my cousin any appointments this morning?"

"None of which I am aware." Pinney raised a telling eyebrow. "He hasn't yet risen for the day, though."

Noel frowned. "Another late evening spent with Baron Pierson and Mr. Debenham? And he with no head for drink."

He should be glad of it, glad Ash had decided not to allow his Quaker fastidiousness to keep him from socializing with his fellow peers. For the sake of his family name and reputation, an earl needed to cultivate strong relationships with other men of his own rank. Even if such cultivation included the occasional bout of gentlemanly dissipation.

Somehow, though, Sheba's disappointment if she were to discover Ash's religious principles falling by the wayside kept satisfaction at bay.

Noel tapped the edge of Miss Gabbidon's note against the blotter. "Perhaps a ride to Clapham this morning will convince our earl that staying out until all hours of the morning is not in his best interest."

Pinney chuckled. "Indeed, sir. Shall I send his valet to rouse him?"

"Yes, and tell the groom to ready three horses. We'll ride to Clapham within the hour."

No footman, only a maid, answered the door at Miss MacKay's Select Seminary for Young Ladies. Noel waited for Ash, as the highest-ranking gentleman, to announce them and their business to the wide-eyed girl. But his cousin's inexperience as a rider, not to mention the sore head he was nursing, had him vociferously protesting every rut and rock in the road from Mayfair to Clapham. Ill-humor must have made him forget the lessons in manners and precedence their grandmother was still struggling to instill.

"The Earl Silliman to see Miss Gabbidon," Noel said, pulling a card from his cousin's coat pocket and handing it to the girl. The tiny thing looked to be not a day older than ten. Not an establishment with a full complement of servants, then. Had Mr. Gabbidon not been able to afford anything better? Or were all the truly select girls' schools unwilling to accept a Black child as a pupil?

"Very good, m'lord," the girl said with a wide-eyed, deferential bob. "If you will wait here in the parlor?"

Pinney and Noel settled on a serviceably-upholstered settee, but Ash, restless even after their four-mile ride, paced before windows that faced out onto the wide expanse of the town common. "I don't know why you had to drag me to Clapham, Noel. This Miss Gabbidon of yours can have no business with me."

"Perhaps not. But Hippomenes needed exercising."

Ash shook his head, grimaced, then rubbed a hand against what was likely a throbbing temple. "I've asked Joshua to take the horse out every day."

"Why should we incur the expense of keeping a horse in town for you if you refuse to ride it?"

"You were the one who insisted a gentleman needs a horse. I'd have been just as happy to walk—"

Before Noel could remind him of the eagerness with which he'd visited Tattersall's, a woman of middling years and scantling height bustled into the room. She glanced all three men before turning to Noel and curtseying. "Lord Silliman? I am Miss MacKay, the headmistress of this school."

"Mr. Griffin, ma'am. My cousin, Lord Silliman, you see there by the window. And this is Mr. Pinney."

"You are come to inquire after Miss Gabbidon?" She eyed Pinney with clear curiosity. "Her father did not inform me she had any relations here in England."

Pinney blinked, clearly surprised to be accounted a relative of the young woman. The secretary must have assumed that since the Gabbidons were friends of Lord Stiles, they must be British, not African.

"Not relations, ma'am," Noel answered. Had Miss Gabbidon shared with this headmistress whatever confidences she planned on imparting to Silliman? The lady's air of puzzlement suggested not. "But Mr. Gabbidon did ask that we call on her after his return to Sierra Leone and offer her our friendship and aid should she ever be in need of them. If you ask the young lady, I'm certain she'll recognize my name."

"How kind of you, sir. Miss Gabbidon's arithmetic lesson concludes in a quarter of an hour, but I can summon her directly if you are not inclined to wait."

"If you would," his cousin said without even a glance at the poor woman.

Noel frowned. If a sore head made Ash treat others with such lack of civility, Noel would have to take more care to ensure his young cousin's bouts of over-imbibing were few and far between.

Miss MacKay did not send a servant, but excused herself to find Miss Gabbidon herself.

Ash refrained from grumbling this time, but still refused to join them. Instead, he crossed the room, staring up the volumes held by a single bookcase on the wall beside the door.

Noel and Pinney exchanged desultory conversation until a young woman dressed as soberly as Miss MacKay stepped into the parlor and shut the door behind her.

Pinney was not the only one who had made an incorrect assumption about Miss Gabbidon, it would seem. The figure before them was no schoolgirl, as Noel had supposed, but a woman full-grown. A few years older than Ash, he'd guess; perhaps Sheba's age? Even more surprising, she looked more like a European than the few Africans he'd met. If he'd not known her father to be Stephen Gabbidon, he might not have thought her to be anything but white. She'd dressed her dark hair, which had none of the curl of Michael's, smooth and straight under a demure white cap. Her skin looked only as tanned as any Englishwoman's might be, after a summer spent traveling in the sun. And her features... Well, her lips were lush and full, but that narrow blade of a nose, the slight cleft in her chin, the lush lashes surrounding golden brown eyes that shaded to green at the edge of the iris, all spoke of European blood. English blood.

Familiar blood...

Noel's stomach plummeted, as if his horse had just clipped a fence and was about to send him tumbling to the ground.

Griffin blood?

Had his father, as well as his grandfather, been keeping secrets? Bloody, bloody hell.

Disturbingly familiar hazel eyes flicked between him and Pinney before settling back on Noel. "Lord Silliman?"

Noel swallowed. "Noel Griffin, ma'am, at your service."

"A brother to Lord Silliman, are you?"

"No, ma'am. A cousin."

She gave him a considering look. "Yes, of course. You look a bit too old, I think."

Noel frowned. "Ma'am?"

But the young woman gave no explanation for her mysterious observation. "He has sent you in his stead? And asked this fellow"—she gave a contemptuous wave in Pinney's direction—"to come along, in some misguided notion that any Black person would be more able to conduct a conversation with another of her own race than he, or yourself?"

"You are mistaken, ma'am," Ash said as he moved from where he'd been hidden behind the parlor door. "I am Earl Silliman. Mr. Pinney is my secretary, here not to serve as interpreter, but to advise us on how best to help you, if you are in need of our aid."

Strong-willed and not easily discomposed, Stephen Gabbidon had described his daughter. Even if it turned out the man wasn't the young woman's actual father, he obviously knew her well. Not at all cowed by the presence of a social superior, she stepped close to Ash, her eyebrows raised. "You employ a Black man as secretary?"

"I do, ma'am. Although I do not see what concern it is of yours."

Noel stepped to Ash's side before his cousin's incivility slipped into outright rudeness. "Was your letter intended for me, Miss Gabbidon, as the friend recommended to you by your father? Or did you truly intend it for the earl?"

Miss Gabbidon's hazel eyes flicked between him and Ash,

wary, eager, determined. "It was intended for whichever Griffin is the son of the man who visited Barbados in the year 1802. The year before my birth."

Noel's chest tightened. His father had been stationed in the West Indies in the years just after the turn of the century.

Ash, wide-eyed, swung between Miss Gabbidon and Noel, and then back to the young woman. "Are you implying that Noel —that Noel's father—is—is yours as well?" he stuttered.

"Both James *and* William Griffin were in the West Indies in 1802," Pinney said, his voice grim.

"But my father was in Nevis," Ash insisted. "Is that not hundreds of miles from Barbados?"

"It is. But if my memory is correct, the estate records show that your father did not only visit Nevis. He spent a little more than a year touring various British colonies in the West Indies, inspecting properties on behalf of his father."

"The Griffin for whom I search had not yet started a family of his own when he visited Barbados," Miss Gabbidon said. "At least, that is what he told my mother before he took her to his bed. I suppose, though, given his subsequent behavior, that also might have been a lie."

"Took her? Or forced her?" Pinney asked, his expression grim.

"It is common practice in the Indies to offer visitors a Black woman upon which they may slake their needs," Miss Gabbidon said. "Whether the woman is amenable or no is of little interest to either, as I'm certain you must be aware."

Ash choked, all the color draining from his face. "Noel? Your parents—?"

"Wed in 1794. I was born two years later."

Ash looked on the verge of casting up his accounts. Could it be true? Could the righteous father whom Ash revered truly have done something so reprehensible before turning Quaker?

"He must not have known," Ash croaked. "Before he left Barbados, he must not have known he'd fathered a child."

"My mother informed him of the fact." Miss Gabbidon was implacable. "She told me her Mr. Griffin tried to purchase her freedom, but her owner would not allow it, especially once he discovered she was breeding. I've often wondered if it was simply a story meant to placate me, or perhaps only to soothe herself."

"Of course he wouldn't have just left her! Leave his own child?" Ash could not seem to stop shaking his head. "I'm sorry, Noel, but it must have been your father, not mine. William Griffin would never have done such a thing. Even if he had… had lain with a woman out of wedlock, he would have helped her when she found herself with child. The man I knew would have moved heaven and earth to bring her back to England with him!"

"And risk being prosecuted for theft?" Michael Pinney asked, one eyebrow rising.

"Yes! Did I not tell you how he was sent to prison for refusing to pay church tithes when I was a boy?"

"But the penalties for theft are far more punitive," Noel cautioned.

"Still!"

"He would risk a ruinous fine?" Miss Gabbidon scoffed. "Being sentenced to the pillory? Being imprisoned for years, not simply months? He would risk being branded, physically branded, a slave stealer? I've yet to meet the European who would ever risk such for an African."

"But my father was a Friend," Ash cried, his hands white and trembling. "A Quaker! Friends once risked *death* for their beliefs!"

Damnation. Noel had almost rather it *had* been his father, if it could have saved his cousin the pain of such disillusionment.

"Ash. Please," he said, schooling his voice to calm. "Once we return to London, I will call at the Admiralty and examine the naval records, to see whether my father's ship was stationed in

Barbados during the year in question."

"You needn't bother." Miss Gabbidon's eyes were fixed on Ash. "The Mr. Griffin for whom I seek was *not* a naval man. A private gentleman, he was, visiting the island in the hopes of purchasing property on behalf of his family, or so my mother overheard."

The clock on the mantel chimed the top of the hour, allowing them all a few blessed moments to catch their breath.

"Your father did not bring you to England from Barbados, Miss Gabbidon," Pinney said once the clock had quieted. "You traveled with Mr. Gabbidon, and with Mr. Griffin's friend Lord Stiles, from Sierra Leone."

"Ah, you wish to claim I am fabricating a tale from whole cloth, do you? But the explanation is quite simple. Stephen Gabbidon was sent to Sierra Leone after participating in a slave revolt in Barbados in 1795. In Freetown, he was able to make his fortune as a publican, and then used his earnings to purchase my mother's freedom. And as my mother would not leave without me, he also purchased my own. The plantation owner who had once refused to release us had since fallen on hard times. Accepting my father's offer might have galled his pride, but it had the benefit of staving off bankruptcy. At least for a few years." There was no kindness, only deep satisfaction, in the tight smile that crossed Miss Gabbidon's face.

Another silence fell over the room.

"Do you have some proof of the connection you claim?" Pinney finally asked. "A letter, or a trinket given to your mother by Mr. Griffin? A lock of hair, perhaps?"

Miss Gabbidon pressed her lips together, saying not a word.

"Then what is it that you want of us, Miss Gabbidon?" Noel asked. As the head of the family, Ash should have been the one to pose the question. But his cousin looked to be in no state to even speak, never mind ensure that the young woman's revelations did not heap scandal on the Silliman name.

"I want nothing from you, sir."

Without question she wanted something. "An annuity? Or preferment of some sort? You must be attending Miss MacKay's seminary as a teacher, not as a student. Could we not help you find a post as governess?"

"I thank you, sir, but no. I am apprenticed to Miss MacKay for three years, and intend to return to Sierra Leone after completing my studies."

"Is it that you wish the family to acknowledge you in some way, then?" Noel hazarded.

"No. I care nothing for the life of an English aristocrat."

"Come, Miss Gabbidon. You did not approach the earl for no reason," Pinney said when the young woman remained stubbornly silent. "You must want something from him?"

Miss Gabbidon paused for a moment, as if not entirely certain of her own motivation. "I simply wanted to see him," she said at last. "To see the man I might have called brother."

"Come, Miss Gabbidon. Surely you do not expect us to believe—"

"Enough!"

Noel blinked. He'd never heard Ash speak with such harshness. Or with such determination.

"Miss Gabbidon is our relation." Ash glared at Pinney, then at Noel. "You will speak to her with all the respect a member of our family deserves."

Miss Gabbidon crossed her arms. "The only respect I desire is the respect you would pay to any lady of your acquaintance."

"But you are not just any lady of my acquaintance. You are my family. Merciful God, my *sister*. I would wish—"

A tentative knock sounded at the door. "Miss Gabbidon? Your geography class begins in ten minutes. Will you be finished with your callers by then, or should I plan on taking the class myself?"

"I will be there directly, Miss MacKay," Miss Gabbidon said. "My callers were just leaving."

The young woman pulled open the door then offered a shallow curtsey. "Thank you, gentlemen, for satisfying my curiosity. Please be assured, I will not trouble you again."

Noel and Pinney exchanged wary glances. Could the scandal her presence threatened be so easily avoided?

"Miss Gabbidon." Ash paused beside her. "Might I call again, when your duties are not so pressing? I would welcome the chance to become better acquainted with you."

Noel stared. Ash's father may not have kept to the paths of righteousness himself, but he'd certainly trained his son to walk in the way of the righteous.

"Sir?" Miss Gabbidon blinked, as if she could not quite believe what she was hearing.

"Please. My given name is Manasseh, but my sisters—all three of them, all younger than I—call me Ash. I would like it if you would do so, too."

He held out a hand, steady now and firm.

She took it, her expression sober, the mirror of his.

CHAPTER 13

Delphie's lady's maid Lacy twirled a lock of Sheba's fair hair around her finger and pressed it against her temple. "Oh, miss, please, just a few ringlets here, and here, on each side of your head—so very charming it would be!"

Sheba had fled Surrey the same afternoon Delphie had dragged her off to Beechcombe—without informing her cousin she was leaving. She'd thought it the best way to make Delphie, responsible chaperone that she was, abandon her foolish retreat and return to town. But five days had passed, and still Delphie had not appeared.

Noel, who had promised her he'd track Spencer down, had finally word yesterday that both Spencer and Delphie were at Hill Peverill, the Earl of Morse's Gloucestershire estate. The two had reconciled, if the note from Spencer that Noel shared with her was to be believed, and planned to return to London in time to attend Lady Silliman's ball this evening.

He'd kept his promise, even despite his anger at discovering Sheba had returned to London by herself. A reliable man, as well as a resourceful one, Noel Griffin. Far more worthy of respect, even of admiration, than she'd shown him to date…

Sheba stared at the unfamiliar face and figure in the mirror in her cousin's Conduit Street bedchamber. She'd absolutely refused to allow the apple green silk gown Delphie had insisted Sheba purchase for Ash's ball to be adorned with flounces or frills or any other extraneous frippery. But the cut of the bodice revealed far more of her décolletage than she was used to seeing, and the way the draping fabric clung to her curves—well, all she could say was that if any of the elders from Leicester Meeting ever caught sight of her in such a garment, days of pained lectures on the dangers of vanity would be certain to follow.

But it would be worth it, wouldn't it? Dressing like a fashionable lady, complete with the cosmetics and curls Lacy insisted were *de rigueur* for attending a *ton* ball, would surely catch Ash's attention. And give her a chance to talk with him about their future.

Ash Griffin is not at all eager to pursue a connection…
If he truly cares for you, why has he not asked for your hand?
Has he ever really wanted to marry you at all?

"Oh, miss, please don't frown. I've a way with curls, I have. You'll look ever-so fashionable, if only you'll allow me—" Lacy pleaded.

Sheba blinked. Yes, a wrinkled brow and drawn-down lips certainly marred the image of the fashionable young woman staring back at her from that mirror.

But how could she not frown? If Delphie spoke true, surely it would be wrong to cling to Ash only because of a deathbed promise.

Even if giving him up would mean endangering all the plans she'd made for his future, and hers.

But if Delphie were wrong?

The frown deepened into a scowl. Oh, why could she not see the true path? She'd tried. Truly tried, every day, every hour, for the last five days, to open herself to the Inward Light, just as her mother had instructed her. Tried to make space for the inward voice to speak the truth to her confused heart. Prayed to be shown the unflinching truth about her life, to understand what she must do to align herself with the will of the Holy Spirit.

But no matter how patiently she waited, how earnestly she listened, that still small voice remained frustratingly silent.

"Miss? Shall I?" Lacy asked as she wrapped a strip of paper around the curling tongs she'd heated in the fire.

Avoid all pride and immodesty in apparel, and all vain, superfluous fashions of the world...

Banishing her mother's voice, Sheba nodded.

"No beads or jewels, you said, but perhaps a single ribbon about your waist? And a single ringlet in the back, curled like so..." Lacy pulled a large hank of hair free of her chignon, slicked it with pomade, then curled it about the tongs.

"You'll be the belle of the ball, miss," the maid declared with a satisfied smile as she pulled one last lock free of the tongs and arranged it to lie on Sheba's shoulder. "Not a single gentleman will be able to take his eyes off of you!"

Sheba shrugged. She'd never be so vain as to wish to attract the regard of *every* gentleman in the room. But if she could draw Ash's eye, she'd be content.

And if not...

She hardly recognized it, that face staring back at her from the mirror. Rouged cheeks. Frivolous curls. Teeth gnawing, gnawing, gnawing at the bottom of her already raw lip. Could that really be Bathsheba Honeychurch? The girl who had wished so hard to grow up and change the world?

She'd never had to imagine a grown-up life before, though, without Ash by her side.

She drew in a deep breath, then another. If Ash no longer cared to stand with her, surely she could find a way to create a meaningful life on her own. She may not have been gifted by God like her mother, but she could still follow Jane Audley Honeychurch's example. And Hannah Kilham's, and all the other women Friends who had forged their own paths through the world.

If, that is, she could be certain about what she was truly being called to do...

Lacy exclaimed with pleasure as she set down her curling tongs and gave Sheba's hair one last pat. "Now, won't that catch Lord Silliman's eye?"

Would it? Or would it only draw the attention of his cousin?

And would she be gratified if it did?

A sudden vision of that gaudy waistcoat he'd worn at his grandmother's rout party, the taunt of an explanation he'd given for wearing it—*I knew it would provoke your sharp tongue*—made her face flame.

He'd not worn anything nearly as showy during any of his brief daily calls since her return to town, to apprise her of his progress in searching for Spencer.

The clock above the mantel struck eight. Only an hour until the ball was due to begin. She pressed a hand against her belly, trying to still the fluttery, empty sensation beating just below her heart, as if the cherubim's had spread out wings not on high, but in the very center of her body.

If *she* had just reconciled with an estranged husband, she certainly wouldn't be in any hurry to rush back to town. Even more so if she hadn't.

But arriving at Silliman House with no chaperone in sight would certainly not endear her to Ash's grandmother. Or to Ash.

Though if Delphie did not return, Sheba could hardly remain here, leaving her best friend to face the *ton* alone—

A bustling from the front of their lodgings halted the sickening whirl of worry. Sheba shook free of Lacy's ministrations and dashed to the door.

The sweet, almost abashed smile with which Spencer greeted her as he helped Delphie off with her coat, the way he whispered in his wife's ear, the sharp flush of color in her cousin's cheeks—no, his letter hadn't lied. Delphie and Spencer had at long last made their peace.

Spencer bowed to Sheba, then hurried down the passageway to his own chamber, leaving her alone with her cousin.

Sheba reached for Delphie's hands. "Well, Philadelphia? Did you take my advice and tell Spencer what you told me? That you love him?"

Delphie's blush deepened as she tightened her hands in Sheba's. "Oh, my dearest. I am the happiest creature in the world!"

"So he shares your feelings, does he?"

A smile the likes of which she'd never seen on her shy, reserved cousin lit up Delphie's entire face. "He does, Sheba. He loves me ever so much. Oh, I'm fair to bursting with the joy of it!"

"Of course he does, you silly goose!" Sheba slipped her arm through Delphie's and led her down the passageway to her bedchamber. "Did I not tell you so?"

Oh, how gratifying, to have played some small role in repairing the breach between two kindred souls, to be a witness to the triumph of love over fear.

"Can you blame me for doubting?" Delphie asked as Sheba pulled her down to sit next to her on the bed. "It always felt as if others only cared about me if I could be of some use to them. My father wished a connection with the aristocracy, so he married me off to Spencer without even asking my opinion of the matter. Lord Morse needed a grandson, so he accepted me in place of Anna, but took control of my child as soon as I'd given birth, and then berated me for not giving him another when—" Delphie looked down at her hands for a few moments, then took a deep breath and raised her eyes back to Sheba's. "And Spencer wanted another heir. Or at least that's why he wanted to reconcile with me, I thought."

"Oh, Delphie, no!"

"At least he tried to court me first," Delphie said with a wry chuckle. "Unlike you, who simply demanded I come to London because you needed a chaperone, and because I was the best candidate to serve."

Sheba yanked her arm from Delphie's and set her hands on her hips. "Philadelphia Audley Fry! I did not *demand* you come to London."

"Did you not? *You must come, and at once! Philadelphia, I beg you!* The exact words of the letter I received from you only two months ago. Have you so soon forgotten?"

Sheba frowned. She'd written that letter in such a rush of anger and fear, she could hardly remember what precisely had flown from her pen. Had she truly been so rash, so demanding? No wonder her cousin had been wary of sharing her feelings with her.

It was Delphie's turn to put her arm about Sheba and give her a comforting squeeze. "Come, my dear, I'm only teasing. You might need me, but I was wrong to think that you and Spencer only wished to use me for your own ends."

"Did I make you feel as if you didn't matter?" Sheba hung her head, her voice cracking.

"You didn't make me feel that way. I convinced *myself* I didn't matter. Losing Spencer, losing my baby—you have no idea how lost *I* was, lost in a slough of grief and pain."

Sheba knelt in front of her cousin and pulled Delphie's hands into hers. "We all knew you were suffering, Delphie. All your Audley cousins—Connie, Elizabeth, even Polly, who's usually so caught up in her painting that she's oblivious to everyone else's feelings—we all worried for you. But then, when your letters returned to their old, cheerful style after your year of mourning, we thought you recovered."

"Because I wanted you to think so."

Sheba laid her chin atop her hands and stared up at her cousin. "Why? Why did you never tell us how badly you were still hurting? We might have helped you, if only you had shared your pain."

Delphie brushed a hand over the top of Sheba's hair. "Because I thought if I kept my own wants, my own needs, to myself, I could keep myself from being hurt again."

Sheba gave a pained chuckle. "That didn't work so well for you, did it? Especially not after Spencer came back to England."

"No, it didn't. Pushing away the people who care for you may shield you from hurt, but it keeps pleasure and joy far beyond reach, too. To allow myself to contemplate the possibility of ever being happy again, I had to risk trusting that if I opened my heart to Spencer, he would treat it with the care it needed."

"And he did?"

"He did." Delphie captured Sheba's hand and squeezed it tight. "I told him how I felt about him, just as you said I should. And he told me how he felt about me. He loves me, Sheba. Loves me, cares for me. Not just for the heir I hope some day to give him, but for me, myself."

The tears shining in her cousin's eyes brought the same to Sheba's own. "As do I, Delphie."

"Yes, I know that now. What you said to me at Beechcombe—accusing me of being unhappy and bitter and alone—your words may have been blunt, but your intentions were kind. I may not have seen it at the time, but I know now that you spoke to me out of love."

"Of love, and of insight. Because I was right not only about you, but also about Spencer, too, was I not?"

Delphie's smile this time was wry. "I suppose I must admit that, at least in this one case, you were."

"One case?" Sheba sat back on her heels and crossed her arms. "Cousin, surely you must know by now that I am always right."

Delphie laughed at the exaggerated braggadocio of Sheba's tone. "Ah, yes. If only everyone would just listen to Bathsheba Honeychurch, the world would be a far better place."

"Indeed it would. And if only you'd listened to me, you could have saved yourself time and trouble, not to mention days of dirty travel running to Gloucestershire and back."

"My lady?" Lacy, a bowl of warm water and a washcloth in hand, bustled into the bedchamber. "Shall you wash away the dirt of the road while I iron your gown? And then we'll have you into your stays and gown and jewels and ready for Lord Stiles in two shakes of a lamb's tail. A happy night for you and for Miss Honeychurch both, is it not?"

Delphie took the bowl and washcloth from Lacy, then gave Sheba a considering look. "You've spoken to Ash, then, have you?"

Sheba scrambled to her feet, then traced a finger over the necklace and ear bobs Lacy was setting out on Delphie's dressing table. A veritable river of diamonds and sapphires, each one larger than the next. Wrong to place any delight in such useless ornaments, no matter how prettily they sparkled in the candlelight.

"No, not yet." She turned her back on the dresser and crossed her arms. "But I will before the evening's over."

Warm fingers squeezed Sheba's arm. "Ah, my dear, do have a care. Be certain, be very certain, that you aren't just using that young man. I don't think he can give you what you want, not anymore."

Sheba swallowed against a lump growing in her throat. She'd never permitted herself, not once, to wonder if Ash's unexpected inheritance might change him, change *them*, in any meaningful way.

Was that why she could not hear the voice of the divine and unerring guide? Because she'd allowed *self* to predominate?

"And even if he could, Ash Griffin deserves to be valued and loved for who he is." Delphie said, her voice far kinder than Sheba's had been when she'd offered Delphie her own home truths. "Not just for what you want of him, or who you wish him to be."

Delphie kissed her forehead then followed Lacy out of the

room.

Sheba sank down and laid her forehead against the bedpost, praying not to mistake the dictates of her own mind for the voice of the true inward guide.

"I'm sorry, Sheba, truly I am. But Lady Silliman promised my hand for the opening set to Miss Debenham. Would you have me embarrass my own grandmother by going back on her word?"

Sheba clenched her gloved hands about the cup of iced punch Spencer—not Ash—had been kind enough to bring her while they waited for the receiving line to break up and the dancing to begin in Silliman House's grand drawing room. If she were to judge only by the unwontedness of his dress, the man standing before her in tight black breeches, immaculate white stockings, and full-skirted tailcoat pulled in tight at the waist and puffed out wide at the shoulders might have been a stranger. But the apologetic expression on his face was all too familiar.

"Certainly not, Ash. But you should have told me before—"

Delphie's cautioning frown, which Sheba caught out of the corner of her eye, brought her scold to an abrupt halt. Embarrassing enough to have her assumption that she would open the ball with him proven so publicly mistaken; even worse to have Delphie and Spencer witnessing her acting the shrew.

She might not be happy about his decision, but she need not be rude.

"Enjoy Miss Debenham's company, Ash," she said as she set her empty cup on the tray of a passing footman. "She's a kind young lady, from what I saw of her at your grandmother's rout party last month."

"Perhaps another dance, later in the evening?" Ash appeased. But already his eyes were wandering over her shoulder. In search of his first dance partner? Or his officious grandmother?

Sheba curtseyed. "I look forward to it."

After throwing her yet another apologetic glance, Ash bowed and took his leave.

She could not quite contain the frown aimed at his disappearing back, even as she felt it tightening the throb of tension in her temples. He may have made the offer only to placate her, but he *must* keep his word. She'd not pressed, had given him all the space he'd asked for to figure out how to reconcile his past and his present. It was more than time they decided what they would make of their future.

"Lady Stiles. And Miss Honeychurch. Good evening to you both."

Noel Griffin bowed, his eyes not on them, but on his rapidly disappearing cousin, his lips pulled tight in disapproval.

Noel would never offer vain promises just to avoid strife.

"Stiles." Noel reached out and took his friend's hand. "A sacrifice, I know, for you and your lady to return to town so soon. My grandmother and I appreciate your show of support for the new Lord Silliman."

"We came for our cousin as well as yours, Griff. Heaven knows not even the scandal of arriving without a chaperone would have kept Sheba away tonight."

She could hear the affection in Spencer's voice, but his words still reminded her of Noel's, when she'd first arrived in London. Accusing her of courting scandal to force Ash into marrying her, his hazel eyes alight with indignation and contempt.

She glanced up at him from under her lashes. Tonight, those eyes contained nothing close to disdain.

Sheba's stomach gave a strange, sideways flip. Had he joined them to ask her to dance the first set?

"Miss Honeychurch, may I introduce you to Sir Harold Butterbank?" A pale-faced gentleman Spencer had pulled into their circle stood next to her, blinking in surprise. "My wife's cousin, Miss Bathsheba Honeychurch, who has been our guest in London this past month, Sir Harold."

Had her mouth turned dry from relief? Or regret?

Her gaze flicked for an instant to Noel's, then quickly darted away.

"Friend Butterbank," she said, turning to greet the newcomer. Closer to Ash's age than her own—could this be his first ball, too?—Sir Harold offered her an awkward bow.

"Cousin," Spencer continued, his voice raised to be heard over the tuning of the orchestra, "Sir Harold represents the citizens of Evesham, and has just taken his seat in the Commons this session."

They were allowing boys into Parliament, now, were they? Well, perhaps a young man might be more open to discussing political issues with her than his elders were.

"Do you take an interest in Wilberforce's efforts to end the inhuman system of slavery prevailing in so many of the colonies of the British Crown, Sir Harold?" she asked.

Sir Harold, eyes widening, gave a quick nod. "Indeed, I do, ma'am. And if you will allow me the privilege of escorting you to the floor for the first two dances, I will be happy to tell you about every petition we've received urging an end to the pernicious practice."

Sheba took his preferred hand.

But as the young gentleman led her onto the floor, all her senses attuned not to Harold Butterbank, but to Noel Griffin, his gaze on her back almost as burning as a brand.

Sheba may not have been the most graceful of dancers, but she managed to avoid Harold Butterbank's toes as he led her through the opening steps of a quadrille. And then the toes of the gentlemen (all introduced to her by Spencer) who partnered her in the reel, the cotillion, and the circular dance that followed. Happily for her, the figures called by Ash's partners before each set were quite simple. Frances Griffin must not only have arranged those partners in advance, but must have also counseled each lady to choose steps easy enough for her inexperienced grandson to tread without embarrassment.

Sheba's lips pressed together in consternation. Frances Griffin hadn't offered any such counsel to Sheba. Ash's grandmother obviously had no intention of the two of them dancing together even once the most important of occasions.

Sheba had little appetite for the sumptuous supper, served on gaudy services of massive silver plate in the front and back drawing rooms at the ridiculous hour of two in the morning. She picked at the pineapples, peaches, and grapes on her plate, lending only a desultory ear to the conversation of the popinjay —the son of some nobleman, she thought Spencer had said— with whom she had been paired for the meal. Spencer must have run out of political friends whom he could cajole into partnering her.

"If you are quite finished, Miss Honeychurch, you must allow me to introduce you to my father," the popinjay declared as he set his own empty plate down on the corner of the buffet table. "I cannot wait to see the earl's face when you greet him as 'Friend Milne!' How very droll!"

Milne? Was the popinjay's surname Milne? Hadn't her cousin Polly abandoned a gentleman of that surname at the altar two springtimes ago?

She examined the dandy more closely. The gaudiness of his dress—and even more so, the impudence of his manner—matched the description of the man from Polly's letters, at least before she'd cast him aside. But since Sheba hadn't attended Polly's not-quite-wedding, she couldn't be certain.

Surely Delphie would never have been so tactless as to pair her with a man their cousin had jilted. But perhaps Spencer had acted without consulting his wife? He *had* been out of the country when the scandal had broken...

Before she could begin to question the fellow, though, she saw

Ash returning his supper partner to her chaperone. Perhaps she could catch him before the dancing began again?

"Thank you, *Friend Milne*, but I fear the pleasure of meeting your father must wait until another time. If you will excuse me?"

Sheba dashed out in pursuit of her quarry.

She caught Ash just on the verge of re-entering the grand drawing room. She gathered her courage, then dashed after him and caught his sleeve. "Ash, may I have a word?"

"Sheba, I need to find my next partner. Can it not wait?"

"Not unless that next partner is me. You promised you'd save me a dance."

Oh, how tired she was of that pained, sheepish expression on his face!

He shrugged free of her hand. "I'm sorry, Sheba, but my grandmother—"

"Enough. I'm done waiting. We need to talk, *now*." She grabbed his elegant sleeve and pulled him down the staircase, away from the noise of the ball. Yes, the library would suit…

"Sheba, this is hardly becoming behavior. What will people think if someone finds us alone?"

"What will people think? Is that all that matters to you now, Ash? What these aristocrats think of you?"

"Of course I care what they think! I have to earn their respect, and their good will, if I have any hopes of being accepted here."

"Here? Then you have no plans to return to Leicester?"

Even though he'd turned his back to her, she could tell his hands were tugging at the bottom of his waistcoat. "No. My grandmother and cousin have shown me how necessary my presence is, both in London, and in Plymouth, too, where the Silliman country seat lies. We plan to remove to Ruxford Hall after the current session of Parliament ends in a few days."

"We?"

"Yes. My grandmother, myself, Mr. Pinney, and Noel."

"And what of me, your intended bride?"

Even in the dim candlelight, she could see Ash's face pale. "Sheba. Surely you've realized by now that a marriage between us—it's not—I can't—"

"You can't what?"

Ash sucked in a long breath through his nose, then blew it out through his mouth. "I can't marry you, Sheba. I know that we talked of it, once, before, when my responsibilities, my life, were so different. But now everything's changed. I have to consider my duty to my family."

The cord of the fan—useless, frivolous thing, but Delphie insisted every lady at a ball *must* carry one—twisted painfully about her wrist. She flicked her arm, forcing the tightening cord to spin in the opposite direction. "Your family? What of your family in Leicester?"

"I will, of course, invite my mother and sisters to join me in Plymouth for the summer if they so wish."

Sheba pulled in a long breath of her own. "And what of our family? The family you and I were intending to make together?"

Ash crossed his arms and stared out the window, eyes fixed on the sooty, moonless sky. "You know it was only ever an informal arrangement between us. Why, the elders hadn't even granted us approval to consider marrying."

"They will, though, if we only remain steadfast," she said, trying to keep the desperation from her voice.

"Steadfast? When we cannot in good faith tell them that we feel a deep inward prompting of the Holy Spirit toward each other?"

"But your father and my mother always prophesied that we would marry one day. Should not that matter just as much?"

"They might have *hoped* we would marry. But even they would not have insisted if one of us did not feel called to it. And I know you do not. Friend Sattherthwaite told me so, after your petition to the Women's Meeting."

Sheba nearly choked. How dare Rebecca Satterthwaite reveal

such a humiliating thing!

"I know it must be a disappointment that I haven't felt such a call," she said, laying a hand on his sleeve. "But I will, Ash. I'm certain of it."

Sheba had never been less certain of anything in her entire life. But the strange tingling in her chest, the spots dancing on the edge of her vision, were somehow making even more untruths spill from her mouth. "You won't be the only one to whom the Holy Spirit has spoken."

Ash shrugged free of her hand, his eyes finally meeting hers. "I'm not, Sheba. Not the only one. I've never felt called to marry you, either. And I don't think I ever will."

What a sudden, sick sense of falling, those shocking words spawned! As if someone had shoved her right over the side of the chalk cliff at Flamborough Head, sent her plummeting toward the frigid waters below.

Sheba pressed a hand below her ribs—as if such a feeble gesture might somehow contain the dizzy, nauseating rush—and stared at Ash, the friend of her childhood. The young man with whom she'd always assumed she'd craft a life, a life dedicated to making the world a better place. He would work as a minster, she as a teacher. She would support him, just as he would support her.

Where was the sadness, the disappointment, at the prospect of such a life never materializing? She saw nothing of either in his eyes. Only determination, pity, and—merciful heavens—something that looked only too much like relief.

Surely she would have known if he hadn't wanted what she wanted.

And I don't think I ever will...

Had he never wished to marry her at all? And she'd just refused to see it?

She grasped the errant fan so tightly, its rivet pin bit into the palm of her hand. "How could you not tell me, Ash?"

He was back to not looking at her again. "You know how I hate to argue. And so do you."

"Me, hate to argue? But I'll debate with anyone, about anything!"

"About political issues, yes. You'll happily take up the cudgels against anyone who disagrees about outlawing cruelty to animals, or who objects to paying labourers what to your mind is a fair wage, or who argues that slavery should be abolished gradually rather than immediately. But you never like to talk about feelings, especially if you think someone doesn't share yours."

Her mind scrambled, sifting her memory for examples to refute his claim. But she could not come up with a single one.

"That's a ridiculous excuse!" she heard herself exclaim, as if she could avoid her own failure by attacking him.

"Ridiculous?" Ash crossed his arms. "Or simply the truth?"

"It doesn't matter," she choked out. "You let me make all those plans, dream all those dreams, and never even once hinted that you didn't want the same. How could you be so cowardly and cruel as to never tell me so?"

"Because you never ask what I want!"

Sheba froze in place as his cry reverberated through the room.

Ash had shouted at her? With a harshness that struck almost as painfully as if he'd actually raised his hand to her?

Who was this stranger who had taken the place of her best friend?

Sheba took one faltering step back, another, blinking and blinking.

But Ash followed, a gloved finger jabbing at her chest. "You never asked me if I wished to work in your father's factory, you just arranged for it to happen. You never asked me if I felt called to the ministry, you just assumed I'd want to fulfill my father's wishes. And you never, not even once, asked if I wanted to marry you. You just assumed that since you believed it would be so, I would, too."

"But still, you could have told me no—"

"No, I couldn't," Ash shouted again. "Because you never let me speak for myself! You're always so sure you know what's right, what's best! And we all just follow along, rats to your pied piper, enticed by the confidence of your utter certainty. But I'm tired of it, Sheba. I'm tired of always doing your bidding. I need to make my own decisions now. And the first decision I'm making is finally saying no to you."

Sheba closed her eyes, blinking against the prickling heat rising behind her eyelids. Surely she wasn't going to *cry*?

Ash sighed, then brought his hands to her shoulders, thumbs brushing both encouragement and dismissal against her clavicles. "Go home, Sheba. Scrub that silly paint off your face, take down those ridiculous curls, and go back to Leicester. Go back home and leave me to decide for myself what is right."

She stared and stared, tendrils of ice unfurling in her chest, crackling like frost on a winter windowpane.

He waited a long time for her to answer. But she could not summon the wherewithal to say a word.

At long last, he stepped back, bowed, then turned on his heel and strode from the room.

CHAPTER 14

"Silliman, what's wrong?"

Noel reached out a hand to slow his cousin, who had almost knocked him clear over the rail of Silliman House's grand staircase in his rush to reach the top. Noel had never seen such an expression on the younger man's face, jaw set, brow furrowed, mouth pinched tighter than an oyster's shell.

"Nothing. If you will excuse me, I have guests to entertain." Ash shook off his hand without even a glance and hurried towards the ballroom.

Noel's eyes narrowed as he stared up at his cousin's rapidly disappearing back, then back down the staircase, over to the door from which he'd emerged. Had Ash argued with Sheba? She'd certainly abandoned Viscount Dulcie, her partner at dinner, with little ceremony. And a decidedly determined glint in her eye, too.

If Ash had told her about Miss Gabbidon, and received a reaction anything like their grandmother's...

He hurried down the staircase, crossed the passageway, then pushed aside the library door.

Bathsheba Honeychurch stood by the window, frowning fiercely at her dim reflection as she scrubbed a handkerchief roughly over her cheeks. The ribbon which had encircled her waist at the start of the evening now lay on the floor by her feet, surrounded by a scatter of brass pins. And the neat coil of hair that those pins had been constraining had fallen, leaving long blonde tresses hanging down over the blades of her shoulders and the soft curve of her breast.

Disheveled. Improper. Utterly unsuitable.

And still his heart flailed about in his chest, helpless as a cod entangled in a fisherman's net.

She must have heard the hitch of his breath, for she spun round, shoving the handkerchief behind her back.

Even in the dim candlelight, he could see the glisten of tears in the corners of her eyes.

He strode into the room, just managing to keep his arms, his hands, to himself. "Whatever is the matter, Sheba?"

She gave an odd sort of hitching laugh. "The matter? Nothing is the matter. In fact, I have the happiest of news."

Noel's stomach plummeted. Surely Ash had not proposed…

"Just what you have been wishing for, in fact, ever since you first caught sight of me," she added when he could not bring himself to ask.

He gave a bitter laugh. "I doubt you have the least idea what I wish."

"No? Have you not told me from almost the first moment we met that I am an entirely unsuitable match for the exalted head of your family?"

His breath caught. "My cousin has broken with you?"

She mistook the eagerness in his tone entirely. "Yes. He has finally told me he cannot, will not, marry me. How very pleased you must be."

His hands fisted. "Miss Honeychurch. Sheba. You must know your disappointment gives me no pleasure."

"And here I thought you'd be crowing over your triumph."

Defiant, those words, but the furrows in that smooth brow, the droop of those usually proud shoulders—no, he had not the least desire to crow.

He took a step closer, in spite of his rational brain warning him to keep his distance. "I may have believed you an unwise choice as the future partner of an earl. But I have not once spoken a word against you, nor encouraged my cousin to drop your acquaintance."

"Perhaps not directly. You're far too crafty for that. A master of artfulness you are, Noel Griffin."

Yes. Far better that she argue with him than sink further into distress. He'd never been very good at offering comfort. "Artfulness?"

"Yes, artfulness!" Her hands—gloves long gone—balled in fists by her side. "You keep Ash so busy with his new duties that he has no time left for himself or for me. You play without cease on what he owes to Silliman family honor, but pay no heed to the family he left behind in Leicester. And you insist on the importance of your ridiculous aristocratic social conventions, conventions that have nothing to do with the religious values with which he was raised. Conventions that demand he marry a lady of rank, and certainly not a lowly Friend from the provinces. Do you deny you have done it?"

His eyes narrowed. "I have no wish of denying it. I did everything in my power to help my cousin reconcile himself to the duties and responsibilities of his new rank."

"Help him? You've turned him into your puppet, directing his every action, his every choice!"

Noel's jaw clenched. "My cousin's choices may often align with mine, ma'am, but I assure you, he is no puppet. Perhaps he listens to my counsel because I take pains to persuade him of what I think is right."

"Persuade? Friends do not persuade! We believe people should be left to their own liberty, and not pressed to act in any way which the guide within does not move them."

He took a step closer. "Of course Quakers persuade, or

attempt to persuade. Why else would they send ministers out to harangue the public about the immorality of their behavior? Why else would you rebuke my cousin like a wayward child whenever he fails to conform to your wishes?"

She stepped closer, too, her hands fisting on her hips. "I do not treat him like a child! I only wish to remind him of what is right, what is true! If he would only listen to the infallible guide within—"

"It strikes me that you'd prefer him to listen to the infallible guide *without*—to yourself. Because Bathsheba Honeychurch is never at a loss to explain what is right and true."

Before he had even finished speaking, her mouth tensed, ready to tear yet another strip off his reprehensible hide. But after he uttered that harsh last sentence, the words died on her lips.

And then, those lips began to tremble. "Ash said that, too." Her blue eyes fixed on him, wide, appalled. "That I always think I'm right. That I never listen to him or ask him what he wants."

She whirled, as if she could not face him a moment longer. Damn, why was he always such a clumsy fool when it came to dealing with people's feelings?

She pressed her palms against the pane of the window, then tipped her head to rest her brow against it. "I truly thought my heart was animated by a sincere and fervent wish for his happiness, not my own. Or not only my own." Her voice cracked in dismay. "Why did I never think to ask him what would make him so?"

The sight of Bathsheba Honeychurch lashing herself with such recrimination—no, it was wrong, wrong to see such a confident, determined woman brought so low. Especially by his own hand, or rather, by the cruelty of his own words. And it wasn't entirely her fault, was it? His cousin had been in the wrong, too.

He swallowed as that hand rose, brushed aside the spill of her hair, then pressed lightly between the delicate blades of her shoulders. Her entire body trembled at his touch.

"I haven't known him for as long as you have, but my cousin strikes me as a person who values the happiness of others far more than he values his own," he began.

She nodded. "His father instilled in him the utter importance of the commandment to love thy neighbor as thyself."

Perhaps because as a youth the man had so utterly failed to live by it himself?

But Sheba had uttered those words completely without irony. Ash must not have confided in her about their latest family scandal.

"An admirable goal," he acknowledged with all the diplomacy he could muster. "Yet it can be difficult to know the truth of such a man, a man who pretends he has no needs of his own."

"Pretends?"

"Yes, pretends. No one, no matter how saintly, can be entirely without needs or desires of his own."

"But if I had only asked him what he wanted, what he needed—"

"Even then, he might not have told you," Noel said. "Not when what he wanted was apparently so at odds with your own wishes."

She frowned at him over her shoulder. "Does not his anger at me for *not* asking suggest precisely the opposite?"

"He grew angry with you?"

"So very angry. Ash Griffin, who has never raised his voice to anyone for as long as I've known him, shouted at me."

Her lips began to tremble again. Noel fought against the urge to chase down his cousin and plant the callow boy a facer.

He grasped Sheba's shoulders and turned her to face him. "He was angry at himself, Sheba, as much as he was with you. Perhaps even more so."

"With himself?"

"Yes. He wants to make everyone happy, but there is no way

he can reconcile your needs with my grandmother's, never mind his own. You should have asked him what he wanted, yes. But if you had, it might only have made the impossibility of pleasing everyone too painfully obvious. He was angry with you for making him face what he's been avoiding—that no matter what he does, he'll end up hurting someone, someone he cares for deeply. I'm only sorry that someone has proven to be you."

She hugged her arms tight across her chest. "I know I'll never make a suitable wife for an aristocrat. But if there were some way the title could be yours, rather than Ash's, perhaps he and I might—"

He shook his head. "It wouldn't matter. Because even if he were only a simple Quaker, you and he still would not suit."

She jerked away, her shoulder hitting the frame of the window. "Whatever makes you say such a thing?"

"Because it's the truth, Sheba! Ash may care for you, may even love you, albeit as a friend. But he isn't the right husband for you."

She bowed her head. "Yes. Because I failed to see what he wanted, what he needed."

"No! You might not have understood Ash, but he doesn't understand you, doesn't appreciate, you, either. Tradition, convention, that's what's he holds most dear. He thrived on following the rules of your religious Society, yes, but once he accustoms himself to them, he'll thrive on following the rules of polite aristocratic society just as well. You, though—well, you've never been bound by meaningless social expectations, by the way things are and have always been. No, Bathsheba Honeychurch, you want to change the world."

He slipped a gloved finger beneath her chin, raising her doubting eyes to his. "And I value you for it, Sheba. Value you, and honor you."

He saw the flicker of recognition in her eyes at his deliberate echo of her own words to him a little over a month ago. The words that had revealed to him the truth of his own feelings for her.

Wishful thinking, to hope they might have anything close to the same effect on her.

She drew in a ragged breath. "Noel, I thought you didn't like me. Have we not been at daggers drawn from the first moment we met?"

His laugh sounded pained, even to his own ears. "Didn't like you? Did I not just explain how a fearful man uses anger to push away someone who forces him to see a truth he's not willing to face?"

"What truth?"

She'd accused him of being crafty, cunning, always planning and scheming to manipulate his way to his own ends. Yet the words that came tumbling out of his mouth had never felt so artless, so utterly beyond his control.

"The passion you have for all your political causes. The directness and honesty of the truths you tell. Even, God help me, that annoyingly, endearingly righteous attitude you take, expecting everyone to live up to the same high standards to which you hold yourself." He laughed. "Not like you? When I can't stop wishing I could be a part of all your causes? Can't stop thinking about how I might work to change the world, too, and perhaps prove myself worthy of one of your approving smiles?"

He swept a finger from the edge of her eye down the curve of her cheek, tracing the white salt trail of her tears. Clear evidence of the pain of being rejected by the man she truly loved.

And still he could not keep the words inside.

"When I can't stop wondering what it would be like to kiss you?"

For long, tense moments, the shock of his admission hovered between them. And then he was staggering, reeling, stunned with unexpected delight as she threw herself into his arms.

Too much. Too much, the sharp bite of anger and disappointment and self-loathing. The pain of Ash's rejection, the trembling terror of the gaping, empty hole which she had always assumed was the firmest of grounds, the ground upon which all her future plans had rested. Too much to take in, to understand, to control. Too much to feel.

And so she threw years of lessons about the evils of fornication, years of cautions and admonishments to self-control, threw it all to the winds. Threw herself at Noel and kissed him, kissed him to feel nothing, anything, instead of the obliterating clamor of self-recrimination and doubt. To stifle it, drown it, deep in the clasp of welcoming arms, the soft-rough press of unfamiliar lips.

"Sheba." The guttural growl of her name, the press of his mouth against the line of her throat. Shivers of awareness coursing through her hands, down her spine, over her entire person. The spring of his hair beneath her palm; the sweet, honeyed spice of his pomade; the secret silky smoothness of the tiny hairs at the back of his neck. She reveled in it, lost herself in sensation, in the present, in the now of her body and his, pressed tight, close, sheltered in a quiet cocoon of belonging.

She pulled away, overtaken by the need to trace her thumb over the bridge of his nose, the wings of his brows. How simple a touch could make a reserved man shudder! And suddenly her own hunger grew, as great as the skies, dark and vast, yet bright with the spark of stars. And she was kissing him again, kissing his lips, the line of his jaw, the shocking softness of the lobe of his ear.

And, to her utter shock, biting that lobe, now, too. Short, sharp nips, warning that if he could make her forget herself, so, too, could she make him.

He jerked and groaned, then tilted his head closer, offering himself up for long, heady moments to the pleasure-pain of her touch. She nudged her nose against the curve of his ear, then bit the lobe again, hard.

Why? Why should she want to tease him but also to hurt him, too?

Because the anger and humiliation of what had come before would not remain at bay, no matter the strength of her wanting?

Her anger-fueled aggression should have frightened him away. Yet it only seemed to excite him further. With a deep groan, he set his arms beneath her bottom and pulled her to his chest, then carried her to a desk beside the library door, the silk of her skirts rustling between them. With a groan of frustration, he bit at the tips of his gloves, yanking and pulling until each finger flew free. She gasped as the unfamiliar heat of bare palms slid along her jaw, beneath the coils of her fallen hair.

"Forget him, Sheba love," Noel whispered, drawing her face close to his. "Kiss *me*."

And she did. Closed her eyes and kissed and kissed, drinking from his lips as if from the wells of salvation. Kissed until her lips fluttered and throbbed, swollen and lush with yearning. Kissed the only person who still seemed to respect her, care for her, want her.

Was she kissing him? Truly kissing Noel Griffin? When she'd never set her own lips against anyone's before? Her male cousins, jackanapes and roysters all, completely unworthy of girlish romantic fancies. The boys of Leicester Meeting, far too self-disciplined to talk of, never mind act on, burgeoning sensuous appetites. And Ash—

No, Ash had never kissed her, had he? Not beyond a friendly buss on the forehead or cheek...

Certainly not like his cousin was kissing her now. Kissing her like a man ravenous, starving, greedy in his need. As if the rational, controlled gentleman he showed the world were merely a front, a blind behind which hid a shockingly insatiable passion. A passion which met her inexperience—her sudden confusion about where to place her hands, whether to pull her lips away and return or to press all the harder against his—with no derision, no dismay. Only with an eagerness as forceful as a torrent, a torrent sweeping her up in its fearsome, welcome rush. Making her forget, forget worries and frustrations, plans and dreams, past and future, everything, utterly, entirely.

Everything except how it felt to be held, to be *wanted*.

Voices murmured from the passageway, distant, meaningless. Nothing to the pounding of her own heart, the pulse of his against the palms she'd pressed to the silk of his waistcoat.

Until the murmur grew into a rumble, and then into the scrape of an opening door...

"And here, over the mantel, you will find the portrait of Lord Silliman's father and his brothers, taken when they were all just boys. Very like, you will find the current earl, very like!"

Noel's hands froze at the jarring intrusion of his grandmother's voice.

"Here, Silliman, give your arm to Lady Wilhelmina while Lord Dulcie holds the cand—"

Sheba blinked, less at the sudden burst of light than at the gasp of dismay from Frances Griffin. Dulcie—the popinjay from dinner—had swept the candelabrum not only forward, towards the mantel, but then backwards, revealing a no-doubt disheveled Sheba perched on the desk. And her grandson—the wrong grandson—pressed tight to her side.

Sheba's eyes pinched shut, as if by closing them she might make the entire awful scene disappear.

But the popinjay would not cooperate. "Lord Ruxf—I mean, Mr. Griffin—and Miss Honeychurch? But did not the gossip mill have it that the chit was hanging out after you, Silliman?" The man's voice nearly squeaked in excitement and incredulity.

Dulcie's words jerked Noel from immobility. Pulling free of

Sheba's arms, he stepped in front of her, as if it were still possible to shield her betumbled state from the uneasily milling guests.

"Dulcie. Of course," he muttered.

Sheba suddenly recalled Polly's dismay at discovering her fiancé numbered among the most scurrilous gossips of the *ton*...

"Yes, Silliman, what is your cousin doing accosting *your* lady?" another supercilious male voice gibed.

"What an insult! And in your own house, too!"

She couldn't bring herself to look at Ash. But Noel—even though she couldn't see his face, she saw his entire body stiffen.

Did he think it a mistake, what they had done?

Did she?

"What are you going to do about it, Silliman?" asked another nattily-dressed young spark.

"No true gentleman would stand for such an affront to his honor," taunted a third, his brows raised in clear scorn.

Noel scowled, then took a step toward Ash. "Silliman. Send these men away so we may talk in private."

"Ladies, please. Let us leave the gentlemen to discuss this matter amongst themselves," one of the older women urged.

"Yes, the final dance of the evening will be starting soon. You wouldn't wish to miss it, would you?" another asked as she guided a younger woman toward the door.

"But I thought she was a Quaker? Are not Quakers the chastest of women?" one of the young ladies whispered, peering over her shoulder at Sheba as her mother—aunt? elder sister?—chivvied her from the room.

Sheba's fingers clutched at Noel's hand as a long, tense stillness enveloped the room. What were they to do?

A low, serious voice finally broke the taut silence. "An insult to a lady under a gentleman's care is a greater offense than if given to a gentleman himself, Silliman. Will you not demand satisfaction from the blackguard?"

Demand satisfaction? Surely he could not mean a duel?

Sheba finally dared a look at Ash. But he refused to meet her gaze, his eyes fixed on the carpet at his feet.

"I would be happy to serve as your second, and make all suitable arrangements, as you are unfamiliar with the conventions," another man offered, laying a hand against Ash's shoulder. "Or Debenham, if you'd prefer."

A tall, dark-haired gentleman nodded. "Certainly, Raikes,"

But Ash remained silent, confusion and indecision creasing his face.

"Surely you won't sacrifice the respect of your peers by allowing this slight to stand, Silliman?" an older gentleman asked, shock and disgust in every outraged syllable.

"Enough!" Sheba pushed with all her strength, sending a clearly startled Noel stumbling into the center of the room. She jumped off the desk, folded her arms, and gazed in turn at each of the young bucks collected around Ash with all the contempt she could muster. "Enough. There will be no ungodly violence here."

"Ungodly violence? Here? Spoken just like a ranting dissenter," a thin, narrow-faced man scoffed. "As if we would hold a duel in the middle of a ball. No, we'll arrange for them to meet tomorrow morning. That is, if Griffin refuses to offer a suitable apology. Whom should I contact as your second, man?"

Noel's hands fisted by his sides. "Someone find Viscount Stiles."

Debenham—or was it Raikes?—dashed from the room, clearly as eager to spread gossip as he was to summon Spencer.

Sheba glared at Noel and Ash in turn, but neither would meet her eye. They stared only at each other.

Sheba's hands slid from her hips, limp, trembling. What had she done? Did they truly mean to engage in a duel?

Noel, lying on the ground, wounded, at Ash's hand—Ash, bleeding, dying, at Noel's—All because of her—

Stupid, impetuous fool! Would she never learn?

Spencer pushed through the crowd of gentleman surrounding them, Delphie close on his heels. "Bathsheba? Noel? What's happened?"

The crowd about them held its collective breath, all eager, bloodthirsty anticipation, waiting for one of them to speak.

No. She had to stop this. Had to stop this *now*, before Ash or Noel said something they couldn't take back.

But how?

Forcing herself to smile her broadest smile, to pitch her voice loudly enough for every single gossipmonger in the room to hear, she held out her hands to Delphie.

"Wish us happy, cousin. Noel Griffin and I are betrothed."

CHAPTER 15

Noel stood by the window in Stiles' Conduit Street drawing room, shifting uneasily from foot to booted foot. In the pocket of his tailcoat, the ring he'd taken from his mother's jewel box perched on tip of his thumb. His index finger flicked it off into the pocket's depths, then searched it out again and slid it on, stopping when it hit the joint of the first knuckle. Slide it on, flick it off, search it out again, over and over while he waited to see if the ring would even be necessary at all.

Nothing about marrying Bathsheba Honeychurch made the least bit of sense. Her longstanding affection for his cousin, his grandmother's dismay at the inferiority of her rank, her commitment to religious beliefs so different from his own—every rational consideration argued against such a match.

Oh, he'd come up with a logical excuse to explain why he hadn't immediately denied Sheba's brazen announcement. Contradicting Sheba would not only damage *his* reputation, he'd reminded his grandmother, but (more importantly to the countess) would set the ugliest of blots on the Silliman escutcheon.

But the truth, he feared, was far less noble. For it wasn't honor that sang in his veins, urging him to keep her to that impetuous proposal. No, it was something stubborn, and selfish, and utterly beyond the control of any intellectual faculty. Something that insisted, no, *demanded*, that for once in his long, dutiful life, he reach out and take what *he* wanted. Something, some*one*, that he could call his own.

He doubted, though, if Sheba's shocking declaration meant she felt anything close to the same.

But if he could persuade her to go through with the charade, perhaps in time she might—

"Miss Honeychurch." A footman held open the door for a far more restrained Bathsheba than the wild-eyed girl he'd embarrassed so horribly only the night before. In his pocket, Noel's hand clenched, the bezel clasping the ring's ruby rough against his palm. Even dressed in a grave gown of sober brown, her hair coiled tightly in a simple knot, she still made the breath catch in his throat. No, no dress she donned, no matter how demure, could ever make him forget the passion with which she'd kissed him, the fervency of her fingers as they'd searched out all the places that made him tremble. The way she'd nibbled, then *bit*, the tender lobe of his ear...

Her eyes locked on his, determined, defiant. Yes, if he were allowed even a small share of that passion—in his bed, in his life—he'd marry her today, his cousin, his grandmother, the gossips of the *ton* all be damned...

A slight clearing of the throat jerked his eyes from Sheba's. Lady Stiles had accompanied her cousin. She gave him an encouraging smile, then took up some needlework at the opposite end of the room. They'd been granted a modicum of privacy, then. But not enough for any unruly passions to land them in trouble again.

"Noel, I'm so very sorry to have entangled you in such a mess." Sheba paced between the drawing room windows, viciously twisting her hands, as if worried he'd only regard her penitence as sincere if she pulled them clear off. "I was awake most of the night trying to think how to free you from this terrible pass. I could apologize to Ash, and to your grandmother, if you think that would suffice? Or would Ash's new friends still insist he challenge you? I fear they have come to have far more influence over him than they ought. If that is the case, I could write to the elders of Leicester Meeting and beg them to send Ash a letter admonishing him against dueling. Friend Farrand might even come to London if he thought the situation dire. Or perhaps it would be better for me to return to Leicester, and allow the gossip to die down? Oh, I did so wish to attend the meeting of the Anti-Slavery Society on Friday, to hear Wilberforce and Stephen and all the other famous abolitionists speak about how best to bring an end to the evil institution. But I would leave town immediately, today, even, if you thought it best—"

"Sheba. Please. All this pacing will do nothing but rub the carpet bare." Of course she would come up with a dozen potential solutions to their situation, and be unable to decide on any of them. "Sit here beside me, and we can discuss which, if any, of your ideas is worth pursuing."

Sheba dropped down to the settee, pressing her palms against her flaming cheeks. "How can you be so calm when I've ruined everything? If only I hadn't thrown myself at you like a veritable drab in the street—"

"Don't say such a disparaging thing about yourself, not ever again!" The harshness of his tone surprised him. But he took care to be gentle as he drew her hands away from her face and cradle them in his own. "You may have begun, but I didn't stop, even knowing the strictures of the *ton* far better than you. The fault is not yours, but mine."

"Yours?" She shook her head, sending stray wisps of hair flying. "You may have overlooked society's rules, but I completely ignored the lessons not only of my parents, but of my church. No person of faith would ever condone such wanton behavior. And yet I did not stop, either."

Confusion, recrimination—and could that be a touch of wonder?—warred in her eyes.

He gave her hands an encouraging squeeze. "Then perhaps we may agree that we were both at fault, and move on to the more pressing issue—what is to be done about it."

"Perhaps." She gave a great, gusting sigh, then glanced up at him with bright, blinking eyes. "Are any of my ideas likely to help?"

"All intriguing possibilities. But I'm not convinced any of them would achieve the desired goal."

"To keep you and Ash from killing each other in a pointless duel?"

"I am not going to fight a duel, especially with my own cousin."

She bent her head and pressed her hands to her face, her relief palpable.

He tamped down the urge to raise that head between his two hands, press his lips to her brow, her cheek, that lush, receptive mouth. No. Not yet.

"What we need is to keep the gossips at bay, and prevent undue damage to your reputation, or to Silliman's," he said instead.

"I don't care a fig about my reputation. But I know how much you value yours. What must I do to salvage it? If you don't care for any of my suggestions, what would you have us do?"

She had a care for his reputation? A bud of warmth blossomed in Noel's chest.

He crossed his arms to contain the unfamiliar feeling and settled back against the settee. "I didn't say I didn't care for *any* of your suggestions. In fact, I believe your initial instinct—to declare ourselves betrothed—to be the most logical path a couple in our situation could take. An illicit passion will preoccupy the gossips for weeks, but one condoned by marriage —or at least, by the promise of an impending marriage—might burn bright for a few days, but will soon be displaced by more salacious scandal."

"But we are not betrothed. I only said it because I couldn't think of any other way to stop you and Ash from fighting!"

"And just how did you come up with such an idea? I didn't think you knew enough about the ways of the *ton* to realize an engagement might excuse, or at least explain, our—our situation."

Sheba gave a small grimace. "I may have little direct experience of fashionable society myself, but my Grandmother Audley certainly has. Each summer she tells me and my Audley cousins the same old stories about the giddy times she spent as a girl in London searching for a suitable husband. When that horrible Debenham man kept goading Ash to challenge you, the memory of one popped into my head. About two of Grandmother's friends, each of whom were caught forgetting themselves with men who were no better than they should be. Both ended up forced to marry the men to stave off a duel. A Lady Something or other, and the Countess of—oh, better not to repeat names. Grandmother always said that both ended up regretting those marriages."

Lady Something and the Countess of—Yes, Noel could fill in those names quite easily without any help from Sheba. Several candidates for each, in fact. Marriage might prevent open opprobrium, but scandal had a far longer memory.

"She meant to caution my cousins to take care during their own future London seasons, I think. But in the end, none of them even had one. Anna died, and Delphie and Connie both married young, before they could even be presented at Court. Polly, traipsing about the Continent studying art with her grandfather, had no desire to make her come out, and Elizabeth's family couldn't afford to give her one." Sheba gave a dull laugh. "Who would ever have thought I'd be the Audley cousin most in need of Grandmother's warnings? Regrettable marriage indeed!"

"You would find a marriage to any man not Ash regrettable?" Noel slipped the ring off his thumb and let it fall to the bottom of his pocket. "Or only a marriage to me?"

She stared up at him, her eyes wide. "Surely you don't wish to marry me?"

Did her words convey dismay? Hope? Or simply sheer disbelief? He couldn't quite tell...

He couldn't acknowledge, even to himself, how afraid he was to even ask. Instead, he summoned the analytical, calculating front he always used to protect himself from complicated, confusing wells of feeling.

"We can't openly deny our betrothal if we wish to avoid scandal. But this—this incident occurred at the very end of the season, not at its height. If we spend this next week or two being seen about town together, the gossips will take our betrothal as confirmed, and the young bucks will stop teasing Ash to issue me a challenge." Two weeks would be better than nothing, though hardly all he wanted.

"I don't understand. Do you mean for us to be engaged or not?"

He leaned toward her, yearning to kiss away each wrinkle of confusion marring that adorably worried brow. A rustle of skirts from across the room reminded him they were not alone. He pulled back, setting his palms carefully atop his knees.

"The *ton* will soon leave London for the summer, scattering to their various country estates. When Parliament reconvenes and everyone returns to town in the fall, Lady Silliman can bruit it about that after spending the summer together, we realized we would not suit. Surely by then, another scandal will have caught the gossips' attention, leaving our *faux pas* to the annals of the past."

"You wish me to pretend to be engaged? To continue the awful lie I started? Oh, what a tangle." Sheba's fingers threaded through her hair, pressing tight against her head.

"It would only be a lie if the betrothal were entirely make-believe."

Her forehead wrinkled. "How could it be anything but?"

If I loved you, and you loved me back?

Noel blinked away the maudlin sentiment. As if he would ever allow such words to pass his lips...

"If we considered it a trial of sorts," he offered instead. "We know we are compatible in certain respects—" His eye fell to her mouth as her teeth bit against her lower lip, suggesting she understood all too well the sort of compatibility to which he referred. "We can use these next few weeks to see whether that compatibility might extend to other parts of our lives."

"Compatibility? Is that all you wish of a wife? Compatibility?"

Noel blinked. He'd never given it much thought, what he might want in, or from, a wife. "What in heaven's name is wrong with compatibility? To mutually tolerate one another's foibles, to meet across the breakfast table each morning and dinner table each evening with no expectation of argument or dispute—yes, compatibility is certainly a worthy goal in a marriage partner."

Sheba frowned. "I will never become a poor passive machine, a mere smiling wife."

They both turned at the sound of a throat clearing from across the room.

Noel shifted closer to Sheba. "Compatibility doesn't require a wife to be any such thing," he objected.

Her head tilted to one side. "Does it not? Were your parents compatible? Your grandparents?"

Noel blinked again. He could barely remember his parents spending any time together at all before they died, even during those rare weeks when his father was not away at sea. As for his grandparents... Well, Lady Silliman had never disagreed with her husband, not in public or in private, had she? But did that mean that she and the earl had been compatible? Or rather that she'd simply stifled her own thoughts, her own needs, in favor of her husband's?

"Were yours?" he asked instead.

She gave him a considering look. "Yes, in fact, I believe they were, although you wouldn't have thought it to look at them. My father is a man of business, which interested my mother not a jot. And my mother's religious calling—he could never understand it, no matter how fervently she preached. Yet a word as tepid as 'compatible' doesn't do justice to what they shared. He mourned her deeply—mourns her still."

And was still so caught up in his mourning that he failed to pay proper attention to his daughter, Noel guessed. Sheba hadn't expressed the least fear, or even worry, about word of the scandal reaching him in Leicester.

It should have made Noel happy, knowing he needn't cajole a doting father into granting him permission to court his daughter. But something inside him ached, thinking of a younger Sheba losing the guidance of not just one, but both parents. Just as he had, himself.

"They respected one another, and loved one another," Sheba continued when he remained silent. "She was his equal.

"Is that what you wish of a husband? To be thought his equal?"

"Not just to be thought it. But to be *treated* as such. I know I'm not nearly as deserving of such treatment as my mother was, but still, I cannot help but wish for a friend, a companion, a true union of minds and spirits."

"'A friend, a companion, a second self; one that bears an equal share with thee in all thy toils and troubles. Then thou hast a wife.'"

Sheba gasped. "How do you know the words of William Penn?"

"Grandmother told me you offered her advice and mentioned his name. I was curious to find out more about a man whose wisdom you found worthy of sharing."

Sheba's steepled hands pressed against her lips.

That his small attempt to forge a connection with her by reading what she admired should soften her eyes so—

Another clearing of the throat sounded from across the room, this one considerably louder than the last. "Have you come to a decision, my dears? Or have your debates about the perfect marriage partner distracted you from your purpose?"

Affectionate, Lady Stiles' smile, yet also pointed. Yes, it was more than time to bring this discussion to an end.

Noel reached into his pocket. "It's common now for a betrothal ring to be made of diamonds, but I knew you'd reject anything so showish. This one belonged to my mother, and to her mother and grandmother before her. It was given to each upon her betrothal. If you wear it, and are seen in my company these next two weeks, you needn't say a word about whether we are engaged or no. Everyone will simply assume it to be so."

He tugged at the two clasped hands at the ring's front, revealing that the ring was actually comprised of three interlocking piecrust bands. On the middle one, hidden behind the clasped hands, lay two gold hearts.

A fede gimmel ring—*fede*, or faith, symbolized by the clasped hands; *gimmel*, from the French *gemel*, or twin, for the interlocking bands held together by a pin. Together, an emblem of the union of two into one.

He snapped the ring shut, then took her hand in his. "I would be honored if you would wear it, too. At least for the next few weeks. May I?"

"I won't lie," Sheba said, thrusting up her chin. "If someone asks me directly if we are betrothed, I will have to say no."

"I understand," Noel acknowledged, silently promising her he'd make every effort to avoid any situation which would force her to.

He waited, then, his stomach tight, as she considered the ring for what seemed an excruciatingly long moment.

Finally, she swallowed, then nodded, and stretched out her hand.

He slid the ring carefully over her ring finger, until it came to rest at the base.

A perfect fit.

"Ladies and Gentlemen, I am afraid I have taken up too much of your time. I have only to add—I trust you will all persevere in this great, this just cause, in which we must act with temper, but at the same time with zeal and firmness."

Sheba's ears rang with the clamor of clapping and cheers as the Duke of Gloucester brought the first public General Meeting of the Society for Mitigating and Gradually Abolishing the State of Slavery throughout the British Dominions to a rousing conclusion. Never in her life had she witnessed such an immense gathering of the politically-minded, not even at last month's Quaker Yearly Meeting. Why, nearly a thousand men, and a goodly number of women, too, must be packed inside Freemasons Hall this afternoon!

When they'd first entered the hall, she'd been taken aback by the wealth of pagan masonic emblems decorating nearly every part of the Hall, as well as by the range of semicircular windows placed far above their heads on the towering walls—to prevent the masonic ceremonies from being observed from adjacent buildings, Spencer had helpfully explained. But none of that mattered now. Because being surrounded by so many people, all deeply committed to the same just cause—why, she had never felt such energy, such a sense of shared purpose.

How inspiring, to hear the son of the great William Wilberforce read aloud the report of the Society! To cheer with the gathered crowd after the next speaker offered the resolution that, as the bondage in which eight hundred thousand of their fellow subjects were held was repugnant to the spirit of Christianity, contrary to the soundest maxims of policy, and a gross violation of the principles of humanity and justice, the members of the Society should pledge themselves to the sacred cause of emancipation. To join the general assent to the call to renounce the use of West India produce. And to listen to the Nightingale of the Commons himself, the renowned Wilberforce, declare how the great cause had obtained such a degree of personal and moral strength that its final and decisive triumph could not but be assured.

The men in the audience had already been standing—the three rows of benches on each side of the long hall were reserved for female attendees only—but the women surrounding her now surged to their feet as well, joining the general acclaim.

So compelling, the speakers had been, she'd nearly forgotten these last few hours to fret over the impossible scheme she and Noel Griffin had concocted between them. A betrothal that wasn't quite a betrothal, meant to save him, and Ash, from the scandal in which she'd embroiled them both. But when she began to clap, the unfamiliar weight of the ring Noel had given her pressed hard against her palm, a smart of reminder that the righteousness of the indignation she felt at others' immoral actions could never banish the guilt of her own.

She glanced over her shoulder, searching for Noel's familiar, solemn face. Though he was not the tallest man in the grand hall, she found him easily in the crowd, standing in front of a square fluted column, Spencer at his side. Delphie's husband was speaking to him, but Noel's eyes were fixed on her. Flaring with intent, just as they had two mornings ago when he'd placed his mother's ring on her finger.

Intent that made her yearn to draw closer, even as her muscles tensed with the urge to flee.

"Sheba, dear, might you move toward the aisle?" Delphie's

hand pressed against her back. "We are keeping these kind ladies from rejoining their party."

"Oh, excuse me," she apologized to the plainly-dressed women milling behind Delphie. "My apologies, Friends."

The women smiled in fellowship as Sheba gathered her reticule and shifted towards the end of the bench, glad for any excuse to shift her attention away from Noel. It filled her with pride, seeing that so much of the audience, especially the women, were clearly Friends. The women Friends took such intense interest in the proceedings, their attention focused on the words of each speaker rather than on the chattering of their friends or the waving of their fans in the over-warm room, as several more fashionably-dressed women seated near them had done.

How satisfying it would be, to join with them in pursuit of such an important cause.

Delphie rose on her tiptoes, trying to see over the heads of the crowd toward the end of the hall. "Where are they? Can you see Spencer, Sheba? Or Mr. Griffin?"

Oh, if she could only not have to think about the coiled tangle of feelings Noel Griffin inspired for a little while longer! Her eyes searched in the opposite direction. Yes! A familiar face.

"Sheba, where are you taking me?" her cousin asked as Sheba towed her toward the upper end of the room. Decidedly away from where she'd last spied Spencer and Noel.

"Delphie, please, I wish to speak to William Allen, whom I met at Yearly Meeting," she explained.

"But he was one of the speakers! Surely he will be too busy to speak a to young lady."

"Oh, Delphie, you still do not understand the ways of Friends, do you?"

Sheba pulled her cousin through the crowds until they reached the older man. "Friend Allen, hello! My cousin Delphie Burnett and I wished you to know how glad we were to see you amongst the speakers today. Though your words were few, oh, how they inspired us!"

"Friend Honeychurch," the grey-haired man acknowledged with a kindly smile. "Friend Burnett. How good to see that you, and so many other women Friends, feel called as I do to protest the cruel traffic in human lives."

"Your advice to diffuse light and information on the subject within the utmost range of our influence struck me as particularly apt," Sheba replied, not pausing to correct the man's mistaken assumption about Delphie. "It is just as you say: if all gathered here would only spread the word, then when the Colonies came to the Ministers for support of the system of slavery, those Ministers *must* say 'It is impossible to bolster your system any longer; the people of England will not endure it.'"

"Yes, Friend Honeychurch. All the good we have heard this day, and all that is contemplated, will depend on the exertions which shall be made throughout the kingdom by such respectable persons as yourself."

"Yet so many here insist on the necessity of gradual, rather than immediate, emancipation," Sheba repined. "Each time a speaker cautioned against freeing the enslaved all at once, I had to press my lips tight to keep myself from crying out in protest." Oh, how every ounce of her being thrummed to speak out against the cowardice of the gradualists!

Soon, though, she'd be able to share Elizabeth Heyrick's pamphlet with each of those speakers, nay, with every single person in this room. Friend Phillips had come to an agreement with several other Quaker booksellers, as well as two Evangelical firms, to share the risk of publishing.

If only everyone in this room knew what she knew, what her teacher had made her truly see, they'd have to demand freedom for all men *now*, rather than at some unspecified date in the future. Immediate emancipation was the only stand a truly moral person could take.

A sudden stillness quieted the whirl of her thoughts. Was she meant to remain here in England, advocating for the anti-slavery cause, rather than travel abroad to minister and teach?

Was this what a leading from God felt like? Her mother had always described being called to the ministry as a private feeling, a message from above received in the deep silence of solitary contemplation, or when joined with others in quiet prayer. How odd, if she were to receive such a calling in the midst of a bustling crowd.

Or was she simply allowing the zeal of today's crowd to distract her from what God was truly calling her to do?

"Allen!" Another of the speakers, one whose name she couldn't recall, waved from the front of the Hall. "The Duke wishes to have a word."

Friend Allen patted her on the hand. "If you would excuse me, my dear."

Sheba frowned, watching a clutch of men bow and scrape to the froggy-faced brother of the king. As if the Duke of Gloucester's participation in today's proceedings should matter more than any of theirs, or hers. Why should so many people take his embrace of gradual, rather than immediate, abolition, as permission to keep ignoring the present sufferings of the wrongfully enslaved? Just because he happened to be a member of the royal family? Hadn't Spencer laughingly said many of his peers called the fellow "Silly Billy"?

How many of the people here today shared the duke's views?

Did Noel?

Surely not. A man who embraced the gradualist approach would never have come up with a way for Friend Phillips to publish Elizabeth Heyrick's pamphlet without endangering his publishing firm.

And she'd never really thanked him for that, had she?

"Sheba."

Sheba started at the murmur of Noel's voice, so close to her ear. Surely the simple thought of him had not drawn him to her side?

"Lady Georgiana, might I have the honor of introducing to you Miss Bathsheba Honeychurch?" he inquired, drawing forward a stylishly dressed young woman close to her own age.

Ringlets of dark hair bobbed against the woman's wide forehead. "A pleasure to make your acquaintance, ladies," she said, her voice pipingly sweet.

"And yours," Sheba answered. Why had Noel had taken the trouble to introduce her to such a fashionable creature? And why should she feel a sudden urge to scowl at the sight of such a beautiful woman by his side?

Would he scowl if she addressed this fine lady as "Friend Georgiana"?

Noel, perhaps guessing her dilemma, bowed to Delphie. "May I also introduce Lady Stiles, Miss Honeychurch's cousin? Or are you already acquainted?"

"I don't believe I've had the pleasure," the young woman said. "The wife of Lord Stiles, son of the Earl of Morse?"

At Delphie's nod, the lady grasped Delphie's hands and gave them a quick squeeze. "Oh, how glad you must be that he has come back home! I would never have consented to marry a diplomatic man myself. How very distressing, to be forced to choose between traveling so far from home or parting from my dear George for years on end!"

"Lady Georgiana married George Agar-Ellis, Lord Clifton's heir, two Seasons ago," Noel explained. "Mr. Agar-Ellis was the gentleman who moved today's first resolution."

"You are married to one of the abolitionists?" Sheba asked. "Oh, how eager I am to become acquainted with others committed to the cause!"

"So I understand from Mr. Griffin," the lady said with a gracious smile. "I am holding an evening conversazione Tuesday next, if you would care to join us. You and Lady Stiles both, of course, although I fear I cannot extend the invitation to Mr. Griffin. The conversazione will be for ladies only. But he has promised me, Miss Honeychurch, that your quick mind will be certain to enliven our discussions."

"Promised? Or warned?" Sheba asked, risking a glance up at Noel. But nothing disdainful, nothing even the least bit mocking, marred his features. And though he did not offer her a smile, something far different than disdain seemed to enliven his expression, his eyes. Affection? Admiration?

She dropped her eyes, the fingers of her right hand twisting the ring he had placed on her left. How odd, to feel such an unfamiliar, and uncomfortably disconcerting, shyness with a stranger. Had Noel truly sung her praises to the woman?

"You are very kind, Lady Georgiana," Delphie said. "But I fear we may have left London by then. My cousin's father wrote me only last week, urging me to make arrangements for her return to Leicester."

Sheba pulled at the strings of her reticule. She *had* promised her father she'd return home after attending today's Anti-Slavery meeting. But to have come all the way to London, only to miss an evening's conversation devoted to discussing the anti-slavery cause with like-minded women? Especially when Noel had made such an effort to procure the invitation for her—

Sheba grasped Delphie's arm. "But we've made no fixed plans of yet, have we? We could easily spend a few more days in town."

"Indeed," Noel added. "I've several engagements that will not permit me to travel until next Friday at the earliest."

Sheba blinked. "You plan to come with us?"

"Of course he does," Lady Georgiana exclaimed, tapping her fan against the ring on Sheba's finger. "A letter begging permission to pay his addresses to a man's daughter may do for *some*, but a true gentleman will always wish to make his request in person."

"I've already discussed the matter with Stiles, and he has no objection to the delay," Noel said before the urge to disavow the woman's assumption could escape Sheba's lips.

She stared up at him, her eyes no doubt filled with questions. Did he truly mean to travel to Leicester? To speak with her father?

But he knew she'd never ask such questions in the midst of a crowd.

She looked down, then, and toyed again with the ring he'd given her, her fingers playing over the piecrust band, the clasped fingers hiding the two tiny hearts. What would Noel think of her father? And what would her father think of him?

"Then we thank you for the invitation, my lady," Delphie said with a curtsey. "We would be pleased to attend."

"I look forward to furthering our acquaintance, then. But for now, I must bid you good-day. Poor George is like to have his ear talked clear off if I don't rescue him from all this political tittle-tattle! Lady Stiles. Miss Honeychurch." And with a curtsey of her own, and a rustle of lace and silk, the elegant lady disappeared into the crowd.

Noel offered one arm to Sheba, the other to Delphie. Her cousin chatted amicably as he guided them with care through the crowd still milling in Freemason's Hall, but for once, Sheba remained completely silent.

That he'd taken such pains to please her—that he had *known* what would please her—she couldn't think when she had ever been at such a loss for words.

Or when she had ever felt such a giddy lightness in all her limbs, as if she might fly away like a dandelion clock at the merest puff of wind...

CHAPTER 16

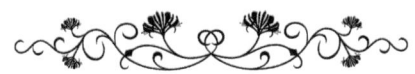

"Ash? A word, if you will?"

Noel's cousin paused on the landing of Silliman House's grand staircase, flicking his whip against his boot. "Might we do this another time? I'm late for an appointment."

Noel wished he had a whip of his own to lash about. Both honor and duty demanded he offer Ash an apology for his appalling behavior at the ball, but he'd barely caught sight of his cousin all week. Oh, Noel had expected him to decline the invitation to the Anti-Slavery meeting. But sleeping through breakfast? Riding out on Hippomenes instead of attending the appointments Pinney had arranged with the Rackhams? Carousing with young Davenport-Devenport and Pierson and Raikes until well into the small hours of the morning? It was almost as if Ash felt compelled to act the part of the dissolute young nobleman to the hilt, to make everyone forget that his standing amongst his peers had been called into question only days before.

Or had he simply been avoiding Noel?

"I'm afraid this can't wait." Noel gestured to the door of the drawing room. "I won't detain you for long."

Ash gave a quick nod, then turned and paced into the empty room.

Noel followed, shutting the door behind them.

"I owe you an apology, Ash," he said, forcing himself to meet his cousin's eye. "I'm ashamed of acting in such a thoughtless, ungentlemanly manner. And at your first ball, too. Could there have been a worse time for me—for that—for—"

The closed-off look on Ash's face disappeared in the face of Noel's fumbling, replaced by his usual open good humor. He snorted, then dropped onto the settee and crossed his arms. "Sheba would remind me that it is only disguised pride, seeking for superiority, that demands an apology before offering forgiveness. But I confess I am glad to have one from you nonetheless."

Yes. Sheba. It was her, as well as his cousin, whom he'd harmed. "I should never have endangered the reputation of a lady under your protection, Ash. Nor endangered yours, either," he said, finally finding the right words.

"And I should never have blown up at her so. In the middle of a ball!" Ash gave a rueful shake of his head. "You're not the only one who wasn't thinking in an entirely rational manner."

"Perhaps. But my behavior was far worse than yours. I still can't believe I did—I thought—Well, I hardly know what I was thinking."

Ash gave a wry chuckle as he crossed his booted feet and set his arms over the back of the settee. "I'm guessing you weren't thinking much at all. Except, perhaps, how comely a woman in distress can be?"

Comely? That glorious tumble of hair, the slope of those defeated shoulders, the arch of that still-proud neck—even in distress, the word comely hardly did justice to Bathsheba Honeychurch's exquisitely vibrant beauty.

"Indeed," Ash concurred, as if Noel had spoken his thoughts aloud. "She's always been like a sister to me, but I'd have to be blear-witted not to see how pretty she is. Or how drawn you are to her."

Noel opened his mouth to deny it. But the knowing, affectionate look on his cousin's face told him any such denial would be futile.

Ash laughed at what must be a comical look of consternation on his own face.

Damn, it felt good to be back in his cousin's good graces. He dropped into a chair opposite the settee and pushed his hands through his hair. "Yes. Damn me for my sins, I'm drawn to her."

"And will you have her? Or, perhaps the more relevant question, will she have you? Am I to wish you joy?"

The drawing room creaked open before Noel could answer. Grandmother, unbecomingly pale, slowly made her way into the room.

"I'm so glad to see you up and about again, Granny," Ash said, rushing over to take her arm. "But don't overtire yourself. Sit down right here next to me."

Embarrassment, rather than illness, had likely kept Lady Silliman confined to her chamber for the last three days. Yet Noel kept up the polite lie. "Are you quite over your indisposition, ma'am?" he asked.

"One never quite knows with these things," Grandmother answered, then gave a heavy sigh. "Genteel women are so prone to nerves, are they not? I do wonder at Miss Honeychurch, venturing out only days after—And in such a public venue, where anyone might see—Well, they do say the lower orders do not feel as strongly as the genteel, do they not?"

"Grandmother—"

"Did you not promise to pay a morning visit on the Debenhams, Silliman?" Grandmother continued, neatly cutting off Noel's protest at her implied slight to Sheba. "You and the eldest Miss Debenham made such a handsome couple at the ball, did they not, Noel?"

"Oh, indeed!" Ash said, saving Noel the trouble of having to respond. "The Debenhams. I had almost forgot."

"Morning visits cannot very well be dispensed with, sir," Grandmother advised. "Not if one desires to cultivate a large circle of proper acquaintance, as only befits an earl."

"Certainly not, Grandmama." Ash tipped his head toward Noel. "Shall you accompany me, cousin?"

"Wiser, perhaps, to go on your own?" Lady Silliman offered. More statement than question, in spite the diffidence of her tone.

"Even though it would show everyone that Noel and I have made our peace?"

"You have? How good of you, Silliman."

"How could I not, when he apologizes so handsomely? You've taught him well, Grandmama."

"Have I, then?" Grandmother gave Noel an appraising look. "Even so, Silliman, I would have a word with your cousin before the morning is out."

"As you like, Belldame," Ash said with a sunny smile for their grandmother. "But I would have a word with you too, Noel, if you'll still be here this afternoon? I've an apology of my own to make, and a plan for making it, but I can't implement it without your aid."

An apology? To Sheba?

"To be sure, cousin," Noel said with a nod.

"We'll talk then," Ash said, then dashed from the room, a cheery whistle on his lips.

Noel had risen from his chair at Ash's invitation. But when Frances Griffin gave a delicate cough, he lowered himself back onto the wool cushion. No doubt Grandmother expected him to apologize to her as well as to Ash.

Taking up her workbox, she pulled out a stitching pattern and a handful of grey wool. "Ash's secretary tells me you have been calling upon Miss Honeychurch these several mornings," she said as she set a wooden tapestry frame on her lap.

He gave a short nod.

"I did so wish that something would happen to detach the

young woman from your cousin. But I hardly imagined you would take it upon yourself to engage her affections in his stead."

"It was not my intention, ma'am, I assure you."

"It was all her doing, then? I confess I am relieved to hear it." She pulled a needle from a velvet pincushion and threaded it with a strand of the wool. "For all their other faults, females of the Quaker persuasion do have a reputation for chastity. I would be disappointed to discover my grandson had chosen to importune an unwilling gel."

Noel ground his teeth. How little his grandmother knew him, if she'd suspect for even a moment that he'd force his attentions on a lady against her will. But Grandmother had never understood him, had she?

"Imagine if you and Ash had actually been forced to measure your swords against one another!" she said as she plied her needle up and down, up and down, through the tightly stretched canvas. "Although I suppose pistols are far more common today. How many young men of my acquaintance once took up their swords to defend their honor! I was but a gel then, myself, though. And dueling is hardly a respectable course of action in these more enlightened times."

"Happily, Miss Honeychurch's quick thinking saved us from such a scandal."

"As if a Griffin betrothed to a Quaker were no scandal!" The wool between her fingers pulled taut, so taut that he feared it might snap.

But then she took a breath, and the tension on the thread and in her face both eased. "It would be unforgivably rude to deny Miss Honeychurch's declaration, at least during these last few weeks of the Season. But after everyone has left town for the summer..."

He stared at the gray cat perched on a red cushion emerging from Grandmother's canvas. Expecting him to be as placid as that feline, she was, to fall into place without argument, without her even having to give voice to her demand. To put his duty to his family above all, just as they'd both been trained to do.

"I cannot speak for the lady," he said to his grandmother's bent head, her attention carefully turned to her needlework. "But I have no intention of breaking off our agreement. In fact, I plan to do everything in my power to convince Bathsheba Honeychurch to be my bride."

The hand above the canvas stilled for the merest moment before taking up its steady motion again. "Truly, Noel? You think to marry a Quaker? If you have no respect for your religion, you should at least consider your position in society, the standing of your family."

"The family's standing did not crumble when Ash's father married a Friend."

A pained expression flickered for the merest instant across his grandmother's face. But her composure did not falter.

"Because we kept William's missteps from reaching the ears of the *ton*. Something impossible to do in your situation, I fear."

"But I don't really matter any more, do I? I'm no longer the heir apparent, only the heir presumptive. And not even that for long, if you are successful in convincing Silliman of the importance of an early marriage. You and he and his future wife will uphold the family's reputation, without any help from me."

"Upholding the standing of the Griffin family has always been my primary concern. But your cousin was not brought up to value it as you were, Noel. He still needs to learn to put the interests of the family and the estate before all else."

"Does he? Or are there other things more important?"

"More important? Such as taking up with those who oppose the family's West Indian interests? Yes, I know how you spent your time yesterday, and with whom. Has Bathsheba Honeychurch so much influence over you already? Oh, Noel, how it pains me that I ever set you in that hoyden's path."

"Miss Honeychurch's influence? You quite mistake the matter, ma'am. Have I not long spoken of my admiration for my father's commitment to combatting the slave trade? Of my abhorrence of the institution itself?"

"High principles are all well and good, Noel, but the eldest Mr. Rackham suggests that you have been advising Ash to act in a way that will endanger the estate's financial standing. Have you truly been urging him to consider disposing of our West India holdings, no matter the financial loss? Or has that presumptuous pretender you were foolish enough to introduce him to already blinded him to his duty to his actual family?"

Damn Rackham for an interfering gossip! And blast Frances Silliman for refusing to even consider Sarah Gabbidon's story. Impossible that her beloved middle son would have defiled himself, defiled their family, by laying with a slave, or so she had insisted when Noel and Ash had tried to explain the existence of another grandchild she had yet to meet.

Pressing Frances Griffin again about Sarah Gabbidon, though, would do nothing to change her mind about those plantations. Better, for now, to ignore that cruel dismissal of her own granddaughter and confront the issue of the estate's slaveholdings head-on. If he could bring grandmother to see reason, win her to their side, then their combined will might force Rackham to do what they wished about those loathsome West Indian holdings, despite Ash not yet being of age. Something he suspected Sarah would appreciate far more than being grudgingly acknowledged by an English grandmother she had not the least interest in knowing.

"Does it not seem the height of hypocrisy, ma'am, for a son to rescue enslaved Africans from captivity while his father, and now his nephew, forces others to labor uncompensated for his benefit?" Noel asked. "And under the most inhumane of conditions?"

"The trade in slaves has been outlawed, yes, and so it is only right and proper to prevent those who would break the law from so-doing," she said, setting her tapestry frame aside and folded her hands neatly in her lap. "But Mr. Rackham tells me the Africans on our plantations are never ill-treated. We give them food, shelter, protection, and the benefits of Christianity. The conditions the men in our factories here in England must endure are far harsher than those of any planation worker. Only a fool would listen to the canting and lies of the *saints*, as Mr. Rackham says the abolitionists are scornfully termed."

Noel's hands fisted at his grandmother's easy dismissal of the reprehensible institution. When he'd first read the pamphlet by Sheba's teacher, he'd thought Elizabeth Heyrick's arguments for immediate, rather than gradual, abolition overwrought. But perhaps emotion, rather than reason, was what was needed in the face of such complacent acceptance of the morally reprehensible practice.

"But ma'am—"

"Enough, Noel." Lady Silliman waved a cutting hand through the air. "Your grandfather respected Mr. Rackham's advice, and I expect you to do the same."

Noel couldn't contain a snort at the absurdity of *that* assertion. Grandfather, respecting anyone else's advice but his own? Lady Silliman only showed how little she knew of her husband's business practices if she would claim any such thing.

Grandmother did not take kindly to his inadvertent protest. She rose from the settee, narrowed eyes fixed on his. "And if you cannot—if you continue to pay more credence to the dissenting babble of Bathsheba Honeychurch and this Gabbidon woman than to the sound advice of Mr. Rackham and his family—I will be forced to demand you no longer act as advisor to your cousin."

Noel jerked from his chair. No longer act as Ash's mentor? But then what was he to do with himself, with his life?

"And if you go so far as to actually marry that ill-bred chit, you will have to find a new place to live. For you will no longer be welcome under this roof."

And with that uncharacteristically bald pronouncement, Lady Silliman swept from the room.

A gust of wind whipped at Sheba's bonnet strings, threatening to pull her hat completely from her head. Any other day, the thought of it might have plagued her with worry. But on a sunny summer First Day, riding in an open carriage beside Noel Griffin after worshipping together at Wandsworth Meeting—why should did she care if the silly thing went flying?

The rush of cool air against her cheeks, the tap-too of the wheels of the two-seated carriage, clack, clack, clacking over the cobblestones, even the familiar stink of the cloth and iron mills lining the River Wandle—all sent the strangest giddy exultation dancing throughout her every vein. Anticipation of the upcoming tea with Lady Georgiana and her fellow abolitionists, the inadvertent nudge of Noel's elbow as he guided his horses down Wandsworth High Street, the warmth of his thigh, pressing scandalously close to hers—everything she thought, everything she felt, all inspired such vivid glories of delight, she could hardly recognize herself.

If her bonnet wished to join the festive fray, who was she to deny it?

Because in the small brick building that housed the Wandsworth Friends, while they all sat together in silent worship, she'd heard it again. The call that had first whispered to her so unexpectedly at the end of the Anti-Slavery meeting, to give over the false concern to educate those abroad, and to teach instead right here in England. Not letters, or numbers, or even the Gospel, as she did in the small school she'd established in Leicester. No, Sheba felt a growing concern to show those who championed a gradualist approach to ending the pernicious institution of slavery how their stance did more to hinder than to help the cause.

What racing, bounding joy! Joy at having Noel offer to bring her to the Wandsworth Meeting House; joy at racing through the village by his side atop a carriage fit only for two; joy at catching sight, at long last, of a way to cooperate with, rather than fight against, the gifts God had given her! As soon as Friend Phillips and the other booksellers and publishers finished printing Elizabeth Heyrick's pamphlet, Sheba would take it to every Friend, every would-be abolitionist in the city she could find.

And Noel Griffin, her not-quite-betrothed, had made it all possible…

It wasn't right, to keep staring at him so. But she needed to do something to relieve this rush of feeling—

Leaning over the side of the carriage, she pulled her hand free of its glove and thrust it out over the door. The ring he'd given her winked in the summer sunlight. If only she might capture the blitheness of the wind in her open palm….

"Oh, it's just how the angel flying in the midst of heaven must have felt, preaching the everlasting gospel from above to them that dwell on the earth," she declared, her fingers dancing in the air. "How I wish I could drive a carriage and wing over the roads whenever the spirit moved me!"

Out of the corner of her eye, she could see the sun glinting off of Noel's golden brown hair, burnishing it with flecks of gold. "Not a carriage, a phaeton. Named after Phaëthon, the son of the Greek sun God Helios. His father warned him he'd not be able to control the sun chariot's horses, but Phaëthon begged to drive it anyway. Predictably, the foolish boy drove erratically, scorching and freezing parts of the earth in turn. Zeus was finally forced to strike him down dead with a thunderbolt to save the rest."

"A strange name for a carriage! Or is the story meant to be a warning, that a lady should not even think of taking the reins of such a vehicle herself?"

"Not at all. Would you truly like to learn?"

Sheba felt her eyes grow wide. To feel such control, such freedom, herself? She didn't have to think twice before nodding her fervent agreement.

"Then pick a day this week, and I'll bring Galatea and Leucothea to call." He gave a light—might she even say, affectionate?—flick of his whip over the rump of one of the mares in question.

"Galatea and Leucothea? More of your irreverent mythology?"

"Indeed. Goddesses of the sea, the both of them. Not very apt, I know, for two creatures of the land."

"When you named them—you were thinking of your father, were you not?"

Noel's eyes flicked to hers for an instant before turning back to the road. "Galatea, who calms the sea. Leucothea, who aids sailors in distress."

Careful not to interfere with his driving, she laid a light hand on his sleeve. Wishing, somehow, she could give him the same sense of comfort that his presence at Wandsworth Meeting this morning had given her. He'd not just left her at the door of the Meeting House, but had come inside, and remained for the entire First Day Meeting, his tall hat standing out like a beacon amongst the flatter, wide-brimmed felt ones worn by male Friends. How very high his eyebrow had risen when she reminded him that Friends did not remove their hats, not even when entering a house of worship. Yet he'd not argued, or even hesitated, just placed that elegant beaver back atop his head, respecting the conventions of the Society even if he himself did not follow them.

For your sake, her heart had whispered.

His eyes flicked down to her ungloved hand resting lightly on his arm, lingering on the piecrust band of gold he'd placed on her finger—only a few short days ago? Then up to her face, fixed there for a few taut moments before once again turning back to the road. Had her touch truly made him sit up a bit straighter in his seat?

"Is that not the turn back to London?" she asked as they barreled past the turning to Battersea Bridge.

"You've a splendid memory. The road to Mayfair there; the road to Clapham ahead. Did you forget we're to meet Spencer and Delphie there to call upon the Wingfields?"

Sheba sighed. If anything could put a damper on her high spirits, it was poor, dutiful Connie trapped in her Clapham cottage, dancing attendance on her sickly, irritable husband. If Noel did teach her to drive, perhaps she could call upon Con and offer her a few moments of respite.

Not that she would be in town long enough to do anything like.

Or remain betrothed to Noel long enough to become anywhere near proficient at the reins.

Sheba's breath hitched. Why should the thought of their false betrothal coming to an end discomfit her so?

She pushed her hand back into her kidskin glove, then set it atop her flapping bonnet. No, it would not do, after all, to allow the thing to be carried away on the wind…

She remained silent for the rest of the drive to Clapham, and only smiled her thanks when Noel brought the carriage—phaeton—to a stop in front of Connie's cottage, jumped down to hand the reins to the footboy, then held out his hand to help her down from her seat.

But when the footman opened the door to Connie's small drawing room, revealing neither her two cousins nor Spencer, but a completely unexpected presence, she could not but exclaim in surprise.

"Ash? What are you doing here?"

She rushed over to her familiar friend, hands held out, until she remembered just when—and how—they'd last parted.

Halting abruptly, her face flamed as she turned her eyes back towards Noel. She could tell from his lack of surprise that he'd known his cousin would be here. Had in all likelihood arranged it himself. Why? Because he thought it best for their first meeting after the scandal to take place as far from the gossips of the *ton* as possible?

She fidgeted with the strings of her reticule, preparing herself for Ash's rebukes. After all, she had engaged herself to his cousin, had been *kissing* his cousin, when only a few moments before she'd been pressing him to marry *her*. He had every right to be upset with her. More than upset. Infuriated.

Her old friend's expression contained no sign of anger, though, not even a hint of disapproval, just his usual open, affable cheer. Had he already forgiven her, then?

But then she saw him yanking at the bottom of his waistcoat in that fidgety way of his. Did he think he needed to apologize to *her*? What had he to be ashamed of?

"Sheba." Ash wrapped an awkward arm about her and gave her a quick hug. "Noel and I thought your cousin's home might be the best place for me to—What I mean is, will you permit me to introduce my—our—a, a lady who particularly wishes to be known to you?"

A rustle of skirts alerted Sheba to the presence of yet another person in Connie's drawing room. A woman stepped up beside Ash and dipped into a deep curtsey, as if Sheba were Ash's grandmother rather than simply his friend. But as she rose, hazel eyes in a deeply tanned face roved Sheba's face and person with an interest far from deferential.

"Sheba, may I present Miss Sarah Gabbidon?" Ash laid what looked like a protective hand on the young woman's shoulder.

"Your—your friend?" Sheba stuttered. Had Ash already found another woman to court?

A pang of something—sadness over what would never now be? Embarrassment over the foolishness of a fantasy she'd once held so dear?—tightened her chest.

Noel stepped close and set a hand on her back. She leaned into its stability, its comfort, holding on to that pang for one final moment before setting it, setting herself and Ash, finally free.

"Miss Honeychurch. I hope you will forgive the imposition. But Lord Silliman thought I would—thought you would..." Sarah Gabbidon trailed off, the oddest expression crossing her face as her glance flicked back to Ash. "My lord, are you certain?"

"Quite certain," he said, taking up her hand and pressing it into Sheba's. "Why would I not want my oldest, dearest friend to meet my eldest sister?"

Basking in the warmth of an affection that had been missing from Ash's gaze for far too many months, it took several seconds before the sense of his words made any impression on her mind. When they finally did, she stared at him, then at Noel, then at Sarah Gabbidon, hardly able to form a sensible thought.

She stepped back, her hand dropping to her side. "But this is not Patience."

"No, not Patience. Sarah is my eldest sister."

Sheba's hand pressed against her breastbone. "Sarah—This woman—She is your *sister*? But who—but how—"

Noel's hand slid from her back and took up her hand, squeezing, squeezing so hard it hurt. But the pain of that squeeze finally brought her back to some sense of herself.

"It seems my father was not always the paragon of virtue we all thought him to be," Ash said before she could give voice to the apology forming on her lips. "In fact, before he joined the Society of Friends, he traveled to the West Indies on his father's behalf, in search of a promising plantation in which the estate might invest."

He pulled his shoulders back, clearly encouraging himself to not shy away from her gaze. "While he was there, he fathered a child on an enslaved woman in the West Indies. He then left that child behind when he returned to England. Miss Gabbidon is that child."

Sheba felt the color leach from her face. Ash's father, who had served as a model of piety and righteousness to them all, had committed such an appalling sin? Every fiber of her being yearned to deny it. Yet when she looked at Sarah Gabbidon, the green-brown of the woman's eyes, the familiar slant of her jaw, the way she tugged at the edge of her blouse, just like Ash tugged on his waistcoats when he was upset or worried—no, she couldn't deny how strongly this young woman resembled her dearest friend.

Oh, how hurt Ash must have been, to discover such a terrible thing about so revered a father!

And how painful for this young woman, to know her father had abandoned her, had created an entire family once he'd returned to England from the West Indies, one that did not include her.

West Indies? Merciful heavens. Had Ash's sister, like her mother, been *enslaved*?

Sheba swallowed, swallowed again. "Ash. How long have you and your—your sister been known to one another?"

"Barely a week. Sarah is two and twenty, the same age as you are, Sheba. All these years, and I've never even known she existed." He bit his lip and blinked, clearly fighting back tears.

"And had you known of your brother, Friend Gabbidon?" Sheba asked the strange, yet strangely familiar, young woman. "Of Ash, and your other sisters?"

"Ah, Sarah, I see you've made the acquaintance of yet another of my cousins." Connie, a tray rattling with teacups and spoons in hand, shouldered aside the drawing room door before Sarah Gabbidon could answer. A slightly sheepish-looking Delphie, followed by a more composed Spencer, trailed behind her.

Sheba frowned. Had they all known of Ash's sister before Sheba had?

"Please, everyone, take a seat, and I'll pour out." The mundaneness of the act, as well as the evenness of Connie's tone, eased the tension in the room just the smallest bit. "How do you take your tea, Miss Gabbidon? Milk? Sugar?"

"No sugar." The flatness of Sarah Gabbidon's voice brought the tension roaring back. Sugar, of course, was the primary crop of Britain's colonial slave plantations.

"We do not allow West Indian sugar in our house," Sheba declared. But in the presence of an actual human being who had witnessed, had perhaps even been forced to participate in, the coercive labor that produced goods she so easily eschewed, the pride she had once taken in proclaiming that stance struck her as painfully self-aggrandizing.

"When I first met Miss Gabbidon, at Miss MacKay's Select Seminary, I had not the least idea she'd connections to so many of my own friends and relations," Connie continued, as if nothing untoward had just happened. "Do you know that she and Spencer sailed on the same ship to England from Sierra Leone?"

"And that her father asked me to keep an eye on her during her time in England?" Spencer gave Miss Gabbidon a friendly smile as he took a seat beside her.

"Sierra Leone? You spent time in Sierra Leone, Friend?" Sheba asked, clutching at the lifeline Connie and Spencer offered.

"Freetown is my home, ma'am. My father—stepfather, I suppose you would call him, although he has always been the father of my heart—he was exiled to Sierra Leone as punishment for his participation in a slave revolt. But freedom was no punishment. He earned enough to buy his own tavern there. And since Englishman who owned the plantation where we were enslaved had fallen on hard times by then, Father was able purchase my mother's and my freedom, too. I plan to return to them both after I complete my apprenticeship here in England with Miss MacKay."

"A plan which I hope you will help me convince Sarah to give over, Sheba." Ash moved forward in his seat, eagerness in every line of his body. "I've told my sister she is more than welcome to make her home with me here, at Silliman House."

Sheba shot a glance at Noel, unsurprised to find the wariness of her own expression mirrored in his. Even if Ash's sister did wish to remain in England, she doubted punctilious Frances Griffin would welcome this previously-unknown granddaughter into her own house. Acknowledging that Ash and his sisters were members of the Society of Friends had been embarrassing enough; claiming a granddaughter whose mother had been enslaved—no, she couldn't picture Frances Griffin ever opening herself up to such scandal.

"You are very kind, Lord Silliman," Sarah Gabbidon said, civility not hiding the dismissal in her voice.

Ash jumped from his seat to pace the room. "You see how little she believes I am in earnest. And why should she, after how her father—our father—treated her mother? I've asked Mrs. Wingfield and Lord Stiles, whose opinions I know she trusts, to vouch for the sincerity of my proposal, to no avail. But if you, Sheba, you who have known me since I was a babe, tell her I would never make such an offer if I didn't mean it, she'll have to believe me."

Mrs. Wingfield? When had Ash started to use such honorifics?

Sheba set down her cup and drew her friend closer to the window, out of hearing of the other guests.

"Ash, have you truly considered the wisdom of such a course?" she whispered.

"What, do not tell me you of all people, Sheba, think it wrong to acknowledge my own sister! Just because she has African blood—"

"No, that is not at all what I meant," Sheba murmured. "I would only ask you to consider, as I think my mother would if she were here, whether you're making your newfound sister such an offer for her sake, or for your own?"

His brow furrowed. "For my sake? In what way would it be for my sake?"

"Because you feel so dreadfully guilty for what your father did, you think to relieve your own feelings by making up for his sin yourself?"

Ash crossed his arms and turned his back to her, staring blindly out the window. But she could tell he was still listening.

"I understand your need to prove yourself different from your father. But in so-doing, are you not placing your own wishes ahead of your sister's?"

Sheba shot a glance at Sarah Gabbidon. The set of the young woman's face, the self-sufficiency and determination in every line of her body—no, she doubted Ash's newfound sister would be swayed, even by the assurances of her brother's oldest friend. "I don't believe she cares much for your grand gesture of repentance."

Ash glanced over at his sister, too. "Welcoming a family member into one's home is no grand gesture," he protested. "It's simply common decency."

No, his pain would not allow him to see what was so clear to Sheba.

"Are you so very certain this is what you are being called to do?" She gave a self-deprecating smile, hoping it might soften the sting of her words. "It would pain me to see you following the poor example I set, acting as selfishly towards your sister as you accused me of acting towards you."

"And yet you continue to advise and admonish me in spite of it," Ash scoffed. "When did you become such a sensible, weighty Friend?"

Sheba flinched, then hung her head.

"You're right. I'm no weighty Friend. But what you said to me at the ball—since then, I've been trying, trying to make sure any guidance I offer is given in the peaceable spirit of truth and not just to gratify self, as my mother often advised." She gave a self-derisive chuckle. "But it's hard. The words want to fly past my lips without giving me a chance to reflect on the wisdom of offering them. I'm sorry if I've gotten it wrong again."

"Oh, Sheba." He sighed and hung his head. "I never should have spoken to you in such anger."

"Offered in the wrong tone, perhaps, but those words were only too apt. I do find it exceedingly hard to keep my much-loved self from standing in the way of recognizing the needs of others. Especially yours. And for that I apologize, my dear friend."

"Thank you, Sheba. But still, you know it has never been *my* besetting sin, not understanding the needs of others," Ash said with a quirk of a smile. And then, in a quieter voice: "Please. I fear I will never have peace if I lose her again."

The pain in his voice, his face, nearly brought tears to her eyes. "I would never wish such an evil to befall you," she whispered. "Of course I'll help."

With a brisk step, she set herself in front of Ash's newfound sister. "Friend Gabbidon. I—"

"Please, ma'am," the young woman interrupted. "Call me Sarah if you would. It feels odd to be termed 'friend' by one whom I've only just met."

"Very well. But only if you will call me Sheba. Members of our Society do not stand on ceremony."

Sarah nodded.

"Perhaps if you were more familiar with the world in which Ash moves, you might be better able see yourself taking a place in it. Might you care to accompany us to a conversazione to which Delphie and I have been invited this coming Third-day?"

"Tuesday, she means," Connie explained.

Sarah Gabbidon's posture stiffened. "I'm afraid my teaching responsibilities—"

"But this is an evening gathering," Sheba interrupted. "Surely your Miss MacKay can do without you for one night?"

"Especially if I ask her," Ash said with a waggish tilt of his eyebrow, his earlier pain nowhere in sight. "Though I demonstrated appalling petulance at our first meeting, the good woman seems to have forgiven me for it since. In fact, she appears quite taken with my handsome face and winning manners now, do you not agree? And if I send my carriage to collect you, and to bring you back, and if Mrs. Wingfield were to come too, so you wouldn't have to travel alone, she could hardly object."

"But I couldn't leave the colonel," Connie demurred.

"Spencer and I will come and keep him company," Noel offered. "The conversazione is for ladies only, you see."

"One evening, Sarah? Just to see?" Ash pleaded.

Sheba had rarely been able to resist such a look from her best friend. But his sister had not known him nearly as long as she…

Sarah Gabbidon gazed at each member of the gathered company in turn before her eyes at last came to rest on Ash.

"One evening," she finally offered. "But I cannot promise you more."

"There, then. It is all settled." Ash held out a gloved hand to his sister. "Now, I believe you are due back at Miss MacKay's within the hour. Make your curtseys to the ladies and I'll walk you back across the Common."

"Is he always this high-handed, Miss Honeychurch?" Sarah Gabbidon asked with a laugh.

"Sheba, please. And only when it comes to his sisters."

The two exchanged tentative smiles before Connie led Sarah into the passageway to collect her hat and gloves.

Once his sister—sister! She still could hardly believe it!—had left the room, Ash came and took Sheba's hands between his.

"I don't believe I've offered you my felicitations on your betrothal to my cousin," he said, smiling over his shoulder at Noel. "I hope the two of you will be very happy."

Sheba blushed. "Ash, you must know I didn't intend—"

"I know, Sheba," he whispered. "But as I believe my father would remind us both, 'There are many devices in a man's—or a woman's—heart; nevertheless the counsel of the Lord, that shall stand'."

That he could speak of her betrayal with such understanding! And remember the goodness of his father, not only his sin and shame...

She could not help but wonder, though, if guilt over that sin and shame had driven William Griffin to prove his righteousness every single moment of his remaining life. Prove it not just to his fellow Friends, not just to his family, but most urgently, to himself.

When I am no longer here to guide him, let him draw on your strength, help him to walk in the truth and the light. Swear it, Sheba!

But in that final moment, to not accept her simple *yea*, to insist she swear, contrary to what Friends held right—had guilt and fear won out over love?

Had he demanded from her what she never should have promised?

Ash kissed her cheek, then, and let go of her hands. "Thank you for your help with Sarah today, even though it all must have been a great shock. But you are of firm character, Bathsheba Honeychurch. I knew I could rely on you."

What a very good man he was, her old friend. And how much she still loved him.

Even if he was not the right man for her.

"Always, Ash," she whispered.

She squeezed his hand for a moment then released it, both acknowledgement of friendship and bittersweet farewell.

And then stepped back to Noel's side.

CHAPTER 17

Sheba flipped through the freshly-printed pamphlets the printer's boy had just delivered, smiling in spite of the stench of turpentine, soot, and some kind of woody oil emanating from their pages. How pleased Elizabeth Heyrick would be when she received her copies! Now that *Immediate, Not Gradual Abolition* had been reprinted in cheap form (only 4 pence sewn!), Elizabeth's arguments would reach a far broader audience than that of the original pamphlet she'd published earlier this spring in Leicester.

How clever of him, to bring so many different people together to further the cause...

She'd been so wary of the tug of personal attraction she felt for him. An attraction she hadn't even recognized, or at least allowed herself to acknowledge, until the night of Ash's ball. After that, though, the tug became a wrench, plucking and pulling at her not only while in his presence, but when she was alone with her thoughts, thoughts occupied all too often by him.

Prefer the Person before Money, Virtue before Beauty, the Mind before the Body, she had often heard the elders advise, echoing the words of the American Friend William Penn. That Noel could refer to the same passage, but cast such a different light on the man's words—it had taken her aback. Led her to take up

Penn's *Reflections and Maxims* herself. How astonished she'd been to find his first maxim on Right Marriage to be *Never marry but for love, but see that thou love'st what is lovely*. And even more so by his advice on differentiating base lust from love: the former is volatile, the latter fixed; love grows, while lust wastes away after its indulgence.

And then, these shocking words: *Let not Enjoyment lessen, but augment Affection*. Which, as they followed a warning against searching out pleasure in forbidden places, suggested that "enjoyment" meant enjoyment of the physical passions.

While Penn also cautioned that lust is only a *Union of Sense*, Sheba could not help thinking a true marriage might mean not only the Union of Spirits, as wedding Ash would be, but instead a Union of both Spirit and Sense combined.

Because while Noel clearly felt an attraction to her person, he also seemed drawn to her mind, her beliefs, her convictions.

Perhaps, even to her soul?

"Sheba, love, Lord Silliman's carriage is at the door," Delphie called from the front of their lodgings. "It's a warm evening, but we still shouldn't keep Connie and Miss Gabbidon waiting."

Miss Gabbidon! Sheba had never felt close to any of Ash's sisters—the younger ones too coltish to be her playmates, Patience, the elder, far too practical and unimaginative to stomach Sheba's grand schemes and fancies—but she hoped it might be different with Sarah Gabbidon. How many questions she wished to ask her, this woman who looked so like Ash but whose experiences of the world had been so very different from his own...

Stuffing a few copies of Friend Heyrick's pamphlet inside her reticule, Sheba dashed down to Delphie and followed her out to the waiting carriage.

"Connie. Miss Gabbidon." Delphie greeted the carriage's occupants as she settled on the seat beside their cousin. "A pleasant evening for a drive, is it not? The light lingers so long this time of year. But the moon will be nowhere close to full this evening, I fear. Can we not persuade you to stay over in town until morning?"

"How kind of you to offer. But I fear we cannot," Connie said, ostentatiously pulling her skirts out of the way as Sheba stepped into the carriage. As if they were in danger of being trampled! Con sat on the far side of the carriage, nowhere near Sheba's admittedly less-than-dainty feet.

Opposite Connie, Ash's sister, her neat gray gown nearly as plain as Sheba's, gave a nod. "I, too, must decline your kind invitation, Lady Stiles. My duties at Miss MacKay's begin quite early in the morning."

Sheba shivered. Not only did Sarah Gabbidon look like Ash, she sounded quite like him, too. Unsettling, it was, to see such a familiar expression on the face of a relative stranger, to hear the cadence of his voice in her own slightly higher tones.

Unworthy, to allow any such unease to interfere with her promise to champion Ash to his newfound sister.

She lifted her chin and offered a smile. "Sarah. How very pleased I am to see you again."

Sarah nodded and offered a smile of her own. One far more tentative than Sheba's, though.

"Are you quite certain you cannot stay the night?" she asked as the carriage rocked into motion. How better to befriend the young woman than by spending as much time with her as possible?

"Sheba, do not tell me you've forgotten your gloves again!" Connie took Sheba's bare hands and turned them critically in her own before releasing them with pained sigh. "And I'm sorry, but no. The colonel's wounds often trouble him in the night, and he often calls out for me to soothe him back to sleep. Lord Stiles and Mr. Griffin assured me they would send word if I am required."

Sheba gave a silent huff as she pulled a pair of wrinkled gloves from her reticule. As if two men could not keep a fretful invalid entertained for a few hours! But then, Con always did so need to be needed...

Unkind, such a thought. Constantly being at the beck and call of a demanding husband could hardly be pleasant. Poor Con's face looked quite tired and drawn.

Instead Sheba opened her reticule and pulled out two copies of the printed pamphlet. "You won't be able to read it in the carriage, but I've a pamphlet here that I hope you will find of interest. Written by my teacher in Leicester, Elizabeth Heyrick, on the need for immediate, rather than gradual, abolition of slavery."

"What are we to do with such a thing now?" Connie's nose wrinkled, at the unpleasant scent, or at what she considered Sheba's impertinence, Sheba couldn't say.

"You champion the cause of emancipation, do you?" Sarah Gabbidon asked, an ugly note of suspicion in her voice. "Is that why I am here tonight? To reassure those who argue that my people are in no condition to make a right use of freedom? That we can in fact be 'civilized'?"

"Sarah, no! I had not the least idea—" Sheba stuffed the pamphlets back into her reticule, then reached out a hand, a hand suddenly far too warm inside its over-tight glove. But the anger and disgust in Sarah Gabbidon's voice made her think better of it. Presumptuous, to think a touch, especially from someone against whom she entertained such awful suspicions, could offer any reassurance.

"Miss Honeychurch. Lady Stiles." Strips of light from passing streetlights traced over Sarah Gabbidon's face, light and shadow, light and shadow. "Mrs. Wingfield has already agreed to my request that no mention be made of my relationship to Lord Silliman this evening. I understand that, because of his religious views, he has had some trouble finding his place in society since coming into his title, and I would not wish the existence of an illegitimate half-sister to make that task even more difficult. I would be most appreciative if you'd simply name me a friend of Mrs. Wingfield's, one interested in the opportunity to partake of intelligent female conversation. Heavens knows I have little enough chance of such amongst Miss MacKay's schoolgirls."

"Certainly, Miss Gabbidon," Delphie said. "We will be happy to introduce you however you prefer."

The carriage drew to a stop before Sheba could offer any further apology.

"Lady Stiles, Miss Honeychurch. How kind of you to join us this evening," Georgiana Agar-Ellis greeted them after her footman had taken their wraps. "And to bring us more ladies devoted to the arts as well! Oh, how lively we all shall be!"

Sheba clutched at her reticule, making the pamphlets inside crinkle. Ladies devoted to the *arts*? Was not the evening's *conversazione* to be about abolition?

The footman nodded at Sarah. "Your maid is welcome to bide in the kitchens until you are ready to leave."

Beside her, Ash's sister stiffened.

"You quite mistake the matter, Friend. Sarah Gabbidon is our companion, not our servant."

Sheba moved to draw her arm pointedly through Sarah's, to depress the footman's impertinent presumption. But would such a display be for Sarah's benefit, or for her own?

Instead, she crooked an elbow towards Ash's sister, allowing the young woman to accept or ignore her invitation as she would.

Sarah stared at her for a moment, then took up Sheba's hand, lacing it through hers.

"And this, Lady Georgiana, is my cousin, Constance Wingfield," Delphie said, dispelling the tension with mundane civility. "Her husband served in the action at Waterloo."

Their hostess dismissed the erring footman with a curt nod, then gestured them across the wide marble-floored hall. "Are you fellow devotees of Erato, Mrs. Wingfield? Miss Honeychurch?"

"Connie has always loved verse, but I fear Bathsheba would be as likely to recognize the muse of lyric poetry as she would the Duchess of Devonshire," Delphie said with a fond smile.

"Oh, how she would frown whenever we stole a novel away from the library at Audley Priory," Connie exclaimed. "And do you recall, Delphie, how we would take it in turns to recite lines from of our favorite poems to torment her? Ah, 'May Heaven so guard my lovely quaker,/ That anguish never can overtake her; / That peace and virtue ne'er forsake her, / But bliss be aye, her heart's partaker.' "

"Ah, 'To a Beautiful Quaker,'" Sarah Gabbidon said. "A lovely bit of verse, although perhaps not amongst Lord Byron's more intellectual endeavors."

Sheba frowned. It had been years since her cousins had teased her with that profane poem. As if she should dream of no greater joy than imagining a worldly versifier falling in love with her from afar.

"But very apt," their hostess said as she gestured them into a drawing room filled with fashionably-dressed ladies of all ages. "For Byron is to be the subject of our conversazione this evening."

Sheba froze on the sill of the drawing room door. Poetry was to be the topic this evening? And not poetry in general, but the works of a reprobate so pernicious, his name was even recognized by her?

"I know you Quakers tend to frown upon poetry." Georgiana Agar-Ellis gave a sorrowful shake of her head, as if she could barely imagine the ignorance of one who embraced such a fusty view. "But now that poor dear Byron is gone, we will do our best to persuade you to look more kindly upon his works. You won't be scandalized, will you, Miss Honeychurch, if we read some of his lyrics aloud this evening? I confess, I am quite eager to hear a Quakeress's opinions of his work."

A Quakeress's opinions of his work? What would she, or any Friend, know about frivolous, profane versification? Did Georgiana Agar-Ellis mean to make a fool of her in front of her friends?

What a waste of an evening. Was one truly meant to mourn a villain whose name was "linked with one virtue and a thousand crimes"? Or take pleasure in men tortured by unnamable sins? Or in endless paeons to physical, rather than spiritual or intellectual, female beauty?

More than once during that hour, Delphie's restraining hand had been all that kept Sheba from storming from the room.

"Thank you, ladies, for sharing your favorite verses with the company," Georgiana Ellis at last declared, finally bringing the painful recitations to an end. "Let us adjourn to the drawing room for refreshment and discussion of the literary merits of what we have heard."

Sheba and Sarah shared a long-suffering glance. Sarah, she thought, had no more love for such drivel than she.

"Have you ever read Caro Lamb's *Glenarvon*? They do say her protagonist is modeled after Byron," a young woman behind them whispered.

"As if my mother would ever allow such a scandalous novel into our house!" another replied.

Sheba tried to move out of hearing of the silly chatterers, but the gathering pressed too close.

"At least Lord Melbourne never divorced her for taking Byron as her lover."

"If only Byron's wife had been as wise!"

"I would have forgiven him anything, if ever he wrote such as thing as 'Fare Thee Well' to me!"

"Even knowing he fathered a child on his half-sister?"

Beside her, Sarah gasped.

Was this the society into which Ash wished to introduce his sister? When he'd been brought up to observe the precepts of the apostle, to not let corrupt communication proceed out of his mouth?

Before she could tell these silly girls what she thought of their mindless gossip, Sarah grabbed her arm. "Excuse us if you please."

Sarah elbowed her way through the throng, pulling Sheba in her wake, until they reached the blessed quiet of the passageway.

"You were about to ring a peal over those silly creatures, weren't you? Just as I would have if I ever heard such words on my students' lips," Sarah said. "But young women of the *ton* are not schoolgirls in need of our correction."

"But such appalling behavior should be denounced—"

"Such appalling behavior would be nothing to the scandal of Lord Silliman's cousin's Quaker betrothed presuming to scold the daughter of a duke, I fear."

Sheba sighed and sank into a chair—meant for a footman, not for a *lady*, no doubt—and tipped her head back against the wall. Why should it still be so difficult to curb this need to admonish and scold?

"I am so sorry, Sarah, for insisting you come tonight. I could hardly have chosen an event less likely to entice you into accepting Ash's offer, could I?"

Sarah gave a wry smile. "Nothing you could do or say would change my mind about that. I am glad to have met him, and hope to meet his sisters, too, before I leave England. But my heart yearns for my own country, my own people."

"You are determined to return to Sierra Leone when your apprenticeship is done?"

"I am. The children rescued from the slavers need teachers who respect them, not ones who regard them as uncivilized, ignorant heathens."

Another young woman, passing by on her way to the retiring room, paused at Sarah's words. "Surely you do not regard evangelizing as disrespectful, Miss Gabbidon?"

"Yes, will not those children benefit from learning the lessons of Christianity from our missionaries?" Sheba frowned. Had she been mistaken in that, too?

"Perhaps. I do wonder, though, what you would think if a group of Mende or Temne came and set up a colony in England, then insisted Christianity was nothing but heathen superstition? Would *you* feel respected if they demanded you give up your religion and convert to theirs?"

"Give up their religion? But all the missionary papers I've read say Africans have none," the young woman asserted, doubt making her dark curls dance.

"Do they not?" Sarah smiled. "I wonder who benefits by promulgating such an obvious untruth."

"But even if they do, is not a false religion far worse than no religion at all?" Sheba asked.

"Is not the faith of one's oppressors, if used as a tool to maintain their oppression, the most false religion of all?"

"But Christianity is meant to liberate our brethren from oppression, not maintain it!" Sheba exclaimed. "Does not the Bible say 'There is neither Jew nor Greek, there is neither bond nor free, there is neither male nor female: for ye are all one in Christ Jesus'?"

"Does it? No such line appeared in the Bible the Barbados missionaries shared with us. No, we were far more likely to hear 'Servants, be obedient to them that are your masters according to the flesh, with fear and trembling, in singleness of your heart.'"

"Someone abridged the Bible?" Sheba exclaimed, her eyes widening. "Who would dare?"

"Those who feared its words might prompt a desire for freedom. Oh, do not look so shocked," Sarah said. "I understand that Quakers believe there is that of God in everyone, but surely you know not all Christians share that view."

"Are you not a Christian yourself, Miss Gabbidon?" the other woman asked, her tone somewhere between amazed and appalled.

"I am," Sarah replied in an even tone. "But I do not see the good in forcing my beliefs onto others. Especially when I see how wary the Igbo and Yoruba and Hausa children are of accepting the teachings of those who look just like the evil men who stole them away from their kin. How can they not but wonder if such wicked people do not also serve a wicked god?"

A wicked God? Had not Michael Pinney said almost the same?

Their companion, though, looked not curious, but scandalized, at Sarah's challenge. "But it is your duty as a Christian, Miss Gabbidon, to teach them how wrong they are—"

"Miss Wilberforce," Georgiana Agar-Ellis interrupted before their raised voices could draw the curious into the passageway. "I see you have met Miss Honeychurch, our Quaker guest. Although as your father numbers many members of the persuasion amongst his political allies, perhaps such a meeting is not as novel for you as it has been for many of the ladies here tonight."

"Miss Wilberforce?" Sheba exclaimed. "A relation of William Wilberforce, the great antislavery crusader?"

"My father, yes," the young lady acknowledged with a nod.

Sheba had been ready to dismiss the woman for her rudeness to Sarah. But how could she not take advantage of such a chance to form a connection to the famed anti-slavery advocate?

"Did you attend the great meeting on Friday, Friend Wilberforce?" Sheba asked. "I admired your father's speech exceedingly."

"As did I," Georgiana Agar-Ellis said. "What an honor for Mr. Wilberforce to be given the task of offering the motion in praise of the patronage and condescension of His Royal Highness the Duke of Gloucester."

The young lady's eyes skittered back towards the drawing room. "My parents did not think it seemly for a young, unmarried woman to attend such a public gathering. Perhaps after I am wed, they will think differently."

"Oh, are you soon to be married, Miss Wilberforce?" Sarah asked.

Friend Wilberforce colored and smiled. "A private understanding between myself the gentleman as of yet. But one I hope will be formalized quite soon."

"A gentleman with good connections, one hopes?" their hostess said with a raised eyebrow.

"And with a pleasant manner and countenance?" Sarah added.

Friend Wilberforce's blush deepened.

"As a married woman, you will be in a better position to advocate for the greater involvement of the ladies in the work of the Society," Sheba said, attempting to turn the conversation back to more important topics. "And if more ladies insist on taking up a role, surely we can persuade the gentlemen of the need for immediate, rather than gradual, emancipation."

"Immediate emancipation? How can you think of such a thing?" Georgiana Agar-Ellis frowned. "What slave is in any condition to make use of his freedom, were it suddenly restored to him?"

"What right do you have to say that because one has been enslaved, and thereby degraded and debased, you will continue to hold him in bondage until he has acquired a capacity to make use of his liberty?" Sarah countered.

"The spirit of accommodation and conciliation is naught but a spirit of delusion," Sheba agreed. "The cause of abolition has been weakened, not strengthened, by it."

"But the West Indian planters warn that immediate emancipation will only lead to insurrection," Friend Wilberforce exclaimed. "Are they not in a better position to judge than we?"

Sheba's eyes widened. Did one truly need to explain such

things to the daughter of William Wilberforce?

"Is it not hypocrisy for us to praise Byron, who extols the resistance of the Greeks, and deems it an act of virtue, nay, of Christian charity, to supply them with arms and ammunition, to enable them to persist in insurrection, while at the same time fearing the same of those we enslave?" Sheba opened her reticule. "Here, if you will just read this pamphlet—"

"Elizabeth. Your parents will be wondering at our long absence," an older woman interrupted. Not a relative—she looked nothing like Wilberforce's daughter—a companion, perhaps, or a chaperone? "Lady Georgiana, will you ask a footman to call for our carriage?"

Elizabeth Wilberforce was leaving? But Sheba had barely had a chance to discuss anti-slavery work with her at all!

Sheba rushed after her, holding out the copy of Elizabeth Heyrick's pamphlet she'd finally managed to pull free of her reticule. "Will you share this with your father, Friend Wilberforce? It was written by a Quaker lady of my acquaintance, on the need for immediate, rather than gradual, emancipation."

Elizabeth Wilberforce gave an apologetic smile. "My father has enemies enough, Mother says, without taking up such a radical stance."

"Please, Friend Wilberforce?" Sheba begged. "I am certain he would find it of interest."

The sweet expression on the face of Wilberforce's daughter disappeared, replaced by a look of pity. "My mother says it is best to leave politics to the men, and concern oneself with one's home, and the state of the poor in one's parish. Good evening, Miss Honeychurch."

As she watched Elizabeth Wilberforce's departing back, Sheba suddenly realized how quiet the room behind them had become. Had the company all been watching her importune the great Wilberforce's daughter like a fishwife in the street?

But when she glanced back, the ladies had all returned to the drawing room and their own conversations.

But for the remainder of the wretched evening, not one of them offered either Sheba or Sarah another word.

CHAPTER 18

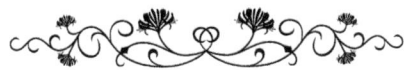

Noel shouldered his way through the press of naval officers and curious members of the public gathered in Old Palace Yard, all awaiting the ceremonial launch of the most complete piece of workmanship, in the iron way, that London had ever witnessed: the *Aaron Manby*, the first iron steamship built to ply the open ocean, rather than just a canal or inland waterway.

Months earlier, at Michael Pinney's insistence, Noel had requested an invitation to the exhibition from Captain Irby, a friend of his father's, in the hopes that the innovative technology might intrigue him enough to invest. And Noel had been intrigued, especially after Pinney had arranged to have plans of the ship's design sent to Noel for his review. He'd even asked Pinney to arrange a meeting between himself and Captain Napier and Mr. Manby, the naval officer and the engineer behind the project.

But now that Noel and Sheba were engaged—or on their way to becoming so, if Noel could but make her regard his suit as something more than simply a sop to scandal—the immediate surety of income from an estate, rather than the potential future profits of a yet-to-be proven engineering innovation, seemed a far wiser financial course to pursue.

Yet he'd not wished to disappoint Captain Irby by cancelling their appointment. And when it had come up in conversation with Sheba that Irby and his father had both served off the coast of West Africa, intercepting slaver ships, she'd begged for an invitation, too, despite being in the rush of packing to remove to Leicester two days hence.

Something inside him settled as he caught sight of her, up on her toes, trying to peer over the heads of the milling crowd in search of him.

With a nod of thanks to Spencer, he took Sheba's hand from where it lay on his friend's arm and placed it atop his own. "And how was your evening at Lady Georgiana's?" he asked as he nodded his good-byes to Spencer and then guided her across the paving stones of the Yard.

"Oh! How very many people there are!" Sheba exclaimed, ignoring his question, her gloved fingers dancing on Noel's arm. "How are we ever to find your father's friend?"

Before he could ask why she'd shied away from his own question, his name, bellowed in a loud, deep voice, rang out from across the courtyard.

"Well met, sir, well met!" Captain Frederick Irby, in an even louder voice, called, and waved a bicorne hat high above the crowd.

Noel felt Sheba's fingers slip from his arm as Frederick Irby shook his hand, then pulled him into a rough embrace.

Noel stilled for an instant—how long had it been since any fatherly figure had shown him physical affection?—then raised his own arms to clasp Irby in return.

But he still kept half an eye on Sheba, ready to catch her back if curiosity tempted her off into the crowd.

"Captain. A pleasure to see you again, sir," Noel said.

"And you as well, my boy, you as well. Look more and more like your dear mother every day, God rest her soul," the ruddy-faced sailor declared as he pulled away to examine Noel from head to toe.

"You look to be in fine trim yourself, Captain."

Irby's laugh made his entire body shake. "Finer than that sorry excuse for a craft we've come to see. Why any man with knowledge of an actual ship would want to invest in such a lumbering barge, I cannot for the life of me imagine. What an ugly, ungainly thing here is, by way of a boat!"

Irby gestured with his hat toward the bottom of Parliament Stairs, where lay the object of his scorn: a flat-bottomed ship about one hundred feet long, sporting no sails, only a narrow towering funnel propped up by wire guy-lines, steam and smoke belching from its stack. Ugly, yes, but Noel could not help the rill of excitement the sight of that ship instilled. Irby might not think much of it, but Noel could see so clearly how a ship not dependent on the whims of the wind, able to maintain a constant speed and a predictable schedule, would be a major attraction to many trades.

Anyone who invested would likely reap the rewards a hundredfold—

"But who is this you've brought with you? A young lady? Scupper any chance with her, my boy, taking her aboard such a pitiful excuse for a ship as this *Aaron Manby*."

"You are quite mistaken, sir," Sheba protested as she stepped away from the jostling crowd. "Did not Noel tell you how I begged him for an invitation once I knew *you* would be in attendance?"

"Ha! A charmer as well as a stunner!" Irby's full-bellied laugh sent the fringe of his epaulettes a-flutter. "What would a pretty young creature like you want with an old salt like me? Introduce us if you would, my boy."

"Miss Honeychurch, may I present Captain Frederick Irby, late of his Majesty's Royal Navy?" Noel said, shaking off visions of the future. Such investments were not for him, not any more. "Captain Irby, Miss Bathsheba Honeychurch, cousin to my friend Lord Stiles, who is visiting from Leicester."

The Captain frowned, straining the gold buttons on his tight-fitting coat. "Leicester? A land-locked place, is it not? How anyone can bear to live so far away from the sea I'll never fathom."

"One cannot pine for what one does not know." Sheba offered Irby her most confiding smile. "I'd never seen the ocean before this visit to London. And I confess, to my shame, I've still yet to set foot aboard a ship."

"Never set foot on a ship? And you think to introduce her to seafaring by way of this laughable excuse for a vessel?" Irby waved a dismissive arm toward the Thames. "For shame, my boy, for shame! If only they hadn't broken up the poor *Amelia*, ma'am, I'd show you what a proper ship can do."

Noel grimaced. Injuries in battle, as well as the ill-effects on his health by his service in Africa, meant the older man hadn't captained a ship since the end of the Napoleonic wars.

A loud whistle from the riverside brought the crowd to expectant attention.

"Ah, the *Manby* seems ready to take on passengers," Captain Irby said. "Shall we make our way down to the river?"

Sheba smiled and took the captain's arm. "If you promise to tell me all about your work pursuing slavers off the African coast while we wait to board."

"Ah, now I understand," Irby said, raising an eyebrow at Noel. "A fellow abolitionist. Well, met, my dear, well met! Did Noel tell you the story of our encounter with the *Lindeza*, a Portuguese slaver with more than a hundred and forty poor Africans aboard? It was the year eleven, I believe…"

The two chatted like magpies as they followed the crowd down Parliament Steps and onto the *Aaron Manby*. Noel trailed behind, well-satisfied at having given such pleasure to the woman he loved.

Yes, loved. Something restless inside him settled at admitting the truth of it, at least to himself.

If only he could devise a strategy that would make her love him too…

Noel joined Irby and Sheba by the rail of the *Manby* and let his eyes wander as the boat steamed past the stone wharfs and gas works, Tothill Fields and Millbank Penitentiary perched on the north side of the Thames. Would she admire him more if he, too, had joined the navy, had risked his life as his father had to chase down slave ships?

When his grandfather had first taken him from school, Noel had begged to be sent to the Royal Naval Academy rather than trained up as the next Earl Silliman. Grandfather had refused. Only a fool would wish the command of a single paltry ship when he was destined to command government, nay, command society itself, as one of its leading peers, or so grandfather had sneered. Noel's failure there had taught him the futility of challenging the head of his house, taught him the necessity of keeping his needs, his desires, safely to himself.

Could a lady so open as Bathsheba Honeychurch ever come to care for a man as cool, as aloof, as that?

The admiration with which Sheba gazed up at Irby—Noel frowned at how quickly pleasure shifted to jealousy. Did he truly have to fight the urge to march over and snatch her away from the far-too-entertaining fellow?

Yes. Yes, he did.

Once he had got his ill-bred urges under control, he stood silently and listened as Irby spun tale after tale, all putting himself in the most flattering light. Breathed in the starch and humidity as they passed the Steam Washing company, the biting alcohol and juniper of the London Gin distillery, the stench of the New Chelsea Water Works. Watched the spin of the *Manby*'s paddles churning the water behind them.

He took out his pocket watch—yes, the ship was well on its way to meeting the times its owners had predicted to sail from Westminster to Battersea.

"Irby? Is that you, old fellow?" Another middle-aged officer slapped Irby on the back as they sailed past the Chelsea Botanical Gardens. "How many children has that new wife of yours given you, eh?"

"Go, go, Captain," Sheba said as Irby glanced between her and the newly-arrived officer. "You've no need to entertain us for the entire exhibition."

Sheba turned to Noel, then, her eyes glossy with excitement. "I would almost think it worthwhile, joining the Navy, if one could but spend all of one's time rescuing those taken so unfairly from their homes and families. Captain Irby tells me his ship alone secured the liberty of more than seven hundred souls."

"You would likely have been dead before you had the chance to engage in such grand rescues as Irby likes to relate," Noel heard himself say. His hands gripped tight against the rail.

"Dead?" Sheba's eyes widened—in shock? Or disbelief?

No, he'd not lie to her, not even to gain the respect and admiration of those bright blue eyes she'd so easily bestowed on Captain Irby. "So many sailors, and even more of those liberated by them, grew ill on those ships, my father wrote in his letters to my mother. Perished from dysentery, smallpox, Yellow Jack and other fevers—more than one hundred and twenty during a single cruise, I was later told—that the *Swiftfire* was obliged to limp back to England to take on more crew."

"Is that how your father died? Not in battle, but from disease?"

Of course she would see right to the root of his anger. He jerked his chin, stared out at the coal and ferry wharves—both too small for a ship the size of the *Manby* to dock.

He felt her step closer, set her hand atop his. "Then I'm doubly happy your grandfather prevented you from joining the navy," he heard her say. "Because I would regret all my days not having had the chance to know you, Noel Griffin. To account a man worthy as you my friend."

She must have seen it in his eyes, his humming need to take her in his arms, press his mouth against the oh-so-serious line of those dear, dear lips. For she took a step back, deliberately lightened her tone. "And what think you of the *Aaron Manby*, Noel Griffin?"

Noel cleared his throat, pulling his wayward hands behind his back. "I'm more curious to hear your opinion. The owners think to persuade the navy to purchase, but companies interested in passenger service strike me as a far more likely market. If, that is, ladies such as you would consider traveling in such a vessel?"

"Yes, would you ma'am? I've heard from all the navy fellows, but what does a young lady think of my ship?"

They turned from the rail to find a broad, dark-haired man in a blue captain's uniform eyeing them with interest. He gestured toward the river as the *Manby* turned in a tight circle before the narrow timber spans of Battersea Bridge. "Does she not maneuver in a very superior style?

"*Your* ship?" Sheba asked. "Did you design her, Friend?"

Of course, she took not the least umbrage at an unfamiliar gentleman striking up a conversation. Noel stepped between Sheba and the stranger, making it clear that the lady was not without protection.

But the fellow didn't even seem to notice. "Captain Charles Napier, at your service, ma'am. I'm the financial half of the partnership, with Mr. Manby and his son serving as the engineering half of the concern." The man bowed, sending the ends of his clumsily-knotted cravat spilling down his wrinkled front.

Napier? Irby had warned Noel that many in the navy found the captain who had financed this iron steamship more than a little eccentric. Another reason to give over the idea of buying into the project.

No matter how the possibilities intrigued…

"Bathsheba Honeychurch, of Leicester. And my—my friend,

Noel Griffin."

"Griffin? The same Griffin who wrote to ask about investing in our little project?"

"I did think to do so at one time." He glanced quickly at Sheba, then back to the captain. "But my circumstances have changed in the interim."

The captain shook his head. "Too bad, too bad. After today's demonstration, and the channel crossing we plan to make in the fall, the orders are sure to flock in."

"From the Admiralty?" Noel asked.

"Not during peacetime, no. But give us another war, and iron ships will become to the Navy what the cavalry is to the Army—the post of honor."

"I cannot help but believe that such a ship would be better employed for commerce than for war," Noel said. "Those who needed to transport perishable foods, livestock, mail, they are your likeliest customers. Perhaps companies interested in developing quick passenger service."

"If I could be assured of reaching my destination more quickly than by coach or sail," Sheba said, "I would certainly travel on such a ship."

"Ah, doing our work for us, are you? Absolutely certain you're not interested in investing, sir? Between you and your lady, you could convince even the Admiralty itself to purchase."

"I wish I could, captain. But I've other obligations."

"I see, I see," Napier nodded, casting a significant glance at Sheba. "Family first, eh, young man?"

Both he and Sheba seemed to be waiting for the other to correct the man. But neither said a word.

The captain frowned, his black side whiskers bristling as a cluster of admirals standing at the opposite rail cast him dark glances. "Shortsighted, narrow-minded bunch, the lot of 'em. As if the introduction of iron and steam would somehow strike a fatal blow to the naval supremacy of the empire! Won't hear a word in favor of either. Just like they refuse to grant our men proper wages and pensions, then scratch their heads over why sailors prefer to work on merchant ships than one of theirs. Pigheaded, blear-witted bunch, the lot of 'em."

Noel glanced over the captain's shoulder, where the knot of admirals gazed at Napier in obvious disapproval. Did the fellow have no sense of tact, to be making such disparaging remarks in public, and in such a carrying tone? No wonder Irby had called him "Mad Charlie."

"And if you want to be considered a true eccentric, just dare to suggest discontinuing the punishment of flogging," Napier added, his frown deepening into a grimace. "Little do they care that the worst character subjected to such punishment receives commiseration from all seamen, or that the feeling uppermost in their minds is disgust at the brutality of officers sentencing him to such a punishment, not disgust at the infractions of the one being flogged."

Even knowing how little Sheba needed yet another cause to take up, Noel could only marvel at the snap of indignation in her bright blue eyes. So vital, so *alive*, she was, crusading against all the wrongs of the world.

Sheba placed a hand on the captain's wrinkled sleeve. "You should take pride in the title of eccentric, captain. Speaking out for what is right, especially when others shun you or cast aspersions against your character, takes true courage, my mother always said. Especially when surrounded by those whom you *thought* shared your beliefs. My mother never faltered, but I cannot help but feel disheartened when I see so many caring more for being polite than for telling the truth."

Noel frowned as the light in Sheba's eyes dimmed. Was this why she'd turned the conversation every time he'd ask her about the evening party at Lady Georgiana's? Had she been her usual outspoken self? And had the ladies there shunned her because of it?

Or was she avoiding the subject because she felt guilty at not living up to her mother's impossibly high standards?

A young man not in uniform—the younger Mr. Manby, perhaps?—pulled on Napier's sleeve. "Captain. Viscount Melville wishes a word."

Napier sighed. "Ah, well, won't do to keep the First Lord of the Admiralty waiting, no matter how much of a nuisance he thinks me. If you'll excuse me, ma'am? Sir?"

Sheba turned back to the boat rail, eyes shifting away from the factories on the south side of the bridge to fix on the far more pleasant scene of Battersea Field's Flora Tea Gardens. Noel caught his breath as the vision of her lips closing about one of the fine-flavored strawberries grown there dashed through his brain.

"I've always been taught that those who wed for money cannot have any true satisfaction from marriage," she said as he rejoined her at the rail. "But perhaps I should have asked you at least a little about your financial situation. Is that why you can no longer invest in Captain Napier's project? Because Ash's gain has been your loss?"

Noel frowned. "It's true, I no longer command the riches of the Silliman estate. But my father left me a small inheritance, which will be more than enough to support a wife."

"To support a wife? But not also to invest in a project that fires your imagination?"

"Fires my imagination?" How could such an imaginative flight of fancy ever be applied to him?

"Yes. Because when you look at this ship, your eyes light with the fire of possibility. Of what could be, what will be, if you could only lead other people to see it, too."

"Just as yours do, whenever you hold one of your teacher's pamphlets in hand, ready to share it with anyone who doubts the merits of the abolitionist cause?"

They looked at each other, then, for long moments, over the

rail of the ship. The shock of being so well understood by another slowly gave way to acknowledgement, then acceptance, and then to a giddy lightness fizzing and popping in his veins.

Sheba laughed, then, a peal of astonishment and delight. "Why was I so certain a marriage could only work if a husband and wife shared all the same interests, the same goals? My parents certainly didn't, and yet I doubt anyone would call their marriage a failure. Perhaps it is even better if each party has his own projects, his own passions…"

The lightning-flash of a kingfisher, skimming over the water. The belch of smoke and steam from the wharfs and timber yards and iron works of the south bank of the Thames. The thrill of a dream suddenly, tantalizingly within reach. Alive, alive, alive…

"Perhaps. If each will still bear an equal share with the other in all their toils and troubles," Noel said, threading his fingers through hers and squeezing tight. A wordless, ardent invitation to join him on the precipice of possibility, to spread their wings and fly into a soaring, limitless future. Together.

"Beg your pardon, miss."

The footman's words jerked Sheba free of her distraction. She'd been standing on the pavement outside their Conduit Street lodgings, staring up at the windows, the strangest heaviness weighing down her chest. Would she truly miss living in London?

"I'm sorry, Joshua." Sheba stepped away from Spencer's traveling coach, where another footman struggled to secure trunks and valises atop the vehicle's roof. "I didn't mean to stand in your way."

"Not atop, miss. Lady Stiles wishes this"—the footman shrugged a shoulder, on which a small trunk perched—"to ride inside."

Sheba opened the coach door then scrambled aside again, allowing the footman to set Delphie's trunk on the floor. Still plenty of room for both Sheba and Delphie to sit comfortably during the journey back to Leicester, even if Spencer or Noel occasionally chose to ride inside with them rather than on their mounts.

Yes, Noel Griffin was accompanying them to Leicester. She twisted the ring he'd given her so the clasped hands and stones lay on the palm side, then pulled on her glove over it. She'd considered their betrothal a ruse, even though he'd said otherwise when he'd given the ring to her. But a man like Noel Griffin would hardly lie, merely to protect his reputation, or hers.

And neither would she…

The carriage horses whinnied, and Sheba startled again. Not from the sound, but from a touch, a soft, damp huff of air nosing against her neck.

"Amphritite! Behave yourself, miss!"

Sheba glanced over her shoulder to discover the large, liquid brown eye of a horse staring at her. Atop the animal sat Noel, immaculately turned out for a long day of riding.

Why should the weight in her chest lift at the mere sight of him?

With a jingle of bridle and spurs, he dismounted.

"My apologies, Bathsheba. Amphritite is usually better behaved. A lovely day for a journey, is it not?" He raised her hand and set a light kiss atop it.

Thank heavens she'd remembered her gloves. She didn't want to think what such a kiss would have felt like pressed against her bare skin…

"Noel, well met!" Spencer—when had he come out of the house?—clapped his friend on the shoulder. "We should be able to make Woburn, perhaps even Northampton, by dinnertime, if we don't dawdle."

"Ah. I wonder, Stiles, if you might be willing to make a slight change of plan?" Noel drew a letter from inside his coat and handed it to Sheba. "We've been invited to pay a call in Uxbridge on our way out of town."

"Uxbridge? Who do you know in Uxbridge?" Spencer asked.

Unfolding the sheet of paper, Sheba skimmed the invitation addressed to Noel, barely able to stifle her gasp when she caught sight of the signature at its bottom. Two capital w's slashing sharp points on the paper—

Spencer read over her shoulder, then raised an eyebrow at Noel. "Wilberforce? The very fellow Sheba has been longing to meet ever since she came to town?"

Noel nodded, his gaze glancing toward Sheba before fleeing back to Spencer.

"Why Uxbridge? You couldn't have wrangled an invitation when the fellow was in town?" Spencer grumbled.

"Mr. Wilberforce's time is not his own when he is in London."

"Oh, please, Spencer, may we stop?" Sheba pulled on Spencer's sleeve. "Surely Uxbridge will not take us so far out of our way."

Spencer crossed his arms. "West instead of north, and at least fifteen miles if memory serves."

"But surely it won't matter if we reach Leicester tomorrow evening instead of mid-day," Sheba pleaded.

"Well, if you don't mind making your father think you care more for an old politician than you do for him, who am I to object?" Spencer's mock sternness gave way to a wide grin. "Just let me tell Delphie and the coachman of our change in plans."

Spencer dashed up the stairs, leaving her alone with Noel. Sheba stared down at the note, hardly able to look at him, fearing what she might see in his face, in his eyes. "You did this —for me?" she whispered.

She felt rather than saw him nod. "You must know by now there is little I would not do to ensure your happiness, Bathshe

—umph!"

She threw herself into his arms, her own wrapping tightly about his neck, the letter crumpling between them. She heard her reticule thud against the pavement. But what should she care for such trifles, when Noel Griffin said such a thing!

His arms slipped about her back, squeezing her close against his chest. She closed her eyes, basking in his steadiness, his warmth. In how unexpectedly *right* it felt, to be encircled in his arms.

"Sheba, sweet." His lips whispered against her ear, sending a shiver down her spine. "Please don't tempt a poor fellow so. Not unless you wish me to scandalize all of London by kissing you within an inch of your life."

Her face warming, Sheba forced herself to pull free of his embrace.

What could she do to hide her embarrassment? Her eyes lit on the reticule she'd dropped, its contents now spilled about the pavement. She crouched to scoop up her coin purse, a fan of Delphie's, and a thimble that had escaped from her rosewood sewing *etui*.

"Friend Wilberforce's daughter did not seem very interested in what they could do to forward the cause of abolition. But surely not all the ladies of his acquaintance share such indifference. I wonder if he has ever considered all that women could do for the cause?"

Noel crouched, too, gathering a handful of hairpins and two copies of Elizabeth Heyrick's pamphlet. "Be careful not to expect too much of the gentleman. When his opponents may term him and his fellow Evangelicals 'The Saints,' it's meant to be ironic, not because they believe him a paragon of every virtue."

"Doubt William Wilberforce? When he has done so much for the cause? I would as soon doubt that the stars shine in the heavens as doubt such a man."

"You might be disappointed, then, if you argue that ladies

should play a larger role in championing abolition than they have in the past. I'd also suggest you avoid thrusting your teacher's radical proposals in the man's face."

Sheba frowned. "Why? Would not Elizabeth Heyrick's proposals be of more interest to Wilberforce than to almost any other man in the country? Why should I not share a copy with him?"

"Because before Lady Georgiana would agree to facilitating this invitation, she made me promise I would keep you from pressing your pamphlets on him as you did on his daughter," Noel said with a sigh. "Did you not realize that you'd embarrassed her, Sheba, talking to the ladies so?"

Sheba's throat tightened at the memory of the women at Georgiana Ellis's party, their gazes heavy with amused disdain. She had so little in common with them, and even less respect for them, those gossiping, irreverent ladies of the *ton*. Foolish, then, to still be stung by their scorn...

Why had she not answered when Noel had asked her about that evening when they last met? If she'd talked to him of it, told him the truth before he found out from someone else, he might not think so ill of her now. His disapprobation, thinking she didn't about care about the feelings of his friend—how surprisingly painful it felt!

A sudden, appalling thought struck her.

No. Surely not.

But what if it were? What if her desire to remain in England was no true leading of the spirit, but instead a selfish yearning to bask in the approbation, nay, the admiration, of Noel Griffin?

"Am I not allowed to speak to Wilberforce about the pamphlet's arguments, either?" she asked, defensiveness and doubt banishing the apology she'd initially intended to voice.

"Sheba. I'd never tell you what you can and cannot say. But you make it more difficult for yourself, bellowing and roaring like a bull in a china shop when others don't immediately see things your way."

Sheba jumped to her feet, crossing her arms and glaring down at Noel. "What, you think I should pretend I agree with the public's craven championing of a gradual emancipation of those poor souls, the wrongly enslaved?"

"Not pretend, no. But I would advise you to stop speaking out in favor of immediate, rather than gradual, emancipation," he said as he rose from his crouch. "Especially to Mr. Wilberforce. The man's spent his entire life championing the enslaved. Who are you to suggest his current approach is wrong?"

Sheba grabbed the pamphlets he'd collected and stuffed them into her reticule. "Who am I to remain silent, when the Spirit tells me advocating such a course is not only foolish, but immoral?"

Noel sighed. "You assume that if everyone just knew what you know, they'd believe exactly what you do. But the world doesn't work that way, Sheba. People have different interests, different needs. Something Mr. Wilberforce, canny politician that he is, knows full well. Can you not follow his example, and deploy diplomacy to artfully manage others?"

"Artfully manage others?" she huffed. "What, I should pretend to sympathize with the gradualist position, even though I find it abhorrent? My mother would scoff to see me stoop so low."

Noel threw up his hands. "Better that than insulting and shaming those who hold it. Can you not see that haranguing people only makes them hold even more tightly to their own views?"

Sheba's breath caught. His abhorrence of his family's West Indian holdings; his frustration at not being able to act to mitigate the suffering of the people on them; his guilt and dismay at unintentionally harming Michael Pinney by making him work in the presence of that portrait—of course she'd assumed he shared her convictions about immediate, rather than gradual, emancipation.

But he'd never said any such thing, had he?

"And what is *your* view of the matter?" she asked, struggling to keep her voice even. "Do you believe Africans have a right to their liberty, a right which is a crime to withhold? Or do you share the Duke of Gloucester's opinion that no man—no British man—should wish for immediate emancipation?"

"Of course I believe slavery to be morally wrong! And if I had the running of the world, I'd outlaw it immediately, just as you would."

She grasped her hands tight, to keep them from trembling in relief. She'd been wrong to doubt him. So wrong—

"But Sheba, I'm not the king, or the Prime Minister, or Wilberforce," he abruptly tacked. "And neither are you. If you ever wish to bring the evil institution to an end, you need to bring public opinion to your side. And the best way to do so is to address people's worries and fears. Worries and fears that a gradualist approach acknowledges."

Our moral code must be maintained in all its original purity. No compromise shall be made between the law of the world and the law of God.

How many times had Sheba heard her mother preach those words?

"No compromise between the law of the world and the law of God...

But he'd promised! Declared and affirmed he'd bear an equal share of her toils and troubles—

She tried to dismiss the frantic buzzing in her head. But it would not be quieted. A buzz that kept asking, what if, like so many other worldly men, he only meant he would do so when it suited him? That she must compromise whenever he would not?

How could she live up to her mother's expectations if she married a man who would not allow her to speak out for what she believed?

As she stared up at Noel, an icy sickness curdled every bit of joy in her heart. Of course a man of worldly spirit might admire the passion, as well as the person, of a Friend. But could anyone not a member of their Society truly understand and value her uncompromising principles? The principles which were the most important part of who Sheba was?

What a fool she was, to trust an outsider to understand.

Even more a fool to allow herself to begin to care for him. To allow this overweening lust to distract her from the righteous path...

Trembling, Sheba peeled the glove off her left hand, twisted free the ring he'd placed on her finger, and set it on her palm. With slow, deliberate calm, she extended that palm to him.

"As you must recall, Noel Griffin, our betrothal was only meant to be temporary. Now that it has served its purpose, I believe it is time for it to come to an end."

His face paled. "What? Surely you do not—"

"Your grandmother will be pleased that our ill-considered association has concluded," she cut him off. "And that you no longer have cause to travel to Leicester, and so can remain here with her and your cousin in town."

"Sheba, please—"

Sheba longed to deny her own words, to banish the hurt from Noel's voice, his far-too-dear face. To throw herself back into his arms, to revel in their safety and warmth.

No compromise between the law of the world and the law of God...

She turned her back on him, so he would not see the weak tears pricking at her eyes.

"I will never compromise, never disappoint my mother so," she whispered, then climbed up the steps of the waiting carriage and shut the door.

CHAPTER 19

Sheba stood at the front door of The Chestnuts, the small house to which William Wilberforce, seeking refuge from the dirt and sprawl of London, had recently moved. Sheba's hands felt far too warm inside her kid gloves, and not only from the early July heat. She was finally going to have the chance to speak to the famed Wilberforce herself!

She'd anticipated such a moment for months. Her mind should have been focused on the questions she wished to ask the Nightingale of the Commons. Not on this fierce longing to have Noel Griffin by her side while she did.

But she had sent him away.

Now her hand felt not only too warm, but too bare, denuded of the ring she'd so quickly become used to wearing...

Sheba shook off the unwelcome pangs, turning instead to inspect the building before her. Some might have assumed William Wilberforce would reside in a house that reflected his position of influence in British society. But the unassuming white brick Uxbridge house before them stood only two stories high and five windows wide, with three small dormers poking through its tiled roof.

An almost sacred space, it felt, as an ancient butler let them down the passageway that would lead them to the great man himself.

"Lord and Lady Stiles, ma'am, and Miss Honeychurch," the butler intoned.

A bright-eyed older woman—Wilberforce's wife? Barbara, wasn't she called?—jumped up from the drawing room sofa, needlework, threads, and scissors all falling in a jumble to the carpet by her feet.

"Ah, my Lord, my Lady, come in, come in! You find us quite at sixes and sevens today, I'm afraid. I did hope the servants would be finished unpacking by now, but alas—"

The lady threaded a friendly arm through Delphie's and led them into a drawing room crowded with letters, papers, half-emptied boxes, and far more people than Sheba had anticipated. Why, there must be more than a dozen visitors in the room! Not a family quiet at home, as she'd pictured, but a noisy, sociable gathering.

"One always forgets, does one not, how long it takes to settle into a new home?" Delphie sympathized.

"Especially a home so inconveniently small! Do you know, we must send some of the servants and most of our guests to the inn a mile away to sleep?"

Wilberforce's wife led them past a poorly swept hearth, an unpolished brass fire grate. How Sheba's mother would look askance upon such lackadaisical housekeeping!

Delphie gave Wilberforce's wife a sympathetic smile. "Removing from one house to another can be quite tiresome. But you have a charmingly cozy room here, with a lovely view of the Common."

"Yes, but when one takes up residence in a place more like a hutch than a house, all of us squashed inside like so many rabbits, the view matters little, I think. And to have to become used to the ways of new tradesmen, and new servants—oh, how troublesome it all is! But here is Mr. Wilberforce, eager as always to form new acquaintances. My dear Wilber, Lord and Lady

Stiles, and a young cousin of theirs, a Miss Honeychurch, whom Lady Georgiana Ellis commends to your attention."

How very small he was, this man who had seemed such a towering presence on the raised dais at the Anti-Slavery meeting! Far shorter than Noel, slighter even than Sheba herself, hunched in his chair, a curling comma of a spine.

Why should she be so shocked to discover him such an old man? He'd spent decades on the national stage advocating for political reforms.

Intelligence still sparked in his eyes, though, intelligence and patience and good humor. Even before he'd said a word, Sheba had no trouble imagining him swaying audiences with the wisdom those knowing eyes promised.

"Mr. Wilberforce. An honor, sir." Spencer bowed. Beside him, Delphie offered a curtsy.

If Sheba were to give deference to any human being, it surely would be William Wilberforce. Yet though her knees knocked together, they would not bend.

It gave her courage, imagining the admiration in Noel's eyes at witnessing her remaining true to her principles.

Sheba frowned. What had put a such misguided vision in her head? If he admired her for that, she'd not have needed to return his ring, or send him away...

The old politician himself did not seem to care, or even notice, Sheba's marked lack of deference.

"Stiles, Stiles, Stiles," he murmured as he pulled on a pair of spectacles and scrambled amongst the papers on the table beside him. "Where did I put that letter? Ah, yes, here it is! And my memory did not prove false. Sir George *did* say you had spent time in our African colony. Come, my lord, come and sit beside me and tell me who you think should be named governor there, now that poor MacCarthy has met such an untimely end."

Delphie pressed Sheba into a chair, the weight of her hand against her shoulder a clear warning against trying to wrest the conversation toward her own concerns.

Sheba shrugged free with a frown. As if she would ever show such disrespect to the great Wilberforce! Of course one of the men who had been behind the founding of Sierra Leone would wish to hear about Spencer's time in the British colony, and discuss its future governance. Sheba *could* exercise patience when it was called for, even if Delphie, or Noel, might doubt her capacity for forbearance.

Besides, one would have to be stone-eared to not be enthralled by Wilberforce's mellifluous voice, let alone by the questions he posed Spencer, or the stories he told in his turn. As riveting as any preacher she'd ever heard, even her own mother. Little wonder everyone in the room quieted to listen to his conversation with Spencer.

Until, that is, an elderly man, one far older than Wilberforce, shook his walking stick at a servant. "What, are we to have no bread and butter? You, there, bring some bread and butter, plenty without limit," he roared.

The interruption did not discompose Wilberforce in the least. "Oh, Mr. Beasley, thank you, sir, thank you kindly for seeing to these things," he called to the old fellow. "Mrs. Wilberforce is not strong enough to meddle much in domestic matters."

Wilberforce bent close to Spencer. "My former Secretary, Beasley. Too troubled with cataracts to read anything now, poor fellow, but we keep him on because he is so grateful. And his wife, too, because she nursed poor darling Ba—our eldest daughter, you know—during her final illness. But I trust our dear child is now rejoicing in heaven, though her mother and sister miss her sorely."

Sheba shot Delphie a worried glance. The Wilberforces were not the only ones here today who had lost a child.

But she needn't have worried. Spencer had already taken up her cousin's hand, holding it tight between his.

If each will still bear an equal share with the other in all their toils and troubles—

"May I refresh your cup, dear?" Spencer asked his wife after the condoling murmurs abated. He gave her shoulder a comforting squeeze before taking up her cup and carrying it to Wilberforce's wife. And then caught Sheba's eye, tilting his head toward the seat by Wilberforce he had just abandoned.

Bearing a share of not only his wife's toils and troubles, but of Sheba's, too. Sheba smiled her gratitude before setting her own teacup on the table.

"I had the pleasure of meeting your daughter Elizabeth at Lady Georgiana's, this Tuesday past," she said as she slipped into the stiff-backed chair. "Is she not with you today?"

Wilberforce blinked, then gazed distractedly about the room. "As I can barely see much past the end of my nose, miss, you would know better than I whether Elizabeth is present. Or rather, should I say *Friend*? You are of the Quaker persuasion, are you not?"

Sheba nodded.

"May I compliment you on demonstrating all the self-possession of a Friend, as well as much natural politeness, in allowing an old man to monopolize the conversation so?"

"It requires little politeness on my part to listen to a person so very interested and amused by everyone and everything." Sheba offered him a warm smile. "Whatever such a person says naturally becomes interesting and amusing itself."

Wilberforce laughed, light and joyful as a chiming bell. "And so I will take an interest in *you*, Friend. You are returning home —to Leicester?—from a visit to London?"

"Yes, my first."

"And how long did you reside in town?"

"Since the beginning of May."

"Only two months! Hardly enough time to even scratch the surface of such a teeming metropolis as ours. What did you enjoy most about your visit?"

"Attending the meeting of the Anti-Slavery Society, and hearing you and the other abolitionists speak."

Wilberforce chuckled. "And here I thought Quakers did not engage in the convention of flattery, my dear. Although I wonder if it was quite wise, Lord Stiles, to bring your ladies to such a public event," he added as Spencer took up a stance behind her chair.

"I only speak the truth, Friend Wilberforce," Sheba insisted. "Your admonishment not to trust to individual zeal or effort for accomplishing the abolition of slavery struck me as particularly apt. We certainly must all work together if we are to achieve our goal."

"Indeed, my dear. Creating coalitions, even with those whose views do not precisely match our own, is the only way forward. That and negotiating with those who disagree," he said, his eyes twinkling.

Sheba bit her cheek. Why should it trouble her, to hear him promote the same methods Noel had?

She shook off the uncomfortable feeling. "Do you not think ladies particularly suited to such work? We may have no voice in Parliament, no chance to speak for the cause in public meetings, yet we have a voice and an influence in a sphere, which, though restricted, is no narrow one. To the hearts and consciences of our own sex, at least, we have unlimited access."

Wilberforce blinked. "All private exertions for such an object become their character," he said as he reached for his tea, leaving her hand to drop to her side.

She leaned forward, her heart pounding in her throat. "But what of *public* exertions? Do you not think we ladies should form an auxiliary of our own, to support the work of the larger Anti-Slavery Society?"

"Ladies to join political associations?" Barbara Wilberforce exclaimed. "Is that not unbecoming?"

Sheba frowned. "Only if such associations are conducted in an unbecoming manner. And if William Wilberforce would but declare his support—"

But Wilberforce was already shaking his head, his grey curls bouncing. "No, no, my dear. I own I cannot relish such a plan. For ladies to meet, to publish, to go from house to house stirring up petitions—these appear to me proceedings unsuited to the female character as delineated in Scripture. Does not St. Paul command 'suffer not a woman to teach, nor usurp authority over the man, but to be in silence'?"

"But does Paul not also tell us of many women who spread the word of God?" Sheba protested. "Does he not say Euodia and Syntyche labored with him in the gospel? And account Phebe a servant of the church for carrying his letter to the Romans from Greece? Does he not mention the work of Priscilla multiple times, most often naming her before her husband Aquila?"

"I cannot but admire a young lady who knows her Scripture," Wilberforce said with a gentle smile. "But the examples of a handful of unusual women do not refute the general precept."

"But Paul never says that only certain gifts or callings are for men, and others for women," Sheba protested. "All are called by the Spirit to spread the Word of God. My own mother heeded that call before her own death, traveling throughout the country to spread the word of God."

"A female preacher?" Barbara Wilberforce's eyes flew wide. "Imagine if our dear Elizabeth had taken such a strange start! Mr. Pinney never would have had her then, would he?"

"Pinney?" Spencer set his cup and saucer down on the table with a sharp click. "Of Bristol? A relation of John Pretor Pinney?"

Sheba frowned. Who was *John* Pinney? Some relation of Michael Pinney's?

"Yes, John Pretor Pinney's son, Charles. Quite pleased we are with the match," the proud father said. "A pious gentleman, quite devoted to our girl. Her focus will be on domestic concerns, not on the warfare of political life."

Sheba flinched, even though the man's words had not been directed to her.

"But are you not aware that much of Mr. John Pinney's wealth stems from holdings in the Indies?" Spencer asked.

Barbara Wilberforce sat further back in her chair, a mulish expression overtaking her round face. "Mr. Charles Pinney is a banker, not a proprietor of lands and slaves. As he informed Mr. Wilberforce himself, his late father sold his plantation to a neighbor just as soon as the slave trade was made illegal."

"A banker, yes. But one who grants mortgages to West Indian plantation owners, if we are speaking of the same gentleman," Spencer said.

"Oh, but we've been assured that mortgages are not at all like the slave trade," his wife explained.

"But if those mortgages are not repaid, does he not by default become owner of those plantations, as well as the people enslaved on them?" Sheba asked.

"Of course Mr. Wilberforce should prefer for any one he loves to be without such possessions," his wife asserted. "But having been born to them, a man must do his duty by them."

"It is difficult to move in society without encountering someone with West Indian connections," Wilberforce said. "And it is such a comfort for an old man, knowing my child will be loved and cared for when I'm no longer here to watch over her."

Sheba stared at the great anti-slavery advocate, hardly able to believe her own ears. What a feeble excuse! Would William Wilberforce, who had worked to tirelessly to end the slave trade, truly allow his daughter to marry a man whose family fortune, no, whose own wealth, had been built on slavery? The man who had called his fellow members of Parliament to account with the words "you may choose to look the other way, but you can never say again that you did not know"?

Be careful not to expect too much of the gentleman...

Sheba jerked to her feet. "Friend Wilberforce, you cannot—"

"Surely it cannot be two already?" Delphie stepped in front of Sheba and laid a hand on her arm. "You've kept us all so wonderfully entertained, Mr. Wilberforce, we've quite forgotten the time. But if we are to make Woburn before dark, I fear we must be on our way."

Their host, obviously in some pain, rose from his chair far more slowly than they had. "So kind of you to make time to visit with an old man, my lady. I'm always happy to form new acquaintances, especially ones who share so many of my own interests."

"Sheba, would you go and ask John Coachman to ready the horses?" Spencer's words were more command than question.

Sheba rushed from the drawing room, blinking away the tears that burned at the corners of her eyes. Blinking away the sight of the man whom she had revered nearly all her life. Almost as much as she revered her own mother.

No matter how admirable, he was but a man. A man with feet not only of iron but of far too breakable clay. Shattered now all to pieces, just like the statue in Nebuchadnezzar's dream. Or like the chaff of the summer threshing floors, destined to disappear at the first stray gust of wind.

Noel had warned her not to make a graven image of a mere man, hadn't he?

Their idols are silver and gold, the work of men's hands... They that make them are like unto them; so is every one that trusteth in them...

Had she made an idol not just of Wilberforce, but of Noel, too?

She shuddered to a stop in the passageway, her breath catching in her throat. Is that why she'd pushed him away? Because she couldn't value him for who he was, instead of the impossibly faultless idol she believed he should be? Because he was not an idealized angel on earth, but just a man, with all the complexities and imperfections inherent in the human state?

No compromise between the law of the world and the law of God.
You're always so sure you know what's right, what's best!

Sheba squeezed her eyes shut, pressing her back, her shaking hands, tight against the wall. Her mother's admonition, Ash's accusation, the hurt in Noel's eyes—the visions fluttered wildly about her brain like a flock of leaderless geese.

Had she been wrong to push away the one man who seemed to value her for who she was, rather than for the exemplary woman she could never seem to be?

And if she was, what was she going to do to make things right?

"Please thank your father, Sheba, for his kind hospitality to us this past week." Delphie folded a petticoat and set it atop the gowns already resting in the half-filled trunk. "We would have so liked to stay in Leicester another fortnight."

"I know, Delphie." Sheba sat down on the bed by her cousin and gave her a comforting squeeze. "But Con needs you, and Spencer, whether she's willing to say so or not."

Since the arrival of Connie's express with news of her husband's death, the residents of the Honeychurch household had been all at sixes and sevens, rushing to help Delphie and Spencer prepare for a far earlier return to London than had originally been planned.

Sheba laid her temple against Delphie's shoulder, blinking away an unexpected rush of tears. She had no reason to cry for Colonel Wingfield. As her mother would surely preach, the Lord had received his soul into the mansions of glory, where the wicked cease from troubling, and the faithful are at rest.

No, this strange pall of sadness had been plaguing her days, long before Con's letter had arrived.

Since calling on Abiah Griffin and her daughters, and being so foolishly surprised at not finding her best friend in his usual seat by the hearth? Since being greeted by her father with his usual absentminded affection, and not the least bit of curiosity about her time in town? Since the crushing disappointments of her encounter with Wilberforce?

Do not fear the truth, her mother's voice whispered in her ear.

Sheba shuddered, her hands clenching tight in her lap. The truth?

Sadness had been her constant companion, ever since she had given Noel back his ring…

"Poor Connie!"

Sheba's head fell from Delphie's shoulder at her cousin's deep sigh. "We could all see how much the colonel's injuries pained him, but not even she imagined him in any real danger."

"No," Sheba agreed, rising from the bed and striding over to the dressing table. She snatched up Delphie's best bonnet and nestled it inside a hatbox. "Do you think Con will wish to remain in Clapham now that the colonel is gone?"

"The more pressing question is will she be *able* to remain in Clapham. Connie writes that she has no idea what provision, if any, her husband made for her in the event of his death."

"Did her father not negotiate a marriage settlement with the colonel before they wed?"

"Apparently not."

Noel Griffin would never have left a wife so unprotected…

Delphie grimaced, her eyebrows pinching tight over her brow. "Oh, how I wish we had tried harder to convince her not to marry in such haste!"

Kneeling at Delphie's feet, Sheba grasped her cousin's hands in hers. "It is not your fault, Delphie. Not yours, nor mine, nor Elizabeth's or Polly's. Con might enjoy giving all of us cousins her advice, but you know she never listens to ours."

Delphie squeezed Sheba's hands, then gave a decisive nod. "Well, if she cannot stay in Clapham, I will ask her to come to us at Beechcombe Park. Do you know, I once thought it the dearest wish of my heart to invite her, and you, and all my Audley cousins to live with me there?"

Sheba gave a wan smile. "As if you wouldn't be wishing us all back home within a fortnight, the way we bicker and quarrel."

The hinges on the bedroom door seemed to squeal in agreement. Delphie's lady's maid shouldered into the room, a stack of Spencer's shirts in hand.

"I've done with the ironing, my lady. Why do you not let me get on with the packing?"

Delphie nodded, then gazed about the room. Searching for any last stray belongings, no doubt.

"Now if I could just remember where I put my copy of *The Scottish Chiefs*…"

"Weren't you reading it to Spencer in the drawing room last night?" Sheba asked.

Delphie blushed, as if reading mightn't have been all she and her husband had been doing downstairs after Sheba and her father had retired for the evening.

Sheba's lips burned at the thought, jealous, wanting. Yearning for the press of Noel's against her own…

She bit her bottom lip, hard, almost hard enough to draw blood. "I'll find it for you," she said, rushing out into the passageway before Delphie could remark on the sudden flush crimsoning her cheeks.

"Bathsheba?"

Sheba paused on the stairs. Was that her father's voice?

"Might I have a word?" he called from the library.

Though her father had played civil host to her cousin and Spencer since their arrival in Leicester five days past, he'd barely offered more than a nod to Sheba. Not so different, then, from their usual state of affairs since her mother's passing.

But several times she thought she'd caught him staring at her, his brow furrowed in confusion, as if she were one of the Roman antiquities he so enjoyed collecting, but one he wasn't quite sure how to catalogue. But he'd look so quickly away, she couldn't quite be sure...

She pushed open the library door to find her father sitting behind his desk, flipping through a small bound volume. Not one of his scholarly tomes on antiquities, or one of the ledgers from his hosiery factory, but something that looked more like—a diary?

Father had never kept a journal, had he?

No, but Sheba's mother had...

She placed a hand against her suddenly fluttering throat.

"Sit down, child. I've something I wish to say to you."

"Father?" Sheba perched gingerly on the edge of a wooden chair.

He stared at her for long minutes, his eyebrows gathered in tight. When had they turned so grey?

"You are not happy, are you?" he finally said.

"Not happy?" she echoed. How had her unobservant father noticed *that*?

"No. Not happy. Because your agreement with Manasseh Griffin has come to naught?"

Sheba's eyes fixed on her fingers, plucking at a seam in her gown.

"No, I thought not," her father said when she made no answer. "But disappointed in love all the same. I recognize the look. The same one your mother wore when she thought a match between us impossible."

Sheba's eyes jerked to her father's. "My mother—disappointed in love?"

"Difficult for you to imagine, I see," he said with a melancholy smile. "Perhaps not being born a Friend made her so determined to serve as exemplar to you, to embody the perfect model of unerring Quaker behavior. I thought it a mistake, not sharing her struggles with you, especially as you grew older. But she did not agree."

"Struggled? My mother?"

"Yes, struggled," he exclaimed, his hand slamming down against the cover of the journal. "Because we lost her before she could share those struggles with you, you've put her on a pedestal, practically made an idol of her. And I won't have it, not any longer."

Snatching up the journal from the desk, he rose and strode to Sheba's side.

"She asked me to give this to the Meeting, ask that they consider publishing her words. But grief made me selfish. I didn't want to share her, the woman I loved. Not with them. Not with you."

His face lined with regret, he held the small book out to her. "But I think it's time you knew Jane Audley Honeychurch the woman, not just the virtuous paragon she wished you to see."

Hours later, Sheba stared at the familiar sights of Leicester through the library window, her mother's journal clutched tight to her chest. A group of boys played in St. Nicholas's churchyard, daring one another to climb the rude, unequal forest stone and brick of the ancient wall which stood on the church's west side. On the first day of their visit, her father had taken Spencer and Delphie to view the Roman ruin, but neither had cared to join the great antiquarian debate about whether it was the last remaining wall of what had been a temple to Janus, or a great gateway to the Roman town that had once stood on the site.

Would Noel's curiosity have been piqued by the controversy? She didn't know if antiquities held any interest for him. But then, she'd never known they intrigued her mother, either.

She could picture him now, not masking his inquisitiveness as her mother, fearful of taking an interest in anything the Meeting might deem too worldly, had, but taking one side or the other, impressing her father with his intelligence and wit. Or joining the weekly debate with her father's friends, a group of men who, despite their business interests, took an eager interest in literature and philosophy, too. Or sharing her father's fascination with his collection of Roman coins, many dug up right here in the parish in which they lived—

At a knock at the front door, her heart gave an odd, uneven pound.

No. Longing for Noel Griffin would never make him suddenly appear on her doorstep.

Far more likely to be Rebecca Satterthwaite or Mary Tanner, come to ask her again about how she'd spent her time in London. The elders hadn't seemed satisfied with their brief discussion of the subject yesterday, after First Day Meeting. She sighed and placed the journal safe in her father's desk, trying to ready herself to listen with an open heart to what would likely be their many criticisms and admonishments of the worldly behavior in which she'd indulged while in town.

But when she pulled open the door, a far younger Friend stood waiting on the pavement.

"Ash? Whatever are you doing in Leicester?" she exclaimed.

"Besides calling on my oldest friend?" He gave her a quick embrace, then moved back and glanced over his shoulder, his usual amiable smile flickering. Both Sarah Gabbidon and Michael Pinney stood behind him, neither looking at all comfortable.

"I wished Miss Gabbidon to meet the rest of my family," Ash stammered. "*Our* family..."

Sheba's gaze flicked between Sarah and Ash. He'd wanted her to meet his sisters, something Sarah had wished, too. But had she not been expecting her half-brother to arrange such a gathering so quickly?

"Come in, come in," Sheba said, opening the door wide. The surprised glances being thrown at Michael Pinney by curious passers-by surely must be discomfiting. Almost forty thousand people made Leicester their home, but very few of them were of African descent.

"Did you insist on keeping up the pretense that you are unrelated?" Sheba asked Sarah as she gestured her to a seat on the settee. "Or did you allow Ash to inform his family of your true relation?"

Michael Pinney raised an amused eyebrow. "As direct and blunt as always, I see, Miss Honeychurch."

"I appreciate Sheba's directness," Sarah protested. "Far too many people here in England prefer to dance around hard truths."

"As I've discovered these past three months, much to my own chagrin," Ash said with a wry grimace.

"And I did not wish to make you into one of them," Sarah said to her brother before turning back to Sheba. "So no, Sheba, I did not agree to come to Leicester just so I might spy on my relations behind their backs."

Sheba might have chuckled at Sarah's dry humor if Ash's expression had not looked so pained.

"You did not write in advance, to give your mother some warning?" she guessed.

The corner of his mouth rose. "Cowardly, to leave such news to a letter. No, I thought it best to inform her in person."

"How difficult it must have been, to tell them what your father had done."

Ash grimaced. "Difficult, painful, and deeply upsetting, especially for my mother. You know in what high esteem she always held him. Learning he'd kept yet another secret from her —I fear it's shaken her faith, even though she would never admit as much to me."

"Ash's—*our*, sisters seemed pleased to make my acquaintance,"

Sarah said. "At least after the first shock of discovering a sibling about whom they had no previous knowledge suddenly on their doorstep. But they've been so curious about my apprenticeship, and eager for my advice about their own teaching. Patience and Abigail will be sad to give it over, if you decide to return to it now that you have come back to Leicester."

Would she be satisfied, overseeing the small school again? When her ambitions had been to change the world, not just this small corner of it?

"How long are you to be in town, Ash?" Sheba asked instead, banishing such questions for now. She would need time, and reflection, and above all, hope, if she were ever to discern a true leading about her future.

"Miss MacKay's Seminary is closed until August," Ash replied. "My sisters are hoping Sarah will remain with them for at least the next fortnight, if not to the end of the month. Which is the real reason for our call. Would you stand Sarah friend whilst she resides here in Leicester? Speak out against the gossip that is all too likely to flare?"

"Since I've no desire to mix in society, I've no need of any defender," Sarah demurred. "All I wish is to become better acquainted with your sisters."

"But the Griffin sisters, at least the elder two, are hardly in the habit of remaining quietly at home," Sheba said. "And even if they were, Friends' homes are not places of retreat and seclusion from public life, as the homes of the worldly are. You are bound to meet far more people than you anticipate."

Sarah's forehead creased. "Ash, why did you not tell me so? I doubt I'd have agreed to stay longer than you if I had known."

"Longer than your brother?" Sheba frowned at Ash. "Will you not be here, then, to smooth your sister's path?"

A conscious flush rose on Ash's cheeks. "No. Noel and I must return to town by Saturday."

Sheba's heart flew up into her throat. Noel was here, in

Leicester? Why had he not come with them?

The look of pity on Ash's face—on all of their faces—served as explanation enough.

Sheba swallowed, hard.

"I wish you still had some influence with him, Sheba," Ash finally said. "You might have persuaded him to accept one of the estate's properties I promised to deed him when I come of age. But Noel refuses to accept a penny from Silliman funds."

"He's hardly impecunious," Pinney reassured. "Captain Griffin's prize money amounted to a very pretty sum."

"Prize money?" Sheba said. "What is prize money?"

"When our Navy captures an enemy's ship, the ship and its cargo are sold. The resulting monies are then distributed among the crew of the ship that made the capture," Pinney explained. "The ship's captain is awarded the largest share."

"Not only of the prize money, but of the head money, too," Spencer called from the passageway. "At least for ships assigned to the West Africa Squadron, as Noel's father's was."

Sheba frowned. "Head money?

"Yes, the bounty sailors gained from liberating Africans from slave ships." Spencer set down the valise he'd been carrying and entered the room, bowing to their guests. Delphie followed—in search of the book Sheba had promised to retrieve for her?

"Noel must be so proud of his father," Delphie said as she picked up the errant volume. "It's quite a dangerous posting, I understand. The constitutional courage of its seamen is anchor of Great Britain, is it not?"

"But where does this head money come from?" Sheba asked. "Surely our government does not *sell* the people they've just liberated?"

"No. The money comes from the Crown," Spencer said.

"I believe the going rate is £40 for a man, £30 for a woman, £10 for a child under 14," Sarah said, her voice laced with bitterness.

Delphie frowned. "Do you think it wrong, Sarah, to reward our brave sailors for their work to suppress the shameful trade in human beings? Especially given how harrowing such work must be. Should we not take pride in their honorable sacrifices?"

"Honorable sacrifices?" Sarah huffed. "If only you had heard them, toasting their successes in my father's tavern. Crowing not over saving so many souls, but over how much prize money they'd gain."

Spencer gave a wry grimace. "From what I heard, ships with only a few captive Africans aboard caused even more excitement than the full ones."

"Why?" Ash asked, his brow furrowing.

"Because such ships were usually on their way *to*, rather than *from*, Africa, and so filled with trade goods to sell before they went a-slaving," Spencer explained. "And unlike wrongfully imprisoned Africans, cloth and spirits and other goods taken from captured ships *can* be sold, and the profits split among the crew, typically for a far greater amount than any head money they'd earn from rescuing a ship full of captives."

"Yes, the presence of only a handful of enslaved sailors aboard such a ship gives the Navy the right to capture it, but doesn't require all the trouble of figuring out what to do with the hundreds of mistreated and often ill human beings aboard," Sarah scoffed.

"It wouldn't matter, if they actually helped the people they purportedly freed—"

"Purportedly?" Sheba's skin began to crawl.

"Yes. The Crown reserves the right to enlist all recaptives in the military, or to bind them as apprentices, whether they will or no."

"More in name than in actuality, this freedom you are all so proud of bestowing." Sarah's lips curled with disdain.

"But we take such pride in our navy's role in suppressing the trade," Ash exclaimed. "How is it that the public knows nothing of this?"

"Never mind the public." Sheba's eyes whipped between Ash, Spencer, and Sarah. "Does Noel know?"

The three exchanged questioning glances. "I've never spoken with him on the subject," Sarah finally said.

"Nor I," Spencer concurred. "Noel has always spoken of his father with pride, but I've never heard him speak in particular about his work in the African Squadron."

"Then you must tell him," Sheba said, vehemence forcing her from her chair. "Tell him the money his father left him is tainted!"

"Sheba, please sit down." Delphie laid a quelling hand on Sheba's arm. "Such censorious language hardly seems warranted."

"Even if our sailors did gain pecuniary rewards for their efforts," Spencer agreed, "those efforts still kept hundreds of wrongfully imprisoned Africans from a lifetime of forced and inhumane toil."

Sheba's fists tightened, her fingernails biting into her palms. How could they justify such equivocation?

She opened her mouth, bitter reproaches poised on her lips—

Can you not see that haranguing people only makes them hold even more tightly to their own views?

Sheba blinked, then dropped back into her seat, struggling to contain her frustration.

"Perhaps," she forced herself to acknowledge. "But should not Noel be told before deciding for himself? Ash, will you speak to him about it?"

"If the topic ever comes up, I won't lie. But I don't see there is any cause for me to introduce it in conversation myself." Ash bit his bottom lip. "Why tarnish his father's memory to no purpose?"

Sheba's breath hitched. The pain of living with the tarnished memory of a once-revered parent hung heavy in her friend's eyes. No, she couldn't insist he tell his cousin, could she?

"If you think it so important that Mr. Griffin be told, then why should you not be the one to do it?" Sarah asked. "Difficult news comes best from those who love us. And from those whom we love."

Sheba stared at Sarah, the words a whirligig in her brain.

Those whom we love?

Sarah offered a kindly, if far too knowing, smile. "You do love him, do you not?"

Sheba clutched the arms of her chair. *Did* she love Noel Griffin?

Why had she never thought to ask herself such a thing before?

Never Marry but for Love—the first of William Penn's maxims on "Right Marriage."

As she considered the question, the restless, striving dissatisfaction that had been her life-long burden whenever she struggled to discern her personal path abruptly dissipated, giving way all at once to a growing surety, the same surety she usually felt about only her moral and political beliefs. That deep inward prompting of the Spirit that had always been lacking in her feelings towards Ash—yes, she felt it now, but not for her oldest friend.

For his cousin.

How strange, but also how so very fitting, that wayward Friend Bathsheba Honeychurch should be granted such a divine leading, calling her to link her life to such an entirely worthy, yet entirely unsuitable man.

"I do, don't I?" she said, the words more statement than question. She, Bathsheba Honeychurch, loved Noel Griffin.

What wonder, to be the recipient of such a deep, soul-affirming truth...

Delphie squeezed her hand. "Then do you not think he deserves to know that, too? Just as much as the other?"

CHAPTER 20

Noel stood with his back to the small burial ground beside Leicester's Quaker Meeting House, staring out over the rippling summer meadows that lay to its west. A few butterflies, and even more bees, flitted between the flowers peeping out between the tall grasses, the River Soar the merest hint of silver beyond. A clump of honeysuckle climbed the wall between the grounds and the field, the sweet, light scent from its abundant blooms not quite covering the musty, damp, earthy decay of the graves.

Except for that slight hint of unpleasantness in the air, and the modest stone lintel at the gate marked "1682," Noel would hardly have known he was in a graveyard, so different was it from where his grandfather, along with the rest of his Silliman ancestors, had been laid to rest. He'd hardly expected grand monuments or vaults in a Quaker cemetery, never mind anything like the elaborate cyclopean mausoleum at Ruxford Hall. But not even simple gravestones marking the sites of the dead? How was he to know where the redoubtable Jane Audley Honeychurch lay?

His lips curved in a self-mocking grimace. As if holding a one-sided conversation with a dead woman could help him better understand her living daughter…

"Cuck-oo," a lone bird called from a stand of white willow by the river.

Noel snorted in agreement. Yes, yet another fool's errand, coming here today. As was this entire trip to Leicester. What was he thinking, still pining after the woman who in no uncertain terms had given him his congé?

A desperate urge, it had been, to insist on accompanying Ash and Sarah despite having no clear strategy for how achieve his goal. Hardly even knowing what goal he should be striving for...

He began to wander aimlessly through the churchyard, wondering how he could devise a strategy, or even a plan, when the woman he longed for wanted nothing to do with him? Not because she didn't care—he'd swear she did, at least a little—but because she'd been nursed on the uncompromising self-righteousness of a mother who controlled her even more firmly from the grave than she ever could have if she'd lived?

Wrong to damn such a pious, beloved preacher. But Noel damned her all the same.

"She's over there, by the west wall."

A voice, achingly familiar, caressed his ear. He closed his eyes, fearing his longing had gotten the better of him. As if the mere thought of the woman who haunted his dreams could bring her to his side...

The peal of a clock bell tolling the hour made his eyes flick open. But when he turned in search of its source, he found Bathsheba Honeychurch instead.

"The worldly use gravestones as a sign of respect for the memory of those who are gone. But Friends do not believe such monuments a proper way of honoring the dead," she said, her voice careful, diffident.

Of course she guessed he'd come in search of her mother's grave. Almost as if she could see inside his brain without his ever having to say an awkward word.

Was that why he loved her so?

"Why should a tombstone be improper?" he asked. Far better

to discuss philosophical abstractions than to plague her with his own inconvenient and unwanted feelings.

"Because it is human nature to praise those whom we love, more particularly when we have lost them. And tombstones and monumental inscriptions all too often abound with extravagant, undeserved praise." Her eyes flicked to the corner of the burial ground. "'False as an epitaph,' as my mother always used to say."

How apt. The inscription on the lintel over the door of the Silliman family mausoleum—"Good deeds are the best memorials"—hardly applied to the last Lord Silliman, did it?

"How, then, do Friends honor the dead?"

She gestured to a path winding toward the river. "Walk with me and I'll tell you."

He fell into step beside her, setting his hands in the crook of his back to keep from reaching for hers.

"The life and remarkable sayings of any Friend eminent for his or her labours in the ministry are often written up by a member of the Meeting to which they belong," she said, her eyes fixed on the path before them. "Then they are published as incitements to piety for our rising youth. I have a shelf full of such volumes in my bedchamber at home."

"Given to you by your mother, I assume."

She nodded.

"But are not longer written accounts just as prone to exaggeration and false praise as shorter ones?" he asked. "Perhaps even more so?"

"Not when any such account must first be presented to the Meeting, which examines it for truth." As they reached the river, she turned to follow its tow-path northward. "Only if it is approved as true will it be shared with the Quarterly or Yearly Meeting and published."

He moved a low-hanging branch out of her way, earning a quick glance from those bright blue eyes. His pulse pounding in his throat, in his temples, made him feel a touch lightheaded.

He swallowed. "Ah, but what is truth? Most of the accounts of notable personages I've read only discuss a person's admirable qualities. Do Friends employ the same conventions in their encomiums? Or do you believe that moral advantage may be derived from recounting the faults and foibles of their eminent subjects, as well as their praiseworthy traits?"

"Our accounts do often include a person's missteps in youth, a period of profligacy before the inner light appears—"

"Those are past faults, though," Noel interrupted. "What of present ones? Say, for example, you were to write an account of Wilberforce—would you recount not only his kindness and generosity, his eloquence in support of the cause of abolition, but also his poor business sense? His overly extravagant generosity? What of his doubt about the ability of ladies to make any significant contribution to antislavery work?"

Sheba's chin lowered for just an instant before those blue eyes rose to fix on his. "You tried to tell me he wouldn't favor a plan to start a ladies' anti-slavery auxiliary. But I wouldn't listen."

He pressed his lips together for a moment. "From all I've heard of the man, I suspected as much, yes."

"Is that why you told me not to share Elizabeth Heyrick's pamphlet with him? Not because you wanted me to pretend to be something I'm not, but because you didn't wish me to be disappointed?"

"You thought I wanted you to hide who you are?"

Her immediate nod gutted him.

"Sheba, no! I'd never ask you to lie!"

She came to a halt by the side of an elegant stone bridge, her chin tipped high. "You may not have told me so directly, but you discouraged me from speaking out for what I believe."

He stared out across the river, at the ruins of Leicester's ancient abbey on its opposite bank. She believed he didn't respect her principles because they differed from his own? That he would only respect her if she agreed with him? Made herself lesser? Hid the truth of her honest self?

Was that why she had sent him away? Because a woman raised to believe herself the equal of any other person would never marry a man who demanded she give over any belief that did not match his own?

He'd been raised to expect as much from a wife. Not just consideration of his feelings and beliefs, but deference, even submission, to his superior male views, in both public and private. His mother, and even more his grandmother, had outwardly conformed to the views of the men they had wed.

But did *he* need such self-abnegation from the woman he married?

No. Didn't need it, didn't even want it. Especially if that wife were Bathsheba Honeychurch.

A restless movement by his side jerked him from his questions. He raised his eyes, searching the face that had grown so dear to him in spite of all he'd done to keep himself from wanting her.

He'd never been very adept at sensing other people's emotions, but he could read Sheba's as clearly as glass. Almost as if she were a mirror, reflecting back his own. Hurt, and regret, and a deep, pained longing for something, someone, she couldn't, wouldn't allow herself to have...

"I owe you an apology, Sheba," he said, taking her hand, and his own courage, in his. "I'm so used to hiding my own thoughts and feelings, to pretending to be what I'm not. I didn't realize how appalling my advice to be more diplomatic would sound to one raised to value plain speaking."

"No, don't apologize. Or at least not for that." Sheba shook her head, then pressed her back against the side of the bridge and stared down at the ground. "My mother so often preached that compromise with the world should be anathema to a true Friend. That one must be uncompromising with oneself, as well as with others, who fail to live up to their testimony to truth."

Her eyes turned up to his, then, tight with a pain he didn't understand. She'd must have forgotten to tie her bonnet ribbons again, for it now lay between them on the ground. He gave in to the impulse to sweep a hand over the silk of her hair, encouraging her to continue her story.

"But then when I came home, I read her journal. And discovered that I hadn't understood at all what she truly meant."

"Your mother kept a journal?" His hand curled about her neck, cupping her nape.

"A spiritual journal, yes. Many in our Society do, as a means of self-reflection."

"Had you not read it before?"

"No. My father had been using it as a talisman of sorts, holding it tight as a way to contain his grief. But when he saw how melancholy I seemed since returning home, and guessed it might have something to do with an unhappy heart, he felt called to share it with me."

It looked painful, the way her fingernails scraped at the mortar between the stones of the bridge. He brushed a thumb against the apple of her cheek, assuring her he wanted to hear more.

"Jane Audley Honeychurch—she was such a vision of perfection in my mind, someone who never compromised, never doubted. I'd put her on a pedestal, thinking her more saint than human. And I was so afraid I'd never live up to the example she had set."

"Oh, Sheba," he whispered, wishing he knew how to take away the weight of such an unfair burden.

"Upsetting, then, to discover how wrong I'd been."

"Wrong?"

"Yes, wrong. That journal—it showed me that my mother struggled each and every day, struggled almost as much as I do, to discern a true calling, to allow the will of the Spirit rather than her own to be her guide." She pressed her hand against his, as if she couldn't bear the thought of his pulling away. "Noel, she judged herself as harshly as she judged others when she fell away from the truth."

"And through her example, taught you to judge yourself just as harshly, too."

"Yes. But she never taught me—or perhaps she tried, but I was just too young to understand—that truth alone is never enough. In so many entries in that journal, she'd be in the midst of castigating herself, or another Friend, only to stop and remind herself of Friend John Woolman's words: 'Let love be the first motion.' Perhaps if she had lived longer, I might have learned not just self-righteousness, but kindness as well. That I, like every other Friend, have a duty to advise and admonish those whom I see straying from the truth of our beliefs, but I must do so only when motivated by love. Not ambition, not righteousness or indignation, but love."

Noel frowned, working to see the connection. "Is that just the Friends' way of saying 'be diplomatic'?"

She laughed, then, rich strands of amusement and pain and relief. "Yes. If only I could be as succinct."

He laughed, too, but quickly sobered when she pulled free of his hand and turned toward the river.

"If I'm not to apologize for counseling diplomacy, then," he asked, joining her by the river's bank, "can you tell me what I've done to offend you?"

She gazed back at him over her shoulder. "You asked me to give over my beliefs in favor of yours."

"What? I never asked such a thing of you!"

"No? You did not wish me to give over my radical beliefs? To pretend to embrace more moderate, more socially acceptable views? Because I won't, Noel. I can't. I may have been wrong about how best to persuade others to join the cause for immediate abolition, but I will never compromise about the rightness of that cause itself."

"Bathsheba Honeychurch. I would never ask you to lie about your principles. Or to hide your light under a bushel."

"You wouldn't?"

He took her hands—her fingertips red and rough from scraping against the bridge's stonework—and pulled her close. "You wouldn't be the woman I loved if you did."

Those unblinking, lash-lined eyes—he'd never imagined how wide they could grow.

"You love me?" she whispered, those blue eyes finally turning up to his. They roved his face, as if she could not make the least sense of his unexpected words.

He took her hand and pressed it against his lips, then his heart. "I do, Sheba. My rational brain has been listing all the reasons I shouldn't, almost from the moment I first set eyes on you, a whirlwind of flying pamphlets and untidy hair and impetuous, interfering passion. The precise opposite of anyone I'd ever been told I should, or could, want. But the ardency of my feelings for you, they turn rationality to dust, blow it away on the wind. Because in spite of all our differences, something in my soul cries out to yours."

His heart pounded as she stared at him for what seemed like eons, her eyes fixed on his, her mouth rounded in an "O" of surprise.

It pounded even more frantically when those lips turned down into a fierce scowl.

"But *I* came to apologize to *you*!" she exclaimed, pounding tight fists against his chest. "To tell you that *I* love *you*! What are you about, stealing my thunder so?"

His expression must be as flummoxed as hers had been, so unexpected were her words. Gradually, as he disentangled the wonder of their meaning from the harshness of the tone in which they'd been spoken, his lips quirked, first into a half-smile, then into a full-faced grin. And then he laughed, laughed harder than he had ever laughed in his entire life, a rush of joy burbling from his mouth like a brook overflowing from the melt of the harshest winter's snow.

He grasped her fists, pressing them tight against his chest. "Oh, my dearest, loveliest Sheba. You can make an argument out of anything, even a declaration of love. How lucky I am, to have gained the regard of such a fierce, spirited woman."

He kissed her, then, kissed those contrary lips, the flush of those high cheekbones, the infuriating curve of her brows. And then her lips again, bussing and pressing and nipping until with a groan of need she opened to him, opened her lips, her soul.

He almost stumbled when she pulled away.

"No!" She shook her head so fiercely, the hairpins keeping the locks aloft flew. "We can't. You have to go—"

Noel caught her hands before they could push against his chest. He wasn't going to let her send him away again, not now that he'd gotten a taste of the future he'd once feared even to imagine.

"Why? You doubt that I love you?"

"No! You are no liar, Noel Griffin."

His heart settled at the certainty in her voice. If she believed him in that, then anything else was only a temporary stumbling block, easily overcome.

"You fear I won't treat you as an equal, as a man raised amongst your community would? I promise, Sheba, you'll have no cause to rebuke me on that accord."

She shook her head.

"You think I'll demand you convert to my religion? I won't."

She shook her head again.

"Because I am not a Friend? Because marrying someone not of your faith will lead to excommunication?"

Sheba huffed. "Friends do not practice excommunication, even against one who marries contrary to discipline. I will likely be publicly disowned, though."

"There's a difference between being excommunicated and

disowned? One that is meaningful to you?"

"Yes! Excommunication is something done *to* an offender, depriving him of an indispensable channel to the grace of God. But disownment is a message from the Society to the world, a message about what it means to be a Friend, what behavior is and is not consistent with that identity. It is done to maintain the Society's self-definition, not to punish the person who has erred. If I am disowned, I won't be able to attend Meetings for Business any longer, but I'd still be welcomed, nay, even encouraged, to attend Meeting for Worship."

Noel tapped a considering finger against his lips. "Not religion, then. Is it because you fear I can't support you financially? I've not the wealth that my cousin has, but I assure you, I do have means of my own."

Her wince told him he was getting closer. If she would just tell him what the matter was, he could set his mind to fixing it…

"That's why I came in search of you. To talk about those means."

"Oh? And here I thought you came to apologize, and to declare your love."

She ducked her head at that, trying to hide her ungainly snort at his painfully weak sally. Oh, he was lost, wasn't if he, if even a snort could strike him as winsomely charming?

"Noel Griffin can tease? Who would have ever thought?"

She smiled, then, but far too wanly to suggest he'd banished her concerns.

"I fear the urge to tease will disappear after I tell you the truth of your inheritance," she finally said.

"Inheritance? Do you mean the money my father left me?"

"Yes. "She looked up at the sky for a long moment, then sunk to her knees beside a honeysuckle bush off to the side of the path, pulling him down beside her. "You see, it's tainted."

"Tainted?"

"Yes, tainted. I thought men of the Navy so brave, so selfless, fighting to free cruelly captured Africans from evil slavers. But Spencer and Sarah, they've been telling us it's not—that they aren't—" She broke off, hands flying in frustration.

"Are you referring to the fact that men like my father are paid for each enslaved person they free?"

"Not just that. It's that they aren't even freed, not truly!" she exclaimed. "They're forced to serve as apprentices, or to enlist in the army. As if they owed us a debt for recapturing them."

"All of them? Even the children?"

Sheba sat back on her heels, her breath gusting out in clear relief. "You didn't know, then."

Noel shook his head. No, his father had never said as much, at least not in Noel's hearing. But something had always held Noel back from investing those funds, hadn't it? Some unconscious discomfort at gaining from the losses of innocent others?

"I am not sure, about the children," Sheba said. "But Sarah, or Spencer, will likely know. Does it truly matter, though? If your father's money comes at the expense of even one unfairly treated human being, is it not just as tainted?"

Noel traced the flight of a sparrow hawk wheeling over the ruins of Leicester Abbey. How different the winged creatures here in the Midlands were, compared to familiar sea birds around Ruxford Hall.

But Ruxford Hall no longer belonged to him. Never had, if only he'd known. Leicester, and Bathsheba Honeychurch, were his destiny now.

If she'd still have him...

"You don't wish to be tainted by association," he said flatly, half question, half assertion. "You'll refuse to marry me if I don't relinquish my inheritance."

"No. I won't tell you what to do, not anymore. Not even after I'm your wife."

His *wife*? She meant to marry him, then?

He couldn't stop himself from kissing her again, a smacking press of soft lips against her cheek, before shifting to her suddenly ravenous mouth.

They kissed, and kissed, and kissed again, the sun lowering in counterpoint to their rising desire.

She'd pulled free his cravat, and jerked his shirt free of his trousers, warm hands roving the naked skin of his back with abandon before he had sense enough to realize what she was about. What a scandal, if she were discovered making love out of doors in her own home town.

Keeping his arms about her, he pulled his lips from her lush mouth, then set a gentle buss against each dear temple.

"How I love you, Bathsheba Honeychurch," he whispered through love-swollen lips.

But before he had a chance to smooth her tumbling hair, or re-tie the drawstring on the front of her simple bodice—when had he pulled it open?—she had jumped to her feet, grabbed up her skirts, and was racing back down the towpath towards town.

He could only shake his head and marvel as he watched that lithe figure winging down the path, a skylark dull of plume but blithe of spirit, gifting him a gladness he'd never thought to know.

He laughed at himself, then. It must be love, if cold, aloof Noel Griffin had been reduced to such flights of versifying fancy...

"Aren't you coming?" she called. "I have an idea—no, two or three, maybe even more—for ways you, or we together, can make it right."

Life married to a lady as vibrant, as spontaneous, as so wholly *alive* as was Bathsheba Honeychurch—well, he'd never have cause to term it dull, would he?

He scooped up the bonnet that had flown from her head, set a hand atop his own hat, and soared down the path behind her.

December 1824

> A small party of Friends being in earnest conversation upon the subject of the Slave Trade, each exclaimed—"What can I do for the cause?" It was universally agreed that every soul in this United Kingdom, from the king to the peasant, could do something. What that something may be, each Individual must define for himself, according to the measure of his zeal and the extent of his ability; but without doubt, if the whole nation sets to work in this manner, the great task will be accomplished...

Sheba set the press proof down on the drawing room table and checked on the progress of her two collaborators in this new publishing venture. That Elizabeth Heyrick and her old friend Susanna Watts, both of whom had multiple books and pamphlets already to their credit, had not only looked favorably on Sheba's suggestion that they take extracts from some of the weightier anti-slavery publications and republish them in periodical form, but had also invited her to join them in the task —she still could hardly believe it. Even with the first proofs of the venture scattered about the room of the cosy house on Wellington Street which she and Noel had agreed to purchase shortly after their marriage. Not with his father's prize money, but with a portion of her dowry.

She should have known, though, in how high esteem

Elizabeth Heyrick held her. Sheba's former teacher had attended her wedding to Noel, even though Leicester Meeting's elders, unsurprisingly, had not allowed it to be held in the Meeting House. "Worth a rebuke, to share such a happy day with you, my dear girl," Elizabeth had whispered as she signed the wedding certificate resting on the table in Joseph Honeychurch's house.

Because even if she couldn't be married in the Meeting House, Sheba would never wed in a church. A determination which had caused Noel no little consternation. After arguing over the matter for days, they finally agreed to compromise, inviting their small collection of family and friends to the home in which Sheba had been raised, exchanging vows first, for legality's sake, in front of a priest (*No child of mine will be born illegitimate!* Noel had insisted), and then in the Friends' way, with no mediator but God between them.

Sheba had felt the presence not only of her mother, but all her audacious Audley ancestresses, silent witnesses as Noel declared to the collected company, *Friends, I take this my friend Bathsheba Audley Honeychurch to be my wife, promising, through divine assistance, to be unto her a loving and faithful husband, till it shall please the Lord by death to separate us.*

"Have you found any errors, Bathsheba?" Elizabeth asked, interrupting the happy memory.

"None." Grimacing, she wiped the ink from her fingers with a handkerchief. "You, Friend Susanna?" Sheba asked.

"Just plain Sue," the older woman chided. "You know I am no Quaker."

Friend Susanna had already invited Sheba to call her so several times. But Sheba doubted she'd ever be able to refer to an elder by such a pet-name.

"No, no mistakes. A meticulous printer, Albert Cockshaw." Susannah Watts sighed. "If only he would stop asking if we are quite sure about the title."

"He frets so that *The Humming Bird* will put us in danger of furnishing the anti-abolitionists with a pun." Elizabeth took off her glasses and wiped away a smudge with a handkerchief. "It's all a *hum*, all *humbug*? He fears those fond of repartee may take advantage."

"Why may it not put one in mind of the *humble* instead?" Susanna asked.

"Let the shafts from the quivers of ridicule strike our little plumed messenger!" Sheba protested. "I'll not object to being punned into notice."

"I agree," Elizabeth declared, gathering the pages Sheba and Susannah had been proofing and tapping them against the desk until they aligned. "I do wonder, though, if we truly need to include other material completely unrelated to the abolitionist cause?"

Her older friend frowned. "But—"

"Oh, I don't refer to your poems, Sue," Elizabeth reassured. "But this account of the monastery of St. Bernard? And next month, didn't you say you wished to add a piece on the art of writing?

"And one on the natural history of the humming bird. Yes, I did." Susannah folded her hands on the table, mulishness banishing her usual placid expression.

"Noel and I talked about that, just before he left to pick up the post," Sheba said with a quick glance toward the window, a barely contained smile bubbling on her lips.. Her husband—husband! She could still barely believe herself in possession of a husband, even three months after their wedding—had been gone since just after luncheon, and it was nearly three already. The post office was only a few streets away. What could be taking him so long?

"And?" Elizabeth asked, pulling Sheba from her silly worries.

"He reminded me that the West Indian interest often complains, quite rightly, of the terribly canting nature of most anti-slavery publications," she explained. "Repetitive, dry, dour writing does little to draw those not already committed to our cause. Why not allow poetry and science to entice those who might otherwise avert their eyes?"

Susanna chuckled. "Bathsheba Honeychurch, arguing for the importance of meeting people where they are? I never thought to see the day. Now, if you could only persuade Bess here to follow your example..."

"Humph," Elizabeth sniffed, although the crinkling of her eyes suggested she took no offense.

The slam of the front door drew Sheba to her feet.

"Ah, Bess, I believe it's time to take our leave," Susanna said, tilting her head toward the front of the house. And then, much to Sheba's embarrassment, broke into song.

"*Young Love liv'd once in an humble shed / Where roses breathing, And woodbines wreathing / Around the lattice their tendrils spread...*"

"They're worshiping to romantic ballads in the Baptist church these days, are they?" Elizabeth asked, eyebrows rising.

"Oh, you know how hard it is for me to resist a cheery tune," Susanna protested.

"Be sure to let me know as soon as you hear from the Birmingham ladies about their letter to Thomas Clarkson," Sheba said as she gathered up the proof sheets and tucked them into Elizabeth's reticule. She usually enjoyed listening to the old friends bicker, but if Noel had come back—

"A wonderful idea, that, to ask the old campaigner for advice about establishing a female Anti-Slavery Society," Susanna said as she shrugged into her coat.

"I'm glad they heeded your advice to write to Clarkson, rather than to William Wilberforce," Sheba said to Elizabeth as she handed her old teacher her bonnet and gloves.

"Yes. At least we know Friend Clarkson believes women, especially female Friends, can be both rational and useful. Ah, Friend Griffin," she said as Noel stepped into the drawing room.

"We were just taking our leave."

"Do not hurry away on my account," Noel said, although his eyes rested not on the visitors but on Sheba.

Noel. Quiet, honest, devoted Noel. Dressed not in the showy garb of a London swell, nor the sober attire of a male Friend, but in a suit befitting the provincial businessman he was working to become.

To think she'd nearly allowed her own worries to outvoice the Spirit leading her mind and soul to him! How wrong she'd been to believe she knew what he expected of a marriage partner, then to dismiss him when those false assumptions did not match her own beliefs. So afraid, she'd been, of not living up to her mother's example, her mother's expectations, she'd let herself be guided by fear, not by faith.

No longer. In Noel Griffin she had found a true companion, one nearer to her than all the rest of the world. And in their marriage, a union of mind and spirit, just as she'd been taught to expect. But something more, too: a union of bodies, a mutual rendering of the "due benevolence" that Delphie had argued all those months ago in London must play a role in any true marriage of equals.

She laced her hand through the crook of his arm and smiled, welcoming home the man she loved.

"Ah, but we know how eager Bathsheba must be to read those letters you've brought," Elizabeth said.

What? Oh, yes. Noel had gone to collect the post, hadn't he? Sheba felt her face pink.

"And you are expecting a business associate of Mr. Griffin's later this afternoon, did you not say?"

Were they?

"Bid you farewell, Friends. We will let ourselves out."

Sheba's fingers twitched against Noel's waistcoat, even as her friends chuckled. Noel, at least, waited for the door to close behind them before setting his lips to hers.

"My apologies for taking so long," he said, pulling back with obvious reluctance. He tipped his forehead to rest against hers, as unwilling as she to break the connection entirely. "The letters from Birmingham were late. You wouldn't have wished me to miss Pinney's last missive before sailing, would you?"

Though their grandmother had frowned upon it, Ash continued to call upon Noel for guidance and advice, even after his marriage and move to Leicester. Between them, they'd hit on the plan of sending Michael Pinney to Nevis to make preparations for the emancipation of the enslaved on the plantations owned by the Silliman estate, so that it needn't wait a moment longer than when Ash came of age in a little over a year. No matter how much his grandmother and the trustees protested, Ash would not be swayed.

"And in the London post, a note from Sarah, one from Delphie, one from your cousin Elizabeth, and two from cousin Connie."

Sheba flipped quickly through the pile Noel handed her. "None from Ash?"

Noel brushed a wayward curl behind her ear. "No, dear. Not today."

Sheba set her cheek against Noel's waistcoat, taking solace in his slim but comforting bulk. Ash had been happy to allow Noel to use his father's prize money to pay for Michael Pinney's trip to Nevis, but he'd been far from pleased to discover Sheba and Noel had gifted the rest of Captain Griffin's prize money to Sarah, for the funding of a school upon her return to Sierra Leone. He'd not sent Sheba a letter since.

She'd been tempted to write first, cautioning him not to allow guilt to blind him to Sarah's needs. But it was no longer her place to admonish him. When Sarah's teaching apprenticeship came to an end, she prayed he'd accept, nay, even be happy, that his sister had a will of her own.

Sheba started to slip her arms around Noel, but stopped as

something crinkled in his pocket. "Oh, you forgot one," she said, slipping a hand inside.

"No!" He slapped his hand over the pocket, but she'd already drawn out the folded sheet. Not a letter—it had no address, no seal. But on the outside, her name—in Noel's handwriting? Why was her husband writing to her?

She glanced up and saw the tips of his ears turning red.

"Noel? Is it not for me?"

That lopsided smile—all shy and self-deprecating and vulnerable—oh, how it made her ache with love.

"Yes, it's for you," he said, ducking his chin to avoid her gaze. As if he need hide from her. "A silly commemoration of first Christmas together."

"Christmas? Should I not open it now, then?"

He gave a diffident shrug. "Perhaps it's better this way. For I'm not sure I'd have summoned the fortitude to share it, when the time came…"

With eager fingers, she unfolded the sheet.

Four intertwined hearts, he'd drawn, in the center of the sheet, each with words—a poem?—running through them, and through straight and angled borders along the sides. In the center, a drawing of their Leicester house. Inside each heart, an abolitionist pamphlet. In the triangles between the straight and angled borders, tiny little boats, replicas of the ships his father had captained as well as the *Aaron Manby* and the other steamships Noel and Captain Napier planned to someday build. And framing the whole, a twisting honeysuckle vine, hummingbirds flitting from blossom to bloom.

Two lives, two souls, joined as one.

"A love token?" Admirers had given such things to several of her Audley cousins, but she'd never expected to receive one herself.

"A true love knot," he corrected. "Popular amongst some of the Quakers in Pennsylvania, or so Captain Napier tells me. I intended to show it to him tonight, ask him if it comes anywhere close to the ones he's seen. Probably not, I'm guessing. If boys are taught to draw at all, it's only so they might make maps, not actual art. And I've even less skill at versifying—"

"Stop." Sheba stepped closer, hoping he could see all the love in her eyes. "It's beautiful. And I haven't even read what you've written yet."

Now not only his ears, but his entire face flushed. "Perhaps I should take it back, before I truly embarrass myself—"

Sheba set a hand against his waistcoat. "Please. Let me?"

He placed his hand over hers—for courage?—then gave a quick nod.

She began to read, turning the paper to follow the flow of the words as they wound between each heart.

This knot of love which I do send
Is, like love, without an end.
Its turns and crosses many you see
So hath your love, dear, challenged me.
Yet thoughts by day and dreams by night
Rest still on you, my heart's delight.
Mountains shall melt, the seas run dry
The stars run lawless through the sky,
The sun at midnight shall appear,
Ere I prove false to you, my dear.
Turning arms, exchanging kisses
Each partaking other's blisses
Laughing, weeping, still together
Bliss in one is Mirth in either.
Never breaking, ever bending,
This is love and worth commending.
Still beginning, never ending,
This is love and worth commending.

"Oh, my dearest Noel," Sheba whispered, setting her hand against his still warm cheek. "My dearest, dearest love."

She drew his head down to hers, pressing all the hope, all the peace, all the joy in her heart into her kiss. A kiss acknowledging their shared beliefs and many differences, the value in which they held one another because of both.

Love, and truth, and light.

THANK YOU

Thanks for reading *Not Quite a Scandal*. I hope it gave you as much pleasure in the reading as it gave me in the writing.

Would you consider writing a review? Reader reviews on Goodreads, LibraryThing, and other social networking sites are especially valuable. I'm grateful for all reviews, critical or admiring, and if you take the time to write one of *NQAS*, you have my thanks.

If you'd like to know when my next book becomes available, or to find out about discounts, giveaways, and other Bliss Bennet-related info, sign up for my newsletter at http://www.blissbennet.com. You can also see what I'm up to by following me on BlueSky, liking my Facebook page (www.facebook/com/blissbennetauthor) or Instagram page (http://www.instagram.com/blissbennetwrites).

AUTHOR'S NOTE

On Quakers, or The Society of Friends

Historical romance, like historical fiction, looks both forward and back: not only to what people in the past believed and valued, but also to the present, to the beliefs and values of its readers today. And what current-day readers of male/female romances clearly value is a strong, self-actualizing female lead. Today's historical romances abound with feisty feminist protagonists, women who speak up, speak out, and fight against injustices that seem obvious to us now, but that in the past were far more likely to be regarded as just the way things were. Anachronistic, perhaps, but who wants to read about characters who espouse outdated sexist and racist views, rather than the more progressive values we currently embrace? And, after all, isn't historical romance *romance*, a fantasy of the past, not something that requires the rigor of complete historical accuracy?

And yet…

I can't help but wonder if encountering so many proto-feminists and social justice crusaders in the historical romances I read does a disservice to the actual, and quite rare, women in the past who *did* act against the norms of their times. Does the prevalence of kick-ass historical romance heroines who also get to marry their dukes (or marquesses, or earls) lead me to assume that there was little to no cost in rebelling against social norms? Do I end up believing, unconsciously if not explicitly, that it was easy for women in the past to run their own business and spy rings and detective agencies, rescue children, wives, and pets from violent abusers, and publicly advocate for women's rights, the abolition of slavery, and labor reform? And does that belief lead me to look down on women in the past who *didn't* break the rules? Because if it was so easy to be a rebel, why didn't more women rebel? Were they just lazy, or weak, or morally lacking? And does it encourage me not to see, and thus not to appreciate or celebrate, how very valiant, how very brave, those women who *did* break the rules truly were?

These questions are often on my mind whenever I start thinking about a potential female protagonist for a new book. And so while I, too, like so many other historical romance authors writing in the 2020s, tend to create female protagonists whose values mirror my own rather than the ones more typical of their age, I also try to give them real reasons why they choose not to conform. And to show through their stories not just what they gained, but also what they lost, by rebelling against the more commonly accepted values of their times.

Which is one reason why I decided the heroine of my next book would be a Quaker, or, as they call themselves, a member of the Society of Friends. Since the religion's founding in the seventeenth century, Friends have believed that all human beings have the ability to experience "the light within," or a personal, unmediated connection to God. This belief demanded a concomitant belief: a belief in the spiritual equality between the sexes. A revolutionary idea in seventeenth-century England, gender equality, a time when many were being taught that women had no souls at all.

From the religion's founding, female as well as male Friends were allowed to speak on religious matters during Meeting for Worship, to write and publish religious tracts, and to travel as itinerant preachers to other Meetings throughout the country, or even overseas (Since Friends believe there is no need for an intermediary between a person and God, they refused to ordain clergy; anyone, male or female, called by the Spirit to preach could and should do so, and to travel where the Spirit leads them). In wider British society, female Friends gained a reputation as bold, and more publicly visible, than many of their female contemporaries. As Thomas Clarkson, an Anglican, noted in his 1806 *A Portraiture of Quakerism*, "The Quaker women, independently of their private, have that which no other body of women have, a public character. This is a new era in female history" (vol. III, p. 246).

In no small part because of the disturbingly unconventional behavior of their female members, early Friends were often viciously persecuted by the dominant English society. Such persecution had largely abated by the early nineteenth century, but the Society's pacifism, as well as its early rejection of slavery, "a traffic so unmerciful, and unjust in its nature to a part of our own species made equally with ourselves for immortality," continued to set Friends apart (*Extracts* 177-78). By the early nineteenth century, outsiders still often regarded "Quakers," especially women Friends, as unnatural radicals, derisively dismissing them for "quaking" in the throes of an overly-enthusiastic religious extremism.

Might female Friends be the real kick-ass heroines of the historical past?

Unlike most Regency-era children, an early nineteenth

century girl brought up as a Friend would likely not find it odd, or even exceptional, for a woman to be granted authority and respect. Such a girl would surely expect that she, too, would be treated as an equal when she came of age. Especially because Friends frowned upon mixing with the "creaturely" world, fearing its corrupting influence, such a girl would likely not have been much exposed to English society's far more constraining gender norms.

And thus I began to imagine what might happen if such a girl were to find herself abruptly thrust into the wider world, and the idea for Bathsheba Honeychurch began to take form....

I've listed several of the books I found most useful in researching Regency-era Friends in the *Sources* section below. You can find a complete list of sources on my web site: blissbennet.com/books/NQAScandal.

On 19th century British Anti-Slavery

On a Gentleman saying that,
Some ladies, who were zealous in the
Anti-Slavery Cause, were brazen faced.

Thanks for your thought—it seems to say
When ladies walk in Duty's way,
They should wear arms of proof;
To blunt the shafts of manly wit—
To ward off censure's galling
And keep reproach aloof:—
And when a righteous cause demands
The labour of their hearts and hands,
Right onward they must pass,

Cas'd in strong armour, for the field—
With casque and corselet, spear and shield,
Invulnerable brass.

—Susanna Watts

At the 2019 Romance Writers of America conference, author Courtney Milan led a panel discussion called "So You Want to Talk About Race." During that panel, which was attended by a sadly small number of writers, Milan encouraging the white authors in the room to stop worrying so much about being accused of racism when they contemplated whether or how to include characters of color in their books, and to instead start by thinking about whiteness as a racial category, and how it functions in their stories. Ironic, given RWA's appallingly racist treatment of Courtney Milan later that year (see Aja Romano and Constance Grady's Vox article, "Romance is publishing's most lucrative genre. Its biggest community of writers is imploding," if you're unfamiliar with the history). But I'll forever be grateful that I had the opportunity to hear Milan's bracing call to action. Because it inspired me to research early nineteenth century British abolitionists, in the hopes of depicting them not just as the nobly righteous white-savior heroes that so many history books, and historical romances, present them as. But instead as the messy, conflicted, equivocating, and often quite racist human beings they actually were.

One such figure is the renowned British abolitionist William Wilberforce, who makes a cameo appearance in *Not Quite a Scandal*. Wilberforce is rightfully lauded as one of the most influential politicians of the Regency, and is perhaps the best known of all the British abolitionists of the period. In

1787, Prime Minister William Pitt reportedly asked the young parliamentarian to lead the political push to outlaw the slave trade, a push that took twenty years to accomplish. But by the 1820s, the abolitionists had to admit that the Passage of the Slave Trade Act of 1807 had not ended the institution of slavery itself, as they had expected. Instead, the trade simply shifted to other countries, and the numbers of African men, women, and children captured and transported against their wills by Europeans actually increased rather than decreased. So in 1823, the old abolitionist guard, joined by a new generation of activists, created another abolitionist society, this one focused on ending the institution of slavery altogether.

The name of this new organization—The Society for the Mitigation and Gradual Abolition of Slavery throughout the British Dominions—suggests both its members' commitment to abolition and also the tentative nature of their calls for emancipation. "Mitigation" of slavery, or, in other words, the initial championing of laws to make slaveowners treat the people they purportedly owned less harshly than they had heretofore been allowed; "Abolition" of the evil institution, but only at a "Gradual" pace, a pace that would not prove too threatening to Britain's politically powerful Caribbean plantation owners. Today many would likely view such a tentative approach to the abolition of slavery as craven, even racist. But in the 1820s, the majority of British abolitionists urged a gradualist approach.

Why? In part out of fear of the negative impact immediate emancipation might have on Britain's economy, and in part because of the powerful influence of colonial interests in Parliament and society. Alexandra Franklin has identified eighty six men who both served in the British House of Commons and owned colonial slave plantations between the years 1790 and 1820 (see Franklin, Alexandra. *Enterprise and Advantage: The West India Interest in Britain, 1774-1840.* 1992. U of Penn, PhD dissertation, p. 82). In fact, it was difficult to move in genteel British society without interacting with those who supported themselves on the forced, uncompensated labor of enslaved Africans.

Even Evangelical William Wilberforce could not insulate himself completely from such social—and even closer—interactions. The engagement of his daughter Elizabeth to Bristol banker Charles Pinney, depicted in Chapter 19 of *Not Quite a Scandal*, actually happened (although in 1825, rather than 1824, as it does in my book). In 1762, Charles Pinney's father had inherited several Nevis slave plantations; while he sold them in 1808, well before his son proposed to Elizabeth Wilberforce, much of that son's own wealth stemmed from the mortgages his bank held on Caribbean plantations. If such mortgages went into default, not an uncommon occurrence, the bank became the owner of the foreclosed estates, including the people enslaved on them. As Anne Stott, who recounts this surprising incident in *Wilberforce: Family and Friends* (Oxford UP, 2012) notes, "slave holding, it turns out, could not be abandoned so easily" (234). Wilberforce, taken by Pinney's overt piety and wishing Elizabeth happily settled, disregarded the potential bad press the marriage of the great William Wilberforce's daughter to a man tied, even indirectly, to slavery would inevitably bring. Only after being chastised by old friends and fellow abolitionists did Wilberforce finally write to Charles Pinney that he'd suddenly developed qualms. Pinney broke off the engagement soon after.

Wilberforce's conversation with Sheba about the role women should play in the anti-slavery cause also reflects his actual views. In an 1826 letter to his fellow abolitionist and old friend Thomas Babington, he wrote of his fears that women's involvement endangered both their characters and the cause:

> Macaulay giving me useful intelligence. We differing about Female Anti-Slavery Associations. Babington with me, grounding it on St. Paul. I own I cannot relish the plan. All private exertions for such an object become their character, but for ladies to meet, to publish, to go from house to house stirring up petitions—these appear to me proceedings unsuited to the female character as delineated in Scripture. And though we should limit the interference of our ladies to the cause of justice and humanity, I fear its tendency would be to mix them in all the multiform warfare of political life." (Quoted in *Life of William Wilberforce, by his Sons,* volume 5, p. 264-65)

Not all abolitionists agreed with Wilberforce's view. Thomas Clarkson, almost as influential an abolitionist as Wilberforce but far less well-known today, championed the participation of women in the cause. Perhaps influenced by his familiarity with the Society of Friends, who believed in the spiritual equality of women and embraced female preachers, Clarkson, unlike most men of his day, believed in a woman's right not only to an education, but also to a voice in public life. Clarkson had toured Britain during 1823-4, promoting the formation of local anti-slavery societies for men, groups that would be auxiliaries to the national organization.

Birmingham Evangelical Lucy Townsend wrote to Clarkson in 1825 for advice on founding a female Anti-Slavery Society. Clarkson encouraged Townsend, agreeing that "there are many ladies in different parts of the Kingdom who would embark in committees of this sort" (quid. In Midgley, 47). He also offered advice on what to call the new society, and sent her anti-slavery pamphlets from the national group to share with other ladies.

Real-life Leicester teacher and writer Elizabeth Heyrick had no need of such pamphlets. Heyrick's parents, Leicester hosiery manufacturer John Coltman and Elizabeth Cartwright Coltman, a book reviewer and poet, were both religious Dissenters (John a Unitarian, Elizabeth a Methodist), and from an early age, Elizabeth (or Bess, as she was known by her family) showed a deep concern for others, especially those unfairly oppressed by those with greater influence and power. After a brief marriage, the widowed Elizabeth returned to Leicester to live with her parents. In 1807, she became a convinced member of the Society of Friends (known to outsiders as the Quakers), a religious group that believed in the spiritual equality of women and men, as well as in a woman's right to an education and a voice in public life. Elizabeth spent the rest of her own life teaching and writing —not children's books, or poetry, or even novels for adults, as many literary women of her period did, but fiery radical political pamphlets protesting the major social injustices of her day. Cruelty to animals; the exploitation of factory workers; the inhumane treatment of prisoners and vagrants— all were subject to her witty, caustic condemnation. Family records suggest she penned at least twenty pamphlets, although many have been lost or were never printed.

Heyrick's 1824 *Immediate, Not Gradual, Abolition; or, An Inquiry into the shortest, safest, and most effectual means of getting rid of West Indian Slavery*, was the first published work by a white author to challenge the gradualist stance adopted by the majority of British abolitionists (Black Briton Ottobah Cugoano had first called for total abolition in his 1787 autobiography, *Thoughts and Sentiments on the Evil and Wicked Traffic of the Slavery and Commerce of the Human Species*). Heyrick took the gradualists to task for being "too slow and cautious" in their calls for emancipation, for "accommodating" enslavers, and for encouraging the government to negotiate with plantation-owning colonists rather than outlawing slavery immediately. People needn't wait for government action, she urged; ordinary men and women could take matters into their own hands by boycotting sugar produced on colonial slave plantations.

Heyrick's radical pamphlet proved surprisingly popular, with thousands of copies circulating widely in both Britain and the United States in the 1820s and 30s. It also proved unsurprisingly disturbing to Wilberforce and the other gradualists of the national Anti-Slavery Society. Some historians claim they tried to suppress its distribution, and that Wilberforce instructed the national organization to ignore the female anti-slavery societies that Heyrick and other women began to organize from 1825 onward (Rappaport). Difficult to do, since the national organization relied heavily on contributions from the Birmingham Ladies' Negro Friend Society and other female anti-slavery auxiliary associations.

The unpublished poem at the head of this note, by author and fellow abolitionist Susanna Watts, a close friend of Elizabeth Heyrick's, suggests that Wilberforce's negative opinion of women's participation in the cause were all too familiar to female anti-slavery activists. But Heyrick and Watts never let such disapprobation keep them from doing what they believed was right. They canvassed far and wide in Leicester, urging their fellow citizens to boycott West Indian sugar, a technique also adopted by other female anti-slavery campaigners. And, as depicted in the final chapter of *Not Quite a Scandal*, the two women (with Heyrick's sister, Mary Ann Coltman, not the fictional Bathsheba Honeychurch) edited and published *The Humming Bird*, the first anti-slavery periodical.

"Having heard all of this you may choose to look the other way but you can never again say you did not know": a reproof purportedly offered by William Wilberforce to his fellow members of Parliament for failing to abolish the slave trade. Though the quotation is all over the Internet, the words appear to be apocryphal; I've not been able to find them in any printed speech of Wilberforce's. In my mind, then, I choose to imagine them being spoken not by the gradualist Wilberforce, but by the "brazen-faced" radical Elizabeth Heyrick, my inspiration for Bathsheba Honeychurch.

SOURCES:

Clarkson, Thomas. Letter to Lucy Townsend, 30 March 1825 and 30 May 1825. In Lucy Townsend, "Scrap Book on Negro slaves": 115-18. Rhodes House Library, Oxford University. https://archives.bodleian.ox.ac.uk/repositories/2/resources/12375

———. *Portraiture of Quakerism*. 3 volumes. Longman, Hurst, Rees, and Orme, 1806.

Franklin, Alexandra. *Enterprise and Advantage: The West India Interest in Britain, 1774-1840*. PhD dissertation, U of Penn, 1992.

Holton, Sandra Stanley. *Quaker Women: Personal Life, Memory and Radicalism in the Lives of Women Friends, 1780-1930*. Routledge, 2007.

Larson, Rebecca. *Daughters of the Light: Quaker Women Preaching and Prophesying in the Colonies and Abroad, 1700-1775*. Knopf, 1999.

Midgley, Clare. *Women Against Slavery: The British Campaigns, 1780-1870*. Routledge, 1992.

Shuttleworth, Rebecca Elaine Christie. *Life Writing in the Midlands' Dissenting Circle of Elizabeth Heyrick (1769-1831) and Susanna Watts (1768-1842): 'We preserve the best part of departed friends.'* MPhil Thesis, U of Leicester. 2018.

Stott, Anne. Wilberforce: *Family and Friends*. Oxford UP, 2012.

Wilberforce, Robert Isaac and Samuel. *Life of William Wilberforce, by his Sons,* volume 5. John Murray, 1838.

Wilson, Ellen Gibson. *Thomas Clarkson: A Biography*. William Sessions Ltd., 1989.

ACKNOWLEDGEMENTS

No novel is ever completed without the help, encouragement, and good will of so many people besides its author. My deepest gratitude to:

Lucy Saint-Smith at the Friends Library in London for help with research on early nineteenth-century British Quaker life and history.

Andrew Lewis, researcher, who visited the Friends Library in London on my behalf and photographed relevant documents, including the minutes from the London Women Friends Yearly Meeting of 1824.

My romance writing friends and colleagues, in particular my fellow authors in the New England Romance Writers and Regency Fiction Writers communities. I appreciate all the knowledge and expertise members of both groups share with such generosity and good humor.

Readers and critique partners who continue to offer just the right proportion of praise, criticism, and suggestion: Gail Eastwood, Karen Kaletka, Wendy LaCapra, AG Meiers, Jess Russell, and Tricia Woods.

Courtney Milan, for leading the panel discussion "So You Want to Talk About Race" at the 2019 Romance Writers of America conference.

Laura Kinsale and Mary Jo Putney, for modeling how to write historical romance protagonists grappling with religious convictions (in *Flowers from the Storm* and *Thunder and Roses*, two of my all-time favorite historical romances).

My publishing support team, including editor Wendy Muruli, who provided an early-round sensitivity read, a mid-book developmental edit, and final draft line edits with insight and grace; and designer Elena K. of L1Graphics, who created yet another stunningly gorgeous book cover with equal parts craftsmanship and despatch. Thank you both so much!

My toddler dinner neighbors, still supping together at least once a month even though all the toddlers are now off adventuring in the wider world. Thanks especially to Anita for long walks and conversations both philosophical and practical, and to Jessica for the lovely cover model photos.

My gym ladies, especially Dura, who looked beyond my resting bitch face and invited me to coffee with the other ducks. Thanks for letting me play English prof. during book club....

Dan B., for helping me figure myself out when my brain was not at home to me.

My oldest friend, Deb, for letting me borrow daughter Rachel for my cover model. And to Rachel, for taking to the job with equal parts interest and good cheer.

Mr. Bennet (my own, not Elizabeth's), who continues to support me with awful puns, timely flowers, and a deep respect for my writing. The best place in the world is truly inside your hug.

My own young Miss Bennet, to whom I dedicate Sheba's story. I respect and admire you so much, my own sweet star.

And last, but certainly not least, historical romance readers, and all the Bookstagrammers, BookTokers, librarians, bloggers, and reviewers who champion the romance genre. Thank you for the patience with which you wait for this very slow writer to come out with each new book. A mild case of Covid which turned into a year-long bout of brain fog and debilitating fatigue made the wait especially long this time round. I'm grateful for your continued support, especially when there are so many other forms of entertainment vying for your attention. I continued to be honored that you chose to spend some of that valuable time with my story.

SOMETHING ABOUT BLISS

Bliss Bennet writes smart, edgy novels for readers who love history as much as they love romance. Despite being born and bred in New England, Bliss has always been fascinated by the history of that country across the pond, particularly the politically-volatile period known as the English Regency. Though she's visited Britain several times, Bliss continues to make her home in New England along with her spouse and an ever-multiplying collection of historical reference books.

Bliss's Regency-set historical romances have been praised as "savvy, sensual, and engrossing" by *USA Today*, "catnip for the Historical Romance reader" by *Bookworlder*, "romantic, funny, touching, and extremely well-researched" by *All About Romance*, and "everything you want in a great historical romance" by *The Reading Wench*.

Turn the page for more books by Bliss Bennet

EAGER FOR MORE FROM BLISS BENNET?

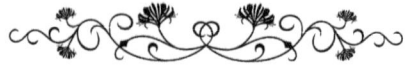

THE AUDACIOUS LADIES OF AUDLEY

Delphie and Spencer's story: *Not Quite a Marriage*

Spencer Burnett, Viscount Stiles, once swore he'd left England for good. Yet after five years of self-imposed exile in West Africa, he's no longer the same spoiled, selfish boy who ran away from a domineering father, a disappointed grandmother, and a decidedly unwanted wife. Proving himself to the family he abandoned will be no easy task. But he hardly expects his formerly docile wife will be the hardest to convince. When Philadelphia refuses to accept his apologies—or to allow him back into her bed—Spencer finds himself tempting her into a bargain he cannot afford to lose.

Philadelphia Burnett's desires were once as vast as the sky. But now, after suffering one devastating loss after another, the only thing she allows herself to want is a home. When Delphie's estranged rake of a husband returns from a five-years' absence to claim the estate promised to *her*, Delphie resolves to fight him every step of the way. Beechcombe Park will be a sanctuary for her, and for the wayward Audley cousins she promised her sister she'd always protect. She cannot, will not, suffer even one more loss. Especially not the loss of her heart...

THE PENNINGTONS

Kit's story: *A Rebel without a Rogue*

A woman striving for justice
Fianna Cameron has devoted her life to avenging the death of her father, hanged as a traitor during the Irish Rebellion of 1798. Now, on the eve of her thirtieth birthday, only one last miscreant remains: Major Christopher Pennington, who both oversaw her father's execution and maligned his honor. Fianna risks everything to travel to London and confront the man who has haunted her every nightmare. Only after her pistol misfires does she realize her sickening mistake: the Pennington she wounded is far too young to be her intended target.

A man who will protect his family at all costs
Rumors of being shot by a spurned mistress might burnish the reputation of a rake, but for Kit Pennington, determined to win a seat in Parliament, such salacious gossip is a nightmare. To regain his good name, Kit vows to track down his mysterious attacker and force her to reveal why she fired on him. Accepting an acquaintance's mistress as an ally in his search is risky enough, but when Kit begins to develop feelings for the icy, ethereal Miss Cameron, more than his political career is in danger.

As their search begins to unearth long-held secrets, Kit and Fianna find themselves caught between duty to family and their beliefs in what's right. How can you balance the competing demands of loyalty and justice—especially when you add love to the mix.

Sibilla's story: *A Man without a Mistress*

A man determined to atone for the past
For seven long years, Sir Peregrine Sayre has tried to assuage his guilt over the horrifying events of his twenty-first birthday by immersing himself in political work—and by avoiding all entanglements with the ladies of the *ton*. But when his mentor sends him on a quest to track down purportedly penitent prostitutes, the events of his less-than-innocent past threaten not only his own political career, but the life of a vexatious viscount's daughter as well.

A woman who will risk anything for the future
Raised to be a political wife, but denied the opportunity by her father's untimely death, Sibilla Pennington has little desire to wed as soon as her period of mourning is over. Why should she have to marry just so her elder brothers might be free of her hoydenish ways and her blazingly angry grief? To delay their plans, Sibilla vows only to accept a betrothal with a man as politically astute as was her father—and, in retaliation for her brothers' amorous peccadillos, only one who has never kept a mistress. Surely there is no such man in all of London.

When Sibilla's attempt to free a reformed maidservant from the clutches of a former procurer throw her into the midst of Per's penitent search, she finds herself inextricably drawn to the cool, reserved baronet. But as the search grows ever more dangerous, Sibilla's penchant for risk taking cannot help but remind Per of the shames he's spent years trying to outrun. Can Per continue to hide the guilt and ghosts of his past without endangering his chance at a passionate future with Sibilla?

Theo's story: *A Lady without a Lord*

A viscount convinced he's a failure
For years, Theodosius Pennington has tried to forget his myriad shortcomings by indulging in wine, women, and witty bonhomie. But now that he's inherited the title of Viscount Saybrook, it's time to stop ignoring his responsibilities. Finding the perfect husband for his headstrong younger sister seems a good first step. Until, that is, his sister's dowry goes missing . . .

A lady determined to succeed
Harriot Atherton has a secret: it is she, not her steward father, who maintains the Saybrook account books. But Harry's precarious balancing act begins to totter when the irresponsible new viscount unexpectedly returns to Lincolnshire, the painfully awkward boy of her childhood now a charming yet vulnerable man. Unfortunately, Theo is

also claiming financial malfeasance. Can her father's wandering wits be responsible for the lost funds? Or is she?

As unlikely attraction flairs between dutiful Harry and playful Theo, each learns there is far more to the other than devoted daughter and happy-go-lucky lord. But if Harry succeeds at protecting her father, discovering the missing money, and keeping all her secrets, will she be in danger of failing at something equally important—finding love?

Benedict's story: *A Sinner without a Saint*

When an honorable artist...
Benedict Pennington's greatest ambition is not to paint a masterpiece, but to make the world's greatest art accessible to all by establishing England's first national art museum. Success in persuading a reluctant philanthropist to donate his collection of Old Master paintings brings his dream tantalizingly close to reality. Until Viscount Dulcie, the object of Benedict's illicit adolescent desire, begins to court the donor's granddaughter, set on winning the paintings for himself . . .

Meets a hedonistic viscount...
Sinclair Milne, Lord Dulcie, far prefers collecting innovative art and dallying with handsome men than burdening himself with a wife. But when rivals imply Dulcie's refusal to pursue wealthy Miss Adler and her paintings is due to lingering tender feelings for Benedict Pennington, Dulcie vows to prove

them wrong. Not only will he woo her away from the holier-than-thou painter, he'll also placate his matchmaking father in the process.

Can sinner and saint both win at love?
But when Benedict is dragooned into painting his portrait, Dulcie finds himself once again drawn to the intense artist. Can the sinful viscount entice the wary painter into a casual liaison, one that will put neither their reputations, nor their feelings, at risk? Or will the not-so-saintly artist demand something far more vulnerable—his heart?

www.ingramcontent.com/pod-product-compliance
Ingram Content Group UK Ltd.
Pitfield, Milton Keynes, MK11 3LW, UK
UKHW042002230426
12048UKWH00009B/498